WELCOME TO

The Abyss line of cutting-edge psychological horror is committed to publishing the best, most innovative works of dark fiction available. Abyss is horror unlike anything you've ever read before. It's not about haunted houses or evil children or ancient Indian burial grounds. We've all read those books, and we all know their plots by heart.

Abyss is for the seeker of truth, no matter how disturbing or twisted it may be. It's about people and the darkness we all carry within us. Abyss is the new horror from the dark frontier. And in that place, where we come face-to-face with terror, what we find is ourselves.

"Thank you for introducing me to the remarkable line of novels currently being issued under Dell's Abyss imprint. I have given a great many blurbs over the last twelve years or so, but this one marks two firsts: first *unsolicited* blurb (*I* called *you*) and the first time I have blurbed a whole *line* of books. In terms of quality, production, and plain old storytelling reliability (that's the bottom line, isn't it?), Dell's new line is amazingly satisfying . . . . a rare and wonderful bargain for readers. I hope to be looking into the Abyss for a long time to come."

—Stephen King

Please turn the page for more extraordinary acclaim . . .

PRAISE FOR ABYSS

The Language of Fear

Stories by Del James

INTRODUCTION BY W. AXL ROSE

A DELL BOOK

Published by
Dell Publishing
a division of
Bantam Doubleday Dell Publishing Group, Inc.
1540 Broadway
New York, New York 10036

ISBN: 0-440-21712-1

Printed in the United States of America

Published simultaneously in Canada

February 1995

10 9 8 7 6 5 4 3 2 1

Dedicated to the memories of

TIMMY MEESKE, TODD CREW,
AND JOHN DUNAI, JR.

They say that nothing lasts forever.
Well, I say that they're wrong because
no one can ever make me forget you,
and my ink will never fade.
Neither will your memories.

ACKNOWLEDGMENTS

I would like to take this opportunity to thank the following people for making my life a little easier and a lot more enjoyable.

My mother Carmen for all her patience and love.

Debbie Woodworth, a queen in a deck loaded with jokers. Without you none of my dreams, especially our daughters, would've ever come true.

Sneaky Peter Pace, Tricky Dickerson, Paulie Curtin, Ronnie & Liz Rella, Scrapdog Jeff, John Maloney, Straydog Ray, Jeff Goodrich, Ritchie Garofalo & Urchin Cycles, Elisa Colleri, the Zack brothers, the Meeske family, Angelo, Big Pete and the Brothers from the Bronx, and the rest of my two-wheelin' family in Westchester, New York. . . . W. Axl Rose, Slash, Duff McKagan, Dizzy Reed, Matt Sorum, Gilby Clarke, Doug Goldstein, John Reese, Tom Maher, Chris Jones, Alex Evezich, and the *entire* GN'FN'R road crew, Stuart Bailey, Amy Bailey, Wendy Laister, Blake Stanton, Lisa Maxwell, Gene Kirkland, Robert "The Godfather" John, Earl Gabbidon, Ron Stalnacker, Truck, Dr. Steve Thaxton, Sabrina Okamoto, Mike Clink, Agust Jackobbsson, Karen Klichowski, Tim Fraser, and the rest of my extended GN'R family. . . . Tony Gardner and all the people at the Tantleff Agency, Jeanne Cavelos and all of the people at Abyss and Dell, Tim Propersi, Mark "Mookie" DiGiacomo, Scotti Capizzano, Steven Werner, Jimmy Waring, Masa Sogano, Kevin Quinn, Kory Clarke, Jimbo Barker, Big Kenny, Riki Rachtman, Joey Meade, Steve O', Kevin & Soul, Lisa Flynt, Ricky Warwick & The Almighty, Max Boseman, Jason Greenfield, Jonni Tegarden, Julie Rexroad, Traci Mikolas, Michelle Lund, Kristy Crella, Arlette Vereecke, Shelly Krueger & my pal Jason, Micheal Oppenheim, Gregg Specland, Tom Zutuat, Patricia Fuenzalida, Suzanne Filkin, Michelle Young, Bryn Bridenthal, Greg James, Robert Benidetti, Jeff Sacharow, Sebastian Bach & Snake & the Skids, Beta, Carlos Booy, Sid Riggs, JJ, Greg Strempka & Elyse Steinman & Raging Slab, Hans Haevelt, Cesca Adonetti, Ronnie Schneider, William Howell, Pat Hoed, Karen Brennan, Kat Turman, Kristina Estlund, Craig Jones & all at RIP, Lonn Friend, Bobbi Kaminski, Kristal Peckham, Jody & Cheryl Woodworth, Nick Savedes, Drake Woodworth, Kevin Dillon, Red Ed & Petey Hopkinson, Steven Huff, Tyla, Ann Marie Partenza, Dennis Dibuno, Cricket, Jo Jo Zauck, Raz, David Velez, Lisa Reveen, Terry Nails, 40, Mary Kenny, the Drunk Fux, West Arkeen, John Pappas, Randy Piwowar and the Hell House survivors, M. D. Conati, Stretch & all the Mamaroneck Fellas, Maria Ferraro, Chuck Billy & Testament, D. C. Clarke, Gabby & Adrianna, Dox Haus Mob, Jennifer Perry, Josh Lewis, Crystal Long, Marc Canter, Shawna Levell, Ian Astbury, John Huffman, Brandy Schaffels, Tiny Buiso, Leigh Johnson, Mike Sudano and the entire A.P.P.L.E. staff, Joey Perri, Paul Kelly, Damon Romanelli, Juan Ayaso, Firm, Michael Katz, Phillip Schmidt, Keith Shaw, and the entire Richbell road crew.

Contents

Introduction

I called Del James around the time that our album
The Spaghetti Incident was coming out and wanted
to see if he had any ideas for a video for the song
"Ain't It Fun." We rapped for a while about the song
—it's a cover of a song originally done by the Dead
Boys, which has a very desperate feel to it. Toward
the end of our conversation, Del said that he saw it
"dark, dreary, and addicted."

"Isn't that how you see everything?" I replied,
half-joking.

In your hands is Del's first published work of fiction, *The Language of Fear*. After you've read a few
stories, you'll know what I mean. In these stories
there's a real sense of the damage that can be done
whenever an individual takes things too far. There's
healthy doses of extreme violence, perversions, inse-
curities, addictions, infidelities, and other themes
regarding the darker side of human nature. He
paints a very vivid picture of people going down the
tubes and spares no expense when it comes to using
red. There's a real depth there, and he enjoys exploring it. Del's the guy who calls me after writing
something particularly disturbing and says "I'm going to Hell" and then reads or faxes me what he's
written. Personally, I think he just likes to scare the

Hell out of himself. *The Language of Fear* is very up-to-date, modern fiction by someone who started this type of writing for fun. He likes to confront taboo issues, and since he's an avid horror fan, there's more of an understanding of what young horror fans enjoy and want. It gives a taste of all kinds of different areas of life and things to avoid. He writes about subjects, no matter how dark, that interest him. There's also a sense of rock 'n' roll in these stories because when he started writing them—and some of them, like "The Nerve" and "Mindwarp," had rough first drafts written in '86—we were all involved in the rock 'n' roll club circuit and living on the streets. Back then, we were all definitely romanced by the darker side of life. We were all trying to get somewhere while having fun with all the wildness. We got through those experiences, and we're lucky we survived the lessons with only the amount of scars that we have.

A lot of Del's insight comes from his personal experiences, taking them even further in a fictional form. These stories tap into the self-destructive side of things that have actually helped me not be self-destructive. While some of these stories are just horror-for-fun type stories, others were inspired by real-life personal situations. He'd express his feelings and emotions through horror stories because there were a lot of times when we didn't realize how scary our real lives were. Del's writing is a way he's dealt with his own personal emotional developments, battles with substances and decadence, and then adding a horror slant. Del's been turned on by things that weren't necessarily good for him, but the birth of his two daughters has helped him deal with that and now he steers clear of those things, except in his stories. I've watched him battle with alcohol and drugs, and I've also seen him become a father and the love for those babies and the desire for them to live happy, successful lives has overtaken his self-destructiveness.

Back when we first met in the summer of '85, food, shelter, and relief from boredom constituted survival. Del has always been the one to find something to entertain himself faster than anyone else, whether it's a hockey game, horror movies, a video game, or *The Simpsons*. It's amazing to me that considering the self-destructive nature in each of us, our relationship helps us avoid self-destruction. There are a lot of times when Del helps me work through something that is emotionally too huge for me to deal with. That helps me to not self-destruct and in the process take GN'R or anything down with me. He's always talking me out of stupid shit that I really wouldn't want to do but I think about doing because I'm frustrated, hurt, angry, or embarrassed. We've both saved each other's lives a few times. Back when we had no clue of what the other one was going to do in life and whether or not we were going to succeed, we still had respect for each other. Now we help inspire that success in each other, and with the successes in each other's lives there's been a sense of compassion for whatever the other guy is going through. We value each other's opinions and have found a way so that our lives work together. If I need Del, he's going to be there for me, and if he needs me, I'm going to be there for him. He treats people the way he would want them to treat him and a lot of people aren't like that. That's who Del is.

Del's is also the guy who called me and said, "I just wrote my best friend's death." For me, the short story "Without You" helped me focus on what could happen in my life and sometimes what was happening. Although Del was being inspired by situations that were going on in my life, it was his way of helping me acknowledge and deal with a painful situation. It stopped me at different times from going too far. When people are looking for their own identity and things aren't going well, they'll settle for being the bad guy or the loser and create an identity that way.

Although the story "Without You" was written before our first album, ('87), the video for the song "November Rain" ('92) where you see Del's name at the end of it is just a piece of "Without You." Things that were predicted in the story actually happened in my life. The goals set before GN'R's first album came out were to get to the levels of success described in "Without You." It's the ultimate rock 'n' roll/self-destructive fantasy.

In the story, Mayne Mann writes a song called "Without You," and around this time I started writing "Estranged." I remember calling Del after finishing "Estranged" and going "I wrote that song," meaning a song that means so much to me, the way "Without You" does to Mayne. I also would end up being haunted by that song as Mayne is. I think it's amazing that the female character, Elizabeth, is the good character, and yet she gets the last word in (don't worry—I won't give it away) by doing something knowing it'll severely fuck Mayne up. I think there was some spite in there, and there's a lot of self-blame in the story on the part of the rocker. Everything is Mayne's fault and he flips out, which is something that I can relate to. There's a lot of personal pain on Mayne's behalf regarding why can't he get a certain love to work.

For years, we've been thinking about making either videos or a full-length movie based on "Without You," and that kept me focused on not wanting to become the character, Mayne, although I basically was that person. There were things involved in the character that had a lot of elements of Del as well as a lot of elements of me. "November Rain" is actually the set up for the short story rather than for the "Estranged" video. We were going to try to bring out more of the "Without You" story and elements in "Estranged," but Stephanie Seymour had other plans so we had to change ours. The story actually helped me for a long time, and I would have loved to have filmed it, but right now it's better for me to evolve and transcend the close similarity to my life and let the story live its own life.

At one point Andy Morahan, who directed "November Rain," and I were asked to do an episode of *Tales from the Crypt*, so I asked Del to write the script, based on one of his stories. It would have given me an opportunity to do something that interests me—act. It would've given Del an opportunity to do something he wants to (and will) do, which is write for the screen. And it would've given Andy an opportunity to film it. Del didn't feel he necessarily had the right story for *Tales from the Crypt*, so he wrote a short story called "The Immortals," which I thought would've been cool to adapt, but then we found out they had to base their episodes on existing comics books. It never came to pass, but the story exists. When I think back about the *Tales from the Crypt*, Del's story was really exciting, and that's what it was all about: trying to figure out how to film that. Any story of Del's that gets adapted into a screenplay is going to be intense, especially if he's involved.

Del has a personal knowledge about most of the

situations he writes about, and he has a love of the gutter from having been there. The short story called "Bloodlust" has a pretty vivid fight that you won't easily forget. "Adult Nature Material" was actually a sick idea of mine. I don't want to give too much away, but at the time he wrote it, Del was working in a porno theater and that's where the story takes place. "Saltwater and Blood" is something close to Del's heart, since he is an avid opponent of gill net fishing. What I enjoyed most about that story was the description of the main character's fear and desperation as he's trying to figure out what the fuck is going on in his mind.

Del is constantly exploring his own mind, and I'm always blown away when I read something he's written and realize how much thinking Del does about what goes on in other people's lives underneath the surface. He asks the questions most people don't like to think about, and he will always push certain boundaries. I've watched Del grow as an individual through his writing while constantly pushing his mind. There's a delicate balance of sympathy and disgust for the evil that makes each story interesting and different.

Personally, one of my favorite horror books—and I haven't really read that many in quite a while—was Stephen King's *Night Shift*. I'm not claiming to be a horror expert, but that book was a helluva lot of fun, and so is *The Language of Fear*. Years ago, I believed Del had a special talent, and after I'd finish reading one of his stories I'd be like, "Hey, are you going to get on this?" and try to motivate him to take it seriously. Well, he did and I've had a blast with these stories, and in my opinion, *The Language of Fear* is the start of Del James's career as a fiction/

horror writer. Be ready for some raw and emotionally disturbing horror.

Sincerely,
W. Axl Rose
November 21, 1993

THERE ARE NO COINCIDENCES
ONLY CHANCE AND FATE EXIST

A Tale of
Two Heroines

Unrelenting precipitation hung over San Francisco like a moist cloud, a heat fog found inside an oven that's been left on too long. For the last ten days, the temperature had remained lodged in the nineties and was showing no signs of weakening. In one decayed section of town, a series of bus graveyards filled block after block, the stripped carcasses bleeding rust. German shepherds patrolled the lots and kept vagrants and runaways from living inside the buses, which technically were still city property. At the end of the graveyards stood a shabby apartment building, a memorial to this dying place.

Inside the apartment, a sick man was trying to decide whether he was dead. The piercing wails of a crying two-year-old bored their way into his skull, reemphasizing that he was unfortunately still alive. Veins he didn't know existed pulsed, pounded, and threatened to burst out of his body. A migraine tore at his skull, while his eye sockets throbbed. He was wrapped in fever, and the ribs on his right side threatened to snap every time he upchucked. Even his teeth hurt. Every time the child cried, it felt like someone set off an air-raid siren inside Frank Banks's cranium.

He felt like the ill-fated survivor of a shipwreck floating in an invisible sea of distress and nausea. Waves of misery slapped against his skull. There was no hope for his future, only prolonged suffering. Try as he might, he couldn't get off the couch because his weary bones ached too much.

Frank's battered stomach felt wrenched, squeezed. It felt like someone was forcing a thick, hairy hand down his throat. No air or relief would come as the hand slowly made its way down into Frank's stomach. Greedily, the large hand scooped up fistfuls of his intestines and pulled his guts back up his throat. He tried closing his eyes, but they were stuck open. They had been for over sixty hours. He desperately wanted to be free of his dark, crawling flesh. Frank leaned forward, mouth opened wide, and braced himself as yet another small amount of sour bile came out.

He wanted to be high right now.

For the past fifteen years, he'd been fighting a losing battle with drugs. Today marked the third day he'd lasted without any smack. The first day hadn't been that bad, but now he had some serious shakes and sweats. He vomited at least six times an hour, or tried to. The dry heaves were worse than vomiting. His throat was raw and his mouth ached. He couldn't remember the last time he had put food in his system but the concept of eating was unimaginable. Again the baby's screams threatened to grind his skull into powder.

"SHUT THE FUCK UP!"

The baby's volume increased.

His watering eyes stared blankly at the syringe in his bony hand. He'd melted down and injected some sedatives, trying to calm the withdrawal symptoms. He knew through experience that only smack could take his pain away. He played around with the point in his hand, hoping for some miracle to happen. Of course, nothing did. The jones was only going to get worse.

He didn't want to quit heroin. It was what he lived for. It was his meaning, his reality, nothing else mattered. He didn't love his woman, and he sure as hell didn't love the child in the next room. There is no room for love when survival is the name of the game. The kid had cost him money, and money equals drugs. Drugs were essential to Frank's survival. And besides, the child didn't even look like him.

He'd met the bitch through a mutual friend, and there seemed to be something there. For her, he was someone, anyone, to be with. Everyone needs love, or so the story goes. At seventeen, she'd been hooking for the past two years, and it had taken its toll on her. Her youthfulness had been sold off in the front seat of cars and inside fleabag motels. She looked chiseled, stale, twice her age. For him, Lisa Lewis was just another scam, and it wasn't very long before she was supporting his habit. Pimping was the only type of work Frank knew, although he really wasn't a full-fledged pimp in the true sense of the word. He was a fast-talking junkie fooling a silly girl. Like any good bullshit artist, he had her believing she was better off on her knees than in school.

She also believed that in his own strange way he loved her.

Frank had only one love in life, drugs. If Lisa was willing to sell herself to support his habit, more power to the cunt. He was willing to run the lovey-dovey game on her and had for almost two years.

But if she really loved him, then how could she do this to him?

Another painful surge of dry air rushed out of his O-shaped mouth. Twitching uncontrollably, Frank's beady eyes searched around the apartment for something, anything, to sell. The tiny, stinky apartment was a roach motel. There was nothing besides scattered garbage and diapers. No TV, no stereo, no telephone. Everything was already in hock except a loud humming refrigerator that nobody wanted and the tattered couch that he was glued to.

"SHUT THE FUCK UP!" he yelled, clutching his right side.

Another burst of nausea swept through him as yellow liquid rushed up his throat and landed on the floor. He stared at the small puddle of bile on the rug and left it for Lisa to clean. Fuck it, it was her fault he was in this condition. Why should he have to suffer just because she wanted out of prostitution? If she hadn't decided to try something as stupid as finding a job, she'd be out pounding the pavement, sucking cocks for cash. Hatred became the focus of his thoughts, and he wanted her to feel the way he felt right now. He wanted to hurt her so badly that she'd never pull this shit again. Uncontrolled rage flowed through his pin-cushion veins, and using all the strength left in his weak body, Frank lifted himself off the couch. An unspeakable thought flowed through his mind.

He knew how to hurt the bitch and get a fix.

He tried erasing the thought but couldn't. It actually made sense in a perverse way. He dragged his feet along the littered floor, pacing back and forth until he reached the bedroom doorway. This was insane. How could he even think what he was thinking?

Easily. Never trust a junkie.

Frank's bowels, which had been constipated cement for months, began to drip ever so slightly as he looked down at the crying baby. He felt no instinctual familial bond between them and even less hesitation. He scooped up the wet, crying baby and hightailed it out the front door.

Overflowing garbage cans decorated the front sidewalk. The putrid stench rising from the cans made Frank gag. Each step made his head pound even worse than it already was. Open pores released buckets of sweat, and the T-shirt he wore quickly soaked through. For all the sweat it caused, the twenty-pound child could have weighed two hundred pounds. The invisible monkey on Frank's back was an additional burden, especially when it began biting Frank. Thick phlegm floated up his dry throat, and every few steps he hacked loudly. He felt shin-splint aches as he dragged on. His calves were throbbing, every vein and muscle ached. The shakes immediately intensified. One tiny injection, and all this pain would be gone, he thought, desperately trying to keep focused. Squinting painfully, he made his way past dingy, decaying redbrick apartments.

After an eternal ten minutes, he finally reached his destination. The apartment building was another run-down excuse for low-income housing, improperly maintained and dirty. Rubbish and empty crack vials were strewn everywhere, as were thousands of discarded cigarette butts. Drug fiends frequented the building's basement, roof, and hallways every hour of the day. The building's graffiti-caked stairways were a revolving carousel that never stopped spinning.

Slippery and desperate, he sneaked into the five-story building. The lobby smelled of urine. Miraculously, the baby girl stopped crying. Frank heard her burp and hugged her, trying to comfort her. She

softly cooed her thanks before dozing off. For a split
second, the addict thought about what he was doing
and almost stopped. As rotten as it was, he continued blaming Lisa. She'd forced him to take these
drastic measures. He found the empyrean stairway
and began ascending. The steps seemed to be made
of thick, wet sand. With every painful step, he sank
farther into the stairs.

Marbles of sweat ran from his pimply forehead
down his ski-slope nose. Snot was dripping from his
nostrils. Frank tried using his shoulder to wipe his
nose, but the movement made the baby burp again.
When he finally reached the third floor, he had to
stop, puke quickly, and catch his breath. He walked
down the hallway and stopped at door 308. The
double-reinforced steel green door was well known
by Bay Area junkies. It sold the much-needed medicine twenty-four hours a day. Heart thumping, he
softly knocked four times.

"What?" asked the voice from behind the steel
door.

Frank was stuttering uncontrollably. Whole
words refused to come to his mouth. More snot
dribbled out of his nose. Finally he blurted out, "It's
Fra—it's Fra—Frankie Banks."

The hinges squealed as the door slowly opened.
Frank stepped back, wiped his runny nose, and
smiled at the huge doorman, who stood well over
six feet, at 260 pounds. A thin black beard surrounded his large bulldoggish face.

"I, um, I—I gotta see Ramon," Frank declared
nervously. He ran his bony fingers through his
coarse hair, trying to act calm. His pantomime of
cool was fooling no one, and he half-expected the
door to slam in his face.

" 'Bout what, Frankie baby?" the large man

asked. His voice sounded metallic, like a robot's. Frank took a step backward, trying to compose himself, and almost threw up on the baby. He felt like bawling. All he wanted was some smack, and it was no secret that Ramon and his cronies bought just about anything, including small children. Behind the large man, he caught a glimpse of another familiar face, Haji. Haji was seated at a dingy table with a weighing scale and some drugs. Knowing that drugs were so close by gave Frank a much-needed second wind.

"I, um, I got a present for him."

"I take his present," the doorman said, holding out his large hands.

Frank recoiled, protecting his prized possession. Bulldog-face smiled, obviously enjoying this game.

"C'mon, broham, this is serious!" Frank sniveled as his bowels loosened up again. He couldn't remember the last time he'd actually crapped, and he hoped that no unnecessary surprises were going to start dripping down his legs. After all, how could he make a deal with shit in his pants? From behind the doorman another thick Arabic-accented voice harshly declared something in a foreign language.

"Haji, my man, I got something—a present! I—I gotta see the man, man!"

Dead tears fell from Frank's brown zombie eyes. The doorman's sinister smile returned to his fat face. He loved it when addicts sniveled. He could think of no better feeling, other than smacking some dumb fuck around.

"You useless piece of dog. Why you insist to see Ramon? You disgust him, you! He fucks your woman in the ass," the doorman snapped in English that was far from perfect. His verbal blows had no effect on the spineless man who stood there stupefied.

Frank felt like a coma victim. Although he could see and speak, both senses betrayed him. His will was no longer his—it belonged to the dope man. He tried leaving but couldn't. His legs refused to give him dignity. Simple motor functions left him as the doorman's piercing stare froze him in his tracks. He felt trapped like a fly in a spider's web, smiling a dead fly's smile. Bulldog-face held out his huge hands. Defeated, Frank handed him the baby in the blanket. The doorman took her and carried her to another room.

Smiling like a moron, he waited patiently, afraid to enter the dealer's apartment. Haji's cold glance kept him at bay. After a silent eternity, the doorman returned. In his hand he held two packets of heroin. Frank's rotten-tasting mouth began to water. The doorman taunted him by showing him the drugs but not giving them to him right away.

"You smelly piece of nigger shit," the doorman barked, disgusted. "Ramon never wants to see you after this."

Frank stood silent as his eyes continued to register the two packets of dope, mentally estimating how much was in each.

"Scum! Take and go," the doorman said, and placed the bindles in Frank's greedy hands. He slammed the heavy door in the junkie's face and grinned knowingly at his seated partner. Haji returned the grin. As long as lowlifes were willing to sell children, they would gladly trade heroin.

"Halle-fuckin'-lujah!" Frank said joyously, raising his middle finger at the closed door. He left feeling like the Super Bowl MVP, off to Disneyland. He quickly made his way to the stairway. Then he remembered he couldn't return to Lisa's. Not after what he'd just done. He shrugged his shoulders. It didn't matter—he'd been a junkie longer than most. He had places to go, people to burn. He entered the stairway and stopped. On the dingy walls were thin streaks of blood, HIV graffiti.

"Yo, Frankie, what'cha got going on, homey?" a familiar voice yelled out. He didn't reply and quickly left. The user harassed him about being a tightass who was cheap with his drugs. More insults were directed toward him, but he couldn't care less what was being said. It was knowing there were approximately four grams—about five hundred dollars' worth of dope—in his pocket that gave him strength. And knowing his pain would soon be gone made Frank a strong man again.

He started walking toward Lisa's.

What could she do? She'd freak a little and then get the money to buy her daughter back. If she really got out of hand, he would fuck her shit up. It wouldn't be the first time. A small pimp strut returned to his stride. Fuck that stupid bitch, he thought to himself, wishing his feet would move faster.

In less than ten minutes, he was back at the apartment. A slight feeling of apprehension swept him as he climbed the stairs. If she wasn't home, he could do a healthy shot and then nothing would matter, but if she was . . . He arrived at the door and listened. Trails of termite tunnels surrounded the ravaged door frame. He put his ear to the scuffed-up door.

No one was home, but the silence was not as comforting as he'd imagined it would be. Frank double-locked the creaky door behind him and silently examined the scummy apartment. He went to the

noisy refrigerator and removed a small, squeezable
yellow lemon juice container. A quick surge of cool
air escaped from the refrigerator. Instead of cooking up his dope with water, Frank squeezed a little
lemon juice into his spoon. Lemon juice is a better
mixture when cooking up Persian smack. It cooks
smoothly. He dropped a large amount of dope into
the spoon. Over the stove, he heated the combination until he knew it was ready, then placed a tiny
piece of cotton in the spoon and drew the drug up
into his syringe.

Then he heard something.

Frank arched like a cat and listened. Someone
was in the hallway, walking toward him. All his
scamming and hard work felt like it had been
flushed down the toilet. Seconds turned into days
and back into seconds as whoever it was walked
past his door. He crept into the living room and sat
down on the couch.

He needed this, he reasoned. If he wasn't as resourceful as he'd been, he'd probably be dead. And
a man like Frank wasn't about to die without a fight.

His arms were out of the question; most of the
veins had collapsed, leaving only loads of small
white scars where scabs had once been. While high,
he had a nasty habit of picking at the scabs until
they bled. Excited and slightly worried about his inevitable confrontation with Lisa, he found a reason-
ably usable vein on the back side of his left hand and
slid the needle home.

The drug took instant effect, hitting him in powerful waves of intoxication. Sonic rejuvenation was
his. Pain and illness had been nullified. Swirls of a
much-welcomed death danced behind his heavy
eyes, but it was the heroin that had ensured that he
would live a little longer. Frank was really rushing

out as the dope erased all misery and sickness. This was what he lived for, and there was nothing better. He left his works on the table in front of him. If Lisa wanted some, she was welcome to it but not too much. Hell, he still had another packet hidden in his back pocket. If she was mad, maybe a peace offering would help. Lisa understood dope.

He sat there corpselike. No matter what ill effects drugs had on his life, this sensation was worth it. He was heavily rushing out as reality faded to black. In less than two minutes, Frank was out cold.

Frank never double-locked the front door, and it surprised Lisa to find he had. Maybe one of his cronies had come by with some drugs, she thought, but knew deep down he had no one besides her. Annoyed and sweating, she dug through her purse for her keys. Small drops of sweat ran down the side of her tarted-up face and fell into the purse.

It's amazing how much trash accumulates inside my purse, she thought, digging through the rubble. Her hand hit something and she seized it. It was the handle of her Charter Arms .32. The five-shot revolver with a two-inch snub-nosed barrel was a foolproof way of getting even the most hostile john to back the fuck off.

For over a year, Lisa had been living in serious fear. Frank beat her up at least twice a week. Besides drugs, it was one of the few things he did with any regularity. Once when he thought she was holding out on him, he almost beat her to death with an unopened can of Campbell's chicken soup. The ten-and-a-half-ounce can fucked her up "mmm-mmm good." She could still remember the sound of the can bashing against her face and head. It was a small miracle that after all the bruises finally disap-

peared, there were no permanent scars. Many a
night she had contemplated shooting him in his
sleep, and many a night she tried but couldn't find
the inner strength to pull the trigger. It wasn't like
she was afraid or anything. She'd already capped
two men during her career as a streetwalker, but for
some reason she loved the useless fucker.

But the time to quit drugs and move on, even if
that meant moving away from California, had arrived, and she'd refused to be intimidated. Surprisingly, Frank had only beat up on her once since she
told him of her plans, and even that fight hadn't
been too bad. Maybe deep down he knew that having the mother of his child walking the streets
wasn't a good environment for the kid. Maybe, without actually saying it, he knew that she was doing
the right thing.

She slipped the key in.

The humid apartment still smelled like a musty
laundry room and bad produce. Even though every
window was open, the dank room was relentlessly
muggy, but Lisa had goose bumps as she entered.
Instinct that had been honed by an education on the
streets told her something wasn't right.

Sprawled out on the couch was an unconscious
Frank. Lisa immediately knew he was loaded.
Where and with what money did he cop? she wondered. He'd made it obvious he was high and un-
characteristically even left her some. Maybe it was
his way of expressing love?

Then common sense kicked in, and she felt a pain
so horrible that death would've been a vacation.
Something was definitely wrong. It was just too
damn quiet, she thought nervously, trying to stay
calm. She quickly made her way to the bedroom

as her worst fear began to unfold before her very eyes.

Panic swept through her, and tears welled but didn't fall. She wanted to scream out against God. How could God, if there was such a thing, let innocent children suffer? Where was divine intervention when anyone needed it? Frank could beat her up and turn her out, but messing with their, with her, daughter was unholy. Her skin flushed red with hostility, and her ears scorched. This was every mother's worst nightmare and then some.

Then in an instant, she got a grip over her emotions. If she was going to find her child, she'd have to remain calm. Frank knew who had her. Just stay calm, she reminded herself, thinking about how satisfying it would feel to blow him away. More than anything she'd ever wanted out of life, she wanted to peel his cap.

"Where's my fuckin' kid???" .

"Sold it," Frank answered weakly, scratching his face. His pupils were nonexistent. Lisa couldn't believe what she'd just heard. His callousness froze her dead in her tracks. How dare this poor excuse for a human sell their daughter?

And to whom?

"WHATTT?" she screamed, making believe this was a bad trip.

Frank was once again drifting off into la-la land. The junkie pimp mumbled and moaned something, but the only word Lisa understood was Ramon. Drool pittered out of the corner of his thick lips as he crumpled Jell-O-like onto the couch. He was scratching uncontrollably, mumbling, falling in and out of consciousness. She reached into her purse and dropped her bag so that everything spilled out.

Everything except her gun. That was firmly in her hand.

Just stay calm.

Right.

Trembling, she aimed at his head. His eyes were closed, his head slowly moving back and forth, his dirty fingernails scratching down his thin cheeks. Everything froze as her sights were set on the scumbag who tormented her so. Here was a chance to eliminate the lowlife who'd sold her on the streets for chump change just so that he could feed his arm. In her shaking hands was an end to all of the pain he'd put her through.

Although his lips moved, she could no longer hear him. She was locked in a private world no bigger than her and him and the gun. This was the point of no return—if she didn't break free from the evil bastard now, she never would. The revolver was wobbling, and she tried steadying herself. Frank's left eye opened, and he saw the gun. His expression didn't change. He just kept scratching his face.

Lisa tried to squeeze the trigger but couldn't. Her forefinger refused. She lowered the gun and began scooping items off the floor and back into her purse. She thought she heard a tiny laugh escape from the couch. There was no time to lose if she ever wanted to see her daughter again. She put the gun back into her purse and walked over to him. Sounding like a lame Clint Eastwood, Lisa warned, "If those fuckers hurt one hair on her head, I'll blow your brains out, you cocksucker."

"Be careful, there's sharks in dem rooms," Frank mumbled before nodding out. As fate would have it, Lisa's eyes again noticed the packet of heroin on the scratched-up, filthy coffee table.

A shot would feel so good right now.

Trembling, her hand reached out for the precious powder. She grabbed the bindle and brought it up to her face. She could easily snort a few fingernail scoops. She could almost taste the powder in her nose, dripping down her throat. She could almost feel her pain erased.

A single tear fell down her skinny face. Disgusted with herself for even thinking about getting high and wanting even more to hurt Frank, she poured out all the powder, letting it fall freely onto the dirty green rug. She wished she'd be around when Frank awoke, jonesing, wanting more dope, only to find it wasted.

It took her minutes, but it felt like hours before she arrived at the building where Frank had sold her child. Luckily no one was there except for a prone man who looked dead. Addicts were always dying in or around this building. She rummaged through her purse for a handkerchief. Upon finding some tissues, she wiped sweat away from her face as she caught her breath. She examined herself with a pocket mirror. Miraculously, her makeup hadn't run too badly. There were the always-present dark circles beneath her eyes, but that didn't matter. She knew if she was going to get her child back, she'd first have to catch Ramon's hyperactive, loveless eyes. She sprayed hairspray into her dyed blond hair, noticing that her roots were beginning to show. With brittle fingers, she teased her hair upward.

She'd prostituted herself to Ramon before. Until recently she didn't mind and even liked him. That really wasn't true—she liked his drugs. She'd always suspected something was odd about him. Even when she gave him her goods, he acted strange. He liked her pale flesh, but more than that, he liked hurting her. At first she thought he was trying to be kinky, but looking back there was more: innuendos about certain sexual desires, certain fantasies that went beyond weird. She could take it up the ass, or make it with another woman, or even smile while being urinated on, but looking back . . . It was reality clouded by addiction and fear of offending her supplier that had kept her from putting it all together.

But why did he want her child?

She knew why. Small children equaled big bucks on the black market. The exploitation of children was a sacred rite among the perverted, and someone had to properly prepare and serve these defenseless delicacies. Greed could make a person do just about anything.

Lisa climbed the stairs, taking three at a time. Winded, she made it to the steel door and knocked four times. Every user knew that code. The oafish doorman asked who it was before opening up. Lisa slid inside as he quickly closed and locked the deadbolt behind her.

An awkward, silent half-minute passed before Lisa broke the ice. The doorman's beady eyes were fixed on her breasts.

"Where's my honey Ramon?" she asked nervously, trying to be seductive. The doorman was still staring at her tits.

"Resting," the monotone monster replied.

The man who was usually behind the desk making drug packages wasn't there either. This was very unusual, Lisa thought, smiling sluttily, scheming how to work this situation to her advantage. She moved closer to the doorman and noticed he seemed uncomfortable with her obvious advances. This wouldn't be the first time they'd been intimate.

Well, as intimate as a blowjob in the hallway or in the back seat of a car gets. Suddenly the room got smaller, and again she smiled. Lisa knew how to work small rooms.

"I have to see Ramon. And you know me, I'll do anything," she said like a low-grade pornographic temptress. She stared at his bulge and licked her lips. He stood there wondering how bad this whore was craving. In return, she wondered how bad this pig was craving.

"Anything?"

"Anything," she repeated with emphasis.

A wicked smile crept onto the large man's face.

"Where's Haji?" she asked, almost pinning him against a wall. The doorman shrugged his large shoulders. Of course he knew where Haji was but wasn't telling. Not yet anyway. Ramon's employees were not allowed to talk, let alone flirt with the females he favored. Such actions could cost him his job or even his life. But the doorman couldn't erase the memories of her doing him. It wasn't like he saw that much action on a regular basis. Of all the whores who came here, Lisa was definitely one of the top ten lookers. And the only white one who would do him.

The big man was getting flustered as she smiled her well-practiced bitch smile, asking, "Are we alone?"

If only his partner was here, then he could take this slut to his car, he thought, calculating how long it would take Haji to return to the apartment. It would be a while, and time wasn't on the doorman's side. Mouth agape like a bear, he lunged toward her and began working over her breasts with his large hands. She didn't resist. Expertly, she moaned softly as their pelvises ground together and fought off the urge to offer him a breath mint. His hot breath stunk like Liver Snaps.

"Are we alone?" Lisa panted, licking her slick red lips. Her thin fingers rubbed his penis through his suit pants. For a monster of a man, he had an unusually small cock.

The brute didn't answer. His heavy breathing threatened to smother her. The room was pulsating, pounding back and forth. Lisa knew the score. She continued stroking his joint. When she tried to undo his zipper, he grabbed her hands.

"Think with your dick," she said, smiling falsely. "Your big, fat dick. . . . Daddy, I need some dick. Let me put it in my mouth. Please. . . . Are we alone?" she whispered as her tongue worked over his large earlobe. She was determined to find her daughter.

Passion threatened to get the better of the doorman. He couldn't control himself as he began stammering and finally blurted out, "Stop. . . . Ra—Ra —Ramon is here. He rests, so be quiet. He kill us."

The room temperature was increasing with each passing moment. Lisa freed one arm and seductively sucked his middle finger while her other hand was still active on his crotch, rubbing, tugging, teasing. The doorman's barrel chest heaved. If she didn't loosen her grip, the big man was going to shoot his wad. Smiling, she eased off a little, but it was too late. Bulldog-face groaned as lust turned to hostility. Lisa had played this scene hundreds of times before. She tried cooing to him softly, telling him it was okay, offering to do him later.

With a maniacal look in his eyes, the doorman spun Lisa into the steel door. The back of her head hit the door as the huge man cocked his fist back and let go. Instantly, she was on the floor looking up. Through watery eyes she watched the large man remove something from his jacket pocket. She immediately recognized the weapon in his burly hand as a Bowie knife.

Frank awoke disoriented. His beady eyes immediately found the bindle on his coffee table. He snatched it, but there was nothing left inside. Then he began to remember the morning. He got off the couch, entered the bedroom, and peeked inside the crib.

"Holy shit."

Disgust swept through him as he stood staring blankly at the empty crib. Of all the low-down, dastardly things he'd done, which were too many to count, this was unthinkable. He had finally sunk beneath the lowest of scum.

Frank didn't realize it, but his finger was tracing the outline of the packet in his back pocket. No matter how awful he felt, his finger never stopped fidgeting. It was as though the digit was a separate entity. Finally he fished out the second bindle. He stared at it ashamed, but was afraid to let go. Nothing was real besides the drugs in his hands. And even that wouldn't last very long. How could his life turn to such shit? Again his thoughts drifted to Lisa and their daughter. He'd blown it really badly. After all, with both of them gone, how was he going to get more smack?

I'll deal with that later, he thought as he went over to the kitchen and began preparing another fix.

After hearing the blast, Ramon came running out of his bedroom with an Uzi and took aim at Lisa. She in turn raised her .32 at him in a standoff.

Neither moved for fear of being shot.

"What the fuck?" Ramon yelled at the hooker pointing a gun at his chest. He thought about blowing her away but reconsidered. Even if she did manage to hit him, the odds were stacked in his favor, but the concept of taking a bullet—and even worse, having the law snooping around his drug den—was not worth the risk. He doubted that the single shot that had dropped his doorman was enough to make anyone in this building call the cops. Such were the ways of the ghetto. A barrage of machine-gun fire was a completely different story.

"I want my baby," she pleaded in a tone that was sheer desperation bordering on hysteria. She took several deep breaths and tried holding back the tears.

"What?" he asked, thoroughly confused.

"Please, all I want is—I want my daughter back."

"You mean the nigger baby?" the confused dealer asked while his hateful eyes burned deep into Lisa's frightened soul. Ramon started putting two and two together. After all of the initial commotion and confusion, his memory was slowly coming back to him. He did a double-take as he recognized the woman standing before him.

How dare she point a gun at him?

"All I want is my baby," she explained, answering Ramon's question before he became enraged enough to cut her down. She knew she was in way over her head, but it was too late to turn back.

Ramon was slowly starting to understand what was unfolding. This was not a drug burn or a hit on him—this was a mother's love for her child. Not that matters of the heart held much weight in his world. After all, he was a criminal, but there was a certain romantic beauty to what she was doing here and what she was willing to do to save her child. It was this type of loyalty, where the prospect of death brought no fear, that Ramon admired more than money. He could only wish his cronies to be so loyal in the line of duty.

Amazed, the dealer silently sighed as he looked her over from head to toe. Though he'd just as soon snuff the pistol-toting bitch before losing face, something inside him felt compassion for her. Ramon did not want the blood of a mother defending her child on his hands.

"There's been a misunderstanding. I paid five hundred for the baby. That baby was brought to me by Amir," Ramon explained, pointing at the stiff on the floor. "Obviously he had no right bringing me this child, so I'm gonna return it to you."

With guns still pointed at one another, Lisa and Ramon slowly walked into the bedroom where the baby was. It had slept through the entire drama. Ramon pointed at the child with his Uzi.

"If I wanted to kill you or your child, you'd both be dead. Take it and get the fuck outta here before I change my mind," the drug dealer warned.

Lisa shook her head in acknowledgment. She quickly picked her daughter up and within seconds was gone.

As she carefully closed the front door behind her, the dirty hallway looked like heaven. Strange situations bring on strange results, she reasoned. She'd risked her life coming here, killed a man in the process, and was leaving with her daughter. She hugged her baby and headed for the stairs. Lisa would not be returning home tonight, or for that matter ever again. Like a condemned actress, she'd played out her final scene with the lowest ranks of humanity and knew it was time to move. Very far away. And she held the ticket to a new life in her hands.

Adult Nature
Material

He reached his left hand out into the darkness of pure black but quickly pulled it back. It was times like these, alone and in his bed, when he was the most frightened. It was a fear everyone has experienced but no one admits. Although there was nothing wrong with his twenty-twenty vision, he felt completely blind. His straining eyes tingled in the gloom as they searched for sight that was impossible. After several nerve-wracking seconds of unadulterated vulnerability, he leaned forward again, left hand extended.

"This is getting really stupid," he nervously joked to himself.

Then something grabbed his arm and yanked.

His feet were pulled from the safety and support of his warm bed as he began plummeting. Cold tears formed in his unseeing eyes. Warm wind pushed his features taut. His thin hair blew backward, electrified.

Thirty unending seconds into the descent, he continued to drop. The force against his chest was tremendous, and he found it nearly impossible to breathe. The grip that held his left wrist was relentless and threatened to crush his bones. If only he could scream. . . . Trapped in the uncertainty of pure darkness, he couldn't tell what had him. Was it human or monstrous? Did it have shape, or was it invisible? Was it smiling hideously?

It's probably for the better that I can't see it, he thought, and continued falling, faster and faster. Velocity and inertia took on new dimensions. Then the unseen grip let go of his arm. With his testicles slamdancing in his gut, Jimmy knew he was going to crash.

SPLUTTT!

He landed in a thick, oozing slime and sunk. He couldn't breathe as slime engulfed him. He felt like someone trapped in a pool filled with Chun King duck sauce as he continued sinking toward the seemingly bottomless bottom. The thick substance burned his nose and eyes. Phlegmy goo choked out what little air was left in his struggling lungs, but sinking in the putrid jelly substance was better than falling endlessly. His drop had slowed to the extent that if there were something to grab hold of, he could've stopped. But there was nothing so he continued sinking, waiting for something to happen.

And then it did. He fell through the bottom of the gelatinous cortex.

Jimmy dropped ten feet and crashed with a heavy thud. Sharp pains jolted through his out-of-shape body. Every bone felt broken but nothing was. He was just banged up pretty good. Then more slime— the same slop that had been holding him moments earlier—came raining down, inundating him in a downpour. It felt like the world's largest bird had let loose a massive turd on him. He wiped honeylike goop away from his face. It smelled familiar, but he couldn't quite identify it. His hands, along with the rest of him, were totally drenched in the gel. After shaking off as much as possible without the benefit of a towel, he stood up, sore and bruised.

All around him he could feel an ominous presence. Not like a pair of eyes watching him, but rather, more like he was walking inside the eyeball. He took small subdued steps. It really made no difference which direction he chose—direction was a forgotten concept wherever he had landed, and he couldn't see a damn thing in this abominable darkness. He kept his slightly trembling hands extended in front of him, making him look like one of George Romero's zombies.

He heard a faint noise.

Throwing caution to the wind, Jimmy began to run. After all, whatever had grabbed him was still out there. Behind him, the surface he stood on crumpled and fell into more black nothingness. It was like crossing a frozen pond that had begun to thaw. But instead of water beneath the ice, there was nothing, a void. He could hear the surface shattering as his pace increased. Then as though he'd passed through an unseen door, there was a dull, orange-red glow engulfing him. He felt as though he'd walked into a softly setting sun. The pastel lighting stung his unaccustomed eyes and made him flinch.

This new area radiated warmth but not in a physical sense; he now felt somewhat safe. Well, not safe, but better than he had. At least he could see. Looking down, he noticed that the glowing surface on which he stood was solid.

After his vision settled, Jimmy noticed something up ahead. Awaiting was a figure. He could not make out whether it was male or female since it was completely covered in thick, purplish slime, sort of like a melting grape Popsicle.

Oh no, the Cavity Creep's got me, he thought, trying to make head or tail out of the shape.

Jimmy stopped before the figure and after several seconds of indecision accepted its inviting hand. Beneath the slimy covering was a soft, friendly hand. It had long, bony fingers. Their fingers interlocked and squeezed out some of the muck.

Using its free hand to wipe away some of the slime from its covered face, the figure revealed that it was female. She led Jimmy farther into the orange light where there were other slime people. All were writhing about, intertwined. He felt like an intruder at an orgy. Sensing his unease, the female who held his hand directed it toward her pert breast, which took very little coaxing to get him inspired. Memories of summers past spent on beaches chasing well-greased beach-bunnies were revived. As was he. He no longer hurt from his crash.

The female let go of his hand and tore off his slime-drenched clothing. She grabbed his waist and pulled him toward her. He didn't resist as she stroked his waking penis, working her slippery hand up and down. She had a firm hold on his stiff member, and if she didn't loosen her grip, he was going to come. He tried pulling away but she held fast. Instead of fighting, he let her have her way, which was really his way anyway. He squeezed her firm buttocks, sliding his fingers in between her slippery cheeks. She slowly dropped down to the ground, guiding him toward her, never letting go of his cock. He wound up on her chest sliding his dick through her mushy cleavage. She didn't make a sound. She pushed her breasts together, giving him more to slide through. Stimulated to the point of throbbing lust, Jimmy wiggled out of the tit-fucking toward her pelvic area. After a little teasing and squirming, he was inside her.

He wrapped his arms tightly around her and squeezed. She returned the gesture with a hug of her own. Her vagina was slick with joy juice, and the circular motion of their hips did not last very long. If she had expected some studlike marathon fuck session, disappointment was hers. Jimmy was too excited and exploded inside her. That was the first time he heard her make any sort of noise. Her tone made him uneasy. It seemed as if she was giving thanks for his sperm. And if this was true, why? A small grunt escaped from her mouth as her thighs quivered ever so slightly. She held on until he fell out of her.

Jimmy quickly stood up and felt embarrassed. He felt as though all the eyes in the immediate space were upon him. Actually, most were. He covered his dick with his hands. He took a deep breath and asked the female he'd just fucked where he was.

"Home," she answered softly.

"Wha'?"

"You're home."

With that the female wiped away more ooze, and her facial features became increasingly visible. The small nose. The thick lips and well-rounded smile. High cheekbones. Small but soft eyes. All the features that had once belonged to the only woman who had ever mattered to him. A mother he now only remembered through memories since she was dead. Or was she? Jimmy tried screaming as he realized who he'd been with.

"Kiss me," the Mother Thing creaked.

"Freaks. Fuckin' freaked-out motherfuckin' freaks," Jimmy Downey declared to no one, trying not to touch the cold glob of spunk in his boxer

shorts. As he carefully removed his underwear, he
realized that he had to find a new job. Working in a
pornographic movie theater was just a bit too much
for his already-deteriorating mental health. Freaks,
whores, crackheads, raincoat warriors, and devi-
ants were all part of the job description. Nightmares
were not.

Like a chimp, Jimmy scratched away at his flabby
body. There was an itch inside his ear that no matter how deep he dug, refused to subside. Wax piled
up on the tip of his forefinger. He wiped it off on a
bedsheet. Slightly hung over, he felt the need for a
drink.

His mother, the woman in his dream, was someone he hadn't seen in more than five years. They'd
had a falling out over something he couldn't quite
remember. And then she died. The thought of her
made him flash back to the dream, but just as
quickly as he remembered, he was making his way
to the kitchen, preparing to forget. After popping
open a cold Schaffer, Jimmy felt better. He'd feel
whole after a cigarette.

" 'Schaffer is the one beer to have when you're
having more than one,' " he flatly sang, amused
with the beer's jingle.

Outside, it was raining and the sun was almost
down. Jimmy rarely saw the sun since he worked
the night shift at the Pussy Kat Theater. He looked
at a clock on the kitchen wall. It read 7:05 P.M. It
would be less than two hours before another work
night began. He cursed and took another long sip.

Three beers later and wet from where his um-
brella did not protect, Jimmy swaggered through
the large front door of the Pussy Kat at exactly 9:00,
just as Norbert Millen, the usher he was relieving,
was removing his black bow tie. He and Norbert

exchanged minimal greetings before Norbert disappeared into the dreary night. Although it was against public fire ordinances for employees to smoke inside the theater, Jimmy puffed away casually.

He hated everyone, and not too many people liked him. He was a potbellied, opinionated, backstabbing weasel who thought he was superior to everyone except for his fellow Irishmen. And even they didn't enjoy his obnoxious company. As for his few friends, they accepted him for what he was: a lonely drunkard. Jimmy tended to live in a past that was made up of stories of what he could've been if only the chips had landed differently. His drunken tales were about how good an athlete, lover, and fighter he was. Occasionally, he drifted into tall tales of his involvement with the Westies Irish mob. It usually took people who met him less than fifteen minutes to figure out he was a bitter bullshit artist trying to sell the world a shit-stained canvas.

His disposition was harsh, at times quite vicious. He was the stereotypical nasty Noo Yawker, and almost everything that came out of his mouth was unpleasant. His pale white flesh was decorated with freckles and acne. Big clownlike green eyes swam in a sea of red sorrow, and his red-veined nose, which went well with his bright orange hair, was showing signs of deterioration due to years of excessive drinking. It was not unusual for street toughs to disrespect him by calling him Mickey or Howdy Doody.

The city block consisted of tourist traps, fast-food places, and run-down movie theaters. The small, dank 140-seat adult theater was painfully sandwiched between an all-night adult bookstore and a Brew N' Burger. Jimmy took his seat on the tattered bar stool behind the ticket booth's bulletproof window. Rain streaked his view of the decrepit playground known as Forty-second Street. This was a playground where no rules applied. Purgatory's version of ring-a-levio. During the two-year course of his employment at the Pussy Kat, he thought he'd at least heard (if not seen) it all when it came to tales of depravity: politicians ass-fucking little boys, girls sucking off dogs, golden showers, fist-fucking, shit-eating, and worse. Much worse. For $500 admission you could watch someone be tortured to death in a sex booth, and for an additional fee, you could have sex with the corpse.

Or keep a memento.

One of Jimmy's favorite stories he'd heard was of a patron at a live sex show. One went inside an ammonia-reeking private booth, and on the other side of the glass was a semi-nude female. For a five-dollar token, she'll talk dirty while the customer masturbated. Instead of masturbating, this patron took a Ticonderoga pencil, covered it with a Trojan, and painfully inserted it into his urine hole like a catheter.

Oh, the New York groove.

The evening grinded away slowly. Time was the enemy. Carefully stashed in the closet of the ticket booth was a three-quarter-filled bottle of Bushmills. When no one was looking, Jimmy took a swig. It was booze that made shit-hole jobs like this tolerable, but for some reason he never seemed to keep any job, good or bad, for too long. The way Jimmy figured it, when he'd been dealt the cards of life, someone had cheated him. Breaks that were meant to come his way never did. No matter how hard he tried, he never seemed to get ahead so he'd grown complacent—that is, until his big break, like Lotto or hitting the numbers, finally arrived. He looked around to make sure no one was looking and raised the bottle to his lips again before putting it back.

Two stoned-looking Puerto Ricans made their way to the window. In the center of the glass was a grilled speaker, and to its right a small black sign with white press-on letters stating tonight's triple feature, the times they ran, and in two-inch red letters: ADMISSION PRICE $7.00. This week's quality entertainment was *New York Honey*, *Read My Lips*, and *The Secret of N.Y.M.P.H.* After reading the sign, the smaller of the two men spoke into the dingy, silver grill.

"*Quanto?*"

"What?"

"Yo, how much?"

Jimmy pointed at the sign. He'd been through this routine every day for the past two years. Every street urchin expects to receive a discount.

"No, Holmes, how much for two?"

"Fourteen," Jimmy answered monotone, annoyed. Among all of NYC's immigrant dregs, he hated Puerto Ricans the most. Second on his list of top-ten worst ethnic minorities were the dot heads. Third was a tie between gooks, chinks, Koreans, and all the other yellow fucks. Fourth were the kikes. Fifth, spades. Sixth, wops. Seventh, dumbass polacks. Eighth, frogs. Ninth, teabag-limeys. And tenth, anyone else he may have forgotten. Homosexuals received an even deeper resentment just for being "queer."

"What are you, fuckin' nuts? Fourteen fuckin' dollars? I'll go home and pull it for free!"

"Who's stopping you, Sanchez? Pull it till you pull it off, but if you don't like the price, move the fuck away from the ticket booth," Jimmy explained in a take-no-shit voice.

"Yo, man, you gots an attitude."

"Your mother swallowed my attitude," Jimmy countered, baiting the smaller Puerto Rican. He figured he could take this guy—it was his big friend who worried him.

"*Bendejo, maricon!* I don't like you, motherfucker!" the talker declared, and clenched his fist as though to hit the glass. He was getting jumpy and hyped, ready for action. His larger friend laughed and grabbed him before he could do anything stupid. Jimmy picked up the telephone inside the booth and pretended to dial 911. The two men slowly made their way from the ticket booth but not until they bilingually cursed the usher out, with *punk*, *puto*, and *motherfucker* being the three most prominent words used.

"Fuckin' sand-blasted niggers," Jimmy grunted as they left, being careful that they were out of earshot. He knew that all Puerto Ricans smoked crack and carried guns, and he didn't feel like getting capped. Not for this shit job. He lit up a smoke and turned around only to see Juan Clemente, another usher, standing at the booth's entrance.

"What are you looking at?"

"Just checking you out," explained the nineteen-year-old. The movie theater was one of three part-time jobs he held down. Besides this gig, Juan drove a delivery van during days as well as a taxi on weekends, trying to support a small family. Unlike Jimmy's face, which was hard from bitterness and booze, Juan's boyish features were tough from responsibilities. It was his voice that gave him away as a kitten dressed in tiger's clothing. At times his soft, broken English sounded frail, and Jimmy was not above mimicking him behind his back or, if he was drunk, directly to his face. But it was always Juan he went to when he needed something like three bucks for smokes. Juan was an efficient young man who earned every cent of his measly salary and gave thanks to his Higher Power for allowing him to make himself and his family better off than some of those who wandered these streets.

Jimmy told Juan everything was just fine. He wanted to be left alone so he could continue his drinking on the sly. Juan nodded and went on a routine check of the theater's interior. Contrary to popular opinion, porno theaters do not allow patrons to openly masturbate. It's against the law, as Paul Ruebens found out, and if undercover vice happen to catch a patron beating his baloney, the best that can happen is a fine, the worst is the closing of the theater. Females peddling their wares inside hardcore cinemas are a rarity closer to myth. There's not enough cash potential. Nowadays, the prostitutes working theaters are usually transvestites. After watching Stacy Donovan or Jeanna Fine lay pipe, an aroused, potential john will let just about anyone blow him. After ejaculating, many men tend to get hostile over the fact that they let another man go down on them; therefore, fighting occurs.

Jimmy took another quick sip and looked out into the night. Through the rain against the glass he sighed at the city everyone loved to hate. All along the Deuce, Forty-second Street to tourists, were big city bright lights and hordes of hustlers, beautiful people, junkies, cops, and homeless types, all hurrying nowhere. Yellow cabs, limos, and buses dominated the races run on these pothole-infested streets. Litter, drugs, and despair were some of

Manhattan's virtues that even the innocent could
see. And on this particular stretch of concrete, sex
reigned supreme.

The theater was about one-quarter full, as
crowded as it ever got, when Juan returned looking
uneasy. Jimmy read him like an old magazine. Sus-
pecting that he already knew the answer, Jimmy
asked what was wrong.

"I think a man is abusing himself."

It never occurred to Jimmy how lonely someone
might have to be to seek refuge and pleasure in a
sleazy joint like this. Fuck that noise, he wasn't in
the sympathy business. Instead, he grabbed a flashlight and followed Juan to the seat where the customer was. Jimmy took a sadistic pleasure in throwing masturbating customers out of the theater. It
was the inborn bully in him that he would never
outgrow. Juan slinked off into the lobby wondering
if he'd done the right thing. He hated the way
Jimmy berated the pathetic even more than he
hated this job.

Jimmy watched for several moments, feeling a
self-righteous, disgusted rage within him swell. According to the priests who had accounted for most
of his high school education, touching yourself was
wrong. Not that he'd never masturbated, just never
in public, and that was probably what the priests
meant. There were rules to jerking off that are sacred, and public exhibition ranked as a cardinal sin.
Booze and religion almost justified the pleasure he
was anticipating in humiliating another human being. Jimmy looked up at the screen, licked his lips,
and watched the large screen. Tori Welles was
groaning with glee as her head bobbed up and
down. Jimmy found himself staring at her pretty
face lapping away at some stud. There once was a

time when watching a beautiful woman's mouth wrapped around a penis was enough to excite Jimmy. Now it just made him bitter. He hated the fact that he too was among the lonely, and it just wasn't fair that an Irishman like himself should ever have to feel dejected.

Without warning the beast struck, shining his light on the unsuspecting moviegoer. The shocked middle-aged man nearly died of humiliation. Time suspended as seconds turned into hours. Tears welled in his eyes before he could do anything to stop them. Then to top off everything he almost caught his wilting wiener in his zipper.

"All right, you friggin' freak of nature. Get your shit and get the fuck out," Jimmy announced loud enough for the entire theater to hear. Several amused customers laughed as they watched the spectacle. A mild round of applause followed the lion and his Christian as they exited the theater.

It didn't take very long for the routine to return to normal. Juan worked the concession stand that sold stale popcorn, rubber-tasting hot dogs, candy, and flat soda. He also checked the theater every half hour for pot-smoking or dick-spanking while Jimmy managed the ticket booth, chain-smoked, and drank.

And drank.

The night seemed to slowly crawl by on its belly. Large boom-box radios added atmosphere, with the latest hardcore raps bombarding the hearing of everyone in the vicinity. The only real excitement occurred when the two Puerto Ricans he'd had a beef with earlier walked by again. This time, the usher took the initiative and flipped them off. Curses and threats were exchanged before Jimmy picked up the phone, and again the duo left angry.

Buzzing from the drinks, Jimmy watched as hookers of every size, sex, and ethnic background tried hustling up customers. For some reason, the bad weather had brought the working girls out. With no regard to the AIDS epidemic, sexual services were bought in abundance. Jimmy contemplated a quickie during his fifteen-minute break. A little head never hurt anything except his wallet.

As the night grew older, the action on the street began to slow down. Police cars constantly sped by with new passengers occupying the back seat. Jimmy couldn't care less. His bottle was starting to get dangerously low, as was his mood. The more inebriated he became, the nastier he got. He'd lashed out at Juan on two separate occasions as well as having made several rude comments to patrons. It was his racial slurs that often got him beaten up. Regardless of how many poundings he took, he never learned.

Juan emerged from inside the theater and informed Jimmy that there was another man masturbating inside. He blew cigarette smoke in Juan's direction and smiled an unfriendly smile.

"What's a matter? Youse afraid of a jerking-off jerkie?"

"No—no."

"Then what's the fucking problem, Sanchez?" he asked coldly, enjoying himself at Juan's expense.

"Well?" Jimmy baited. He loved making Juan crawl. For several long seconds he waited for Juan to reply.

"C'mon, ya fuckin' hump. Spit it out."

"'I'm uncomfortable, you know,'" Juan explained, unable to meet eyes with Jimmy.

"'I'm uncomfortable, you know,'" Jimmy repeated in a mocking, girlish, high-pitched voice,

raising his sodden body off the stool he was sitting
on and exiting the ticket booth.

"You know something, Juan? I'm gonna start calling you Juanita if you don't grow a spine. I mean,
you're a tough guy, right? I thought all you spics are
supposed to be tough"

Before going into the theater, Jimmy made a
quick stop at the now-closed concession stand. He
ducked down and pulled open one of the drawers
beneath the sink and removed an official New York
Rangers team glass that he bought at McDonald's
for forty-nine cents with a purchase of a medium-
sized soft drink. Juan grew impatient with him but
said nothing as the drunkard filled the glass with
another stash he had hidden.

A man in a cheap suit was milking his lizard for
all it was worth. If he wasn't careful, he'd be blind
by the end of the movie. He looked like every other
faceless person who frequented this type of estab-
lishment. The friction between his penis and palm
made a loud rubbing sound. The man stopped momentarily, spat into his fist, and went back to work.
His fast hand speed increased as he neared orgasm.
He began to moan much like Paula Price, the
woman onscreen, who had an exceptionally thick
dick in her butt.

For a split second, Jimmy zoned out and again
enjoyed the show. There was something decadently
exciting about pornography and beautiful young
girls who are willing to do anything sexually. Then
reality struck down his pleasure as he realized that
he'd never have as physically attractive a woman as
the one onscreen. Much like Juan, he too hated this
job. He hated how dejected it made him feel. He
hated it when he was turned on by the smut because
he no longer felt any better than the men who paid

to be here. And dammit, he was better than every last one of them. From the homeless vagabonds to the college professors and every freak in between, Jimmy Downey was better. He hated the perverts, like this little runt sitting before him, who came in off the street to hit nut and return to their humdrum middle-class routine.

And besides, even the priests said doing it was wrong.

With his left hand, he shined the flashlight's powerful beam directly into the patron's face, freezing him like a stunned deer caught in a car's headlights. The panic-stricken man couldn't even cover himself as Jimmy's right hand dumped the liquid from the Rangers cup into the man's lap. Contrary to Juan's earlier thoughts, it was not booze. Shrieks of agony filled the seedy theater as his flesh began to bubble up. Ghastly blisters quickly multiplied on top of each other as sulfuric acid quickly ate its way through any exposed skin. Blood boiled up and out of his veins as the corrosive liquid burned its way through his erection. The man crumpled, fell off his seat, and began writhing on the sticky floor. Crimson was raining out of his penis. After twenty seconds of high-pitched torture, his screams subsided to something much worse. Whimpering in torment, he begged God to end his misery as he tried holding together what was left of his ruined cock. Juan also began praying, asking for forgiveness. Then he threw up on himself.

Jimmy shook his head, disgusted with Juan's lack of intestinal fortitude. He pointed down at the bleeding man and drunkenly mumbled out just loud enough for the entire horrified audience to hear, "Betcha he never does *that* again!"

The shocked audience began screaming and hol-

lering as they flooded out of every exit. Within a half
minute, every last customer was going or gone. It
only took Jimmy several sobering seconds to realize
that he'd fucked up big-time. While in theory his
plan to stop masturbating customers was effective,
the reality of it was that he'd done something criminal. Very criminal. Alcoholic sweat flooded his
pores. His heart began to pound as adrenaline shot
through his drunken body. After regaining partial
composure, he decided to call it a night. He'd just
go home, black out, forget this ever happened, and
never return.

He viciously shoved the babbling usher out of his
way as he made it toward the ticket booth. Juan
couldn't believe what he was seeing. This wasn't
right, but what was he to do? Jimmy grabbed his
coat and a few other personal belongings, and all
the money he could pocket out of the register.

"Fuck 'em, only a few people know what really
went down. If anybody asks, and they won't, I didn't
do shit," Jimmy reasoned, trying to stay cool under
the circumstances.

The night air felt cold, sobering. With each passing moment, he regained more and more of his wits.
The ground was still wet, but at least the rain had
stopped. Off in the distance, sirens wailed, growing
louder as they grew nearer.

He had to get away.

Outside the theater, a small crowd had gathered
and rumors were already spreading as to what had
happened inside. The tanked usher felt their angry
fingers pointing at him. He looked down, trying to
hide his face, as he headed into the safety of Manhattan's neon jungle. It was easy to get lost in the
shuffle. All he needed was a taxi. Or maybe a subway.

Just as he was breaking away from the growing theater crowd, Jimmy ran into his two favorite Puerto Ricans. Before he could say or do anything, the smaller fellow was all over him, hitting him with vicious lefts and rights. The blows were extremely powerful, backed up by a roll of nickels in each fist. The sound of his face being pounded drowned out all the other street noise. Every now and then the sound of bones cracking occurred, but Jimmy doubted that it was his assailant's fists. He tried covering himself as best he could but the little guy, he was five feet five standing on a phone book, was relentless. His white freckled face was now red, purple, and swollen. The bigger man got in an occasional lick, but he was really there to make sure that his smaller friend won. And all three judges had him winning by a unanimous decision. Then, just like the cavalry, the police came running and separated them.

Thank you, God, Jimmy thought as his battered body fell like a sack onto the cement. Blood seeped out of several openings on his face. He didn't know if his swollen jaw was broken but his nose definitely was. Looking up through his one unclosed eye, he'd never been so enthralled by the beautiful sight of handcuffs—that is, until he realized that they weren't for the Puerto Ricans.

Bloodlust

Tell me, what do you feel when my eyes fall upon you: joy or sadness? Do I make you want to turn away? Is mine a stare that radiates love or intimidation? Do you feel anything? Fear perhaps? Maybe you would rather not look? Is evil inherited or an acquired trait? Is there something about my brown eyes you find disturbing? Tell me. You really shouldn't worry, my eyes are just like yours.

Perhaps.

What propels one person toward creativity and another toward sadism? Why does one man carve a steak while another carves up his family? Why are guns so popular? Who are "random crime victims," and why do they meet horrible fates? How can one person spend an entire lifetime searching for true love while another finds it easily, only to turn their back on it? Why do tools of hatred outsell instruments of peace? Why does one man split an atom in the name of God and science, while another uses that technology to obliterate a country? Where do the forces of violence come from? Where does one draw the line dividing good and evil?

These questions change from person to person, but the answer is always found in their eyes.

I was up with the sunrise. Sleep rarely comes the night before I'm due to perform, and today was no exception. I might have gotten three or four hours of uneasy sleep. I can't tell. It doesn't matter. On nights like last night, sleep reminds me of death, and that's the last experience I want to embrace.

You see, I'm a professional warrior, a high-priced gladiator, a killer. Since the beginning of time man has lusted for blood and has been willing to pay top dollar for it. Wagering on life and death began before Jesus Christ's crucifixion, and unfortunately it has never stopped. We revel in self-righteousness about being humane, being above animals, being rational, but whenever there is bloodshed, like a car wreck, people crane their necks, thrilled that it wasn't their misfortune. My opponent and I will fight until only one of us is left standing. I exist because I kill and will continue killing in order to exist. It may come as a surprise to some of you that fights to the death still occur, but then again, some of you may have attended these exhibitions. The admission price to see us perform is nothing compared with the heavy wagers being laid on our heads. Many spectators have left arenas devastated, not because of the atrocities they've witnessed but because of the large sums of money they've lost on a "sure thing." The only sure thing in life is death and taxes and I don't pay taxes.

My trainer and owner, Saul Kutz, is a kind old man of about sixty who, if judging the book by its cover, looks as though he doesn't have the constitution for this sort of activity. He looks tender, almost vulnerable, but beneath his apparent weakness there is a man solid as nails and a superb fighting strategist. His dull hazel eyes have a certain depth of knowledge that reinforces whatever he's saying as true. I've grown to love this life as well as Saul. It may not be for everyone, it may not be "humane," it may not be legal, but you'll never understand what kind of a rush I feel when I fight for my life, or the gratification I feel standing over my slain opponent. One could say that I'm Saul's slave, but I don't view it like that since I could easily kill him or run away. Thoughts like those have never appealed to me. Saul's always been fair and straight with me, which is more than can be said for a lot of people in this racket. Many trainers dope their protégés and bet against them, making a small killing (no pun intended). Not Saul. He has a real sense of integrity, and I respect him for it. He has always looked out for my best interest and has never placed me in a no-win situation. If I lose, it's because I deserve to.

My last fight was held in a different state. In this business you have to love traveling. Saul has taken me places and shown me things I would have never imagined if I'd led a "normal" life. With the authorities always one step behind, eager to make the big bust, touring is the only way to ensure your freedom. The idea of spending the rest of my life behind bars is much more frightening than losing tonight.

The aroma of Havana cigars gave Saul away as he entered the quarters through a thin gray fog. Quickly I rose and listened as he dealt me the same rap he always did about not hurting myself on the day of a fight. He explained tonight's game strategy, speaking slowly, methodically, making sure I absorbed every word while I stretched out, loosening tight muscles. I've trained every day for the past eight months. My body is a rock of muscle. The hard hours will all be worth it because I don't intend to lose tonight. Saul checked my eyes and reflexes with

his hands. I knew I hadn't overtrained, and it was
apparent that I was ready to test myself in the ultimate form of competition.

Reflecting back on my last match, I had gotten off
rather easily. Sure I bled and was bruised for a few
weeks, but the match lasted less than fifteen minutes. Needless to say, I was in tip-top shape. On the
other hand, my opponent was a seasoned veteran
who was ready to be taken out of the game, and I
felt absolutely no remorse in doing so. After all, it's
a dog-eat-dog world.

Saul explained that I wouldn't be on until eight
o'clock, so we'd take today very easy. I needed a
quick jog to loosen up some more. He let me outside
and told me three times not to overdo it. It took
some real willpower to hold back my adrenaline
rushes when my legs wanted to sprint, but I could
feel Saul's eyes burning holes in my back, making
sure I didn't overdo it. Other trainers kept guns on
their fighters just in case their bread and butter decided to split. Saul and I didn't need anything like
guns.

*"If you pull a goddamn muscle and we have to pull
out of tonight's fight, the fuckin' psycho promoter
will rip my eyes out and piss on my brain!"*

I could still hear his words as I threw caution to
the wind and broke into a quick wind sprint. The
morning sun was blinding, and I almost got hit by a
speeding metallic-green Chevelle that had to swerve
to avoid me.

Good thing Saul didn't see that, I thought as the
car disappeared into the horizon. I continued running. California was like a second home to me. I
never had a real home, but I was born in Cali, and I
did well whenever I fought there. A silly sense of

home field advantage filled me as I trotted back. It really didn't make sense since a killer has no home.

Saul had seen my close call and chewed my ears off. His "I told you so" tone of concern echoed through my brain until breakfast was ready. The little workout had whetted my appetite. I could hear myself making chomping noises as I tore into the blood-rare steak, ripping it ravenously. This could be my last meal, and while I ate like someone possessed, Saul continued thinking, plugging, and planning out tonight's strategy.

Time dragged on the way it always did on fight days. This was what the condemned man standing at the gallows must feel like. Little things started playing with my mind. Would today be the last time I felt the wind blow? Would I ever see moving clouds again? What wonders would tomorrow hold if tomorrow actually arrived? Saul said very little during the ride to the arena, and this made me very uncomfortable. He wasn't being his usual talkative self.

Did he know something I should?

The ride along the 101 South was a slow one as we caught the tail end of the five-to-seven traffic. Cars lined up in four lanes and crawled for miles. People stared at me like they knew who I was, and every time a police car or motorcycle cop came into view, Saul tightened up. When we finally reached our exit, Saul sighed and loosened up just a bit. Carefully, so not to draw any unnecessary attention, the light brown Cadillac that had carried us through most of the U.S. cruised through the maze that was downtown Los Angeles.

The car pulled into a semi-empty side street and eased itself into a large parking lot behind an old redbrick warehouse that would serve as tonight's venue. As a precaution, it had been rented by the promoter under an alias. The building was like countless other ones I'd fought in; nothing special or flashy, and more important, nothing that would raise unwarranted suspicions.

The once-bright sun was fading fast, and the early evening temperature was dropping. Saul shut off the tinny-sounding jazz that came from AM airwaves, and we got out of the car. The air tasted alive and brisk. The street noise sounded like a symphony.

A massive man who must have weighed close to four hundred pounds let us inside the building through a side door. He stunk like he hadn't washed in weeks. A smoldering Kool cigarette hung loosely from his oversize purplish lips. Gray smoke shot out of his wide nostrils as he explained where our dressing room was. He kept a watchful eye on me and stepped back outside.

The room allotted to us was probably an old janitor's quarters. It stank of ammonia and stale beer, the same way an old barroom floor smells. Saul paced the perimeter three times before settling down in an old, torn green Naugahyde chair. He stared at me but said nothing.

The minutes ticked away the final half-hour so slowly that I felt at one with the rust growing on the old pipes that ran down the corner of the dressing room. It felt as though I was trapped in suspended animation. That's the worst part about death fights; waiting for showtime. Saul stubbed out a dark brown cigar and within a minute lit another. Then he rubbed me down. Outside, I could hear the rumble of fans starting to gather. Saul's firm hands squeezed my back, my arms, and my neck until I signaled for him to stop. Then he nervously left to go speak to the promoter.

As usual, there was only one bout scheduled after mine. If there was an overabundance of warriors willing to fight to the death, then the demand to see blood wouldn't be so great. Neither would the purse. I listened to his Florsheim shoes slap floor tiles until there was silence.

Saul quickly walked down the empty corridor. Every five feet or so there was a light brown wooden door. He twisted the dull brass knobs, but they wouldn't budge. He continued until he found a door that opened.

"Hey, puto!"

"Sorry," Saul replied, quickly shutting the door. He continued down the dreary, poorly lit hallway. One of these doors had to be the promoter's office. He was determined to find the man. Although he always had prefight jitters, he had never felt this way before. He felt intoxicated without having had a drink all day. Intuition told him to get out of this fight and fast.

He found the door he wanted, knocked, and entered. Seated behind an olive-green desk was tonight's promoter. He and Saul had done business before, and neither liked the other.

"Saul-ee bay-be." Saul didn't reply but forced a transparent smile out of respect.

The forty-three-year-old promoter was sharply dressed. His tan Pierre Cardin suit looked tailor-made. Around his neck were several gold rope chains, and his front teeth were also made of gold. His dark tan was salon-bought and made his bald head gleam. In his left ear was a tiny diamond stud.

"My fighter's ill, I gotta pull outta tonight's fight,"

Saul announced as fast as the words would fly. He felt his heart pounding hard, threatening.

A red flush rose up over the promoter's face. "BULLSHIT!" he yelled, slamming his fist down on the metal desk, causing a small American flag and several Papermate pens to roll. Agitated, the slick promoter grabbed the flag before it fell off the table. Then he sent everything else—documents, imported cigarettes, and pens—flying across the room. The twenty-four-karat-gold Rolex around his wrist jangled. He stood the flag back up in its appropriate spot and stared at it, bewildered, hardly believing the audacity of the old man before him.

"He can't go on tonight. I never seen him look like this. It'll be a slaughter. Please," Saul pleaded.

"Then it'll be a slaughter," the bald promoter coldly stated. "People pay good money to see a slaughter, and business is business. Jew like you should know that. Personally, I don't give a fuck. If your boy is breathing get him to the ring on time."

A demented smile formed as he removed a fully automatic Heckler & Koch nine-millimeter pistol from one of the desk drawers.

"Or get melted."

Five minutes passed. Saul returned silent, pale, and flaccid, like he'd just tossed his lunch. I began to wonder if something wasn't kosher about this fight. Endless cigar smoke drifted out of his mouth, forming an annoying cloud that didn't rise. When he took the cigar out of his mouth, it threatened to shake itself free from his left hand.

Saul motioned for me, and we left the rinky-dink dressing room. Standing on a tiny runway, he gave me my final instructions and a few corny clichés of inspiration. Try as he might, Saul would never be compared to Vince Lombardi.

Connoisseurs of death fights knew about tonight's matches through several underground publications dedicated to the sport. Spectators who had never seen me fight knew all about my foe, myself, our records, our strengths and weaknesses, and the odds set for tonight's bout. Along with photos, these fanzines printed bogus fight schedules as well as real ones to confuse authorities. Anyone who reads these publications regularly knows how to read between the lines.

We burst through a set of steel double doors, and I trotted behind him. I'd already been announced through a megaphone, and a spotlight was awaiting me. Standing in the center of the "ring" was the ring announcer, who resembled Groucho Marx with a large beer gut. I instantly felt crazed hatred toward this cheesy-looking excuse for a human. I guess he sensed my hostility because before I reached the ring, he was long gone.

The crowd was as mixed as any I'd ever seen. Every ethnic group was accounted for tonight. The promoter was definitely going to make some bucks. There were men in expensive business suits drinking out of silver flasks, their ties crooked, noses red, and pressed shirts untucked. All their faces told the same story: They'd lied to their wives, using the same routines they applied whenever the occasion arose to have some extracurricular sex with nubile, promotable secretaries. Society's elite loved blood, and they'd pay big bucks for it. Next to the Beverly Hills imports were the blue collars: construction workers, clerks, taxi hacks, compulsively chain smoking and drinking beer out of paper bags, money in hand and ready to party. There were very

few women and no children present. There never
were. This was status quo for these twentieth-cen-
tury "games." It was too brutal for the young or
weak-stomached. Warriors like myself serviced brutality, which would always be a macho sport.

Located at each end of the arena floor was a bet-
ting booth run by the promoter. It was a bizarre
combination of OTB and three-card monte. The
odds were posted at the booths. You handed the
cashier your money and received a claim check. If
your fighter won, the claim stub was cashed in. Behind each cashier were two heavily armed security
guards with mafioso loyalty and eager-to-act Uzi
trigger fingers.

The stale air was dense and stung my eyes. Whenever these bouts were held indoors, it was a no-win
situation. If there was air conditioning, after the
bout you'd catch a cold, and if there wasn't, humid-
ity from the spotlights made it difficult to breathe.
Tonight there wasn't any AC, and a thick cloud of
smoke hung lifelessly up by the lights. The "ring"
wasn't a conventional one. It was a fifteen-square-
foot fenced-in area. The roof of the cage was eight
feet high, and barbed wire ran along the top of the
cage in case one of the fighters tried running. There
were two doors, one on each side of the ring, and
they were locked as soon as the match started. Only
one door needed to be opened at the end of the
match.

Saul slowed us down to a very laggard strut. The
crowd stood around the steel-caged ring, eagerly
awaiting my entrance. Since most of these spectators would have to wait a year before they'd witness
another live spectacle, they let their voices be heard
tonight. The majority booed me, which meant they'd

bet on my opponent. This wasn't the first time I was the underdog.

"You over-the-hill piece of shit!" yelled a deep-throated fat man with tattooed hands. I took a slight step toward him, but Saul held me back. The fat man's intoxicated eyes filled with terror as well as amazement.

Forgetting the cup of beer in his hand, Fatty shook his fists at me, showering two people. A small-scale riot almost erupted. Saul usually let me bait hecklers, and his quick action to pull me away surprised me. What surprised me even more was the stunned expression on his face. While I'd been enjoying myself growling and terrorizing the audience, Saul's eyes never left my opponent.

His eyes were death black and merciless. There were too many scars on his face, and it resembled a puzzle of pain. Red marks, gouges, and welts adorned most of face and upper torso. It was apparent that he had been fighting as long as, if not longer than, I had. A long, deep, jagged scar ran along the left side of his face that made him look even more evil than he was.

His eyes were fixed on mine, and I returned the death stare. If I let this psycho know that I was the slightest bit intimidated, I was doomed. Saul always said you can tell who's going to win by the look in their eyes.

The lights around the ring dimmed.

There was a frightening lull as Saul turned to me and said, "Okay, boy, this is it. We've been through this plenty of times before, so don't let me down. We've worked for months, and you know that in order to win you gotta be the aggressor with this fucker. I'm too damn old to be left alone in this miserable world. You gotta get in there and get him. Get him!''

Saul spent a good portion of his life training me, sweating right alongside me. Whenever I got into trouble, and God knew I'd had an uncanny knack for finding trouble wherever we went, he always got me out of it. He inhaled deeply on his cigar and left the ring wearing a nervous look. He tried to hide it, but I saw right through him. Shaking, he locked the deadbolt behind me.

On the opposite side of the ring, a Mexican trainer slapped his fighter in the chops, trying to get his warrior psyched up. His trainer stepped in front of him and began shouting instructions in Spanish. It didn't take a mental giant to get the idea of what was being said. Death is a universal language. It must have worked because he turned around, looked at me, and began snarling. Drool frothed on his mouth and dribbled down in a long, thin stream.

The trainer slapped his fighter again and left the ring. I heard the other deadbolt slam shut.

The show was on.

We stared at one another for several long seconds. It's within these few precious seconds that two gladiators acknowledge one another's courage while their minds fill with hate. My opponent looked ready to give me the challenge of my life. It was that one simple thought: *the challenge of my life.* A higher compliment couldn't be paid.

And never in my life did I long to kill someone so.

We charged at full speed. Muscles pumped, veins pulsed, adrenaline flowed. Power and force combined with speed and energy as the distance between us shortened. With less than three feet separating us, we both lowered our heads and threw ourselves at each other.

Crackkk.

It made a revolting sound, two skulls smashing. Faces in the audience, faces that paid to see this, grimaced and groaned. Our heads had collided in midair, and we both fell backward, stunned. The match wasn't even fifteen seconds old when I felt the warm trickle of blood running behind my left ear. It was an old wound reopened. As quickly as they felt unease at the sound of our heads smashing, the crowd wildly cheered the first drawing of blood.

I regained my senses and locked up with my opponent in a test of strength. Our upper bodies pushed against each other as we jockied for leverage. Knees locked and calves pushed as our feet tried to slide out from beneath us. With a powerful surge, my opponent landed on top of me. We rolled around several times on the cold concrete floor before I finally got out of his grip.

Again we locked up tooth and nail. Every time you lock up with someone trying to rip your heart out, you'd better give 110 percent. Maneuvering to my right, I snuck in and tried to squeeze the life out of him. His hot rancid breath stank, and he squirmed away. We both regained our balance and locked up again. His short stocky arms were extremely powerful, and he managed to get them under mine. With leverage underneath my armpits, my opponent threw me flat on my back, knocking the air out of me. His maniacal black eyes were those of a crazed shark during a feeding frenzy.

I got up quickly, ignoring the pain, and started backing up. My foe cut off the angle and started cornering me against the steel fence. He fell for my plan and charged furiously. Right before he reached me, I stepped to my left. He went crashing headfirst into the solid-steel corner post. It made a dull gong

sound. I pounced on him and held my advantage for
as long as I could.

The impact of the blow busted my opponent's face
wide open. Crimson poured out of his forehead,
covering the disfiguring scars that ran along his
face. I didn't know which was worse, before or after
the bloodshed. A blow as hard as the one he'd just
received would have knocked most warriors out,
but this psycho managed to shake it off. *Maybe he
has a steel plate in his head?*

The sight of his blood excited me, and I felt a
surge of adrenaline. I stayed on top of him, but he
was up to my every challenge. Ten minutes passed
with neither of us showing any signs of tiring. Out of
the corner of my eye I could see Saul, with his ever-
present cloud of cigar smoke, waving his arms and
rooting for me. I tore into my opponent. He de-
fended himself well and knew when to retreat to
regain lost strength. He turned his thick back momentarily, and I leaped on him. I wrapped my legs
around his waist and my arms around his face and
started squeezing. I sank my teeth into the top of his
cranium. A mixture of hair and skin filled my
mouth. I shook rapidly, making his head jerk like a
rag doll's. Blood began to fill my mouth. In desperation, he sank his teeth savagely into my arm. The
sharp pain caught me off guard, and that was
enough for him to seize the opportunity and flip me
over onto my back.

With everything spinning, I saw him crouch and
lunge toward me. With no time to spare, I lifted my
legs and caught him in the midsection. He flipped
over me, got back up, and again we squared off.

The crowd was going wild. I often wondered
whether the police were paid to not investigate
these noises coming from unused buildings. Every-

one in the audience was screaming at full volume, encouraging us to kill. You learn to hate the crowd more than your opponent.

The action continued at a feverish pace for another fifteen minutes. We'd lock up, muscles and veins working overtime, trying to overpower each other. One fighter would gain a temporary advantage, then the other would counter. The lights over the ring made it twenty degrees hotter than hell on a summer day. I was completely exhausted, ready to overheat, and bleeding profusely.

The time had come for one of us to die.

I heard Saul shouting instructions from behind me. Nothing he said made any sense as I was fighting on instincts. All learned skills were gone. Panting heavily, we locked up again and continued the death dance. My opponent's odious eyes were bloodshot with determination as he savagely butted his bloody face against my nose. I fell back against the fence. He pressed me into it, trying to grate me like a piece of cheese. I spun him, returning the favor, and I held the momentary advantage. Each time we tied up I heard sick muted growls coming from his throat. Again, I turned to my right and rolled with him along the fence. Then he mustered up enough strength to spin me. Finally, we stopped shredding one another and staggered back into the center of the ring. With my last bit of energy, I slammed my sore head upward and it crashed into the bottom of his jaw. A tooth and a sliver of pink tongue fell out of his mouth as I opened mine. Stretching my jaw as far as it would go, I clamped down with all my might. Much to my surprise, my upper canines went right through my opponent's throat. My jaw squeezed and spun, brutally flinging him ninety degrees, and he landed on his side on the cold floor. Large strands of flesh remained lodged inside my mouth after I'd let go. My opponent moaned in agony. I stared at my worthy foe, ready for him to leap on me at any given moment. A seemingly endless flow of blood poured out of his severed jugular vein as his left leg spasmed uncontrollably. He tried to get back up, twitched and jerked for several moments, then died.

The stunned crowd began cheering. Most of those who had lost money remained silent out of respect for the dead. Some creeps cried fix, but it took only one look at me, badly bleeding, to know I'd won fairly. Quite a few people lost money on the match. Shocked expressions swept their faces. Even the well-tailored promoter was applauding my effort. The cheering didn't last very long. It never does.

I waited in the center of the ring like I always did. I'd been trained to stand still until Saul came and got me. No matter how hard the people cheered or booed me, I would not move until the time was right. It was this kind of discipline that made me a champion. Exhausted and injured, I heard the deadbolt behind me open and sensed Saul approaching. I turned and saw him counting money. I hadn't let him down. When he patted the top of my sore head, my tired battered body filled with happiness.

Date Rape

If only Judy would drop before the "Till death do them part" part, thought Jason Ronson, then maybe his menial existence could actually have some meaning. Maybe there was something—or more important, someone—out there for him. It wasn't as if he were looking for a meal ticket or anything, busting his balls was what he was accustomed to. He could deal with the commute, the crowds, the anxiety, the monotony, the calculations, his limited potential for advancement up the corporate ladder, and even the shitty coffee, but he was starting to really lose his patience with her. He'd stopped loving her years ago.

And what was there to love?

Judy was more of a nag than a wife. She was an overbearing, middle-class, uptight bitch who loved her position among her gossipy yacht club friends more than the missionary position. The Ronsons had sex once or twice a month, usually after watching an exceptionally steamy episode of *Red Shoe Diaries*, and those sessions were nothing to look forward to. There was neither passion nor lust. To get Judy to give him oral sex was nearly impossible. She rarely finished what she started but when the shoe

was on the other foot, she was more than willing to
spread her out-of-shape legs. It wasn't beyond her
to keep him down there until he was blue in the face
and she was quite satisfied. *But that wasn't the issue.* It was the years of her vicious jabs that hurt
him much more than lack of physical contact. Her
game was control, which meant keeping Jason under her thumb regardless of how cruel or cold she
had to be.

His secretary called in on the intercom but received no answer. It wasn't that he hadn't heard
her, it was almost impossible not to hear Diane
Greider's shrill voice echoing throughout the firm.
Ronson's thoughts were miles away from the numbers that make up a certified public accountant's
daily routine. After softly knocking on his locked
door, Diane gave up.

He'd been anticipating this moment since he
picked up the latest issue of *Hustler* at a newsstand
in Grand Central Station. It wasn't the first time
he'd seen, or for that matter called, the 1-900 number the beauty was soliciting, but every third week
of the new month promised a new photograph of
her. His wife, who would be calling after Regis and
Kathie Lee was over, would throw a third-stage major conniption fit if she ever found out that he read
Swank, Chic, Cheri, or any other magazines of that
ilk. In Judy's opinion, pornography was criminal.
She would keel over and sue him for divorce if she
knew he spent the better portion of his lunch hour
in adult book stores and peep shows. The fact that
she had driven him there made no difference.

For all intents and purposes the magazine ended
on page 115 with three snapshots of ordinary-Jane
types in *Hustler*'s Beaver Hunt section. An over-
weight woman with a vagina that looked like stale

salami was spread-eagled on a chair while the other
two nudes posed on beds in cheap lingerie. All three
shots were taken by their respective husbands, and
as far as Jason was concerned, all were wastes of
paper and trees. After the Hunt ended, there were
an additional twenty-nine pages of advertisements
for everything from hardcore adult videos and magazines to sexual aids. The majority of the ads were
for the billion-dollar-a-year industry of phone sex.
Eye-catching color photos promised everything
from 1-900 VIRGINS who were X-tra naughty to 1-900
CLASSY LADIES who wanted to speak to horny studs.
For an average of three dollars per minute, one
could talk to lesbians, she-males, California dream
girls, dominatrices, well-hung hunks, desperate college coeds, kinky Vegas showgirls, female convicts,
and just about anything else under the sexual sun.
None of these other ads meant anything to Jason—
not anymore, anyway. As he scanned them, he felt
himself growing irritated. He didn't have the time
or desire to spend his hard-earned cash rapping to
an ebony anal nymph or listening to a retired porn
starlet moan. After flipping through twenty-two
pages of nothing, there she was.

About fuckin' time, he thought as he tried focusing
his designer eyeglasses on the beautiful woman inside the five-inch advertisement. There was nothing
flashy about the ad; that was what had aroused his
curiosity in the first place. If anything it was almost
too tame in comparison with the other three ads on
the page. The dim lighting that was used added atmosphere and romance. Definitely not what the
glossy immediate-gratification audience wanted.
Using his mathematical logic, Jason concluded that
the three other "hot" ads made at least five times as
much money from the 1-900 jackoff crowd, which

was just fine by him. He felt a slight sense of machismo knowing that his dream lover was less used, less worn out.

In his mind, he had developed a relationship with her that only a bookworm mathematician could conjure. The frail man with a weak chin and pug nose was her black knight in shining armor. He was her defender, and in return she was always eager to satisfy him. Jason respected the fact that she never showed too much skin in her ads. There was no spread-eagle exploitation, and she always wore antique black lace. The tasteful feminine lingerie always revealed a pert breast or her well-rounded alabaster ass. Unlike all the other lip-licking or wickedly smiling women, his fantasy lover never looked directly at the camera.

The latest ad was nothing short of a masterpiece. It showed her sitting in an antique rocking chair, leaning forward with her right elbow on her thigh, her long fingers holding up her narrow chin. Her bowed face was partially obscured by wavy raven-black locks, and her magnificent chartreuse eyes pierced through the reader. Her thick lips were painted bright red. Her see-through black negligee was revealing enough to give Jason a good view of both breasts.

As always, right above the phone number, 1-900-555-0923, the ad asked: COULD YOU TREAT A WHORE LIKE A LADY OR A LADY LIKE A WHORE?

Jason thought he could do both and reached for the phone.

While the number rang, he removed his eel-skin wallet from his back pocket and pulled out his American Express Gold Card. The call averaged between twenty and forty dollars, but at least this way

it wouldn't show up on the company's phone bill
and there would be no questions.

"Hello?"

"Eva?"

"Who asks?"

"Jason . . . Jason Ronson."

"Hello, Jake," the seductive voice declared ever
so softly. She had called him Jake during their initial conversation, and since then it was her pet
name for him.

She remembered, he thought. No one else had ever
called him anything so mysterious. Jake, a real he-
man kind of name. The kind of man he always desired to be. The kind of man Kelly LeBrock would
want after he put on some Brut cologne. After going
through the formality of taking down his credit card
number, expiration date and all, the two continued
where they last left off.

Her voice was the sedative he needed to get
through this stress-maligned morning. Her tone was
beautifully soothing, like verbal lithium. He removed his glasses, closed his eyes, and listened as
Eva questioned the mores of society. She always did
this. The sex would come later. And after listening
to her actually speak to him, the sex was like dessert
after a marvelous meal. She asked questions like,
Why should Jake Ronson be denied his true identity? Why should he be a slave to his job when ad-
venture was just around the corner? Why should he
be legally handcuffed to a frigid overbearing house-
wife who was unaware of his carnal passion? Why
did his dreams have to be compromises? Why were
his desires unfulfilled? And most important, why did
he have to answer to anyone other than himself and
the laws of nature?

Why wasn't he with her right now? he thought to himself.

"Are you touching yourself?" the raspy, sexy female asked. It was her voice, not his fingers, that he felt wrapping around his cock. It only took a few moments to bring life where there previously hadn't been any. He felt himself growing as she cooed and encouraged him. Her addictive voice kept reassuring him that there was nothing wrong with the way he was feeling. When he was fully erect, the psychic television inside his mind tuned to a channel of erotic images. He knew Eva was tuned to the same station.

Eva was naked, lying on her back on an antique bed. As he kissed away at her tight stomach, she ran her fingers through his thinning hair. Jake was licking his way toward her flower. Eva arched her back as far as it would go and white-knuckled the brass headboard as he parted her with his tongue. Tiny groans of passion escaped her. Jake had never tasted anything so sweet, so beautiful before. Her rosewater juices were the finest nectar from the fountain of youth, and Jake felt rejuvenated. Eva didn't feel too bad herself. Her heavy, raspy breathing increased in volume. It was these love noises that encouraged Jake to do as thorough a job as he possibly could. Her lovely thighs threatened to squash his head like a grape, but he never stopped working her until he was damn sure she was satisfied.

He kissed his way back up her body, giving every inch its due attention. When their mouths met, lips locked and tongues danced passionately. The scent of her sex on his face turned her on, and she licked his mouth and chin clean. Eva smothered him in kisses, then began working her way down his body.

When she reached his midsection, she looked up at him with the hungriest green eyes he'd ever seen. Jake closed his eyes, and Eva continued her descent like only an expert could.

"Good?" she asked playfully. Her voice sounded like it was from a new sexual dimension instead of the other end of the phone line.

"Always."

"Good . . ."

"Wait," Jake barked earnestly.

There was a long, awkward silence before she could force her words out.

"Jake, we've been through this before."

The phone in his hand felt like it weighed thirty pounds. A sense of desperation that had nothing to do with post-ejaculation guilt swept through him. His feelings for her had turned into something more than a mild obsession. And by the inflection in her voice, he knew she felt something for him. There was too much feeling in her tone. It had been at least eight years, the duration of his marriage, since he'd last felt this alive. He hated hanging up. There had to be more to this than masturbating into a wad of tissues.

"Eva, I've been calling you every Tuesday, once a week, for the past three months. I know my soul hungers for more than this. I hope yours does too. Christ, I even know on what days the latest magazines arrive. If it's lust, well, then let it be lust, but I have to see you."

"Jake, you just did."

Well, then I have to feel you," he persisted. Tiny beads of sweat sprinted down his face. He looked at the clock. It was just after ten.

"Jake, you know how this works."

"Name your price."

"I'm not for sale," she quickly retorted, slightly offended. He could feel her hostility, so before she could hang up, he quickly barked his apologies. After a momentary silence, he could hear her breathing into the mouthpiece.

"I'd really love to but—"

"But what? *What???*"

"You don't understand." Eva sighed.

"What's to understand? I want you, you want me. *Only a phone line separates us*. I'm willing to travel anywhere, pay any amount and then some."

"I'm not a toy or an escort. You can't rent or buy my affections. I'm more than that, and I need more."

"What are you trying to say? I mean, think about it. Basically, your job is, well, a phone whore?" Jake stated nervously, trying to sound firm. He waited a few long seconds for her to respond.

"Does using a word like *whore* make you feel any better?"

Silence.

"I didn't think so," she said softly, sincerely. In that instant, Jason felt more compassion for her and her breathy voice than he'd ever experienced. He felt it leaving his body, traveling through the phone lines and diving into her mouth the way he wished he could. Just as he was getting ready to declare his devotion to her, he felt her getting ready to say something, so he quickly clammed up.

"Jake, more than anything I need stability."

"I'm an accountant!"

"It's not about money. If only it were that easy. . . . I may only be a telephone prostitute to you, but money isn't my game. *Not really*. There are things no man will ever understand about my wants. Everything is so obvious to you when it's in mathematical terms, but what about when an unknown X factor is thrown in?"

"Like what?"

"Like me and my needs."

Just as she figured, he was thrown off guard. Most men to whom she asked this question were. She gave Jake his chance and he'd blown it, so she said a silent good-bye and hung up.

It only took seconds before her phone rang again. It was him again, apologizing, asking what he could do to make right by her.

"Jake, do you believe in spirits?"

"Like ghosts?"

"No, more like karma."

"I believe that there is more than what we perceive to be reality. I believe that there is more than mankind. I believe in extraterrestrials, but not like in that *Aliens* movie or the ones they show on the *X-Files.*"

"Do you believe in God?"

"That's a double-edged sword. I don't believe in one God, like a Christian God, but I believe everyone has a Higher Power. If that's God, so be it. Others call it Yeshewa. Goodness can be interpreted as godliness. I don't believe in Satan, but I know there is pure evil. You don't need no Bible for proof—just read the newspaper," he explained, surprised at how easily the words came.

"Is good better than evil?"

No answer. Eva liked the way this was going. Jake had potential. He had made it to the final *Jeopardy!* question. This was for all the money and the grand prize.

"To what limits are you willing to go to be with me?"

"What are you getting at?"

Click.

"Strange woman," he said, hitting the redial button, wondering, but not really caring, how much these calls were going to cost.

"Hello?"

"Don't hang up! Work with me. Tell me what you want."

"Jake, I don't have any expectations of you. I never did. I also don't expect us to ever get together in any other manner than phone sex."

"Why not?"

"You won't understand."

"Try. You might be surprised."

The irresistible voice explained that she was tired of the life she was leading and wanted out. But she didn't need a sugar daddy. Money didn't satisfy the soul. She made plenty of money comforting the lonely, but she too was lonely. She wanted to be more than some man's plaything or conquest. She went on to explain that many men fall in love with the whore during passion, but when the passion subsides, the whore is forgotten and discarded.

He listened with enthusiasm as Eva went over her life history, her fears, her failures, and her desires. She wanted to share emotions with someone. She wanted long walks on empty beaches. She wanted soft music. She wanted to cook the meal before the passion and light the cigarettes afterward.

She wanted everything he did. With each passing sentence, he fell more in love with her.

"Please tell me what I have to do to make this all come true."

"*Really?*" she asked, sounding like an excited child.

"Really."

"Kill your wife, and I'll be yours forever."

The answer didn't faze him in the least. Actually, he was hoping that that was what she was going to say. Their conversation lasted for well over two hours, during which Judy rang twice but was quickly cut off. It was decided that they would meet after dark. If Jake was truly sincere about his love for Eva, then tonight he would kill his wife. He had to be careful and make it look like a random violent crime, like a rape/mutilation or something. These types of crimes weren't that unusual in New York. Then, after all the dust settled, Eva would elope with him, and the world would be theirs. The more he listened to her, the more he knew exactly what he had to do.

Hours flew by with Jason unable to concentrate on any of his work. He kept hearing Eva's intoxicating voice reverberating through his skull as his mind calculated future crimes. Important calls from clients (and five—count 'em, five—calls from his wife) went unreturned. He figured that since he had no previous criminal record, not even a traffic ticket, and held a good position in the community, no one would ever doubt his innocence and take him for a cold-blooded murderer. Whenever he felt weak, Eva's photo gave him strength that before today he didn't have. He could sense her thinking about him, wondering whether he'd go through with it. Even he had his doubts, but one look in the mirror and he could see a transformation going on. He was getting harder, stronger. No matter how crazy this all seemed, somehow it all made sense.

Without warning, it was quitting time—or in Jason's case, time to put up or shut up.

After finally getting a cab, he thought it over one more time. The edgy man in the back seat had the cabbie slightly worried. He didn't look right. Then again, it wasn't the hack's place to wonder, only to drive. The driver tried initiating a conversation, but Jason wanted no part of it. Even if he did, it was doubtful that he could've spoken coherently. He just stared out the wet window like a mutant that's drunk too much coffee.

Outside it was dark, dreary, and raining steadily. During certain stretches of fall, New York could pass for London with a hangover. Instead of letting the weather upset him, Jason was rather amused by it. It added atmosphere to his already cloak-and-dagger day.

The closer he got to the address Eva had given, the more he contemplated running to the safety of the train and forgetting the whole thing. It was his fear of not knowing what was going to happen next that kept him fidgeting. Although he rarely touched the stuff, he wished he had a drink. His heart raced every time he saw a woman who somewhat resembled Eva's photograph. But there was only one Eva, and he was determined to touch the voice.

What if this was some sort of scam and the photographs in the magazines didn't match the voice? What if she was a butt-ugly cow? What if she weighed four hundred pounds or had big crusty sores on her mouth? What if she wasn't all he'd made her up to be? These questions and others flooded his throbbing temples. Just as he was getting ready to abandon the taxi, he heard her. The sexy voice in his head reassured him that everything would be all right, and he believed it true as the car slowly fought through the traffic.

And then he saw her.

Although there was a certain similarity between the woman in the photographs and the woman standing on the street, Jason knew they were not the same person. It didn't matter. The woman waiting for him wanted him, which was more than he could say about his wife. The fact that she was quite beautiful didn't hurt matters either. He didn't know very much except that he was going to see this through. After fighting its way out of a traffic sandwich, the cab pulled over to the curb and the back door opened.

"Hello, Jake," she said seductively as she joined him in the back seat. Her stunning white flesh resembled marble and contrasted perfectly with her jet-black hair and red lips. His ears immediately recognized her tone, and all of his expectations were realized. He could not believe that the voice he so desired was sitting besides him.

Her green eyes twinkled with mischief, and he didn't even try to resist as Eva softly tackled him with a wet kiss. Beneath her full-length black leather coat, she only wore silk panties and a bra, which were off in no time. Even though there was a stranger present, Jake managed to shed his inhibitions as well as his clothing, and the two were immediately fondling and examining the beauty of one another. Within seconds, Eva's hungry mouth found its way to his erection, and she was much better in real life than over the phone. The cabbie was discreetly trying to get a better view of the fine babe, not the nerd she was with. If this chick was a freak, he'd have no problems going second. Jake threw him a mind-your-own-business look.

If you wanted privacy, you should've splurged for a limousine, you cheap suburban fuck, the hack thought, and continued watching.

Jake let Eva's luscious lips work him over for a short while before lifting her up by her raven hair. He brought her beautiful face to his. She even smelled pretty. Hearts racing with excitement, the couple kissed for all they were worth and then some as Eva mounted his rock-hard penis. It took a little positioning, but once they were comfortable, the two worked as one. Their bare chests pressed together as she straddled his lap. From this angle, all the cabbie could see was her long black coat and her constant up-and-down motion.

Jake had never been with a woman who was this uninhibited before. The little noise coming from her throat sounded genuine, nothing like the silence he was accustomed to from his wife. Their bodies seemed to melt as one, and as Jake approached orgasm, he tried holding it off. He didn't want this moment to end. Eva seemed to sense this and softly whispered, "Come on Jake, cum. Please don't hold back. We have forever. . . . Cum inside me, baby."

And so he did.

Since his angle to watch was no longer any good, the cab driver readjusted the rearview mirror. Even with the defrost on, it was hard keeping the rear window from fogging up. The driver didn't care for the car that was too close to his bumper. He tapped the brake, but the tailgater didn't catch the hint. Slightly angered, the driver maneuvered his way through traffic—and more important, away from the asshole riding their rear.

Jake felt like he was on a ride that was spinning too fast. Mister Toad's wild taxi ride or something. Familiar houses and landmarks seemed blurred as the cab approached his house, but one look at the woman next to him gave him all the courage he needed. She could give him life; all it would take was courage.

The ride from the city to the suburbs of Long Island took a little over forty minutes and cost seventy dollars including a chintzy tip. It was well worth it since Jake and Eva were given time to get acquainted. Very little was said in the way of conversation, and this made Jake uneasy. Although she was caressing him, he wanted to hear her speak. He wanted her to reassure him that what he was going to do was right. He wanted to listen as she freed him from his fears. And most important of all, even if she had to whisper, he wanted to hear her talk dirty.

But very little was said as both parties were too nervous to open up. That would have to happen later.

As he told the driver to keep the change, it dawned on him that this was no dream. He was getting ready to kill his wife for a telephone prostitute.

Fighting the rain, they walked past the old-fashioned iron mailbox that had the name RONSON on it in reflective gold lettering. The wet sidewalk led to the front door. Jake's flesh was crawling with nervousness. Even worse, his insides were in knots. On the other hand, Eva looked quite relaxed.

What the fuck am I doing? he wondered as he slipped the house key into its slot and opened the door. The house was warm and decorated with all the modern conveniences one would expect. Judy spent her husband's money without guilt. The duo crept past the living room and the two bedrooms, one being a guest room that rarely saw any use, until they reached the kitchen. As usual, Judy was putting the final touches on supper. She had her back turned to them as they approached.

"Honey, I'm home."

"That's nice," she replied without emotion, turning around. Her face tried to hide her shock as she caught a glimpse of the dripping beauty.

.

"Jason, who's this?" Judy asked in a loathing tone. She received no answer as her husband removed the largest butcher knife in the house from a drawer.

"A close friend. And my name isn't Jason, it's Jake," he declared, stepping forward. He grabbed his wife by the back of her head with his left hand. He'd wanted to hurt her for so long that her frightened face caused him to sneer. Then, with the thick blade in his right, he forcefully pulled it across her throat, severing her esophagus. Blood poured through her fingers as she gasped for air that never would reach her lungs. Judy's throat was now little more than a red hinge. Fighting for her life, she spun around, staggered for a few steps, then fell on the floor. The last thing her disbelieving eyes saw before the blackness took over was an extreme close-up of a sanguine floor tile.

Eva slowly knelt down next to the body. Her slender fingers touched the deep slash as though confirming that Judy was indeed dead. Dead, so that Eva and Jake could begin their new lives together. Dead, so that destiny could be challenged. Dead, so that certain seeds planted might stand a chance of survival. Dead, quite dead. Eva slipped her forefinger even deeper into the wound. Her finger was half buried in flesh before she removed it. Then she rubbed the blood across her thick, regal lips.

Even though she was wet from the rain and wearing death for lipstick, Eva was still the most beautiful woman Jake had ever laid eyes on. In a perverse way, she looked quite sexy right now.

Overlooking the fact that she'd just tasted his wife's blood, Jake squatted down besides her and placed his lips over his lover's. The crimson kiss made his insides tingle. It was the most decadent thing he'd ever imagined. Life surged within the crotch of his pants, and before either of them realized it, they were in the bedroom, naked and tangled together.

His passionate thrusts reminded her of a younger, stronger man. Not so much the force but the enthusiasm behind them. Her smooth skin reminded him of rose petals. She absorbed him as best she could, and it didn't take long for their gyrating hips to match rhythm. Eva's half-opened eyes registered joy as the two bodies worked as one. A slight glaze covered the two lovers as their thrusts became stronger. Jake's tongue danced along Eva's neck as sighs escaped her. Her orgasms came one after the other, and she was quite verbal about letting Jake know how good he was making her feel. This encouraged him to really lay pipe. He felt her fingers digging into his sweaty back. He had never felt so good, so strong in his entire life. Then with a grunt of passion he exploded inside his new-found love, a woman whose voice he used to pay to masturbate to.

He rolled off her and onto his back. The room seemed to be spinning, like he was drunk from passion, and he couldn't have cared less. If this was how lust felt, then he had never felt better. That is, until he screamed.

She's back to haunt me already, he thought.

But it wasn't a she. The figure standing in the bedroom doorway was male and stood at least six feet two and close to two hundred pounds. Even across the dark room, Jake couldn't help but noticing the pistol in his hands. The intruder smiled at him.

"Who are you?" he asked, petrified with fright. His heart was threatening to jump into his mouth. All the vigor and energy that were previously in his body shriveled and disappeared. He never was, *nor would he ever be*, a man named Jake. That was an illusion he couldn't buy. He would forever be square ol' Jason Ronson. And judging the by the looks of things, forever wouldn't last too long.

The voice he wanted so badly to love betrayed him as Eva began to laugh. "That's Burt."

"*What?*"

"My pimp, silly."

"No—"

"Yeah."

"This is too fucking much," Jason replied as Burt flicked on the light.

"At least I waited until you were through," said the pimp.

This much was true. Feeling like the first-ever male victim of "date rape," the accountant was instructed to put his pants back on. Burt explained that he wouldn't hurt him if he took him around the house and showed him where all the valuables were. If Jason did this, *and did a satisfactory job of being honest about where everything was*, then he'd tie up the frail man and peacefully leave with his whore.

The other option was much nastier.

Seeing Burt in the light, Jason understood perfectly why a woman like Eva would go for him. No amount of money could ever buy what he had: an aura of danger. He was handsome in a rugged way and looked natural dressed in all black. Black boots, black stretch jeans that hugged his muscular legs, a black T-shirt, and a black suede blazer made up his attire. His dark complexion complemented his ice-blue eyes, and he possessed a classic square jaw. He scratched his right cheek, using the black barrel of the Walther P-38 in his gloved hand. The semiautomatic nine-millimeter was loaded with an eight-round magazine, and Burt had a backup clip in the breast pocket of his blazer.

His short black hair was unkempt and messy like he'd just gotten off a motorcycle. Even his long nose added character, as did the silver hoop in his right nostril. Although he was handsome, he was not a man to underestimate. It wouldn't have surprised Jason if Burt had served time in prison.

Like a player in a nightmare, Jason showed the duo where all the Ronson family loot was stashed. Jewelry, cash, deeds, bonds, antique knickknacks, credit cards, and finally silverware from the dining area were all dumped into a pillowcase that Eva carried. Even though she was a backstabbing Jezebel, Jason found it impossible to hate her. He knew how he should feel, and although he did feel betrayed, he didn't wish any ill upon her. In the brief time they'd shared, she had made him feel more alive than he'd ever felt. He'd never experienced such excitement before. She'd jump-started his libido and driven him faster than he'd ever known possible. Unfortunately she drove him head-on into a wall. The fact that she crashed his soul wasn't important. What was important was an explanation.

And to hear her voice the way it used to be.

After thoroughly going over the house, the trio wound up back in the kitchen where the dead woman lay. Her blood had pooled out and surrounded her head in a large puddle

I can't believe I did this, he thought, not feeling remorse for his actions, but rather feeling like a sucker for letting Eva fool him so easily. He knew he would've eventually mustered up the courage and cash to go through with a divorce from Judy. This horrible vision before him had never been an option until Eva had asked for it.

"How could you?" he asked, appalled and deflated.

"I'm not the one who killed the bitch," Eva replied matter-of-factly and left Jason to deal with his conscience.

"I'm sorry . . ." he said, staring at the corpse of the wife he had once loved.

"A little late for that," Eva stated, amused. After all, he could fuck her with blood on her lips, but standing over his dead wife now brought tears to his eyes.

"Do you do this type of thing often?"

"It's my job," she explained, then added, "I mean, I wasn't getting anywhere being the Ann Landers for jerking off men."

Torn between humiliation and fear, something else dawned upon Jason. A new dimension of terror swept through his already-mortified body. His face flushed, and he tried not to scream as he realized that although he'd done everything asked of him, his minutes on earth were numbered.

The pimp had not packed a piece to leave witnesses.

Burt went to step over the stiff and slipped in her blood. He didn't stumble all the way, but he needed to put his hands down to catch his fall. He fell to one knee, and that was the break Jason needed. With all of his might, he grabbed Eva and threw her at the pimp. The two collided with enough impact to knock them down. The loot in the pillowcase spilled everywhere. Jake closed his eyes and dashed toward the front door.

"STOP, MOTHERFUCKER, OR—"

Two quick shots rang out just as Jason reached

the door. They missed him by inches as he felt the cold rain on his face. He reopened his eyes and found himself running through the suburban darkness. He kept expecting to hear more shots.

Like a hunted animal, Jason ran with all his might. It had been years since he'd last sprinted like this. Instinct made his strides fluid and he pushed himself as fast as he could. Running with reckless abandon, he made every step count. He kept his chin up and pumped his arms.

That is, until he ran full speed into the mailbox.

His stomach muscles knotted up from the paralyzing pain. He tried getting up but couldn't. The solid iron mailbox had knocked the wind, and the fight, out of him.

"You stupid dipshit," Burt sneered as he made it to where Jason lay. Just as he was getting ready to squeeze the trigger, a tiny smile crossed Jason's lips. He'd put up a valiant fight and would die with honor. It was the only time in his life he'd ever come close to understanding pride. Then, like the arrival of the cavalry, the next-door neighbors' porch light came on. Several well-to-do men and women were coming over to investigate what all the commotion was.

Realizing that this was not the best time or place to off someone, Burt began to brutally pistol-whip Jason. The force behind the blows was enough to rattle Jason's skull, and after the first few hammering blows, he was knocked unconscious. The pimp and his whore quickly slipped into his car and disappeared into the night.

Jason awoke in the cold mud. The rain was still falling, and from his perspective it looked like thousands of stars were falling from the sky. Red lights

were flashing everywhere. Nothing made sense.
Who were all these people, and why couldn't he get
up? Had he been in some sort of accident? Was he
dead and didn't know it? Was he trapped in a coma?
Was he going to jail?

Paramedics carried his wife away in a body bag.
His memory quickly returned as a policeman reassured him that he was all right. The pain in his head
intensified. It felt like his skull had been smashed.
Then he remembered, it had been. After a while
when he was more together, the police questioned
him not as a suspect but as a victim.

Using the same vivid imagination that had gotten
him into this mess, Jason quickly came up with an
alibi. For every question asked, he had an answer.
Neighbors also reported what they had seen. Unfortunately, no one had gotten a good look at the two
suspects.

The police and paramedics treated him at the
scene, bandaging his busted-up head, before preparing him to go to the hospital. Each civil servant echoed the same sentiments, and he agreed that he was
lucky to be alive. He played the role of the grieving
husband and the humble hero equally well. He pre-
ferred the hero. A tiny grin formed as the two attendants placed him on a stretcher and prepared to
load him into the ambulance.

The grin quickly dissolved as he watched a police
officer emerge through the crowd with the murder
weapon in a plastic bag marked EVIDENCE. How the
hell was he going to explain why his fingerprints
were the only ones on the butcher knife? He broke
down and began crying.

"It's going to be all right," a strange voice reassured.

"I'm a coward," Jason cried.

"No, you're not," the voice soothed in a well-practiced tone.

"Yes I am! They made—they put a gun to my head."

"I know, I know. Everything is going to be all right—"

"NO IT'S NOT! THEY PUT A GUN TO MY HEAD AND SAID IF I DIDN'T DO WHAT THEY SAID, THEY'D KILL ME. . . . GOD HELP ME. . . . THEY MADE ME. . . . THEY LAUGHED WHILE I KILLED MY OWN WIFE!"

A gasp of shock escaped all those close enough to hear Mr. Ronson's confession. This was an even more horrible crime than anyone had imagined. Jason closed his eyes and feigned slipping away, wondering if his story had worked.

An attendant rushed to his aid. Judging from the wounds, Ronson probably had a concussion, and it was quite dangerous to let someone with a concussion drift off. He could possibly die. And no one present wanted this already tragic scene to get even worse. Especially after all this poor guy had been through. The aide managed to get him awake.

"Please, Mr. Ronson, you must stay awake!" the voice emphasized.

Again, he smiled weakly as his weary mind acknowledged that his story had worked. Try as he might, he couldn't get Eva out of his badly bruised head. Although he knew he could never touch her again, he did have plenty of time and money. As long as he was paying, he could still make her say whatever he wanted. Right before slipping off into the comfort of unconsciousness, one last thought struck him. Jason silently prayed that his hospital room had a private telephone.

There was a call he was dying to make.

High School
Memoirs

Judy and her two friends could not have crossed paths with Hank's custom 1970 Chevelle 454 SS at a more inopportune time. The fresh suburban air seemed to lose its crispness as Judy gasped. She tried looking away, but it was useless. Their eyes had already met. Confrontation was unavoidable. She quickly lit a Marlboro Light 100 and started fidgeting. Her two girlfriends and fellow high school sophomores, Tracy and Marlene, also lit up and told her not to stress. Judy smiled weakly and explained under her breath that she couldn't help it.

The high school senior slowed the loud car down.

Until three weeks ago, Hank Bugullio and Judy Harrelson had been a hot item. The couple had been your typical heavy high school relationship with no end in sight. Parents had been met, secrets had been shared, and words like *marriage* and *love* had been tossed around freely. Then four weeks before graduation—and even worse, three weeks prior to the senior prom—Judy had cut it off, leaving the barely graduating eighteen-year-old dateless and brokenhearted.

If only she'd given me some kind of warning, he thought, staring at her, white-knuckling the chrome

tilt steering wheel. He wanted to snarl at her, but he
still had feelings for her. Exactly what they were he
wasn't sure. He didn't know whether he wanted to
kiss her or kill her. Such were the dilemmas of being a wounded teenager trapped somewhere between adolescence and manhood. Logic told him he
should carry himself in a more mature manner,
while his heart often got the better of him. That was
part of the problem of starring in a tragic movie
without an ending to the script. He tried carrying
on, but more often than not he got carried away.
Hank took another long swig off his Budweiser Tallboy. He'd already finished three.

In his eyes, Judy was beyond beautiful, and she
had qualities he'd never experienced before. Although she was two years younger than he, she had
really helped him understand the tenderness that
can occur between two people. Her style was
charming, but one shouldn't let the politeness be
blinding. Once the lights were off, she turned into a
passionate lover who enjoyed physical exploration
of every kind. And this too was part of his hurt. Although he was technically not a virgin, until Judy
and he began making it on a regular basis he'd
never known intimacy. And after having been with
Judy, Hank understood that there was much more
to sex than boning some drunken cheerleader in the
back seat of his car.

Or at least there had been.

Rumor had it she was seeing her old boyfriend,
Nicky, a skinny wigger from a neighboring town. In
Hank's mind, she'd dumped him for a gold-chain-
wearing, wannabe-rapper pizza delivery boy.
Nicky's father owned Casa Nostra, the best pizzeria
in Poughkeepsie—or for that matter, all of Dutchess
County—and Nick the Dick was set for life.

The pearl-white mean machine with black hood stripes was nicknamed the Great White Shark. The mechanical beast was the king of the road around these parts, and it had the engine power to back up any of Hank's drunken boasts. He'd drag anyone, especially Nick's TransAm, anytime.

He pulled alongside the three girls, stopped, and let the car idle loudly. It was no secret among the girls that it was the muscle car that had originally attracted Judy to Hank. Sure, he was cute, but damn, his car was bitchin'. And fast! Hank leaned across his seat and rolled down the darkly tinted window.

"Where ya heading?" he inquired nonchalantly, one hand on the steering wheel.

"The Wall," Tracy snapped. She was always the loudest.

"No, not you. You!" Hank said, pointing his beer at Judy.

"Just hanging," she replied, exhaling smoke.

"Yeah? Get in."

"Okey-dokey," Tracy piped, and started heading toward the car, knowing she was getting under Hank's skin and enjoying herself. She'd always thought of him as a putz.

"No, blockhead. Judy. I want to speak to Judy. You know, the girl I used to go out with. Judy."

"*Who?*" Tracy asked enjoying herself at Hank's expense.

"Fuck you!" Hank barked, trying to keep his cool. He knew that losing his temper right now would do him no good, but there were only a few people he liked less on this earth than the bitch currently taunting him. What pleasure it would give him to torture her. He stared coldly at Tracy, trying to send her a silent warning, before saying, "Jude, can I please talk to you?"

"I dunno . . ."

"Come on, nothing funny. Just talk."

The three girls stepped away from the car and huddled in low-volume discussion. After minor jostling, shrugs, and words of encouragement, Judy flicked away her cigarette, stepped forward, and got into the vehicle.

"I'll meetcha at the Wall in fifteen minutes," Judy explained, leaning out the window as the Chevelle spun its racing tires, leaving a thundercloud of smoke.

"C-ya later!" Tracy yelled.

"That one-way bitch," Marlene declared, and Tracy gave her a knowing look. They resumed walking through the suburban town, secretly wishing they were cruising.

"That was real smooth," Judy said sarcastically, locking her door, then reaching for the radio. Hank threw her a sideways glance that told her to back off. No one messed with the tunes. This had been a major stress-causing issue during the five months that they'd gone steady: what station the radio played. Hank had the touch-tone automatic dialer on the Clarion set to all the New York area rock 'n' roll stations. During the mornings he was always dialed in to the Howard Stern show, but at night whatever station had the best tunes going won. Judy could tolerate rock 'n' roll but would much rather cruise to dance music. Whether it was bad 1970s disco or 1990s hardcore rap didn't matter. If it had a beat and enough bass, Judy would move to it, and move well.

"How's Dicky?"

"Who?" Judy asked, caught off guard.

"You know, Nick the Dick—your boyfriend," Hank said, trying to make every word sting. He finished his beer and pitched the empty can out the window.

"For your information file, he's not a dick. And he's not my boyfriend. He's a friend, a good friend, that I occasionally go certain places with—"

"D-d-dancing?" Hank interrupted.

"I think the word you're looking for is *dancing*. And yeah, we go dancing together—and other things," she said, knowing it would irk him.

"But I thought you liked white guys."

"He *is* white. I mean, for god sakes, he's Italian like you," she replied.

"He ain't nothing like me," Hank stated indignantly before taking a sip of his beer. "I mean, what would your mom say if she knew you were dating some wannabe nigger?"

"Leave my mother out of this, and let's drop the subject. If you're gonna carry on like an asshole, then just pull over and drop me off right now."

Hank bit his lip and continued driving. Seated next to him was one of those coveted high school beauties in blossom. Unlike most early bloomers, she had the kind of looks that were only going to get better as time passed. She was already a catch in most young men's little black books. Judy had the charm as well as the fake ID to make most nightclub bouncers ignore the obvious fact that she wasn't twenty-one. Her Irish eyes were soft emeralds that could make even the most hardened man smile, and her complexion was never blemished by youthful acne. Soft brown hair with hints of blond dancing through it fell past her shoulders and stopped right above her well-developed breasts. Her hair seemed to have a life of its own, flowing with energy, en-

hancing her already attractive features. A small
nose and thick succulent lips completed her beautiful face. She was quite thin but not too petite. Feminine but not frail. In another world, she could've
been a princess, since young men like Hank would
die in a flash just to defend her honor.

She used to be mine, Hank thought, checking himself out in the rearview mirror. His windblown,
dirty brown hair was just messy enough to set off his
bloodshot eyes and give him a certain amount of
cool that girls went for. He wore a cutoff denim vest
over his varsity football team jersey. Black wrist-
bands covered both of his thick wrists and drew attention to his well-defined forearms. A small silver
hoop dangled from his left earlobe. He popped the
top off another Tallboy and offered the last one to
Judy. She accepted. Then there was silence, other
than the rumbling sound of the SS 454 big-block
engine and rock 'n' roll music.

"Would you like to change the station?"

"No, it's cool. I like this song," she replied.

"Good 'cause you weren't gonna anyway."

Led Zeppelin's "Dancing Days" faded into Pink
Floyd's "Time." Hank increased the volume to the
point of pain, but Judy did not complain. To moan
would be to give in to this creep, and she wasn't in
the mood. She could be stubborn as a mule when
she wanted, and right now she wanted. If Hank
dared call her a bitch, she was really going to tear
into him.

Hank sang along with Roger Waters as Judy removed another Marlboro Light 100 from her purse.
She lit up, knowing that Hank hated cigarette
smoke. Marijuana was no problem, but cancer
sticks were bad news. It was a nonsmoker's di-

lemma, she figured, ignoring his cold stare and puffing away.

"That's a real disgusting habit."

"What???" Judy replied, pointing at the radio. Hank caught the hint and reluctantly lowered the music.

"Do you have to smoke that in my car?"

"No. Let me out."

"Why are you acting like this?"

"Like what?" she asked defensively. She wasn't three-quarters finished with her sixteen-ouncer, but she was already starting to feel her oats. Silently, part of her desired a confrontation, but like a good boy, Hank changed his tone.

"Them shits are gonna kill ya someday."

Judy laughed her well-practiced bitch laugh and exhaled on cue. Hank took the hint and again raised the volume on the radio. Pink Floyd had faded into Pearl Jam. There was something unique in Eddie Vedder's voice that always managed to stir his emotions. Maybe that's why he enjoyed Pearl Jam as much as he did and for the next three minutes and fifty-four seconds, "Daughter" provided the soundtrack to his life.

"I'm almost out," the driver said, slurring ever so slightly, holding up his can. "Wanna go get more?" He quickly prayed that she'd say yes. It seemed he did a lot of praying these day, but few of his prayers were ever answered. He hoped God was feeling generous, because if he got her tipsy maybe her shitty attitude would change. Whenever she got drunk, she also got very horny, and Hank would never "just say no" to sex.

"Nah, I gotta go meet my friends. Now if you'd been cool instead of a dickhead and offered them a ride—"

"Fuck them. It's not like they have a life or anything. They're in no rush to go anyplace besides the fucking Wall. You know they'll be there when we get back," Hank explained, trying to remain calm yet exert pressure on her to see things his way.

Judy shook her head no. Somewhere underneath the weight of the world, Hank felt like lashing out and smacking his ex square in the chops almost as badly as he wanted to hold and kiss her. Either act would ruin any possibility of a reconciliation. There were a million things he wanted to tell her, a million feelings he wanted to express, but his fear of rejection kept him silent. She would never understand his sorrow. Love, as well as his last beer, was fading.

A red light stopped their forward motion.

"C'mon, just beer?" he asked, meaning "just us spending time together."

"Nah, Hank, that wouldn't be too cool. Like, I already know you've taken the longest route to the Wall possible, and if you did this so we could finish a beer, then cool, but my friends are waiting on me, and I ain't no flat-leaver. Please, let's just go to the Wall," she replied, not giving in to beer temptation.

The Wall was located in a corner of their high school's parking lot, where kids had been hanging out for years. It was actually the back of a small redbrick gymnasium away from the main building. The main function of this building besides gym class was that was where detention was served.

Next to the Wall, in the parking lot, there was a slightly bent basketball hoop, complete with a chain-link net and several metal garbage cans so that youths would not litter, but more often than not, drunken rowdies broke their bottles. Occasionally, the heavy garbage cans were thrown at the graffitied hangout. The Wall was no big secret to the teachers, police, or custodians. After certain regulars outgrew hanging out at the Wall, a new batch of eager replacements always popped up. For over twenty years, it had been the site of many all-night summer parties. This summer would be no different. When the light changed to green, Hank headed off toward the high school.

"What's that smell?" Judy asked curiously. Since the moment she had gotten into Hank's car, there'd been an unusual aroma lingering. She turned around and looked into the back seat. On the floor, in the back of the car, was a two-gallon aluminum gas can.

"Planning on going somewhere?"

"Maybe—maybe Florida," Hank earnestly replied. Judy said nothing. She had no desire to call his bluff.

"Wanna go? Just you and me. We'll take off, tell nobody. C'mon, what do we have to lose? I've got my dad's gas card and some cash. We could be across state lines faster than fuck," he explained sincerely. Judy actually believed him and thought about it for a split second before reality kicked her in the face.

"I can't—I'm only sixteen," she said, slightly ashamed, puffing on her smoke.

"Fuck it, all you gotta do is say go."

"I, umm. I can't."

"But I—I lo—"

"Hank, don't do this."

Another red light caused them to stop. Hank looked at Judy, admiring her raw beauty. It was like he was seeing her for the very first time. His eyes made her uncomfortable, so she stared out the window.

Hank was serious about running away, Judy thought, flattered and excited. She had really never meant to hurt him. If she was drunk enough and there was no way of getting busted, she might fuck him, but she wasn't anywhere near drunk enough to consider that now, and fortunately the Wall was less than a quarter-mile away. Soon the night would return to normal.

"Why'd you dump me?"

Judy was at a loss for words. Why wouldn't Hank just let things go? No response came as she waited for something to tick. She'd known that eventually the conversation would roll onto this topic. She just wished it hadn't. How did you tell someone that the thrill wasn't thrilling anymore? How did you tell someone that they didn't move you that much anymore? How did a person tell someone they loved—and Judy did love Hank in her own way—that it was over?

Sure, Hank had been there for her when she needed him, and she'd never completely shut the door on him. She never intended to hurt him, or for him to take it so hard, but being Hank Bugullio's steady girlfriend was like trying to walk around with a ball and chain on her sexy legs. He may have thought that what they had was an even give-and-take relationship where both parties' feelings were equal, but she hadn't felt that way in a long time. She was no longer satisfied with what they once had and was sick and tired of being dubbed Hank's Chick. It made her feel like property instead of a person. She couldn't make anyone else happy if she wasn't happy, and she wasn't happy with their relationship. It was as simple as that. She was young and still had a lot of living to do. Sure, they'd had some great times together, but as for her and Hank ever being a couple again in the not-too-distant future, forget it.

Judy felt unsteady, like she was coming down from a major high although she hadn't gotten stoned all day long.

Pot, she thought to herself. Pot would give her a much better perspective, and she was sure that Marlene had some. Judy took the last drag off her cigarette, flicked it out the window, and replied, "I didn't dump you. Things were just starting to get too heavy for me. Really—I, things just needed a change. . . . You know."

The light turned green.

"I really want to be friends," she explained sincerely but was surprised that such a weak cliché had actually come out of her mouth.

"You know, I really fell for you," he confessed. If only she knew how much he cared for her, then maybe she could understand his desperation. He couldn't remember the last time he'd actually slept through the night without having a marathon therapeutic discussion where everything worked out and everyone's point of view was understood. But what the hell was her point of view? Had she ever really cared for him the way he cared for her, or had he just been a gullible high school senior to parade around? Was their relationship about love, or was it just lust disguised under the mask of innocence? Why was she treating him this way?

They turned off the main drag into the high school parking lot and slowed down to a crawl. The tension inside the car was high as the redbrick hangout came in sight. There were approximately eight kids, including Marlene and Tracy, hanging around a large beat-up brown pickup truck.

"You know, that gas can is not the brightest idea,"

Judy said, trying to change the subject. "I mean, it smells bad And what if you were in an accident—and I'm not trying to wish anything upon you—your car would blow up and then what?"

"What the fuck would you care?" Hank lashed out, unable to control the words or the tone. As badly as he wanted to be a gentleman in this situation, teen angst had gotten the better of him.

"No, fuck you. All I did was ask a question. And, yeah right, like you're really going somewhere tonight," she snapped, whining just a bit and lighting up another cigarette.

"Yeah, I'm going somewhere—and you're coming with me. How the fuck do ya like them apples?" Hank snapped. On the radio, a commercial rambled on about discount savings for car insurance. When the insurance commercial ended, another commercial for another product of no interest to either Hank or Judy came on.

Judy feigned laughter and slowly blew out a puff of smoke. Hank had tried to buzz-kill her Friday night before it actually started, but there was no way she was going to let him drag her down that easily.

"So then—where are we going, Romeo?"

"Hell, Juliet."

Hank snatched the cigarette out of Judy's mouth and barked, "I told ya these fuckin' things would kill ya!"

Hank bit down on the repulsive cigarette, leaned over the back seat, and grabbed the full gas can. He quickly untwisted the cap and like a madman playing in the bathtub, splashed gasoline about. He shook up the can as vehemently as humanly possible, making sure to get plenty all over himself, Judy, and the car.

Murky, pinkish liquid flew every which way before he began smashing Judy over the head with the heavy can. Each blow was more forceful than the previous one as even more flammable liquid splashed out. After a half a dozen hard whacks, Judy was busted up pretty good, but she was still vainly trying to defend herself. Gasoline landed in her open mouth and eyes as more blows came. She thrashed wildly, blinded, screaming at the top of her lungs. Another blow from the now-empty gas can caught her flush on the nose. She screamed and fumbled with the door. In her panic, she'd forgotten that the door was locked and she was unable to open it. The driver yanked her closer to him by the hair.

Hank smiled, cigarette between his lips.

"No, please—"

He took a deep drag, getting the cherry nice and orange, then dropped the cigarette into the back seat. A large flame ignited. Hank floored the gas pedal. The car's nose was pointed directly at the Wall.

"Hank, stop it, you fucking maniac!"

But it was too late to stop. Both students were beginning to catch on fire.

Judy smacked at herself, but this offered no relief. The open windows added wind currents that fanned and helped spread the flames. Her beautiful brown hair was the first thing to disappear. It happened in an instant. The stench of burned hair hung heavily like a rancid aerosol of death. During the first phase of what would soon become unspeakable agonies, Hank laughed at his now-bald ex-girlfriend. There was a viciousness in his laughter that crucified her more than the flames.

Massive welts and blisters rose and popped, se-

creting their oily juices. Like a live wire, Judy
flopped around the front seat, screaming for the torture to end. Any exposed skin quickly burned away
in long slimy strands. More of her clothing burned
away.

Her face was reddening then blackening at a rate
that her flailing hands could not stop. Everywhere
she touched, skin stuck to her hands. The gasoline
on her eyes caught, and she flashed back to being a
small child in grammar school and making a horrible mess with Elmer's glue, only this time she was
the canvas. A smoldering canvas, that is.

Screams rose and died as she choked on black
smoke that was partially car interior, partially
burned students. Muscles shriveled and withered
from the heat. Her entire body began to crumple as
the fire gained momentum. Hank, looking no better
than Judy, lifted his badly charred melting hand off
the steering wheel. It left a long strand of sizzling
cheeselike skin. The wretched strand refused to
break off. He strained forward and managed to
push the volume knob louder. The commercials had
ended and Steppenwolf were singing about taking a
"Magic Carpet Ride."

"I love this fuckin' song," he groaned through
melting lips. The speedometer read sixty miles per
hour.

The kids hanging out by the Wall noticed the flaming car and quickly scrambled away. All except
Tracy, who was frozen by the horrified knowledge
that she was going to be run over. She tried to run,
but her feet refused to listen to her mind. For a split
second, her bugged eyes locked in on the driver's
melting face. She knew she was at his mercy and
realized it was too late to repent for the way she'd
always pestered him. Using what little concentra-

tion he had left, Hank made sure the speeding car bashed into Tracy before slamming into the Wall.

Off in the distance, Tommy Flynt thought he heard fireworks. It wasn't an unusual occurrence, especially living this close to the high school. His family's house was less than four blocks away from the school. It often paid off living here: It was easy to sneak out when he was grounded or to escape from cops raiding the parking lot parties.

"It's Saturday night. My boys are wound up tight. Slip on a skin. Put the sucker in. Five minutes to go. Ya got a Marlboro? Bust in some joint. Maybe find some points. That's the way we live downtown. Our feet never hit the ground, ground, ground, ground yeah.

" 'Cause I hate my mother, I hate the world. I told my father some more bull. I hate the system and I break the law. But I'm at home when I'm downtown."

Tommy switched off the Warrior Soul compact disc. The tune "Downtown" was his favorite drug-related anthem, although "Junkhead" by Alice in Chains ran a very close second.

Most of the available wall space in his room was covered in posters or pictures cut out of music magazines. He stared at a clock and estimated that within an hour (and as long as there wasn't a knock-down, drag-out fight during dinner), he'd be free. Well, at least until 1:00 A.M., which was his curfew. For a few hours there would be nothing to do other than get stoned, listen to tunes, and just hang out. His friends—and more important, his girl—would all be there. Just when everything seemed to be going according to schedule, his mother burst into his bedroom.

"You've got shit for brains!" the neurotic, over-weight, middle-aged Wasp screamed, causing Tommy to recoil. Shock registered on his surprised face. It was an expression of confused apprehension that teenage boys everywhere share. Helena Flynt enjoyed his reaction and tore even deeper into him: "WHAT KIND OF SHIT ARE YOU TRYING TO PULL???"

"What?" he asked, thoroughly confused.

"I called your high school counselor, Mr. Marko-witz, today and he regretfully informed me that not only have your grades dipped but so has your atti-tude—and I know why. It's that little tramp," Hel-ena bitched as though each word leaving her mouth left a foul taste.

"Leave Marlene out of this. She didn't do any-thing."

"Don't tell me what and what not to do, mister. I'm your mother. I mean, what kind of college do you expect to get into with B's and, ohmigod, C's? Maybe a community college? Maybe you can aspire to become a liberal arts major? Or what about the military? I hear they'll take just about anyone. Or even better, maybe you can stick around for a few years and just sponge off your father and me."

"Yeah, right."

"Don't you 'yeah right' me, sonny. Yeah right, yeah right. I'm sure it's that kind of 'yeah right' atti-tude that Mr. Markowitz was referring to. He seemed like such an intuitive man."

"Yeah, right."

If looks could kill, Tommy would've been dead on the spot with a headstone planted. Birds would've been crying as mourners observed that the boy should have known how many "yeah rights" he could get away with.

The prematurely graying woman, complete with enough hairspray in her wash-and-set brown hair to personally create another hole in the ozone, began to tremble just a little with hostility. Her face had turned a shade of red that with each passing second grew richer and no amount of makeup could hide. This always happened whenever she was flustered. She resembled an angry cartoon. Deep indentations had carved themselves into her loose cheeks, and there were dark circles beneath her glassy brown eyes. Her elastic mouth stretched open and declared some more warnings. Tommy smiled lovingly at her, and this immediately drove her out of his room.

Only twenty seconds passed before she started screaming.

For the past fifteen years, Tommy had been dominated by an overbearing, self-indulgent, inconsiderate, melodramatic, nagging bitch. He hated how good she was at making him feel inept. No matter how he excelled, she always managed to make him feel inadequate. He'd concluded that his mother wasn't well a long time ago. Her half-full glasses of brandy and constant popping of Xanax didn't help matters any. Sedation is a thin excuse for drinking. She was hardly ever legally sober, but that never stopped her from driving. Or driving him nuts.

His father, Thomas senior, was well-to-do but weak in her eyes. She wore the pants and, for that matter, decided when they came off. Helena knew just how far to push and throughly enjoyed exploiting his lack of backbone. Thomas was the type who lived and let live. Often he felt sympathy toward his son, but his wife would never let the boy be. And usually she was wrong. But as long as Helena didn't grate on Senior's nerves, he was content with stay-

ing out of it. He tried to explain to Tommy that if
Mother went wacky on him, he should agree with
her and eventually she'd forget why she was upset.
But the boy didn't always take everything his father
said to heart. Knowing that arguing with Helena
was like shaking a thin stick at the wind, Thomas
senior had learned to shut her off, finding sanctuary
in his work, charities, and male prostitutes.

The phone rang. Helena, who was never too far
from the portable phone, answered it. Like others of
her ilk, she spent too much time on the phone gossiping. Even though the phone was growing roots
into her left ear, she always blamed the ridiculously
high phone bill on her only son.

Five minutes after the phone rang, the bedroom
door opened again. Necklaces, rings, and earrings
threatened to fly off as Helena shook with rage.
Tommy had played this scene out hundreds of times
before as his mom and one of her gossiping buddies
would wind each other up and the children would
bear the brunt of their hostility. Whatever had been
discussed had really lit her fuse.

"Well, just tell me what the hell I've done, and I'll
try not to do it again," Tommy offered without
sincerity.

"First off, don't you dare curse at me, you little
shit!"

"'Don't curse, you little shit,'" he quickly repeated, and laughed. "My whole life has been one
giant contradiction. 'Do this, don't do that. This is
good but this is bad.' How am I ever supposed to
learn anything if I'm housebroken without common
sense? 'Do as I say, not as I do' is a rotten philoso-
phy. 'Don't drink, even though I do. Don't curse, but
I can. Don't smoke, but it's okay for me.' I do what
you ask, and I'm still wrong. I bring home an excel-

lent girlfriend, and you call her a tramp behind her back."

"She is a tramp," Helena said matter-of-factly.

"How would you know?"

"I can tell. I know these things. She has a black soul."

"A black soul?"

"Yes, that girl's nothing but trouble."

"If she was the daughter of one of your church activity friends or yacht club cronies, she'd have your full approval," Tommy countered knowingly before adding insult to injury: 'Even if she had a black soul."

One point for the kid.

Tommy ran his fingers through his hair. He always did when he was uneasy. Verbal sparring sessions like this were everyday occurrences, and he'd gotten quite adept in the art of spoken word self-defense. "I work my ass off and receive no compliments. No rewards, no joy. No credit. Nothing. Nothing, except from outsiders who don't know what it's like having to live under this roof, and then you take all the credit for having raised such a fine young man, like you're some sort of June Cleaver for the nineties," he snapped sharply, refusing to lose his cool.

Two points.

"Awww, poor baby doesn't get enough attention from the evil mommy," Helena snapped, mocking her son. She'd heard the self-pitying neglected-child routine one too many times on *Oprah* for it to dent her armor. The kid, much like his father, was too damn soft for the real world. There were winners and losers, and if she had any say in the matter, she'd make sure her son turned out to be a winner, even if he hated her for it.

"Will you please tell me why you're so upset?"

"IT'S NONE OF YOUR GODDAMN BUSI-
NESS!"

Helena's face had stretch marks on it from years
of hollering over nothing, and her outbursts were
only a few decibels shy of illegal. The woman was
naturally high-strung, but Tommy could tell that tonight she was heading toward an exceptionally bad
fit. With any luck he would be long gone before it
happened.

"When I slip up, and God knows I'm not perfect,
you go ballistic," Tommy explained, trying to be reasonable but not weak. "You act as if it's a personal
attack against you. It's not. Believe me, I have better
things to do than listen to you rant and rave."

"Rant and rave? You little twerp! How dare you?
I'm going to give you one chance and only one
chance. Dinner will be ready the moment your father arrives. I'd suggest that if you have any plans
regarding going out tonight, you hit the books first,"
Helena warned before slamming the door.

The boy fell onto his bed but found no peace on
his pillow. His room was like a cell. After pondering
his meaningless existence for several seconds, his
stomach knotted up. It always did when he was upset. How could anyone, let alone his own mother, be
such an asshole? Visions of his month-long ground-
ing replayed behind his closed eyes. That had probably been the longest month in his life. He had come
home with beer on his breath and received the pun-
ishment. He would much rather have received a
beating with his father's belt than have had to suffer
through thirty days of Helena. He also remembered
being grounded over nothing major the night he
was supposed to attend a White Zombie concert and

having to eat the ticket. He'd kept the ticket and taped it underneath a poster of the group.

The kid rolled onto his side, looked down, and noticed a neat stack of magazines. Comic books like *Cry For Dawn, Hellstorm, Morbius, Faust, The Punisher,* and *Venom* dominated the top of the pile, but well hidden in the middle were several hardcore pornos that until recently were the extent of his sexual outlet. His girlfriend, Marlene, although she refused to let him fuck her, had on several drunken occasions gone down on him, usually puking afterward.

Wishing he were stoned, he nervously ran his fingers through his brown hair. Then he quickly got up, locked his bedroom door, and returned to his bed, where the view of the white ceiling was the best.

"Top three answers on the board. Richard Dawson asks 'What's America's favorite fruit?' My zonked-out mother answers the question quite seriously with 'Guava.' *Baaahhhhhh!* And then she gets pissed at me for laughing. Here's a bit of advice for you, Mother: Never moon a werewolf, you dumb cunt."

Like some sort of secret NASA nag satellite that was tuned to her son's bedroom, Helena started to gravitate toward his door. Tommy heard her footsteps make their way down the hall.

He'd best be studying, she thought to herself as she tried twisting the knob. No dice.

"OPEN THIS DOOR IMMEDIATELY!"

Tommy closed his eyes and wished she'd disappear.

"This is no joke."

"Yes it is, and you're the punch line," he replied, but not loud enough to be heard.

"ARE YOU RETARDED, LITTLE MISTER?"

No answer.

"I said are you crazy or just plain stupid? I don't know and don't care, for that matter. I'm tired of this shit. Do you hear me? What are you doing in there?"

"Nothing."

Something in the tone of his voice told her that he was doing more than nothing, and not knowing what it was angered her. After all, she'd brought him into the world. She had bled and been torn open so he could have life. He should be thankful.

And more important, he should be studying.

"DAMN IT! YOU CAN'T TREAT ME LIKE THIS!"

Inside the room, the boy wondered if all parents treated their kids this way. And if so, why? What was the point of abusing one's authority? What had gone so horribly wrong that adults had lost the ability to communicate with their kids?

Helena kept talking to the door, and the sound of her voice grated on Tommy's nerves when words like *idiot* and *moron* made their way into his room. He stood up off the bed, quietly walked to the entrance, and rested his head against the door.

"Mommy dearest, if you're so smart, then answer me this: Why did the Romans kill Jesus? All he was doing was trying to be righteous, and look what happened. Why? And how can God still love us after what we did to his only son?"

No answer. Over forty seconds passed before he tried another question.

"Is there really life after death, and how would anyone know? You'd have to die in order to find out, and people who are brought back from the dead never really died in the first place."

Again no response. Tommy waited only fifteen

seconds this time before addressing his side of the door.

"Mom, if all things really are woven from the same molecular fibers, where did those materials originally come from? I mean, where did God come from?"

"I don't know, son. I wish I did."

"And most important, where did Vanna White learn to spell so well?" Tommy asked, and then burst out laughing.

"WHAT THE HELL ARE YOU TALKING ABOUT?" Helena screamed, appalled. For a brief instance, she actually though her son had been asking serious questions and was seeking her guidance on issues no mortal can answer. She should have known better than to let the goofball set her up like that.

"What do whales sing about? Where does Ronald McDonald catch those little square fish? And why did the fuckin' chicken cross the road anyway?"

"WHATTT?"

"Why are they called french fries if Americans invented 'em?"

"WHAT'S WRONG WITH YOU?"

"What happened to Mickey Mouse's hands?"

"STOP IT, STOP IT! GODDAMN IT, SHUT UP! I SAID SHUT UP. I'M TIRED. TIRED! AND THAT MEANS YOU'RE GROUNDED. GROUNDED! DID YOU HEAR ME, YOU BRAINLESS LITTLE SHIT?"

Again, silence.

From behind the closed bedroom door, Tommy's facial expression went blank as all promise vanished for a fun Friday night. He moped from the doorway to the mirror above his dresser.

Staring back at him was a kid, just a kid decked

out in blue jeans and a Type O Negative T-shirt. His wavy brown hair was just long enough to cause his mother to complain. His face was neither too attractive nor too ordinary. Turquoise eyes stood out like neon bulbs against his pale flesh. A small, puglike nose sat above thin lips and a weak chin. Until a minute ago, he'd been content with his ordinary appearance. Now he glimpsed through the disguise, and hated what he saw.

He strongly resembled his mother.

Several seconds, or maybe minutes, passed before the boy finally declared, "Fuck this shit."

He dropped to the ground and began fumbling under his bed. She'd pushed him too far. His fingers groped around until he stumbled upon what he was looking for. Then he pulled the long case out. He unzipped it. Inside the light-brown vinyl case was a Winchester .22 rifle that his father had given him for his fourteenth birthday. Unfortunately, he had never had a chance to fire the gun, because they'd never gone hunting or target shooting. Dad, just like the character in Harry Chapin's *Cat's in the Cradle*, was always too busy.

Laughing hollowly, he pointed the rifle at the image in the mirror. It wasn't his reflection that he saw, but rather his mother's. He'd contemplated killing her for several months now but could never bring himself to do it. Like it or not, he loved his mother. Or at least he loved the idea of a mother-son relationship, like the one Bart Simpson had with his mom. Besides, he could never take the bitch away from his father. That would be letting Dad off the hook too easily. He'd married the hag, and that was his cross to bear.

In the mirror, the overlying image of his mother seemed to dissolve, and he was now staring at himself, aiming the rifle at his own reflection. He hated the weakling his mother had helped create. Then he realized what was wrong with this picture.

The mirror was not to blame.

Tommy turned the rifle on himself.

Anxiety swept through him as sweat surged from his pores. His stomach flip-flopped as his mind raced with nothing but suicidal thoughts. Vicious truths unveiled themselves about what life was and how he fit into the big picture. The truth was, he didn't fit in very well. His racing heart skipped a beat as he felt his shaking finger wrap around the cold trigger that he desperately wanted to pull. Never had something felt so right. Instinctively, he jotted a few words on a piece of paper, then unlocked the bedroom door. What's the point of killing yourself if no one could find you?

He tilted the barrel so that it was aimed toward his brain. After the trigger was squeezed, the .22 bullet would rip through the roof of his mouth, through the bottom of his skull, through his brain, and then exit out the top of his head. Of course there was the possibility that that bullet would mosh around the inside of his head, tearing up everything in its path *before* exiting.

His lips were wrapped around the cold steel, and he almost laughed at how ridiculous he looked when he saw himself in the mirror. He'd look ridiculous only for a few seconds. Then reality kicked him hard in the balls as he realized that the gun wasn't loaded. It was never loaded. His father had never given him any bullets.

But the boy wasn't about to give up without a fight.

His frazzled mind began to wander. Then his legs followed. Before he knew it, he was over by his dresser, digging through the bottom drawer. Well hidden, all the way at the bottom, was a small plastic Baggie. Inside were various fireworks, mostly firecrackers, whistlers, and ash cans. Also in the Baggie were six M-80's, a mini-skyrocket, and a Blockbuster. He'd been trying to save the fireworks, especially the big stuff, for the Fourth of July.

He removed the Blockbuster.

The white compact cylinder was about five inches long and four inches thick. When lit, it caused the loudest of explosions because it was packed with a quarter stick of dynamite. Tommy held the Blockbuster with respect. What fun he could have had lighting and flushing the waterproof bomb down a toilet on the last day of school. But that was neither here nor there. After several seconds of contemplation, he placed it in his mouth.

Betcha never got a blowjob before, huh Mr. Badass Blockbuster? he thought before lighting the wick.

The deafening blast echoed throughout the house, causing Helena to jump and drop an entire casserole. Never had she heard such a loud explosion so close by. Her heart threatened to leap out of her flaccid mouth.

As she stood in a mess of broken glass and ruined food, sheer disgust for the thing she called her son filled her entire being. Distress signals shot from her brain to her body, but she wasn't worried about her son. She was worried about what to serve for supper. After all, what kind of a lunatic lights fireworks inside a house?

"When I get hold of you, little mister," she warned as she approached the bedroom door. Expecting to find it locked, she yanked but, much to her surprise, found no resistance.

The room smelled of gunpowder, and there was a

small cloud lingering. Her eyes focused in on the horror show unveiling. It was as if someone had filled several balloons with red paint and thrown them around the room. Tommy's schoolbooks, which were on top of his bed, were layered in gore. Imbrued chunks of brain and bone fragments were violently splattered all over the walls and posters.

Helena's jaw dropped, and she tried to muster up a scream but couldn't. Try as she might—and more than anything in her entire life she wanted to scream at the top of her lungs—no sounds came. For the first time in her life, she was speechless. If only Tommy could have seen her.

Why did he have to do this? she wondered, sobbing aloud. A flood ran down her face and she was trembling uncontrollably. Didn't he understand how much she loved her one and only child? Hadn't she always been there when he needed her? *How could he even consider doing something like this?* she wondered, unable to put together what had driven him to such actions, although she had her suspicions that the heavy-metal music he listened to had something to do with it. Helena wanted to hug her dead baby but was afraid to touch him.

Then she noticed the note on his dresser.

Dear Mom,
I guess you were right all along
I am brainless!!!

Marlene awoke in restraints. She always did. Unlike those in most conventional hospitals, the restraints were not soft leather straps. That was much too modern. Painfully tight strips of material, like a ripped-up bedsheet, held her wrists in check.

How she had ended up in her current situation

was anyone's guess. How long she'd been there was
another mystery. It didn't matter. Nothing had mattered since that fateful night. Everything she'd ever
understood had lost its meaning. Reason made no
sense since logic no longer existed. Everyone she
loved was dead.

"Wake up, sleepyhead," said someone she
couldn't see.

"We're all here," continued another voice. "And
you're one of us. Never mind the screams and the
mess."

We're all here? she thought.

Her shattered mind began to backtrack, and she
began to remember. It was like wading through the
tide of a dream you can't wake up from. There was a
high school boy from a neighboring town; she
thought his name was Harold. He was kind of cute.
He got too stoned and killed his best friend. There
was also the handsome young man who claimed to
have been bitten by a vampire. Some weirdo with a
thing for sniffing glue and the crack-fiend with the
ruined hand were also at this facility. There were
many more on the other floors.

Hell, according to Dante, has many levels.

Located somewhere else there was the clown with
a thing for handcuffing boys. Joe, the shoemaker,
was Thorazined out and mumbling something about
ruling the world. Edmund Kemper was giving lessons on the do's and don'ts in mother-and-son relationships. Martin Plunkett was writing a book, and
if you listened closely you could hear Charlie strum-
ming his guitar.

There were no doors—at least not in the tradi-
tional sense. Marlene stared blankly into the dirty
gray and bloodstained bedsheet that separated her
from the others. Although she could feel no air cir-

culating, the sheet rippled and swayed as if someone had walked by. Most of the pajama-clad zombies who called this place home were either too drugged out or lobotomized from electric shocks to lift their feet. One could always hear them shuffling, but where they were heading was a mystery. She turned away and was pleasantly surprised. To the right, sitting in the chair beside her, was her boyfriend, Tommy. Behind him stood Tracy and Judy, her two best friends.

Or what was left of them.

Tracy resembled a giant smear. Most of her face was caved inward, and her skin was a spectrum of severe bruises. Purple and red were the most prominent colors. Her narrow nose was broken at a sharp angle, hooking until it touched her right cheek. Bloody mucus dribbled out of her nostrils, and with each breath drawn she wheezed. Her mouth was now oversize, loose, and dangling by the flesh hinges of a broken jaw. A perfect Aqua Fresh smile had been shattered, leaving the remaining teeth as jagged points.

Her body had fared no better than her face.

Jagged bones peeked out through her ripped flesh. Both of her arms dangled at odd angles allergic to gravity. It seemed as if her entire body was contorted. For all the damage she'd suffered, one would have imagined she'd been hit by a runaway subway train instead of a car. But if Tracy was a smear, then Judy was an overflowing exhibit of crusty burns and drippy, gravylike fluids.

Judy's flesh, if you could call it that, was black charcoal with speckles of goopy red sores thrown in for artistic balance. The wounds were oozing pus and leaking. She was a mass of burns scorched into one giant gnarled globule. So coarse was she that she resembled a walking crust with an awful odor. Specific body parts, like fingers or ears, no longer existed. They'd melted away. Viscous slime wept from her eye sockets and ran down what would have been her cheeks, coagulating into heinous makeup. Her bald, melted head lolled on her knobby shoulders since her neck could no longer support the weight. In comparison, Tommy looked like he was ready to go dancing, even though black smoke was still softly billowing out of the large crater in his head. His upper lip, his nose, most of his left cheek, and his left eye were gone.

Tommy smiled his perpetual half-smile. Marlene tried smiling back but was too sedated on 150 milligrams of Thorazine to do anything. Instead of flashing her dingy teeth, she drooled and urinated simultaneously.

"Our graduating class is having its ten-year reunion this week," Tommy creaked. He cupped his hand behind his right ear—the left one had been blown off—to hear what Marlene's moving lips were saying. No matter how hard she tried, nothing came out. Tears of frustration welled in her eyes.

"Hey, don't get bent," the half-head said. The last thing he wanted to see was his girlfriend upset. They'd already been through enough.

"Fuck 'em. You don't have to go if you're not feeling up to it. It's a stupid reunion anyway," Tracy explained through the bruises that passed for her face.

A reunion of the damned, Marlene thought but could not say before everything faded to black.

Mama's Boy

A small, muffled burst of laughter escaped from Peter Koch as he typed the last line to his most recent work, *Mama's boy*, a lurid tale about a teenager who wants to have sex with his mother. Why he chose to write this story was, like many things he did, beyond explanation. The words came and so the story was written.

Koch, a thirty-three-year-old beach bum writer who doubled as a model/actor depending on who was listening, pressed the save button on his word processor, and another piece of his fiction was finished. He rubbed his thin light-brown beard and smiled at the now-blank screen.

"Another glorious day for mankind," he declared, mocking himself, lighting a Salem.

The tired writer lifted his well-tanned body off the chair in which he'd spent the better part of the day creating and left his desk. He made his way over to a window. Outside, the sun was dropping out of sight. An eerie semicandescent glow that wouldn't last long outlined the other buildings.

The room was silent. Too silent. Koch needed a drink, but searching the apartment would be useless. He knew what he had. Or didn't have, which right now was anything. He also knew it would be several days before he'd even submit the new story to any of his reliable buyers. Magazines like *Blue Boy, Cavalier,* and *Hustler* all paid decent money for his fiction. Whenever he was down in the dumps, he could always churn out some diabolical tale of satanic groupies with a taste for brain-blood, chain-saw-wielding dentists, killer cars with souped-up big-block engines, or in this case, a motherfucker, and rise above the bill collectors and credit agencies. It was the bill collectors and their threats that he hated the most. After all, who the fuck were they to pressure him?

If only he had a drink. Or maybe a Quaalude.

Soon, he thought, anticipating the intoxicants and the temporary peace his next paycheck would bring. He returned to his desk, sat at the well-worn chair, and contemplated rereading his latest literary effort. No need, he reasoned. Some poor schlep of an editor would fix his typos, and besides, he knew the story by heart. He felt tired, but that should come as no surprise. He hardly ever slept. When he did sleep, his rest was plagued with horrifying nightmares. It was a common symptom most horror writers shared.

Staring into the word processor's blank screen, Koch saw a familiar face, one that helped inspire most of his gore-yarns. "Hello, Mother," he said, no longer an adult, but a child staring at the only adult he'd ever been close to.

He was putting on a windbreaker, getting ready to leave the small two-bedroom apartment in which they lived, when Mother called out, *"Where are you going?"*

"Outside. Play with my pals," Petey replied, feeling slightly ashamed. She always did this when he wanted to go out. She made him feel guilty about leaving her alone.

"Are you dressed warm enough?"

"Yeppp."

" 'Yes' is the proper way of speaking."

"Yes."

"The weatherman says it may rain. I'm not so sure going outside is such a good idea."

"If it starts raining, I'll run upstairs."

"Promise?" she asked.

"Swear to God," the boy replied earnestly.

"Don't take our Lord's name in vain. He hears everything, you know."

He certainly did. He also knew that his mother, much like God and his second-grade teacher, Mrs. Blanchard, heard everything he did, and he didn't like it very much.

"Yes, Mother."

"You will be home in time for supper, right," she instructed, not asking. The boy agreed and headed for the front door. Freedom was only four steps away when she called out again, *"You're not going anywhere near that basement, are you?"*

"Nope," he replied, dashing out the door, putting an end to the inquisition. He knew she meant well, but a boy can only stand so much. It was that damn basement and the story that Petey had repeated verbatim that made him the object of ridicule of the neighborhood.

In an effort to keep young Pete from playing in the dirty, dangerous basement where the older kids smoked cigarettes and stored pornographic magazines, Sandra Koch had told her son a wives' tale about a psychopath who molested, then cut out the eyes of young boys. The story worked well. That is, until curiosity got the better of Petey and he asked a chum two years older than he was, Jerry Hansen, if he'd ever heard the story of the psycho with a thing for young boys and basements.

"Yeah, right"—Jerry laughed—"like the eyeball slicer is really living in our basement!"

The story, like most childhood tales, went through many changes, some bringing Petey to tears especially when the story mutated to such an extent that *he* was the eyeball slicer. *Fuck you very much, Jerry Hansen!*

Fuck you, Mother.

Feeling guilty, Koch wished he could take back that last thought, but it was too late. Remorse for his lack of respect attacked his conscience. What kind of a son tells his mother to fuck herself? Then his feelings of guilt turned to anger. He was angry over the fact that she still wielded power over him, even in his thoughts. Angry at his inability to shed the invisible coverings his mother successfully smothered him with. Angry and getting angrier. Angry at what his mother had done to him (molded him into a subservient errand boy) and how she'd made him feel growing up. The pressures of youth were bad enough, but she made it a living hell with all her rules and regulations. For Petey to make and keep friends, Mother had to approve them. And of course no one was ever good enough for her. No one except his good pal, Jerry.

Right before his anger reached the dangerous levels that occurred when he brooded over his childhood, the images inside the screen subsided and once again Koch was an adult. *A thirsty, uneasy adult at that.* He pulled open one of the desk drawers. Inside, next to an empty flask, several empty vials, and an empty glass pipe, was a straight-edge razor. There was also a set of thin rubber gloves.

"Mother, do you think they'd laugh at me now?"
Koch asked, smirking at the blank screen. Outside,
it was getting dark, dreary, much like a basement.
Once again the day had died.

The doorbell rang.

*How did she always know when he was thinking
bad thoughts?* he wondered as a surge of uncontrolled panic consumed him. He wasn't a kid anymore, he was an adult, responsible for his own actions. This just wasn't fair.

Slightly trembling, his mind kicked into overdrive. He quickly put on the surgical gloves and
grabbed the straight razor. Although it wasn't very
heavy, the six-inch stainless-steel blade was sharp-
ened to the point of perfection. It was capable of
instant relentless brutality, and this wouldn't be the
first time Koch had ravaged an unsuspecting victim.
Not that he had that many bodies to his claim. Actually, it was less than a half-dozen.

Or was it?

"Who's there?" he called out innocently, sali-
vating as he got up and walked toward the door.
Although he knew such things were impossible,
Koch envisioned his mother, half-decomposed from
being buried for eight years, sitting in one of the
living-room chairs. She wore a familiar blue dress
that was now covered with dirt-laden moss. A thick
pile of worms slithered about in her lap. Her
browned bones were brittle and rotted. She raised a
moldy skeletal hand. She turned her decaying skull
in Peter's direction, and her wretched mouth
croaked *"Play nicely."*

"It's the *Daily Times,*" answered the squeaky
voice.

A swell of psychotic joy surged through Koch's
adrenaline-pumped body as he let out a sigh of re-

lief. He wouldn't have to kill again. Mother smiled back, then slowly disappeared. He was glad to see the dead bitch go. She'd been such a nuisance. Nothing he ever did was good enough to satisfy her. Nothing! He felt like he still lived under her microscope. Every flaw was magnified, every success unmentioned. Mother, Mother, Mother, Mother, Mother, Mother, Motherfucker!

His vision tunneled as he grit his teeth. "Why wouldn't you just let me play with the other fucking kids?"

Don't curse, he thought, and again grew furious for letting his mother manipulate his free will. Koch hated himself for being such a jellyfish. How could someone dead strangle his will so easily?

He was descending to the lowest depths when it dawned on him. It was so obvious that he felt like slapping himself. Yes, he would have to kill the paperboy in order to prove that Mother no longer held any claim over him. He'd tried this before with the others with no success, but he had a good feeling about this one. If he could free himself from her overbearing ghost, then maybe the bloodshed would stop. After all, she'd placed him in this predicament. The paperboy was the same type of kid that she had refused to allow him to play with. A dirty, no-account, door-to-door hustler. The type of kid Peter wished he'd been; *the type of punk she loathed.*

Rationalizing what he was about to do, Koch quickly pulled down every window blind and closed the curtains. Prying eyes were everywhere, and it was better to be safe than sorry. The more he thought about the little bastard—a smug, bubblegum-chewing, backward-baseball-cap-wearing, orthodontist-brace-faced, bill-collecting punk with no worries in the world, standing outside his front door —the more excited he became.

"I'm coming," Koch called out innocently, fake smile firmly pressed on. As he made his way toward the door, the straight razor opened silently on its well-oiled hinge. When he reached it, he wrapped a gloved hand around the knob. The right hand, which held the glittering blade, was behind his back.

"It's the Avon lady!" declared Koch's childhood chum, Jerry Hansen, as the door opened. Hansen almost fell down laughing, and if Koch could've seen the look on his face, he would've understood why. He was white as a sheet with bugging-out eyes, and his mouth was frozen into an 0. It had been at least six years since the two had last seen one another, and surprise was an understatement. Hansen, who was always on the heavy side, had gained at least thirty additional pounds since their paths last crossed. Koch wondered if it was an accident or karma that had placed his number-one nemesis, the man who caused him so much angst and aggravation, here right now.

Mixed emotions swarmed through the shaking writer. He was almost happy to see his friend standing there with a six-pack of Zima beer when he realized he was getting soft, weak. After all, it was this moron who had picked on him for more years than he cared to remember. And to top everything off, Jerry the jerk had Mother's approval. She thought he was just the perfect little gentleman, and now look at him: a wrinkled suit, crooked tie, gold-watch-wearing fat bastard.

His grip on the razor grew stronger. He'd show his mother.

"Thirsty?" Hansen barked.

"Yes, as a matter of fact I am," Koch replied with spittle-covered lips. A light ache consumed his balled-up right hand as he raised the straightedge overhead. His wet lips sneered before saying, *"And tired too."*

But regardless of how drained he felt, he was never too tired for an old friend. That would be rude, and Mother had taught her boy to always be courteous, even when killing someone.

In the blink of an eye, an eternity snuffed to some, the blade came down in an arc. The sound of steel slashing through flesh echoed in the fat man's ears before he actually understood what Koch was doing to him. The six-pack he was holding fell to the ground as his hands tried catching the red rain spilling. Using his left hand, Koch grabbed Hansen's green and gold tie and used it to yank him into the apartment. He slammed the front door shut.

The shredded man slumped down to one knee. Everywhere Hansen looked he saw blood, his blood. His horrified eyes pleaded for mercy that would not come as a size ten kicked him in the face, knocking him flat on his back. Koch then pounced on top of Hansen, placing his right knee on the man's heaving chest.

"WHY????"

Hansen had no answer. He didn't even understand the question.

"Why wouldn't you just leave me alone???" Koch barked, nearly hysterical. A thick stream of drool pittered off his lips and into Hansen's gasping mouth. Hansen just stared, bewildered. Why was his best friend doing this to him?

"You know what I'm talking about. All the picking on me in the basement, fucking with me, getting me in trouble for shit you did. WHY?"

Using his last bit of strength, Hansen spat out, *"Didn't—"*

"You calling my mom a liar, shitbag?" Koch asked calmly before running the razor across his victim's eyes. The blade cleanly ripped through Hansen's eyelids, as well as his retinas and corneas, leaving little more than two bloody orbs that now saw nothing. Whimpers of agony filled the small apartment, but death would not come quickly as Koch began carving around his victim's left eye socket. The right would soon follow as Hansen was ravaged by the product of an overprotective mother's imagination.

Mindwarp

Kicking back on the couch, Jeffrey Sweet was drinking his third screwdriver and petting Omar, the beer-drinking, Frisbee-catching Alaskan husky, when he heard Zeke Feinstein's loud Camaro pulling into the driveway. A smile formed on his vodka-moist lips as Zeke stormed in.

" 'Sup?"

"Work sucks, that's what's up," Zeke replied, throwing his tattered black leather jacket on the couch, making his way to the kitchen. He returned with a Molson. Molson was their favorite brew, and the refrigerator was usually well stocked.

"What happened?"

"Man, these fuckin' townies gave me a hassle. They always do. I told Bob, the walking asshole manager, to send Ron, the extra-large delivery dude. Ron said it was cool but Bobbing Head said no. Had to show off his half-inch of Pizza X-Press power. He told me go or quit."

There was a moment of tense silence as Zeke used his teeth to open his beer.

"What'd ya do?" Jeff asked in a slow, raspy tone that most excessive partyers share.

"Put my tail between my frigging legs and did it.

And got hassled. Every single time I go to 454 Bar-
ton Street, I get hassled. It's like an apartment full
of bikers without bikes. Tough guys, as long as
there's a pack of 'em. These fuckers tried to tell me
they ordered it over an hour ago so it's free. Fuck
that noise. This ain't no cardboard-tasting Domino's
Pizza crap. I told 'em no way and if they wanted to
argue I'd leave with the pizza. They threatened to
stomp me, said they were gonna fuck me up. *Twelve
goddamn dollars!* But at least I got the full amount.''

Jeff read Zeke's hostility. This was not the proper
way to start another evening of partying. At this
house every night was a party night.

Jeff's 156 IQ was always threatening to overload,
since he was constantly testing his mind. No mental
challenge was too great or trivial. He toed the thin
line between genius and insanity as his personality
ranged from Fellini to Pee Wee with no particular
favorite.

The tall, lanky kid looked like a nerd who was
trying to be hip. If he weren't dressed in trendy,
stylish fashion, it would be easy to picture him in
corduroy pants and a wool sweater, complete with a
pocket protector full of Bic pens. His blond hair was
done in the latest rage, short in the back and long in
front, and his face was plain. Actually, it was more
like a pepperoni pizza, since it was an acne factory.
His borderline genius mind understood the nature
of his psychological problems, which caused his bad
complexion, but that offered him no comfort. If only
Oxy 10 did what it promised.

''Mellow out, pizza schelp. I got something for
ya,'' Jeff said, handing Zeke the water pipe. He lit it
and took a deep toke.

''This is my pot,'' Zeke said in the thickest of New
York accents.

"Not the pot," Jeff said as Zeke handed him back the bong.

Zale (Zeke) Feinstein was a fairly handsome kid, and his half-mast tawny eyes, shoulder-length brown hair, and soft facial features made him a score in most girls' book. Besides being cute, he was intelligent, but barely made the grade during high school. The work was never the problem, he aced that, it was his attendance and attitude that held him back; that is, until his senior year. After a confrontation with a soon-to-be career criminal left him in the hospital with a fractured skull, Zeke did an about-face. He graduated with honors and with the intention of going to college, but he never found real friends.

At 5 feet 9 and 155 pounds he was solid without being fat, but he didn't care enough about sports to be a jock. He was too considerate to be a hood, too unruly to be a square, and didn't care for the drug crowd even though he probably took more drugs than any of them. He spent years locked inside his bedroom, dreaming about being in a heavy-metal band. The traveling, the fuck-you attitude, the one-night chicks, and all the partying was where he wanted to be. The few kids who shared his musical taste in bands like Accept, Riot, Diamondhead, Black Sabbath, Yesterday and Today, Budgie, The Rods, WASP, Frank Marino and Mahogany Rush, Tank, Waysted, and Trapeze just weren't cool enough. They were trend followers, not true headbangers. He also dreamed about moving to California after college. Maybe someday he would.

"Downs, V's?" Zeke asked with a brand-new attitude. His shitty mood was almost gone. After all, work was over for the night and homework could wait.

Jeff shook his head no because he couldn't speak. He'd lose the smoke in his lungs.

"'Shrooms?" he asked, removing his spaghetti-sauce-stained white work shirt. Beneath was an ancient Kiss concert T-shirt from the '76–'77 Destroyer world tour. That was the first concert Zeke had ever attended, and he still had the tattered shirt to prove it. Again Jeffrey shook his head no.

"*Blow?*" Zeke asked, hoping the answer was yes. Jeff blew out smoke and smiled.

"Nope, no mushrooms, no downs, no blow, but the news should rock your world anyway. Terry and Wizzy came by with some most very righteous acid from the current North American tour."

"Far fuckin' out. Deadhead acid is always the cleanest," Zeke said as Jeff handed him the LSD, which came on a tiny sheet of white paper no larger than a one half inch by one quarter. Unlike a lot of the acid he'd seen around campus, there were no witty designs or insignias stamped on the paper to identify this acid. Some of the more clever designs Zeke had seen (and taken) included Garfield wearing dark sunglasses, Charles Manson, The Grateful Dead's Steal Your Face skull, and the Batman logo.

Jeff rose off the couch and headed into the kitchen for a beer. When he returned, Zeke already had the acid under his tongue.

"Dude, did you eat that whole thing?" Jeff asked, stunned, silently praying Zeke hadn't.

Zeke smiled and swallowed.

"*No way.*"

The silly smile remained painted on Zeke's kisser.

"You complete delinquent, that's four-way acid. You're supposed to cut it into four pieces. Four separate pieces. Each corner is a thousand microdots of mind-boggling chemicals. Four people are supposed to share it. I figured we'd split it and really trip out. Dude, yer gonna fuckin' fry your brains out tonight."

"Get ta bed."

"Zeke, I'm serious."

"No."

"Yeah."

"Well, why didn't you say something?"

"You didn't give me a chance."

"I didn't know you needed a chance. You should've known better than leaving me alone without adult supervision," Zeke countered, amused with the situation. His mouth formed an exaggerated Buckwheat 0. He hadn't known he wasn't supposed to eat the whole thing. But come to think of it, it did look rather large for one hit.

Outside, a powerful wind threatened to tip the house over and send it flying up to Oz. There are two colleges in the Broome County/Binghamton area. The State University of New York (SUNY Binghamton) and Broome Community College (BCC). Often, locals who are stuck in a lower income bracket attend the less expensive and less prestigious BCC, while students with scholarships or money attend SUNY. Needless to say, there is tension. Townies resent the imports and view them as stuck-up yuppies in training, while SUNY students resent BCC students for resenting them in this catch-22. There's anti-Semitism and SUNY is often vandalized, spray-painted swastikas being the townies' calling cards. The annual hockey game between the two schools is a fight-filled frolic with more brawls in the stands than on the ice.

Zeke and Jeff's small two-bedroom apartment on Riverside Drive was a regular party pit-stop for SUNY students. It was a large house divided into four separate apartments. The other three neighbors had to constantly remind them to keep the noise level down.

The interior was a collection of typical college absurdities and was decorated according to whatever drug they happened to be on. One wall was partially spray-painted neon orange. A secondhand coffee table with a large water pipe on it rested in the center of the living room. Discarded fast-food containers and beer cans were scattered everywhere, as were books, paraphernalia, and CDs. The windows were covered in Moroccan shades and long scarves. The door was done in love beads. A set of motorcycle handlebars came out of one wall. There was a poster of Ziggy Stardust next to a poster for *A Clockwork Orange*, and next to that was a basketball hoop. Floating around somewhere was a mandatory-in-college interior design: the half-deflated blow-up doll that belonged, of course, to Jeff.

Their routines were, if nothing else, rather mundane. School during the day, part-time jobs (Zeke delivered pizzas, Jeff worked in the school bookstore), and assigned homework. Then came fun city: smoking, drinking excessively, and doing any and every available drug that entered the apartment.

After a few more bong loads and another beer, Jeff told Zeke he needed to borrow his car to go find more LSD. There were two superb horror movies on cable, and he wanted to trip during both of them.

"What's on, *Dolemite the Human Tornado* and *War of the Gargantuas?*"

"I said horror movies," Jeff explained, feigning exasperation.

"Them two flicks are pretty damn horrifying. Hey, be a real bro and get more beer and some munchies," Zeke said, buzzing, and tossed Jeff the keys to his '68 Camaro.

"Gimme some money. I paid for the, excuse me, *your* acid."

Zeke looked at his roomie and did his worst Jackie Gleason imitation. "One of these days . . ."

"Okay, Ralphie boy," Jeff said, sounding exactly like Art Carney as he took the cash out of Zeke's hand. He went into his bedroom and grabbed his leather jacket and a Talking Heads cassette.

"Dude, I got tunes in the vehicle," Zeke explained, smiling, knowing Jeff hated heavy metal.

"No, my friend, you have noise in your car," Jeff replied, and left.

"Later."

"Much."

Zeke sat there, semi-wasted, and thought about how much he liked his roomie. The dude was weird, way-out weird, but had a heart of gold. He was glad things had turned out the way they did.

Using the remote control, he flipped through the TV channels and settled on MTV, which was showing a classic performance of Jefferson Airplane when the drug first started creeping in. Funny, Grace Slick never looked or sounded better. Zeke mentally debated how many tabs of acid she was on during this performance. After a few seconds (or was it longer?) he concluded she was probably tripping as hard as he would be later.

An unremovable grin froze on his face as his body began to tingle with electric excitement. It was that stupid *"I'm tripping again"* face he'd worn hundreds of times before. He knew it was there, but no matter how hard he tried, Zeke couldn't take the shit-eater off.

The dangling love beads in the doorway began to

sway slowly as the walls breathed. The floor beneath him was vibrating and the patterns on the walls were taking on new dimensions, especially the bright orange one. It looked like an opening into a fluorescent void. With every minute that passed, the drug became more intense as sturdy mental doors became unhinged.

A few more videos came on before he turned to the channel that was scheduled to show the horror movies. The room started humming as Omar sat up on the couch. Zeke ran his fingers through the dog's hair. It felt like the dog was made out of the finest Chinese silk and he could feel the dog's heart pounding through the fur. Or was it his heart? Or was it the couch?

The movie started.

The colors coming out of the TV were mesmerizing trails that danced around the room. Vivid fluorescent spirochetes swirled before his droopy red eyes. The images on the screen made little sense, but he was digging the hell out of whatever was going on. His field of vision had expanded into a new dimension as inanimate objects around the room drip-faded.

Sounds echoed and reverberated through his cranium, but words lost their meaning. He recognized the words but found himself wondering about their sincerity. Everything seemed to have double meanings. He understood everything except what the words were really trying to say.

Does anyone really know what meaning is?

Zeke wanted to get another beer but couldn't sit up. The drug held an invisible grip over him, gluing him to the couch. Of course it was all in his head, but he couldn't stand. His feet refused to acknowledge his thoughts. Silently, he planned his escape route to the refrigerator. He nervously snickered to himself as a light, sticky sweat formed on his face. He constantly had to wipe his face, which more often than not felt like it was melting. Using maximum concentration, he was finally breaking free of the nonexistent restraints.

The dog followed him into the kitchen. He grabbed a brew and asked the dog if he wanted one. The dog said yes and Zeke poured a little beer into his water bowl.

"Thanks," Omar said, telepathically implanting the word into his master's brain.

"No prob," he replied, and caught himself speaking to a canine. Zeke realized what the LSD was doing to him and started laughing while the husky lapped up suds. He grooved back into the living room and sank into the couch.

Reality twisted and melted but he stayed upright. He felt like someone on the verge of a great discovery but he didn't know how to make it come true. It was as if the hidden answers of the universe were waiting to be explained if only Zeke would ask the right questions.

But why bother.

Sitting in the eye of a psychedelic storm, Zeke heard a squeaking noise from behind the images he was watching. It started out quite subliminally but grew louder with each passing moment. Zeke started bugging out as his acute hearing tuned to frequencies that only extraterrestrials and animals can hear. The noises reminded him of something large trying to force itself through too small a space, like something was trying to constrict its way out of the rear of the television. The audible tension increased and grew in volume. Smiling, confused, Zeke wondered if it was just his overactive imagina-

tion or maybe the wind blowing? And then it was
gone.

For the next half hour, he enjoyed the trip. Much
like a surfer conquering a monster wave, Zeke was
learning how to enjoy the ride. At times it was hard
to breathe because his nose was trying too hard.
Exhaling was another sensation that tickled and
perplexed. His head felt as though it was pulsating
with molecular activity that threatened to overload.
Colors swirled and expanded into deeper dimensions of themselves, then evolved into new, more
intense levels of the spectrum. Everything was spiraling, intertwining into meaning. At times he felt
like crying like a loon because he thought he understood.

So he listened.

Then he asked, *"What the fuck am I listening to?"*

And something would answer in an unspoken language in which music was the common denomina-
tor. And so the song would play.

But there was no music, he concluded as another
imaginary tune came to mind. Just as he was ready
to identify the abstract piece, it was gone. It was
closer to noise than what is normally considered
music but this was not a normal evening.

"I feel like the soft spot on top of a baby's head," he
explained to no one, and silently waited for a reply.
The magnificent colors were becoming too intense
as the couch began to betray him with comfort. The
orange spray-painted wall was a void he dared not
look into.

After a few more scenes of surreal chaos and spe-
cial-effects violence, a commercial for Monster
truck racing at the Broome County arena came on.
Zeke watched in amazement as Grave Digger, the
Jersey Outlaw, Bigfoot, and the Carolina Crusher

drove over compacted cars and flew across the screen. He wondered what genius had come up with the concept of Monster truck racing and were they tripping when they thought of it. After thirty seconds of axle-jamming, front-end-smashing, non-stop four-wheel-drive action, another commercial came on.

"I am the monkey man, the monkey man, the monkey man. I am the monkey man, please don't laugh at me," sang a hideously deformed small boy. Although he prided himself on being a master couch potato, Zeke had never seen this commercial and the soft, eerie voice frightened him.

Inside the screen, and trying to escape, was a black-haired boy with a mongoloid haircut. The boy had one normal arm and one infant-sized arm. The small arm looked like rubber. His tiny hand was bent at the wrist in a ninety-degree angle.

With his back arched forward, the boy contorted about. It looked as if he was trying to dance. The spastic movements were frantic and rhythmless. The boy's bulbous head was roughly the size of a small watermelon. It was too large to be confined, and caused the television screen to bulge outward. The screen slowly continued pushing out, bringing the mushrooming head closer to Zeke.

He stared at the boy with both disgust and pity. He tried looking away but couldn't. Dingy yellow teeth protruded from the boy's mouth. Even with his mouth closed, the teeth were still visible. His lips were so badly chapped, Zeke wondered if somehow they'd been burned. The boy smiled knowingly at him, like the two were sharing a secret, and his crusty lower lip split. A honeylike drop of blood slowly dribbled down his chin. He swiped at the droplet with his swollen tongue but missed. No matter how far he stuck his tongue out, he couldn't reach the drop. Frustrated, he shed a tear from his right eye. The boy bashfully waved good-bye with his normal arm before disappearing.

Lights shone in through a window and ran across the room. Zeke's eyes traced the tiny helicopter of illumination until it disappeared. Listening intently, he heard a car door slam. Footsteps slapped pavement until they faded around the corner. One of the other tenants was home. He wished Jeff would hurry back.

"I could've told you it wasn't him."

Zeke looked around for whoever said that. He was beyond paranoid.

"I'm right here."

"Where?" Zeke asked aloud until his bulging eyes found it.

The dog.

The room was really growing small now. Zeke closed his eyes and tried getting a grip but nothing seemed to work. He'd taken acid so many times that he'd lost count but he had never experienced anything like tonight. He opened his eyes again and his gaze was locked on Omar. At least the dog was real.

"Don't act like I just ripped your jugular out. It's really not that big of a surprise," Omar explained without moving his mouth. *"C'mon, man, I mean why do you think we're called Man's Best Friend?"*

There was no denying that Zeke had heard what he'd heard. Regardless of what tricks his eyes might play on him, his ears were perfect. He tried rationalizing everything. Omar was just a dog and he was tripping out. *But there was much more.* He felt it in the dog's eyes. He'd seen movies like this, about communicating with dogs and such, and he was scared because he was now doing it.

"Relax, boy," the dog told him with a look, but Zeke couldn't. His heart sprinted inside his heaving chest and his eyes bulged wide. Fright pumped through his veins. A cold chill tickled his spine. The dog he had raised from a puppy looked *different.*

"Zeke, we've been here for thousands of years. We've seen it all. We've watched you ruin the environment. We've watched you get weaker, full of self-doubt. We've watched you enslave and kill millions of us. Vivisection, don't make me laugh. We've watched you kill the earth."

A low growl came from the dog.

"We know more about you than even you do."

Omar bared his fangs and a stream of drool fell out. He was growling sickly as he backed Zeke into his bedroom.

"And we don't like what we see."

Omar, Stay!"

The dog continued to slowly stalk forward.

"FUCKIN' STOP!" Zeke yelled, sweat falling off his brow.

The dog barked back defiantly.

"FUCK YOU TOO!"

Zeke grabbed a Louisville slugger baseball bat and charged. Omar didn't resist. It was almost like the dog had known Zeke would react this way. Clubbing like a seal hunter, Zeke slaughtered the dog. *His dog.* His full-force swings ripped the dog's head apart. The sound of wood smacking skull echoed through the room. Brain blood rained everywhere. He didn't realize what he was doing until he'd finished and by then it was too late. The room began shifting underfoot, rotating slowly until he was facing the TV screen.

"A little paranoid, aren't we?" the television asked.

"FUCK YOU!," Zeke declared, still clutching the bloody baseball bat.

"No, excuse me, you're fucked," a winged serpentine female countered, snarling through the picture screen. Staring in awe, Zeke acknowledged that she would have made an excellent album cover. He had seen women like this before in the art of Boris Vallejo and Frank Frazetta.

The demon was beautiful in a classic sense. Her angular, flawless face could've belonged to a model except for her lidless reptilian eyes. Long blond hair with purple streaks through it covered her large breasts. She threw her wild hair back, giving Zeke a good view of areolas that resembled tribal tattoos and nipples that were pierced by small silver bones. Her scaled skin was a brilliant bronze until it reached her slender waist. Her shapely legs were gold, black, and light brown, like a boa constrictor.

In the crook of her left arm, the She-demon held an Easter basket overflowing with cockroaches. Not the small ones, but the big ugly ones you find down South. A thick chrome chain ran around her slim waist and through a small wolf skull, which served as her G-string. She removed one of the cockroaches from the basket and let it crawl along her right hand. Then she held her hand by her crotch and the animal skull snapped up the treat. As its jaws chewed voraciously, the woman groaned softly, sexually. Her butterfly had gone mad.

Zeke stepped backward and got ready to rumble as the glistening demon spread her winged arms, sending the basket and bugs flying out of the television. She leaped out through the screen and landed several feet in front of him. The student swung but missed, tripping over the coffee table and spilling the water pipe. A rancid aroma filled the room.

Zeke quickly stood back up. A tango of hatred, with both combatants jockeying around for better positions, ensued. The She-demon coiled, hissed, and lunged at the exact moment that Zeke stepped up and swung the bat. He connected solidly with her face, knocking her headfirst into the wall, tearing the Bowie poster as the basketball hoop overhead rattled loudly.

The serpentine woman quickly got ready for another round of battle but her fearful eyes gave her away as defeated. The first blow had been too much. Her jaw was shattered, leaving her mouth dangling open, unhinged. She staggered forward, winged arms raised, trying to protect her mangled face. Zeke felt disgusted by it. The usually nonviolent student wondered if someone else was programming him, making him act this way. Was he a player in someone else's video game? Why couldn't he use peaceful means to settle his differences?

Why was she still coming toward him?

He raised the bat and smashed away at her winged arms, not so much because he wanted to fight, but because he didn't know what else to do. The baseball bat cracked the thin bones in her wings and after four or five quick swipes, she backed up next to the television. Realizing she was licked, the broken woman spit out a mouthful of blood and jumped back into the screen.

Zeke started crying wildly as drugged-out tears fell freely. The drugs were coming on stronger and stronger and showed no signs of letting up. This was a trip even he couldn't handle. He ran past the dead dog, past the TV, past the orange wave, and to the front door. Shaking, he grabbed the doorknob but was afraid to turn it. Who knew what horrors were on the other side?

"I'm only tripping. This shit ain't real," he told himself repeatedly, trying to convince himself. Then something behind him moved.

The second feature had begun.

"C'MON, FUCKERS!" he declared, making his way back toward the center of the room. It only took several seconds for a group of rotted zombies to appear behind the thick concave screen. The decomposing corpses slowly milled about until one of them took the initiative and made his way toward the screen. Its elongated mouth hung open and there was desiccated gore smeared on its cheeks, chin, and chancred lips.

Judging by the corpse's appearance, it had not died from natural causes. Its clothing had been shredded, giving view to the large bite marks adorning its bluing torso. Lubricious intestines dangled from a gnarled tear along its stomach and threatened to fall out at any moment. Through the miracle of television, the creepy-crawly was only a few inches long, but Zeke was starting to understand how this game worked. If the zombie got out of the set, it would be at least six feet tall.

A close-up showed dead eyes, immune to thought, staring out blankly. There were no thoughts, no worries, no concerns, racing through the zombie's spoiling mind. It only had one primal instinct: to eat the living.

The walking dead creeped forward and stuck two of its arms through the screen. Zeke noticed that several of the zombie's fingers were missing and appeared to have been chewed off.

Finger food, he thought morbidly before smashing at the creature's pasty arms. So forceful were his blows that he broke bones until they were jutting out through the moldy flesh, but that did little to stop the zombie's forward progress. Zeke had seen enough of these movies to understand what he had to do. He stepped back, readied himself, and waited for the zombie's head to come out of the screen. When it did, he swung the bat with all his might, bashing the zombie's skull until it disappeared back into the television.

He kept a close eye on the rest of the putrid zombies but they were in no hurry to venture out of the TV. Instead they gorged themselves on easily scripted prey. Zeke was considering just smashing the television but found the inner strength to restrain himself. After all, it belonged to Jeff and how would he explain his actions?

In his fried mind, he concluded that the extreme dosage of LSD had opened a new dimension and he'd crossed over. The writings of H. P. Lovecraft came to mind. He'd always been hip to the concept of drugs expanding the boundaries of reality and now he wished he hadn't been correct. His veins pumped adrenaline as he reverted into a caveman with a club as his best friend. Knowing that, he wished the people with the giant butterfly nets would hurry up and take him where he couldn't hurt anyone else. Then he saw something: a way to end the madness.

The plug.

How easy could it be? Unplug the television and the horrors inside would end. With a sound like the canned laughter of a studio audience, Zeke started chuckling to himself. The laughter died quickly as he sucked in a deep breath, getting up his nerve. If he didn't keep his guard up, something could attack from behind. He squatted, then quickly stood up. There was no way of getting around it, he had to touch the plug. Time froze as he realized that this could be the end of his life. What if he was fried when his sweaty hands touched something that had electrical currents flowing through it? What if unplugging the set would also unplug his mind?

What if a six were a nine? he wondered, many years after Jimi Hendrix had posed that same question.

He readied himself to do something he didn't want to. As he crouched down, the floor seemed to embrace him. The lower he got, the less chance of falling over. Then he thought he saw a roach out of the corner of his eye. He paid the insect no mind since he had something much more important to worry about. Shaky fingers gripped the plastic plug, and with one fierce yank the plug was out of the socket.

"Ha, what'cha got to say for yourself now?" Zeke asked the dead screen. He stood waiting for an answer but nothing happened. The screen was that ominous unused grayish-green every screen is when not in use. It looked harmless but he knew better. If he let his guard down he was doomed. He cautiously turned away and headed for the couch. Exhausted, he fell onto the couch, and much to his surprise, it didn't grab or attempt to smother him. It felt relaxing, comforting, like a couch is supposed to. He dropped the bloody Louisville slugger with Don Mattingly's autograph on it.

That was exactly what the TV was waiting for.

"YOU CHEATED," the television declared through small, tinny-sounding speakers as it came back to life.

The living room began to spin and sway out of control. Electrical charges, like miniature lightning, crackled overhead. Waves of energy rolled through the air. The TV screen glowed dimly, then where there had just been hundreds of glass dots on the blank screen, thousands of writhing maggots appeared. Through the mass of maggots came a giant fire-charred hand. Its fingernails had been melted into claws, black and pointed. With every passing inch that came out of the twenty-one-inch screen, the hand grew larger as more maggots spilled out of the set. Soon the hideous hand would dwarf the freaked-out collegiate.

Standing on the couch, he couldn't believe the size of the burned hand. The putrid stench of rotten eggs and slimy milk filled the room. Revulsion consumed him as regurgitated Canadian beer shot out of his tunneling mouth. Zeke knew he only had one chance as he dove for the baseball bat. In mid-flight, he swore to God that if he ever came down off the LSD he'd never do any drugs again.

The second he got the bat in his hands, the four-foot-wide rotted hand grabbed him and squeezed into a fist. He never had a chance to get off a good swing. He kicked, squirmed, and swung at the giant hand that was squeezing the life out of him. He felt his ribs snapping one by one.

"Fuck you," Zeke groaned as the hand squeezed. Blood bubbled out his nose and mouth. Just then, his ears picked up the sound of his car pulling into the driveway.

"Help me," he gurgled, trying to spit the words out through the blood in his mouth. They didn't carry very far. The burned hand was slowly dragging him into the television set. In a last-ditch effort at survival, Zeke placed the baseball bat across the screen. During those last few seconds, he saw his young life ending as the wood began splintering.

His mind flashed back to his family and his childhood. He saw the once blue ocean in which he had learned how to swim and all around his floating body were hundreds of syringes. The rusty needles were getting closer and closer when he saw a green golf course. Wet from the ocean, he started walking on the grass. Lined up all along the fairway were discarded antique toys. These swell toys were from another era, before toys were cheaply made of plastic. There were cleverly painted wooden rocking horses, toy soldiers, Lincoln Logs, Erector sets, sporting goods, Tonka trucks, marionettes, electric trains, and all sorts of goodies that Santa would never deliver.

One of the toys, a jack-in-the-box, popped open. Standing beside the teetering jack-in-a-box was the girl Zeke had lost his virginity to. She was crying uncontrollably. Nothing could comfort her and her tears were pooling at her feet. Head down, Zeke walked over to her and in the puddle he saw the tan house he grew up in. The house seemed frail, ready to tip over. And then for some strange reason he saw his latest report card. All A's and B's. It just didn't seem fair that a bright well-to-do young man with a promising future should let one night's partying take everything away from him. He would have done absolutely anything to be back in the comfort of his mother's arms. But all that was out of the question as the tug-of-war ended when the baseball bat couldn't stand the pressure any longer and loudly snapped in half. Then his upper body was pulled into the television.

Feeling like he was covered in macaroni and cheese with sharp teeth, Zeke closed his eyes as the tiny larvae pecked away. Maggots filled his open mouth and flooded down his throat. He felt them wriggling into his nostrils and ears. He felt them chewing on his eyes. No matter how hard he struggled to squeeze them out of his eyelids, more hungry maggots followed. His left eye popped and ocular fluid dripped down his raw face. Then his right eye was ravaged. Quickly, more maggots gnawed through his flesh. Thousands upon thousands of sets of tiny carnivorous teeth ravaged his flesh until it broke open and the larvae poured into the open wounds. He felt his face contorting and expanding from too many maggots trying to fit into too small a space. They tore at the blinded student until he stopped struggling and was completely pulled in. Hungrily, the television chewed Zeke up as he died the death of a crouton in a bowl of maggot soup

A powerful gust of wind helped throw the front door open and there stood Jeff, who couldn't believe his eyes. Beer, Doritos, and Twinkies, fell out of his hands. He'd been gone longer than he'd planned and the entire apartment was trashed. Maybe he should have waited until he'd gotten home to eat his dosage of LSD. At least he hadn't taken as much as Zeke did, only half.

"Zeke, where the fuck are you?" Jeff timidly cried out, but received no answer. The living room resembled a rough-and-tumble biker bar where all hell had broken loose. Most of the furniture was overturned, broken glass was everywhere, and there was a mutilated dog at the bedroom's entrance. None of that really mattered as Jeff feared for his best friend's welfare. Besides the debris, there was fresh blood everywhere. Everything in sight was stained, thrashed, or ruined.

Everything except the television, which, other than the fact that it was unplugged, was in perfect condition.

Saltwater
and Blood

Even during his earliest memories, the ocean was the only place he ever really wanted to be. He felt safe, at ease on the waves. There was a certain peacefulness about the ocean that was only his to understand. He felt like he belonged to some enlightened nautical society and his education about the ocean went back to his expert teacher. His father had been a fisherman and his father before him.

Fishing is honorable. It's a man's job and a man's way of life with no room for snivelers, lackeys, or show-offs. It takes every man working together as a team to properly catch fish. That was probably the most basic (and most important) lesson his father had taught him. If you have a whiner on board, the whiner has two choices: stop whining or start swimming. There is no room for bickering or arguing among fishermen.

But there is a great deal of arguing going on.

Not on the sea but on land.

Roy inherited his commercial fishing boat and the family business from his father. The stern old man had meant everything to him. Fortunately, his father lived a pretty full life, fishing until he was sixty-three. He tried to show his son as best he could the proper ways of the sea. Roy Emerson, Sr., had fished for as long as anyone could remember and was a dammed good mariner. He had an eye like a hungry hawk and could harpoon a pimple off a whale's back without hurting the whale. Then again, if his father had been fishing the way Roy, Jr., fished, he might still be alive today.

A few years after his father died, the fishing industry invented a revolutionary net called the gill net. Gill net fishing was the most inexpensive, efficient means of commercially catching fish. Synthetic fiber nets were dropped at night, each one a mile long, and pulled up the following morning. Easy, right? The theory was if you used a sixteen-inch gill net (each hole in the net being sixteen inches in diameter) then the only fish trapped were large-sized fish that were ready to be taken out of the ocean. If each fish being pulled out had a head large enough to get trapped in a sixteen-inch hole, it would have already mated twice. This way the ocean was drained of older, weaker fish and the young ones were safe from the nets until they were ready to be taken.

There was only one flaw in this theory: *Fish don't know how to swim backward.*

Any fish with a circumference of sixteen inches would get twisted and tangle itself in the net to a point where it could not move. Then its gills seize . . .

Using the gill net, fishing boats reeled in nets filled with hundreds of dead fish. The ocean's floor quickly became a massive open grave, littered with hundreds of thousands of disposed carcasses. Before the gill net, fishermen like Roy's father had used nets, but they had hands-on action. If something endangered or inedible was captured, it was set free.

Roy looked like a fisherman: healthy, tall, buff but not overtly muscular, and clean-cut. His tan was a natural one from years of working in the sun and his large hands were so coarse he could use them to take the paint off furniture. Like his father, Roy was a blond-haired, blue-eyed Republican. He loved America and apple pie. He believed in God, glory, and his right to bear arms. And to fish commercially. But he wondered if depleting the ocean of its fish supply at such a rate that by the year 2000 most of the world's fish would be endangered, was morally correct. Surely if people knew, they would intervene and gill net fishing would be stopped, he reasoned. But where does a person draw the line? Dolphin-safe tuna was little more than a good advertising campaign. Did anyone have the right to commit genocide just to keep tuna prices down? Did the public have the right to know or would they even care?

Would his father approve?

People did know, he reasoned. Hell, he knew and added to the atrocities, but as long as gill netting was as lucrative as it was, he could keep a secret. Roy was one of thousands of poachers who used the illegal drift nets for profit. Halibut, cod, tuna, squid, and valuable swordfish are what commercial fisherman like Roy desire, but the gill net isn't prejudiced. It takes anything unfortunate enough to swim into it. Sharks, seals, dolphins, porpoises, sea lions, and even whales get tangled up in these nets.

Every now and then, a fish that can move just enough to get water through its gills gets trapped in the net. These fish have to be killed by the fishing crew. Since gunfire would bring unwanted attention, baseball bats are the most popular tool used to kill the tangled fish. You can't take chances with a three-hundred- to seven-hundred-pound fish. One swipe of its tail, one bite, and a member of the crew is crippled. The problem is big fish don't die easily. The sound of an aluminum bat smashing against a blue shark's skull will echo throughout the vessel until the fish's head is ruined. A sound that is even worse is the one made by dolphins.

You can hear them crying all night and day.

"That's just lazy fishing."

Roy turned and saw no one. He couldn't even see the shore anymore. He returned his attention to his four-man crew that was hauling that night's illegal catch. Speed and secrecy were vital since the heavy penalties for being caught using drift nets included a revoked fishing license. To this date, Roy knew of no one who'd actually been caught.

Instead of fence-sitting, Roy decided to help his crew haul in the load. It was rough, strenuous work but he enjoyed testing his powerful arms. It wasn't anything like the rush he felt when reeling in a large fish for sport but that was neither here nor there. This was business. He quickly made his way toward the stern of the boat but lost his footing just as he approached the edge. It felt like the ocean he loved had betrayed him. Slow-motion-like, he saw his foot slide through a thin pool of blood. Momentum carried his six-foot frame over the side and into the net.

Trapped in the ice cold water, Roy instinctively kicked off his Vans sneakers but his legs refused to tread water. The sharp cold attacked his senses, paralyzing him. He felt his muscles atrophying. Although he was an expert swimmer, he couldn't use his strong legs; only his mind functioned, the simplest of thoughts traveling through it.

Sixteen-inch circumference, he thought over and over.

Roy sank steadily as large air bubbles shot from his stinging nose and mouth. Inside his pounding head, he heard a symphony of hammers banging, children screaming, fingernails slowly raking chalk boards, and outboard motors. The ice water bit his eyes, licking his wounds with salt. Something slimy wrapped itself around his left hand. He wanted to scream but no sound would come out of his choking throat. Roy ripped at the slime with his free hand. Surprisingly, there was no resistance and the sea-weed let go.

Even through his water-impaired twenty-twenty vision, Roy sensed what was happening. His pounding heart threatened to detonate. All around him were out-of-focus, bloated gray fish. Even though his perception was off, he could tell they were getting closer. A large mass of bodies was floating up from beneath him.

They wanted him.

Get away, you stupid friggin' fish.

They kept coming.

His left foot was tangled in the net. He pulled desperately but couldn't free himself. He knew getting out of the net was a simple process but with his vision whacked and no oxygen he couldn't figure it out. More precious air shot out of his salty, sour nostrils. Arms flailing, he felt like he was being smothered as more ocean forced its way down into his waterlogged lungs. His swollen throat felt as though iron fingers were squeezing it. Every so often he'd feel another trapped fish touching him but there was something wrong with the way they felt. They were more like cadavers than fish.

That night's catch was being hoisted. Through his

panic, Roy understood what his crew was trying to do. He prayed that they'd have him out of the water before it was too late. He grabbed the nylon net and the gill net tore up his palms. Even more foul water forced its way into his coughing mouth when it dawned on him.

He was being raped by the ocean.

For a split second, Roy wondered what his personal heaven or hell would be. Or would he be denied? Would he return to earth as a tree, only to be cut down? Would he ever be reunited with his father? Would he return as an insect that people instinctively stomp on sight? Or would he just float for eternity, tangled and tumescent? It was then that he conjured up his last effort and started thrashing wildly. Green-and-white bubbles created by his flailing arms took over his field of vision. After some frantic motions, his tangled foot became free.

He started kicking and climbing for freedom, fighting his way upward. Through ravaged salt-burned eyes he saw hope. Orange sunlight was reflecting off the top of the ocean.

There were fewer than ten feet between him and oxygen. He tried climbing faster but the more desperate he became, the more slowly his drained muscles moved. What normally would've taken little effort was now almost impossible. His arms were devoid of energy. Another tangled fish touched his right forearm and slipped around it, trying to keep him inside the net. He pushed it aside and realized it wasn't a fish.

Trapped in the net, bloated and blue, was his father. Pasty cataract-white eyes, that reminded him of fried eggs, bulged out of their sockets. His wrinkled face was moldy dead flesh. Small air bubbles streamed out of his decaying nose and what was left

of the old man's scraggly white hair swayed wildly.
Rotted teeth poked through his wretched smile as
he spit black octopus ink into his son's silently
screaming face. The thick oily blackness slowly expanded until it wrapped itself around his face like a
plastic bag. Blinded by the pitch-black ink, Roy felt
clawlike hands wrapping around his throat.

The bedroom was spinning as Roy awoke terri-
fied, coughing out the saltwater still trapped in his
throat. Maybe someday he'd be able to free it. His
dreams were always in color. For a split second he
remembered the murky aqua ocean, his white boat
speckled in red, and something black leaking out of
his father's mouth. Then the dream was gone but
the thud of skulls being smashed rang in his ears
night after nightmare. And every night, a long session of reflections and thoughts followed since sleep
would not easily return.

The nightmares were also occurring during the
day. Fish was no longer a delicacy and Roy could
hardly stand more than a few bites without trying to
wash the bitter taste of fish blood from his tongue.
Even his favorite characteristic of the ocean, its
salty aroma, was betraying him. Now, the water
reeked of death. Too often, he felt his old man walking behind him, sneakers squeaking against the
ship's floor. When he turned to see the man he so
loved, he never caught a glimpse of him, not even in
the sun's reflection on the ocean where the soul of
every loyal mariner was kept.

Even though the rules of the sea had changed, he
was still where he'd always wanted to be and doing
what he felt most comfortable doing; fishing. He
could handle the trappings of success. When he
wasn't on the ocean, he was in his two-story house,
located in a posh private sector of Santa Monica.

Both he and his wife had fairly new cars and Roy was considering buying a pickup truck for work, and more important, as a tax write-off. His six-year-old daughter attended one of the better private schools and her teeth were being straightened by braces that—if not for gill netting—would be unaffordable. Gill netting's low operational cost made the luxurious life affordable. Just like the rest of society, what his family didn't know about the realities of commercial fishing wouldn't hurt them.

Roy eventually drifted back to sleep and before he knew it was enjoying another lazy Sunday. Sitting in his beautiful house—its mortgage payments always on time—his sturdy frame relaxed in his favorite easy chair. The soft seat contoured to his. The images on the thirty-two-inch television showed summer fun, Angels baseball. Earlier, Roy, his blond-haired, blue-eyed wife Laura, and their blond-haired, blue-eyed daughter Cindy, had sat through an incredibly cramped religious service. Personally, he believed that going into the ninth with the Angels winning by three runs was his reward for being righteous. Sunday was his only day away from the ocean. Today, he felt like doing absolutely nothing and the TV's remote control was secure in his right hand, a cold one in his left.

Then he heard the whirlwind of small feet running toward him.

Cindy ran into the living room holding a pint of Ben & Jerry's Chunky Monkey ice cream, yelling, "Put on channel ten, put on channel ten. Quick."

"Little missy, don't you have a television of your own?"

"Please," she pleaded. Roy pressed the two digits on the remote control and the screen now was on CNN, an odd station for Cindy to be interested in.

Roy's blue eyes focused on the ocean he knew so well and listened as the announcer explained.

"Two Pacific gray whales, one male, one female, have beached themselves off the Colony in Malibu early this morning. The twenty-three-foot-long whales weigh approximately one ton each. Rescuers and volunteers have rushed to the private beach in an effort to save the endangered animals. So far all efforts have failed and experts believe that, as the crowd grows larger and more hours pass, the whales' chances for survival are getting slimmer. No one understands why beaching by aquatic mammals occurs.

"During the early part of the century, the gray whale was all but extinct due to whaling off the California coast. Gray whales grow up to forty feet but are slow-moving, thus easier to hunt. Environmental laws protecting the gray whale saved them from extinction, but the loss of two healthy gray whales would be considerable since there are fewer than two hundred left in the world.

"Reporting live in Malibu, Alex Michaels for CNN."

"Please, please, please?"

"Please what?" asked Roy, enjoying the game.

"Please can we go see the whales? Help save 'em?"

"Ummmm . . ."

"Pretty please with sugar on top?"

"I don't know . . ."

"C'mon, Daddy. Pleeeeessssseeee."

"Mmmm . . ."

"Oh stop it, Roy," yelled Laura from the kitchen. A slight sense of hostility flooded him. He hated it when his wife intervened with any disciplinarian tones in her throat. It reminded him of his failed education.

All was not as perfect as it seemed in the Emerson
household. She blamed his libido as well as his
drinking. He blamed overwork, stress, and her,
since this house and every luxury in it was his doing. Instead of yelling back at his wife, he wrinkled
his nose at his daughter, which caused her to giggle
uncontrollably. It was the beauty of her silver smile
that lifted him off his chair.

"Last one to the car is a rotten fish," he declared.

The ride from the house to the beach took less
than fifteen minutes. It was a ride Roy knew like
clockwork. This was his terrain. They were going to
his ocean. The closer they were to the water, the
more excited the young girl grew.

And Roy knew where she'd inherited that from.

A small crowd had already gathered beside the
beached behemoths. It wasn't an unusual sight to
either Roy or Laura. Every few years rescuers gathered in the Colony, fruitlessly trying to save beached
whales. The commotion brought the media that
were always eager to cover the action but rarely
anxious to get their hands wet. As soon as the car
was parked and they were at the beach, Cindy ran
ahead of her parents over to the seashore.

"Don't get too wet!"

"Be careful!" her mother nervously yelled.

Both proud parents watched the six-year-old run
gracefully. She was the diamond in both of their
eyes and all the corny clichés about children were
true. The air smelled a little sweeter when she was
around. She was the rhyme in their poems, the
beauty in their art. Love had taken on a new meaning when she was born. Both parents proudly noted
that Cindy had made their lives worth living, and no
matter what happened between them, they both

were determined to work things out. They had to. Neither wanted to lose custody of Cindy.

When they finally caught up to her, Roy realized that they were in the middle of another unusual phenomenon. Workers and volunteers had given up on the gray whales; both were dead. In their wake more beaching was occurring. Only this time instead of whales, dolphins were running the kamikaze course.

It started off with just a few dolphins. Workers, concerned citizens, and volunteers removed the dolphins from the beach and carefully carried the mammals back into the ocean. But the dolphins weren't about to give up so easily. They'd return to the ocean, turn around, and with even more velocity and determination, run the route again. In a matter of minutes, there were dozens of beached dolphins. Their cries grew in volume as they grew in numbers.

Roy and Laura watched horrified as one dolphin charged out of the water on a crash course toward Cindy. It was as if she was the dolphin's target. She tried running but couldn't. Fear had cemented her legs into the sand. Petrified screams echoed from her small mouth as cameras focused in on the small girl. The determined dolphin landed less than two feet away from Cindy. Recklessly, Roy ran out to the shore and grabbed his hysterical daughter. He returned her to the safety of his frantic wife's arms.

Outnumbering rescue teams two to one, news crews quickly placed themselves at the shore, eager to capture the action. Cameramen jockeyed for positions. Occasionally a dolphin would barrel into a rescuer or a cameraman, and these spills would be replayed over and over. Reporters gave illustrated accounts about what was occurring and the inexplicable phenomenon of beaching as numb rescuers tried desperately and in vain to save the dolphins.

Slowly, the dolphins died.

An exhausted, thoroughly soaked teenage rescuer made his way past the Emersons. Scattered gray fins still poked out of the water. It was as if the dolphins were waiting for the humans to leave so they could continue their suicides. Tears streaked the young man's face as his eyes met Roy's. Softly, the kid's mouth shaped a question.

"Why are they killing themselves?"

Roy shrugged his shoulders. He felt a lump ball up in his throat as he searched for words that wouldn't come. An ocean breeze swept the sweat off his brow. He looked to his wife for an answer, but her face also was blank. The young man, not knowing what to do or say, looked down at the wet sand beneath his sneakers and continued walking away from the fading sun and the sea below it.

Cindy, who was still being held firmly in her mother's arms, started to stir. No matter how frightened she had been earlier and no matter how hard she had cried, the girl absolutely refused to leave the beach. She turned her head so she could yell in the direction of the sad man.

"Maybe the dolphins saw their mommies die."

Off in the distance another dolphin's chilling cries filled the air, only this time they were accompanied by the silent tears of a grown man.

Skin Deep

The red-and-white neon flickered spasti-
cally, making a crackling electrical
sound, a telltale symptom of a short life
expectancy. It seemed as though nothing
around this part of town lived very long. The symptoms were visible; debris and infectious corrosion
were spreading at a dangerous rate. There was a
plague hiding, waiting, and one could smell death
rising from the sewer grates. If one cared to look
closely, one could see it in the yellowy eyes of the
sick and feel it through the heat. It was a condition
the local population had learned to ignore since
there was no immediate cure.

The tattoo shop was located in one of the seediest
neighborhoods in Watts, and after dark, this particular city street was not to be traveled by the innocent. What the small shop lacked in location it made
up for in character. It was a throwback to the days
of comfortable tattooing when men were men and
cars were American. There was nothing Hollywood
about this joint. Slap had passed away several years
ago but Joe kept the name out of respect to his
brother. Besides the alarm system, there was nothing overtly high-tech within the four walls. The tile
floor was a sparkling black-and-white pattern, re-

sembling a giant chess board, and was always buffed and polished. Among the many trinkets collected over the years was a human skull with a WW II Nazi dagger sticking out of it. Above the skull there was a cheaply framed sign. It showed a tattoo gun and made the declaration: I USED TO BE WHITE BUT NOW I'M COLORED.

For over twenty years, the shop had survived this ghetto paradise as well as the test of time. Joe had seen the fires, the racial tension, and the violence of the 60s and 90s. Barring the ignorant few who felt this was a "blacks only" neighborhood, almost everyone who lived around the tattoo parlor respected Joe. He was a stern man of sixty-five or so who kept to himself. His body was decorated in nautical tattoos, mermaids, warships, eagles, anchors, and he rather resembled Popeye. Unlike the unethical jaggers of yesteryear, Joe was an honest man making a living.

Then came crack.

During the 70s, heroin was the area's main concern and even at the epidemic proportions with which it affected South Central Los Angeles, heroin had never led to the problems that crack had. Heroin addicts were relatively passive. They panhandled their time away, borrowed bad fortune, and stole from an already poverty-stricken area. But they rarely killed. When they did kill, it was usually themselves, by accident. On the other hand, dealers, gangsters, and baseheads often enjoyed the violence that came with crack. It seemed like hardly a day passed without an act of violence occurring somewhere nearby.

The quarter-mile strip of concrete had eight, twelve-story deteriorating apartment buildings on each side of the street. Coded graffiti declared who roamed these streets at night. To the naked eye the graffiti resembled scribble but to gang members it gave fair warning as to who they might run into. Dim streetlamps threw off an eerie illumination that made the nighttime inhabitants appear zombielike. Some were. Throughout the Disneyland of the damned, there were at least ten rock houses. These run-down, unsanitary apartments were run by dealers or gangs that rented out base pipes as well as offering junk couches and chairs as hospitality. The hospitality lasted until the user's cash flow ended. There were *Money Men* (entrusted by dealers), who did the daily business of keeping all moneys accounted for. It was their asses that were on the line if the dough came up on the short side. Then there were *Gunners*, who kept their eyes on the rock house clients. The gunners were usually OGs who had proven themselves to be stand-up type people who had no problem taking a life. *Scouts* were lower-level gangsters eager to work their way up the criminal ladder. They dealt drugs around the projects and kept their eyes open for rival dealers, police, or the DEA. On the street were *Runners*, kids that sold crack to passing cars. These kids were usually minors, some as young as ten, and they sold crack for anyone higher up the criminal ladder, receiving a little cash and street clout in return.

Each of the ten known crack houses made at least five thousand dollars a day and double that on weekends. The ongoing crack war in Watts was showing no signs of slowing down. Gangbangers and black Mafia wouldn't let it, not with the kind of money there was to be made. Almost everyone involved in the cocaine business profited if they lived long enough to collect.

And nobody who's poor wants to live forever.

The tattoo shop was right on the corner of
Olympic Boulevard, one of the worst city blocks in
the entire U.S. The tattoos at Slap N' Joe's were
good and so were the prices, but most people didn't
want to chance going there when they could just as
easily go to Hollywood and get some righteous work
done at Sunset Strip Tattoo. Along the rest of the
block was Garcia's fresh fish and meat, a tobacco
shop, a Laundromat that served as a daytime meet-
ing place for hookers, a closed-down print shop, a
closed-down record store, a closed-down bicycle
shop, and an always-open convenience store. Overflowing metal cans in front of Garcia's and the convenience store offered mangy street cats and der-
elicts alike garbage to pick through. The routine of
collecting and disposing of trash in these parts was
never routine. If several weeks passed before the
trash was collected, no one seemed too concerned.

Parked on the sidewalk in front of the tattoo shop
was a ratty-looking, oil-dripping chopper. Outlaw
bikers had their clubhouse on an adjacent block and
often frequented Slap N' Joe's. The bikers kept an
eye on the shop and, if need be, helped Joe and his
staff with any problem that might arise. They liked
and respected Joe and his staff. A phone call to the
clubhouse would bring a one-percenter eager to toss
any troublemaker out of the shop. In return, Joe
gave the bikers free tats.

Archaeologists claim that studies of the Stone
Age, around 12,000 B.C., show evidence of cuttings
and marks made upon the body, but tattoos done by
puncture and the insertion of dye are traceable to
ancient Egypt. To some a tattoo is the ultimate artistic expression, others need tattoos to feel a sense of
importance or to belong to a certain group.

Then there are others.

Oblivious to any peril, the limousine driver held open the door for his passenger. Dressed in a tan three-piece Giorgio Armani suit, Michael Graham stepped out of the car. Looking like he'd be more at home shopping on Rodeo Drive rather than in a tattoo shop in Watts, he casually approached the shop with over five thousand dollars in his wallet. As he opened the front door, a security alarm sounded. It was a short, annoying sound that reminded Graham of the buzzer on a television game show when a contestant gives an incorrect answer. Graham prided himself on rarely being incorrect.

Hearing the buzzing sound, Quinn, the shop's best tattoo artist, turned away from the client he was working on to see who it was. He waved a multicolored arm at his 10:00 P.M. appointment who, as always, was on time. Graham waved back and, although he hated having to wait, forced out a weak smile, and seated himself on one of the two Naugahyde chairs in the waiting area.

"Be with ya in just a bit, okay?" Quinn yelled out, his surgical glove-covered fingers covered in ink and blood. Blaring out of the shop's stereo system, guitar-legend Johnny Winter belted out his unique-sounding Texas-blues rock 'n' roll.

"I am the illustrated man, baby, I got tattoos everywhere. I'm the illustrated man, got tattoos everywhere. I just love my decorations from my feet up to my hair. Got a screaming demon on my chest. Cat face on my thigh. I got naked women all over me until the day I die."

The small room was covered in flashes, tattoo designs on large sheets of rice paper. Some of the pieces were colored in, most were not. There were typical tattoo designs: hearts, roses, dragons, devils, pinup girls, reapers, tigers, etc. Some of the flashes were over twenty years old and looked outdated. Others were tribal-style tattoos. None of the tattoos on Graham's body would ever be found hanging on the walls.

Quinn returned to his work. He was a low-key man with a talent: He could place ink in someone's skin and come away with a piece of art. All of Slap N' Joe's artists did good clean work but Quinn's looked like it could actually jump off the skin. He was a thin man in his early thirties who had a certain youthful quality to him that would always remain unimpaired no matter how many tattoos he had, and most of his body was covered in ink. Even his long neck was adorned with tats but that did not take anything away from his handsome good looks. Short slicked-back black hair offset a small nose with a rosy tint to it. A thin beard covered his strong chin that looked like it had withstood more than its share of sucker punches. His hazel eyes were busy concentrating on the final touches to another piece.

Even with the music playing, the drilling sound of the tattoo gun reverberated throughout the room. It sounded like a dentist's drill, precise and painful. It was horrible to some, addictive to others. Obviously, the art of tattooing was not for everybody. *Who in their right mind would pay someone to use an electric needle to break skin and permanently alter skin cells?*

Michael Graham would.

Well respected throughout southern California's upper echelon and elite community, he had it all: looks, money, and power. There were players and then there were *players*. Graham was a player with an incredible winning streak and he had no problem with his conscience as long as he accomplished whatever he'd set out to achieve. Whether it was closed-door business negotiations or a charity polo match, to Graham and others of his ilk, winning was all that mattered.

At forty-one, his mousy blond hair was showing the first signs of graying, and added to his charm. Tan and physically fit, Graham fancied himself a lady's man. His brown eyes contained sincerity and warmth but also had the ability to turn blood into ice with a stare. After finding the right artist to do his upper torso transformation, he made the commitment and began his half-body masterpiece about one year ago. Tonight would be his final sitting, the moment he'd been waiting for.

He stood up and walked over to the tattooing area. Seated in the chair, receiving a tattoo, was a 260-plus-pound biker. Most of his massive body was already covered in tats and he looked quite at home in the chair. His jet-black hair was braided into a long ponytail. His hard eyes were covered with black biker shades and a long scar ran from beneath his right lens all the way to his chin. On the back of his tattered leather vest were his colors, the name of his motorcycle club, and the club's insignia.

The huge biker sent out a *What the fuck are you staring at* look that didn't faze Graham one bit.

Quinn looked up from the tattoo he was completing, a skull wearing a Viking helmet (which sort of looked like the biker) encased in a flaming swastika, and felt the tension being tossed from behind the biker's shades.

"He's cool, Thor. He's my ten o'clock appointment," he explained. Thor looked quizzically at Quinn, shrugged his wide shoulders, and sent a toothless smile toward Graham. Quinn quickly finished up and covered the new tattoo in Noxema lo-tion. Then, much to the biker's disapproval, he covered it with a bandage.

Thor sat up and stretched out. His dirty T-shirt read: WANTED: ONE SKINNY NIGGER FOR A HARLEY-DAVIDSON BELT DRIVE. His massive fist completely swallowed Quinn's when the two shook hands.

"You're gonna fix the lock on the back door for Joe, right?" Quinn asked confidently, already knowing the answer.

"First fuckin' thing in the morning," Thor growled in his natural growl, his keys and knives loudly rattling as he headed out the door. Graham waited patiently for the biker to start his motorcycle. It took four kicks before the bike woke up the already paranoid neighborhood. He revved the pan/shovel engine, rattling the shop's thick front window. Enjoying all the noise he was making, Thor smoked the rear wheel and was gone.

"Sorry, man," Quinn said, but not really feeling that way. He shut the stereo off on his way to the front door. He turned the OPEN sign around since Graham demanded privacy and anonymity.

Quinn quickly returned to the tattooing area. He removed the surgical gloves, thoroughly washed his hands, and put on another pair. Sanitary conditions are a must in this day and age of communicable diseases. He picked a new tattoo gun and needles and was ready to work.

Graham walked into the tattooing area and took his time removing his jacket. He took off his vest and began unbuttoning his shirt. With every button undone, more stunning colors became visible. It was like the unveiling of a masterpiece. When his long-sleeved silk shirt was off, it was as though his upper half had a separate life of its own. There was only a four-inch blank spot over Graham's heart, and after tonight, his entire torso would be layered in ink.

Graham tattooed his body for one reason and it had nothing to do with art. His reason was simple: POWER. By tattooing himself in a certain manner to appease the gods, he was enhancing his psychic self, both internally and externally. Magic, as any true magician knows, is the scientific means by which one naturally alters state or condition. Why not use the magical symbolism found in tattoos to help set the course for his destiny? He was well protected from every possible angle. Every color, symbol, and pattern had been well thought out.

Graham turned around to place his shirt out of the way and Quinn saw the massive back mural that he'd placed there. Some of his best work could be found on this man. Every time Graham thought he was finished, Quinn's artistic eyes found a swirl or a flame that could be touched up, enhanced. The back is an extremely sensitive area to tattoo but Graham, like a true trouper, never flinched or complained no matter how badly the needles grated his raw, stinging flesh. That tattoo alone had taken over fifty hours and nearly two months to get every detail perfect. The piece was of one of the four crown princes of Hell, Belial.

Belial, the Worthless One, according to the New Testament, rules the earth, and the incredibly detailed tattoo showed a massive, colorful winged demon in a fiery chariot, which took up most of Graham's back. Belial is said to be representative of fallen virtues and was created immediately after Lucifer was cast out of Heaven. His purpose is to deceive all.

Graham sat. Quinn had his inks prepared, Vase-

line, and a squirt bottle filled with water to wipe
away blood.

"Ready?" Quinn asked.

Graham didn't respond, but he had prepared
himself. Whenever Quinn worked on him, Graham
went into a mild state of meditation. After a few
deep breaths, the client closed his eyes and from
this moment on would not open them until the work
was finished.

On his torso was the Lord of Fire and leader of all
fallen angels, Satan, sitting on a flame-encased
throne while nuclear warheads exploded all around
him. The large tattoo occupied most of Graham's
chest area. Satan's left hand was raised and inside
his palm was a silver inverted pentagram. The
Baphomet goat of Mendes covered the left side of
his body. It had the head of a wretched goat with a
human body beneath and large wings extending out
of its back. It bore a silver pentagram on its forehead and two large horns that extended outward.

Abaddon the Destroyer, the king of the bottomless
pit, covered Graham's right trunk. This long-haired
winged demon had a long, very-detailed scorpion's
tail coming out of its backside. The demon was
snarling and had lionlike teeth, caked in blood. All
of Graham's tattoos were combined into one by spiraling flames, whirlwinds, and spirals. Ancient in-
cantations in languages from times long forgotten
filled in spaces all over his torso. There were also
many serpents, skulls, witches, gargoyles, and imps
that added even more atmosphere to the works.
Both of his arms were covered with massive dragons. The right arm had a three-dimensional ice-
white dragon dedicated to Lucifer, the bringer of
Light. The left arm was Leviathan, the crooked ser-
pent of the Abyss, and that tattoo was similar to the

one on Graham's right arm, only more colorful. Every color under the sun was found in his tattoos but the left arm was his most colorful piece of work. The dragon was a vibrant green (four different shades of green ink combined with other colors to give it texture) bursting out of aqua blue water.

Using a Bic disposable razor, Quinn dry-shaved the hair over Graham's heart where the relatively small tattoo was going to go. He dipped the tattoo gun's needle into black ink, stepped on the floor pedal that gave the tattoo gun its power, and brought it to life. It sounded like an amplified electric shaver, and when the needle hit skin you could hear the difference in the tattoo gun's tone as needles struggled to move underneath the skin.

Quinn began to trace the final outline onto Graham's flesh. He moved slowly, making sure every detail would be perfect. He knew that this final piece was very important to Graham and he wanted it to be flawless, but he would also be relieved when this particular client was out of his life. It wasn't that he minded doing demons or sorcerers, it was part of the job; but it was Graham's seriousness about the occult that made him uneasy. The guy was a little too intense for Quinn's liking. Graham had sworn the artist to complete secrecy about the tattoos. It was a secret he would have no problem keeping. The outline was finished in a little over thirty minutes. Then he changed tattoo guns.

Graham's eyes stayed closed but Quinn could tell that they were rolling around inside his head. At times it appeared as though Graham's eyelids were having a hard time keeping his eyes in their sockets. The flesh danced as the client silently mumbled some undecipherable mantra to himself.

Using a shading gun that had eight fine needles,

Quinn began filling in the outline with black, gray, and red. Whenever there was too much blood, he squirted the water bottle and wiped it away with tissues. The outline soon began taking on its own life, becoming a sharp-looking tattoo. The more attention Quinn paid this piece, the more stylized it became. And Quinn was a perfectionist who made sure every tattoo was given its just due and then some.

Concentrating intensely, he finished the tattoo in a little less than an hour. He put the finishing touches on Graham, squirted the tattoo with water, wiped it with more smelly grease, and declared, "Done."

Trembling ever so slightly, Graham rose from the chair in a complete state of meditation. Quinn could feel the strength and confidence flowing through Graham. His work was complete.

Graham's face didn't resemble his normal face, it looked like a skull covered with pale, dead flesh. His eyelids opened but the pupils were gone. Like a man blinded with cataracts, only the whites of his eyes were present. He gazed into the mirror, not seeing a reflection, but seeing something deeper. Above his heart was a scroll with DCLXVI, the mark of the Beast, inside it.

A maniacal smile slowly formed on Graham's lips and Quinn was relieved and freaked out at the same time. Graham certainly was a strange one, he thought. Fortunately, tonight would be their last night together. Then the front door rapidly swung open and the security alarm buzzed.

"ALL RIGHT, MOTHERFUCKERS, GIMME ALL YER CASH!" a skinny teenager named Moses "Mo' Z" Braxton yelled. At fifteen, the boy's mind was cooked on angel dust, ice, and crack. Inside his shaking hands was a Rossi .38 Special with no traceable serial numbers. Graham's eyes quickly returned to normal and stared at Quinn like he could kill him for forgetting to lock the front door.

"YOU THINK I'M FUCKIN' AROUND? I'LL CAP THE BOTH OF YOU!" the L.A. Raiders cap–wearing youth barked. Beneath the hat was a blue bandanna denoting that Mo' Z affiliated himself with the Crips. Other local Crips didn't trust him but he was less likely to shoot someone wearing the same colors, at least in theory.

Mo' Z was something of a hero on Olympic Boulevard and the stories of him staying up for weeks at a stretch and pulling all kinds of crazy acts were legendary. That's where his gangster tag had come from since he could definitely use a few more zzzz's.

His jaundiced eyes were bloodshot and had a sickly look to them. Quinn silently thanked God that he hadn't come in shooting. This wasn't the first time he'd been held up by a basehead. He tried to make his way to his work desk. Inside was a fully-automatic SIG-Sauer nine-millimeter with a nine-round magazine.

Somehow, Graham seemed to know what Quinn was thinking and froze him in his tracks with a cold, hateful look. Then he started reciting softly. Quinn didn't understand what Graham was doing, partially because it was in a language he'd never heard before, but more so because logic told him prayers don't stop bullets.

The chants grew louder in volume as the tone got deeper. It was a low rumbling sound that was getting more and more powerful. With each passing second, Graham's confidence grew. Quinn wondered how loud he could get before pushing the paranoid kid over the edge. Mo' Z didn't even seem to notice and kept the pistol pointed at Graham's head. Instead of a face, all he saw was a giant smirking crack rock.

So he decided to smoke him.

A sonic blast went off inside Quinn's ears as the gun backfired and exploded in the would-be robber's hand. Crimson streamed out of the five sockets that until two seconds earlier had had fingers attached to them. Mo' Z sprinted out of the tattoo parlor as fast as he could, holding his ruined hand, screaming hysterically at the top of his lungs.

Quinn's eyes were wide with amazement as he followed the trail of scarlet along the black-and-white floor and out the front door. Bits of shredded meat and bones were everywhere. On the ground, the drug addict's forefinger, which was the only digit that had remained intact, was wriggling around, looking for its owner.

Graham broke free from his trance. His entire body was layered in thin oillike sweat. He stared at Quinn, wondering whether or not to kill the tattoo artist, and suddenly the two men were locked in a staring contest. Quinn took a deep breath and slowly let it out. Shocked at what he believed he was seeing, Quinn focused in and took a closer look at his client's body. He did a double take to make sure his eyes were not playing tricks on him. They weren't.

The tattoos were moving.

Multicolored snarling demons from the lowest regions of Hell slowly looked around the tattoo shop for more enemies. Evil, fiery eyes scanned about as the beasts drooled in anticipation of more bloodshed, and sweat fell from Graham's body onto the floor. Hatred filled the room as demons feared in the lore of most organized religions manifested themselves. The realistic pictures were alive and eager for more action. Textured tattoo skulls became replete, their jaws chattering, trying to speak. Dragons and serpents writhed with excitement. Spirals and flames whipped about on Graham's torso. On every inch of his colored skin there was some sort of activity.

The tattoo artist closed his eyes, forfeiting the staring contest. He refused to believe what he was seeing. Several seconds passed before he opened them again.

The tattoos were motionless.

Quinn shook his head in disbelief. He needed a cigarette really badly, he thought, head down, afraid to make eye contact with his customer. Spilled blood was everywhere. Graham followed Quinn's eyes over to the robber's still-twitching forefinger.

"That, my talented friend, almost cost you everything," Graham explained slowly and methodically. Another crazed smile came back to his lips as he bent over, picked up the bloody digit, and slipped it into his mouth.

Knowing that he only had a little time before police and curiosity-seekers started gathering around the shop, the client quickly put his expensive shirt back on. Since he'd started getting tattooed, he'd been extremely careful about what shirts he wore. The tattoos might show through a white shirt. He slipped on his tan vest and jacket and stared at Quinn. Feeling woozy, Quinn tried smiling as his strange client prepared to leave for the final time.

"How much do I owe you? Graham asked, digging an eelskin wallet out of his back pocket.

"Usual," Quinn replied, still stunned from what he had seen. He normally charged one hundred twenty-five dollars an hour but since Graham had so much work done, he cut his rate in half.

"Silence is golden, *right?*"

Quinn nodded and held out his hand. Graham stared deep into his eyes and saw that his faithful artist was indeed telling the truth. He gazed deeper into Quinn and decided to give him a glimpse of what would happen if he ever broke his vow of silence.

Graham pulled open his blazer and nonchalantly unbuttoned the vest and three buttons on his shirt. Quinn tried to move but couldn't. He tried arguing but no sound came. He felt like his feet were tattooed to the floor.

Seconds froze into years as a slimy red hand with long, sharp fingernails emerged from his client's chest. Although common sense told him better, he couldn't take his eyes away from the hypnotic horror show. The hand protruded farther and farther as a red muscular forearm became visible. Around the wrist was something that resembled a bracelet. Upon closer inspection, Quinn concluded that it was a rosary, but instead of beads there were tiny teeth. A small inverted crucifix, made up of something meaty, like black rotting intestines, dangled loosely from the unholy rosary.

The forefinger bent, then straightened, signaling Quinn to come closer. The red hand was drawing him toward Graham's open chest. He tried fighting off the horrible sensation but couldn't. He knew he was standing still but felt as if he were swirling against his will, spinning, hand held out in front of him, waiting to be paid, waiting until the deadly trance was broken. His vision began to cloud as he was pulled into the open chest. Then he could no longer see.

This is what dead people see, Quinn thought.

His heart pounded uncontrollably as a warm filth began to fill the area. He felt surrounded by vileness. With each passing second, the stench grew worse. He wanted to throw up. He felt someone, *or something*, approaching. Seconds later, the smothering darkness began to give way. The black was getting softer, less oppressive against his eyes. Then another thought struck him; maybe he didn't want to see what the darkness held.

A hot gust of putrid wind sent chills through Quinn. His bones ached with fear. He felt something getting closer and closer. He wanted to flee but was frozen to the ground. Whatever it was, it was big.

Then it was on him.

In a brief moment of less darkness, Quinn saw the meaning of true evil. What was standing before him was so intense, so unholy, that Quinn wished he had never been born. He recognized certain characteristics of the demon; he had tattooed them on Graham. The muscular beast that he recognized as Belial was at least eight feet tall, with black claws that resembled charred daggers. A sharp chin, coarse cheekbones, and pointy nose extended from the beast's wicked face. Only the whites of its burning eyes showed through its scorched face. Its black flesh appeared slick and wet, like it had just emerged from a baptism in blood.

The grotesque monster grabbed Quinn by the shoulders and slowly lifted him up toward its mouth. A set of massive jaws clamped down around his entire head and black saliva ran up his nose and into his open mouth. It tasted like sewage was being forced down his throat before he understood what was happening to him.

The monster was sucking on his head.

Lips and a giant tongue worked his face much like
a child does a lollipop. He felt himself being turned
and twisted inside the beast's mouth. He was
dragged along ungiving molars until he was at the
back of Belial's rotten mouth. Quinn was in line and
positioned for something far worse than being
licked.

The horrifying sound of his head being chewed up
filled his ears. Then more molar pressure was added
to flatten Quinn's skull. Then it was crunched back
into shape and then again flattened. Teeth masti-
cated and peeled flesh, gnawing on the muscles beneath. Bones splintered and shot out of his torn
flesh. The hirsute beast chewed slowly, just like Graham did when he ate the robber's finger. Then the
massive mouth spit out Quinn's mangled head.

Then he was free.

Graham watched the tattoo artist slowly begin to
regain his senses. He looked quite pale, apprehen-
sive at what might happen next. Graham, who was
buttoned up and ready to leave, fished out his wallet. He removed fifty hundred-dollar bills and gently
placed them in the artist's sweaty palm. A stunned
gasp escaped Quinn's lips as he stared dumb-
founded at the money. This was well over a good
month's salary.

Carefully avoiding the scarlet puddle on the floor,
Graham headed toward the exit. Unlike the street
thugs and dope dealers who dealt in crime for the
almighty dollar, the well-dressed man was the true
essence of evil. Graham was deception personified.
He was the type of person who could be anything he
chose to be, but instead was perverted by his lust for
power. Quinn wondered how many others there
were like him.

Graham stopped dead in his tracks. He slowly

turned to the artist. Quinn was more than half-expecting to see Graham's mouth extend to massive proportions. He felt his blood run cold as a nervous tic under his right eye twitched. It had been years since he'd last experienced this. His hands trembled uncontrollably as fear enveloped him. He'd rather die than star in his own satanic snuff flick again.

Before returning to the crime-ridden streets, which now resembled paradise to Quinn since at least he understood who was who according to the rules of urban survival, Michael Graham smiled *knowingly*, showing off his perfect smile.

The
Atheist Prayer

Maureen hated Mondays with a passion. "I Don't Like Mondays" by the Boomtown Rats could've been her theme song.

She felt like a beaten slave and Monday morning was her ball and chain of hopelessness. Mondays always meant the same: *her two days of serenity had ended and it was back to riding the bus*.

Dressed in standard office attire, a green dress with a matching blazer, she felt slightly uncomfortable. Anytime a young woman has to wait for a bus in a well-traveled area, a certain level of self-consciousness is inevitable. After all, this wasn't New York or Chicago where buses are a socially accepted means of transportation. This was Hollywood: the land of the greedy and the home of the snide. Maureen Howe obviously wasn't a streetwalker but that never stopped the cretins from making their crude propositions, as if "Bend over, I'll drive" was actually going to turn her on. She hated being spoken to like that, especially by married men off to earn the bacon. Didn't pigs eat their own?

At twenty-four, she had the stressed-out look of someone who has seen too many difficulties. Her pretty features, especially her striking eyes, were cautious, wary of strangers. Her slender body often made her feel weak. She tried to carry on with strength and usually succeeded, but every now and then she felt her strength being sucked away. It was during those moments that she felt most vulnerable. Like she did right now. Even though she'd showered and put on fresh makeup, she was unable to wash away the tired look plaguing her face.

The massive orange sun peeked through the smog-laden sky, blinding anyone foolish enough to look directly at it. Airplanes soared through stained clouds above the oversized buildings, which stood side by side at attention. Most of the concrete soldiers wore medals declaring FOR RENT. Others, either not yet completed or being torn down, resembled battle-scarred amputees. More thick industrial smog clung to the tops of these buildings, blocking the view of the mountains. Behind the mountains was "The Valley." Traffic was already steady on Sunset Boulevard and by eight would coagulate to a standstill. Another work week had begun.

A car accident had left her minus a car, *her car*. In Los Angeles being without a car is the equivalent of being a pariah. No wheels equals no life. Your social life dwindles, easy-access places like work, the gym, or the video store become an effort to reach, and, worst of all, from behind the safety of rolled-up windows, snooty people gawk at you at the bus stop like you're less human than they are.

Maureen tried convincing herself that she never threw any self-righteous looks when she had a car, but she knew she was a liar. The petite blonde didn't like the fact that her mint-condition candy-apple-red '68 convertible Mustang was totaled and the other car's driver, some oily-skinned, non-English-speaking woman, wasn't insured. After giving her the runaround, her insurance company had agreed to pay for some of the damages, but in a nutshell it was bye-bye Mustang.

Bye-bye independence.

Hello buses and a strange new world. News reports were always full of bad news about the RTD. It seemed as if three days could not pass by without at least one report of mass transit mayhem. Doper drivers were failing drug tests. Rapes, robberies, and violence were everyday occurrences on public transportation. Maureen had noticed that there were scores of odd characters on the bus: vagrants, transvestites, runaways, wannabe rock stars, hippies, illegal aliens heading to or searching for a day's work, perverts, religious loons preaching about damnation, and other unfortunates without wheels.

Outside and in, the buses were covered with illegible graffiti and were usually less than sanitary. The smell of urine, feces, or marijuana wasn't unusual. Neither was the stench of despair.

RTD buses reminded Maureen of large gray coffins.

She saw one coming.

Maureen stood up from the brown hard plastic bus bench wondering whether or not she'd forgotten anything at home. It was too late for second guessing. As the bus came into view, she saw that it was jam-packed with cranky-looking passengers squashed together like sardines.

Great, she thought to herself, disillusioned. *Maybe if I'm real lucky some freak will grind against me the whole trip.*

Or tell her another hard-luck story about nothing in particular.

During the past few weeks, Maureen had come to the conclusion that bus riders wore a different look than the rest of society. They looked harder, distant,

openly bitter about the hand life had dealt them.
Somehow the bus was part of the reason for their
situations. Low-paying jobs with limited possibili-
ties for advancement, too many mouths to feed, too
many hours worked, miserable social lives, and, in
general, hopelessness; all this was guaranteed conversation on the short ride to work. Conversations
on the return trip home were usually worse. They
were often about the promotion undeservingly given
to someone else, the break that never happened,
and, of course, why the buses were always late. It
was as if these commuters were destined to forever
spin on the RTD carousel. Maureen couldn't wait
until she owned another car, *any car*, just to rejoin
what she saw as normal society.

To her disappointment, the bus driver waved his
leather-gloved hand apologetically and drove past
her. The bus was too crowded for even one more
passenger.

She sat back down, cursing silently, calculating
time on her wristwatch. The mass transit buses
were rarely on time and as a result neither was she.
At work they said they understood her situation but
deep down she knew it was a nuisance. After all, if
Maureen couldn't get to work on time like all the
others, she should quit. She often wondered why
she didn't.

A foul vagrant strolled up to the bus stop and sat
on the bench beside her. The fifty-or-so-year-old
man stunk horribly from not having bathed in God
only knew how long. A thick stench of gasoline was
present. He was layered in filth and grime. His
nappy gray hair was badly matted and was beginning to rope into dreadlocks. Stains of cheap wine
and coffee streaked his thick, wooly beard. The
tramp ran his gnarled fingers through his hair in an

attempt to brush it down, but his fingers tangled up and got stuck. Embarrassed, he smiled his yellowy smile.

He wore no shoes. His left foot was swollen at least five times its normal size. It was the size of a football and looked like elephantiasis was setting in. The large foot with black claws that passed for toenails was a collage of colors. Besides the black dirt, there were purple, yellow, and blue bruises. Open sores with greenish-yellow puslike fluid oozing out were visible. If Maureen had eaten breakfast, she would have tossed it right there. She wanted to get up and leave but couldn't. That would be rude and her upbringing had taught her to always be courteous. That is, unless someone was rude first. Besides, he wasn't harming anybody.

Just don't look at his foot . . .

The vagrant wore an old moldy raincoat. Local weatherman Fritz Coleman had promised that the temperature would rise into the nineties today, but just in case it rained, the homeless man was ready. He always was. From one of the dirty raincoat's many pockets he pulled out a pint-size bottle of Night Train wine and took a long swig of the devil's blood.

"Wanna sip?" he asked, and held out the bottle.

Maureen shook her head no.

"More for me then," he said, laughing the laughter of the deranged, as if the low-grade wine were something to covet. He took another sip, put the dark green bottle back in his pocket, and smirked.

Cars were lining up in both directions, staring at the odd couple as if they were some sort of bizarre museum display sans wax. Unsympathetic eyes swept over them and passed judgment. Maureen felt angry and embarrassed at the same time.

"You waiting on a bus?" the man asked matter-of-factly.

Maureen wanted to reply something sharp to discourage any further conversation. Instead, she smiled politely and nodded. She silently prayed that her uninterested answer was hint enough that she wasn't in the mood to converse. Several moments passed before the wastrel asked her another question.

"You know why it's late, don't ya?"

"No."

"The government puts agents on the road to slow up traffic by driving slow and dumb, causing accidents. Nothing too major. Fender benders. They need accidents 'cause they need the traffic. The more traffic, the more gas that's used. The less gas in the U.S., the higher the price, *silly*."

For a fleeting moment, the vagabond reminded Maureen of a song lyric she didn't quite understand but sang anyway. In his own bizarre way, he made sense. Maureen doubted that the government purposely jammed traffic, but being a commuter and a taxpayer, nothing would surprise her.

Several minutes passed with no buses in sight. If this continued, Maureen might as well turn around, go home, and call in sick. She fooled with the idea but knew she couldn't afford to miss yet another day's work. The foul man started saying something, then paused in mid-sentence. More cars crawled by with coffee-guzzling, doughnut-munching, wide-eyed passengers staring.

"People are afraid of me, I turn them off. They hate me because I'm different. Hate anything that's different. That's why human nature is so fucked. People are afraid of what they don't understand and try killing off, you know, their fears."

Maureen halfheartedly listened to the stranger's paranoid ramblings, ignoring most of what was being said. She had often wondered how people ever let themselves become "street people." It was a concept beyond reason, she thought, still keeping an eye open for the bus. If someone wanted to work, there were jobs. She hated her job but attended it regularly.

What Maureen would never understand was that this vagabond's existence was his by choice. Unlike many homeless people who are certifiable, this man actually chose this type of existence. It made him happy. The man continued on about how the streets were the only place he enjoyed living. How living outside, as opposed to inside a house or an apartment, gave him a sense of freedom that no one could ever take away from him. He didn't have to worry about losing everything in an earthquake. He also explained that he slept with one eye open since someone was always aiming to start trouble for him.

"Ya ever killed anyone?"

The question shocked the hell out of Maureen. This guy was not all there.

"No," she replied timidly, if not a trifle insulted. She lied.

When she was twelve, a rapist violated her. For one long week, this sick individual beat, tortured, and sodomized her. At times Maureen had given up on her life, preferring death over violence disguised as sex. At least in death there was peace.

Maureen's train of thought drifted until she was back in the bed of her youth, cowering with fear. Her bulging eyes were set on the door, praying it wouldn't creak open. How did she ever allow herself to get into such a mess? If only she could sleep, then maybe everything would be all right. Sweating out anxiety and fear that seemed endless, she closed her eyes tightly, praying for sleep to come. More sweat soaked through her pajamas as the wet girl began a ritual she never told anyone, not even her therapist.

"If I keep my fingers crossed, I won't have any nightmares . . . If I keep my fingers crossed, Mom and Dad are okay . . . If I keep my fingers crossed, I'll go home soon . . . If I keep my fingers crossed, I'll fall asleep quickly . . . If I keep my fingers crossed he won't hurt me again tonight."

The door opened slowly, allowing a thin beam of light into the pitch-black room. Maureen kept her fingers crossed, praying that sleep would come before he could touch her.

He slowly crept into the room, his fat belly hanging over his boxer shorts, a thick leather strap in one hand. Maureen's small body convulsed with fright. Her middle finger and forefinger ached from twisting together. She smelled the stench of bourbon before his hairy hands pulled the covers off her.

"If I keep my fingers crossed . . ."

"I love you, Maury," the obese man softly slurred. Her uncle Wayne always said that before having his way with her. If her mother's brother really did love her, then why was he going to hurt her again that way?

For ten painful years, she had tried to figure out the answer to that question and what to do about it. Like most incest victims, Maureen wondered if perhaps it was her fault. Maybe she'd done something to deserve what had happened. *Should she have told her father? Should she have confided in her friends? Should she tell anyone?*

After receiving extensive counseling and therapy, the truth came out. She'd done no wrong. No child, not even Lolita, is to be held accountable for the actions of an adult. Her uncle had done things to her for his own sick pleasure. She tried forgetting it, putting it behind her, but she could never forget. After too many years of mental anguish, Maureen had finally had enough.

She went to her uncle's house with a loaded Smith & Wesson .38 Special.

This was the first time she had ever visited him alone. In the past, she'd been forced to suffer silently through family gatherings, her parents unaware that anything was wrong, her uncle smiling innocently. It was the fact that Wayne had almost fooled her into believing that nothing wrong had occurred that infuriated her the most. With every approaching step she remembered another act committed against her. She wanted to run but couldn't. She'd come too far to turn back. If she fled now she would never regain her self-respect and she was willing to do anything, even go to prison, to regain what was rightfully hers. Knocking on his door had been like willfully opting to go to Hell.

Then the door opened.

Although surprised at first, he invited her right in. It wasn't like he hadn't seen his niece since "that week." They'd spent sporadic time together during holidays, during family get-togethers, and he made sure to always remember her birthday. As far as Wayne was concerned it was their little secret. Since no one ever found out, *no harm was done*.

In the back of his alcohol-confused mind, Wayne wondered what she was doing here looking so beautiful. And beautiful she was, but not in the manner of one of those porno magazine women he kept close by his bed; his niece was a natural beauty. *An inherited beauty* that he knew he should never have touched but never really regretted touching. What's a man supposed to do when some budding beauty flaunts her sex around?

Her uncle looked very different from what Maureen remembered. Although still on the heavy side from years of overindulgence, he seemed frail. His best features, especially his hazel-brown eyes, drooped heavily. He looked perpetually tired and Maureen found it hard to believe that this was the image of her deepest fear. His large red nose had had its best days years ago. Dark brown spots adorned the top of his receding brow and his hairy hands.

She couldn't believe she was back in the same apartment where she'd been violated, face-to-face with her villain, smiling plastically as if all were well. It took every ounce of self-restraint not to blow his saggy face off during the first twenty seconds of their confrontation. Instead, they had a light dinner and casual conversation. Maureen had to hear him out before blasting him. After forcing down several mouthfuls of his repugnant cooking and forcing out counterfeit smiles, she cut to the chase.

"Why'd you do it?"

"What?" he asked innocently, hoping she wasn't going to bring up *that*. So much time had passed. Why harp on the past?

"DO WHAT???" Maureen yelled in disbelief. "Ruin me, steal my virginity, beat the shit out of me so I wouldn't dare tell anyone. Make me a sexual misfit. That's what, you fucking fat bastard!"

He couldn't believe what he was hearing. Every syllable tore at his wounded heart. He would never hurt anyone purposely, let alone Maury. All he had ever done was share his love with his favorite niece. What was wrong with that? Sure, there were laws, but what the hey? Nervously, Wayne started fidgeting. He had no explanation for what he did, no excuse other than he needed someone. Couldn't she understand that he just wanted to be loved.

"Your aunt Sylvia, GOD MAY HER SOUL REST IN PEACE, left me. I was a wreck. A COMPLETE MESS! I needed someone, a woman. I wasn't thinking properly. I was all alone," the elderly man softly explained then added, *"I was wrong. . . ."*

"Your drinking caused my aunt to leave!"

Sorrowful tears started to flow as he quivered in his chair, ashamed. His jowls went red as he shook uncontrollably. For years he had tried making up excuses for what had happened between him and his niece, often blaming her.

"I know, Maury, I know. I'm so sorry, love."

"Then how could you do what you did to me?" she asked on the verge of hysteria but received no answer. The claustrophobic room was getting smaller and smaller. Invisible tremors shook the slowly spinning room. The air supply was dwindling and the temperature was increasing with every passing moment. Time had died. So drained was Maureen that she was getting ready to forgive the pathetic man in front of her.

Then she remembered how much he had enjoyed hurting her. Her mind, which often worked as a VCR of personal abuse, replayed the events. Some acts were more vicious than others and the camcorder of pain got sharp, tight-angled close-ups of this action. She could even hear the playback. The mental replay didn't lie and the digital stereo playback had recorded Wayne's every groan and grunt.

And let's not forget his drunken laughter.

Maureen snapped out of her momentary bout of

déjà-vu and removed the large, shiny pistol from her oversized purse, taking aim at her uncle's wrinkled face.

"Maury, please don't," he pleaded, trembling.

"My name is Maureen."

"Please listen."

"Why should I?" she asked, crying hysterically.

He had no answer. Every time he had done something painful to her, he thought up something worse, more degrading. He was like a snowball in an avalanche, growing larger, out of control. Only this avalanche had a throbbing penis that was revitalized with each act of sexual sadism. She could hear leather slapping her flesh. She could feel her choking mouth stretching around him. When she wouldn't perform what he wanted, he beat her. Badly. And this too was a turn-on. Distressful visions flooded her memory. Fucking, punching, drinking, chasing, slapping, yelling, moaning . . . laughing.

"Because I love you," he answered, smiling slightly through his rubbery lips. She hated that evil smile almost as much as she hated the vile man to whom it belonged. It was a smug smile that denoted victory for the wretched. Perverts everywhere shared this look.

He isn't even worth killing, she thought, and began putting the pistol away. Inadvertently her teary gaze drifted to his polyester crotch. This abomination wasn't sorry and never would be.

A smile formed on Maureen's lips.

The old man wanted to scream but couldn't as sheer terror choked him. And with his fear came Maureen's excitement. The invincible beast who had shattered her peace of mind was now backpedaling. Davey had Goliath by the balls and was squeezing.

An arousal that surpassed normal excitement surged through her.

"You're family, you're blood," he cried helplessly, but the erection underneath his striped pants refused to wilt.

Wayne raised his unsteady hands to plead with his niece but deep down he knew that it was useless. Maureen had the same look her grandfather had worn when beating him. Wayne remembered his dad's deranged smile growing wider and wider as the thick leather belt snapped loudly against his bare buttocks, legs, and back. And the beatings were only the beginning of his silent pain and his father's sacrilegious joy. Recognizing the look, he realized there are some things that are inherited that should not be.

Maureen slowly raised the revolver and took aim at Uncle Wayne. Burning rage swam through her body and soul. She was at one with outrage. It was a hostile rage that went beyond hatred. It was the rage of a child. And that hurt child had grown into a hurt adult.

The recoil startled her since she had never fired a gun before. Uncle Wayne turned a death-white shade of pale as the bullet whizzed past his fat head, lodging itself into the wall. A quiver ran through her and Maureen felt her crotch go wet. She had never experienced anything like this before, and after the initial shock, thoroughly enjoyed the sensation. Even though she had been in several relationships and many one-night stands, Maureen had never had an orgasm. Thanks to her uncle, sex was not hers to enjoy. With the power of life and death shaking in her hands, Maureen understood that she was only going to get wetter. Chest heaving, she was looking forward to it.

"WAIT!" Uncle Wayne pleaded.

"If I keep my fingers crossed, I won't miss this time," she said softly beneath her breath, reciting what she now called the atheist prayer.

Using her left hand to support the right, Maureen crossed her middle finger and forefinger. The excitement between her legs was increasing with each passing second. She steadied her shaking hands. Taking aim at her uncle's crying face, she smiled the smile of a satisfied woman for the very first time in her life.

Maureen's smile faded as her gaze came to rest on the homeless man's diseased foot. She wondered how it had gotten so infected.

"Have you ever killed anyone?" she timidly asked the dirty man.

The tramp shook his head but he too was lying. He had killed just a few nights ago. A hoodlum had doused him with gasoline, but before he could strike the match, the homeless man attacked and sank his rusty knife into his assailant's jugular. That wasn't the first time he'd killed either. After living on the streets for over a decade, almost as long as Maureen had waited to confront her uncle, he'd had his share of encounters with hostile thugs, punks, muggers, and civilians out looking for "kicks." Just because he had no mailing address did not mean he had fewer constitutional rights than anyone else, including the right to bear arms.

He tapped his moldy pocket. The knife was still there. Without ever intending to, the homeless man had become an expert in violence. It seemed that people just wouldn't leave him be and this made him extra cautious of everyone. People just weren't trustworthy and it was better to be safe than sorry. He'd lost too many friends not to be careful. Two long, silent minutes passed with no sight of any buses.

"You married?" the vagabond asked.

Maureen looked at her hands. No ring. "No, not yet. I have a boyfriend."

"Good, a nice girl like you should have a fella, should raise childrens," he told her, tapping the knife in his pants.

If only he knew about her family secret, she thought, and grinned. Before he could smile back, she looked away.

That was the moment he'd been waiting for. When Maureen turned away, the homeless man made his move. His right hand quickly searched his raincoat until he found what he wanted. From one of his many pockets, the derelict removed some crumpled flowers that he'd picked earlier that morning and placed them on the bench for Maureen. Like a shadow, he left without saying good-bye.

A bus was coming.

The Fumes of
Friendship

The arctic wind sent penetrating chills through Bob Reid's well-worn army fatigue jacket. It wasn't just the normal cold of unusual weather, but the chill of alienation. He was the type of person that people loved to stare at but were reluctant to get near. His vibe set people off, so he was cold and alone in the world. *And dammit, it was supposed to be warm*. The angels that often spoke to him explained that the absence of warmth was a warning sign from God. The current state of world affairs had God pissed off and the little hole in the ozone was God's equivalent of an angry man putting his fist through a wall. Worse, much worse, was waiting if God's disillusionment with man continued. God could get pretty creative when pushed. Actually, Bob was one of the chosen few with whom the Lord had no bone to pick.

Bob tried pulling the jacket's zipper up all the way but it wouldn't go past the three-quarters point. A zipper tooth was broken. He tugged upward for what seemed like hours.

Tucked inside the doorway of First Interstate Bank, Bob asked bank patrons if they had any spare change. It only takes about eighty cents a day for a

resourceful man to survive. That wouldn't satisfy
the hunger that had become his constant companion but it would keep him alive. And alive in any
shape translates into victory. Circumstance had
driven him to beg but very few people gave him anything other than indifferent glances.

"All I wanna do is eat," Bob humbly explained to
his invisible friend, also named Bob.

"I know."

Bob's tattered Converse sneakers carried him
shivering from the doorway that blocked out the
fierce winds. He began wandering. His long fingers
wrapped themselves around a heavy slightly rusted
steel spike inside his jacket pocket.

"Goddamn fuckheads always pickin' on us," Invisible Bob told an agreeing Bob as they made their
way toward Sunset Boulevard.

A yellow school bus noisily passed by and they
remembered. *Fuckheads*. That's what Eugene used
to call them, everybody, the rest of society. It was as
though Eugene and Bob had no place in society.
The fuckheads didn't want another limited-potential
spic or a white-trash retard and that was just fine
with Eugene and Bob. They were kept in remedial
classes, spoken to and dealt with as though they
were brain-dead, and shuffled through the system.
Eugene was two years older than Bob but they were
placed in the same grade. He had shown Bob many
interesting things: like how to sneak onto the public
buses through the rear exit door without paying,
that boogers taste like tuna fish, where to fence
stolen car stereos, or if you inhale fumes from the
extra-strong Super Glue the world almost becomes
enjoyable. The numbies, they used to call it. Like too
many high schoolers, they loved smoking pot but
neither of them could afford it regularly, and when

they did have money, angel dust was their drug of choice.

There were other *free* ways to get high.

Eugene taught him how to sniff glue, paint thinner, gasoline, and aerosols to get catch a buzz. He showed him these tricks and every day the two would meet at school, hang out until lunch, steal something to get high with, then leave. Eugene had also tricked him a few times into doing silly things like smoking tampons or banana peels, but those were just jokes. No matter how many times Eugene did cruel things to him, Bob secretly lived to hang out with his one and only friend.

Unfortunately, Eugene was as butt-ugly as they came. The homely hood with the sooched face was definitely a double-bagger. The cards had been stacked against him since birth. Even at an early age, when all babies are cute, he wasn't. Part of the reason he turned out to be such a bad apple was because of his physical appearance. Getting in trouble was one of his only means of getting attention. He looked like a prehistoric boxer that had taken one too many head shots. It was during kindergarten that he received the nickname and stigma that would stick with him for the rest of his life. Eugene Jesus Santiago was known by most as "Ugly Eugene."

Bob's yellowy eyes scanned but saw nothing edible. He badly needed food and thus his search began. Walking through a swirl of urbanites, he remembered the last time he partied with Eugene. They were in some apartment building's basement sniffing paint fumes out of a paper bag. Both were quite high when Eugene nonchalantly announced that he was going to go get a piece of ass. This struck Bob as odd, for as much as Ugly Eugene bragged about the women he'd had, he'd never specifically told him about his homegirls, and as far as he knew, he didn't have any. The next morning at school, Bob learned that his best friend had been arrested for raping a twelve-year-old girl and was being held as the main suspect in a series of violent rapes involving other young girls. Bob had been taken from class to the Hollywood Police Station where he was questioned, then released. That was the very same day he dropped out of school.

And that night he received the first sign that he was doing the right thing.

While he lay sleeping in bed, a cockroach crawled into his right ear. Roaches have an uncanny ability to contort into holes much smaller than the size of their body, but they can't crawl in reverse. Once they climb into a crevice, unless they can turn around, they're stuck.

Another less known fact is that cockroaches make noise. It's a shrill, squeaky noise. Miniature screams if you will. When Bob awoke, he first felt, then heard, something trapped inside his ear. Digging with his finger proved unsuccessful. A Q-Tip also failed to silence the operatic bug. *It was in too deep.* Frantic, the boy started freaking out. He didn't fully understand what was happening to him.

At 3:30 A.M. his father drove him to the hospital. They filled out forms, waited two hours, and were eventually seen by a physician who had treated many cases like this. It wasn't as uncommon or embarrassing an occurrence as they had imagined it was. To kill the roach, the doctor covered his ear with an oxygen mask filled with anesthesia. Harmless to humans but deadly to insects, he let the gas out and the entire process took less than ten minutes. It was the longest ten minutes of the misguided

youth's life and during that span many revelations
came. He finally understood why his family didn't
love him. He now understood why his teachers purposely failed him in school. He knew why the cops
wanted to kill him. He learned why women played
hard to get and that no often meant yes. During
those last few minutes, when the roach realized it
was expiring, its fear-filled shrieks grew louder and
Bob's enlightenment expanded beyond the realms
of human knowledge. Toward the end, the disturbed
boy actually understood what the dying roach was
trying to say. A pair of surgical tweezers pulled the
tiny carcass out of his ear but Bob knew the voices
in his head were there to stay.

Bob attended every hour of his friend's trial. He
was even called to testify in front of all those angry
parents. He said good things about his buddy and it
really surprised him when the old fuckhead in the
black dress sentenced Eugene. The judge found the
punk competent enough to do his sentence in a
maximum security prison, but the fact that he was
brain-damaged from chronic paint and glue sniffing
was taken into consideration, and along with time
in jail, Eugene would receive special counseling and
treatment.

"I'll be out soon, Holmes!" Ugly Eugene yelled to
Bob from across the courtroom

"I'll wait."

And wait he had. For almost eight years, Bob had
wandered the streets of Hollywood awaiting Eugene's return.

Unseen voices guided him down an empty street.
He resumed fidgeting with his jacket zipper. Sooner
or later he'd get the damn thing to go all the way up.
Invisible Bob suggested that they sneak inside
Builders Emporium and steal some "Get High." For

lack of anything better to do, he agreed. Since he and Invisible Bob were one, when they got to the hardware store, Bob also became invisible.

Anyone can become invisible. It's not so much a magic trick as it is a dilemma. For years, Bob had been trying to get people to notice, acknowledge, or just speak to him. He tried fitting in and failed. Unlike the students on *Beverly Hills, 90210*, the kids he'd attended high school with rarely smiled. No one cared except Ugly Eugene. After he dropped out, no one cared. After he'd been arrested on several occasions, no one cared. When he was committed and released, no one cared. *He was invisible.* All he had to do was smile and people looked the other way.

He entered the store knowing exactly where he wanted to be. He'd done this hundreds of times over the years. The store's heat penetrated his frozen, filthy flesh. He felt his aura flowing and wondered if steam were rising off him. The warmth was more soothing than a hot shower. It had been months since Bob had experienced that particular pleasure. Smiling like a pervert in an adult book store, he invisibly walked past the cashiers who were busy ringing up purchases and past customers who stared but saw no one, until he arrived in aisle 4: paints.

"Remember what happened last time you used silver."

He remembered. Eugene should be getting out soon.

Bob stuffed a large spray can of metallic-blue paint into his oversized green army jacket and headed for the exit. He smiled his dark yellow and gingivitis smile as he passed the store manager, taunting the man with politeness. The man didn't acknowledge him. As he left the store, even the chilling winds couldn't remove his smile.

The sun was beginning to fade. A police siren passed close by and Bob instinctively walked in the opposite direction. Sirens were demons summoning one another. He continued up La Brea Avenue until he arrived at a supermarket. The large structure mesmerized him. It looked futuristic; massive windows exposed the front of the building where antlike people scurried about in a shopping frenzy.

Every day, hoards of street people came to this and every other supermarket to sift through the overflowing Dumpsters, which were conveniently located out of public sight. Bob made his way through the parking lot, hoping that no store clerks were back there by the Dumpsters. Apron-clad clerks enjoyed their position of power over the homeless and when they were out back never allowed street people near the Dumpsters. They claimed it was trespassing.

Just as he turned the corner that led to the alley where the massive trash receptacles were, an elderly couple passed him with a cardboard box filled with produce, mostly brown lettuce and cabbage. Bob smiled halfheartedly at them. If they'd already been through the Dumpsters, then all the good pickings were gone. It was his loss for not having arrived earlier. He'd have to find breakfast, lunch, and dinner elsewhere. He waved as they left. Then they were forgotten as his mouth began watering. Rotten eggs, sour milk, diseased produce, all combined to make a lingering, enticing aroma.

Wide-eyed, he scanned the area. No clerks. He spotted an essential piece of paraphernalia lying on the ground and picked up the small limp paper bag. Fortunately, it wasn't too soggy.

He removed the spray can and sprayed into the
bag. He did this for over sixty seconds, saturating
the bottom in metallic blue. A mist rose up from the
inside of the bag as he placed his long nose and
thick purple-tinted lips inside, and began hyperventilating the hallucination-inducing, brain-cell-killing
fumes.

"Deeper, deeper, deeper," Invisible Bob instructed, just like Eugene used to. Bob complied.
His heart began to race like a small block engine
that badly needed an oil change. He felt his pulse
pounding in his veins, threatening to overload. His
hands tingled as did most of his body. His flushed
face felt like a burning coal, but he wasn't going to
put the bag down until he inhaled every fume possible. After all, he was no chump. He could taste paint
in his nose and throat, and this was good. This was
much more intense than the laughing gas dentists
used. His head threatened to explode from the pressure but that was the least of his concerns. Drippy
brain cells crawled upon one another and fucked,
exploding when orgasm occurred. It felt like someone was running a powerful vacuum cleaner inside
his skull. The roaring machine swept up dead brain
cells and insect carcasses. After two full minutes, he
stopped hyperventilating.

The world swirled neon purple. Bob had the
numbies. *His chest pounded, his head felt like it was
filled with helium. He lost his equilibrium and staggered, smiling.* The effect lasted only several minutes, and when the high began to dwindle he
sprayed more paint into the bag and repeated the
process.

Stoned and vibrating, the electric warrior began
taking in the surroundings, although there really
wasn't much to observe. The large Dumpster looked

like an explosion of produce. He thought it looked like a giant salad, but instead of dressing, vomit adorned the top. The brick walls surrounding him were sporadically decorated in graffiti, most of it illegible. Someone, probably a store clerk, had written in silver lettering: RITA GOMEZ HAS A 2-INCH-LONG CLITORIS. Unfazed but curious, he continued inhaling.

"Bitchin'," Invisible Bob declared after receiving a very powerful head rush. Bob agreed and wondered what his only other friend on this planet was doing.

"Probably taking it up the *culo*."

Bob turned, ready to stab. There was no one visible.

"Yeah, man, there's some mean cats in the joint."

"Yeah, well, Eugene's a bad motherfucker too," Bob declared, speaking to the darkening air.

"Oh yeah? If he's so tough then how'd he get caught with his dick in a twelve-year-old?"

There was silence for several long seconds.

"*Shut the fuck up!*" Bob instructed, yelling at a wall. He squared off, fists clenched. Invisible Bob knew he was serious, dead serious. Fortunately, the wall did not respond.

The toxic fumes brought upon many sensations, among them superhuman vision and strength. He felt as though he could rip a small car in half if he had to, and wouldn't stop trying until he died. No fuckhead better mess with him. Within his spectrum of vision, Bob could see every moving molecule, every color within the kaleidoscope. Whenever he moved his hands, a hallucinatory trail like an electric flow followed. Even with his eyes closed he could still see and the two partners continued huf-

fing until the spray can ran out of blue paint and
fumes.

"I hate it when that happens," Bob said jokingly
to himself, laughing happily as he tossed the empty
can away. It was time to leave. As he exited the putrid alley, he thought he heard another mysterious
voice say something.

Maybe a devil wanted to harm him.

With his newfound bionic vision, Bob could see
clearly in this vile utopia. Ready for action, he
quickly turned around. No one was present. Not unless the devils had come up with some new form of
invisibility.

In the parking lot, he slithered past packs of shop-
pers until he thought he spotted a victim, a well-
dressed man with a soft face. He was usually quite
good at reading people.

"S'cuse me sir, do you have any spare change so I
can get something to eat?" he asked, unable to
make eye contact. He never could when asking for
money.

"Why don't you get a fucking job like the rest of
us so you can feed yourself?" the man replied bitterly, and continued walking.

Black hatred pulsed through Bob as his eyes bore
into a crack in the pavement. Raging hostility consumed his every cell. For a second he thought he
saw Hell, but knew better. He lived in Hell.

The iron spike in his coat pocket felt reassuring as
his subconscious horrors came to a boil. The fury of
a psychotic was waiting to be unleashed. He contemplated sticking the long steel rod into the rude
man's eyes and gouging them out. The evil bastard
didn't deserve the gift of sight. It said so somewhere
in the Bible. His fingers tightened around the spike.
When he looked up, the rude man was gone. He felt

relieved that there was no confrontation. After all, he was a peaceful man of good intentions.

He silently wandered along Fountain Avenue to Mansfield. The street of small, shabby-looking houses and recently constructed apartments looked inviting. Piercing winds whistled through his paint-encrusted nostrils. Still disoriented, he heard the voices in his brain directing him north toward the action: Sunset Boulevard.

When he arrived, Sunset was jammed with bumper-to-bumper immobility. Hostile drivers cursed one another by means of their horns. Bob watched the scenario, amused. Lights swirled, colors changed, and the street volume confused him, increasing, then decreasing, as cars and trucks with mammoth stereos blared music, then drove off. For the time being, the cold didn't bother him. He was too enthralled. He felt like Sonic the Hedgehog or some other hectic character inside a video game.

He noticed another street survivor and instantly felt close to the tiny prostitute clad in an imitation leather jacket and purple miniskirt. The young tarted-up girl barely looked fourteen. Her dark Hispanic face was chubby with baby fat. She wore too much blue eye shadow and her thick lips were glazed in red lipstick trying to hide cold sores. Jet-black hair fell halfway down her back. Her legs were shaking. Like Bob, she was another voyager of inner consciousness, ready to struggle the streets for the experience.

Invisible Bob liked her too. His mind began to run wild. He pictured Bob, face buried in her ass, giving her a rimjob. He hoped she was less than sanitary; after all, a woman's dirty rectum is as good a place as any to take communion. Bob started toward her but before he could reach her, she hopped into a black Camaro, ready to trade her goods to anyone with twenty dollars.

"FUCK YOU, DEVILS!" Bob yelled at the black car. It sped away before the crazy man could get too close.

With both hands in his army coat pockets, he walked over to a garbage can. Reluctantly, he began searching for food. He found a Burger King bag and searched it thoroughly. There were no scraps. Deeper in the trash was a red-and-white cardboard box. He said a quick prayer to the roach inside his brain and then opened it.

Inside the Kentucky Fried Chicken box was a half-eaten chicken breast and an untouched drumstick.

The roach had answered his prayer.

Three blocks away was Hollywood High School, Bob's alma mater. Hollywood High was a war zone with fifteen-year-old guerrillas killing one another over machismo and ten-dollar drug deals. The color of a bandanna, red or blue, could be the difference between whether or not you were decorated with bullet holes. Bob knew the terrain like the back of his hand. He remembered an enclosed doorway that was three-quarters surrounded by walls. At least he'd be protected from the unpredictable winds.

From the building's roof, a powerful spotlight illuminated the doorway where Bob would dine. Night school was in session. He silently hoped no power-tripping fuckhead janitor would force him to leave. At least not until after he finished eating.

He opened the KFC container and stared at his meal. His mouth watered over this fine cuisine. It was more than just food, it was another day's existence. Tomorrow, like every day, he'd comb the streets searching for Eugene.

On cold cement, he rested his weary bones in the

windless doorway and prepared himself for an early evening picnic. With dirt-and-spray-paint encrusted fingers he reached into the cardboard box and grabbed the unbitten drumstick.

"NEEDS SAUCE."

Startled, Bob dropped the piece of chicken into the container and gazed dumbfoundedly at Invisible Bob. He'd heard it too. Like a priest holding a sacred object of ancient origin, he lifted the box closer to his face. He held it gently, afraid of offending it. Then a revelation occurred and he understood where the voice had come from. On the side of the red-and-white box Colonel Sanders's mustached face smiled at Bob. Now he understood, but where would he get the needed condiment from?

Then she came into view, walking toward the doorway.

The pretty, dark-skinned woman looked at him like most people did, apprehensively. As things were, she was already five minutes late for class. She couldn't afford to walk around the building to another entrance just to avoid contact with the vagrant. That would make her ten minutes late and she'd be marked absent. Besides, all the homeless man was doing was eating his dinner.

With one hand in his pocket, Bob sat up as if he were going to open the door for her. The cold steel felt inviting to the touch. As she neared him, she clutched her books tightly and smiled. He returned her smile with one of his own that made the hackles on the back of her neck rise. The attractive twenty-six-year-old with her long black hair tied in a ponytail wished she had used the other entrance.

A high-pitched shriek echoed through the cold night air as Bob raised the spike above his head. With all his might, he brought it down, just missing her face. The dull spike tore through her jacket and sank into her soft breast. Schoolbooks and papers flew in every direction. She felt her chest go aflame as blood spilled out. Before she could scream again, her assailant punched her in the mouth with the solid steel spike. She crumpled onto the pavement. Bob viciously kicked her in the head several times, blasting any fight out of his victim, before pouncing on top of her.

Using both hands for leverage, he lined the spike up with her left eye. She tried to squirm out from underneath him but her attacker had too much leverage over her. Tiny croaking sounds escaped her throat.

Like an anxious lover preparing to insert himself, Bob took a deep breath and double-checked his positioning. Veins bulged on his skinny arms as the steel rod popped through her eye. Her face locked up with terror, unable to scream, as Bob sighed loudly and the spike began its slow penetration. Vitreous and aqueous humor mixed with blood spilled out of her overcrowded eye socket and dribbled down her cheek. He forced the rod in as far as it would go and only then did he ease up. A malevolent grin spread across his face as he stared down at his first-ever skull-fuck victim. He waited for her to stop twitching before he withdrew the crimson-greased spike. There was only the slightest hint of gray matter on the spike's tip, but Bob knew brains when he saw them. After all, the woman was attending night school.

With help from Invisible Bob, he began dragging his one-eyed victim toward the privacy behind the school. "Sauce." He sighed, mentally undressing the corpse. Nothing went better with chicken than the taste of a woman.

Even with the door shut, the janitor had heard it. He tried dismissing it as a car spinning its tires but couldn't. He'd heard these screams before. He'd been working night shift for close to four months, and remembering stories told when shifts ended, he apprehensively made his decision. He knew his moral obligation was to go investigate the scream. Before doing so he armed himself with a hammer.

Keys clanking together noisily, the janitor ran to the doorway. He saw no one and felt relieved. Then he noticed the trail of blood on the ground.

Adrenaline pushed him forward, although he really didn't want to go. He began running again, following the faint trail on the ground to the back of the building. Within thirty seconds, he'd located the perpetrator. The man had his half-dressed victim on the ground and was violating her.

"HEY, MOTHERFUCKER!," the janitor yelled, down to kill.

Invisible Bob screamed as Bob looked up from the woman's midsection. He let go of his condiment and stood up.

Both men, Bob with his spike, the janitor with his hammer, cautiously approached one another until they were less than four feet apart. The janitor's right fist white-knuckled the hammer's handle, but before he could swing, Bob lashed out. He was cat quick and all the custodian saw was a momentary flash. It was as if an explosion had gone off inside his eyes. And then pain in his face registered. Instinctively his left hand flew up. Warm fluid covered his palm and ran down his chin, settling in his neatly cropped beard.

Bob ferociously jabbed away at the left side of his foe's face. The janitor's hand partially blocked the blows as the dull point sank into his hand. Skin split

and small bones broke as a jolting charge of agony
shot from his hand to the rest of his body. Another
solid punch connected and the custodian doubled
over momentarily, leaving his bloody face exposed
again. With all his might, Bob brought his spiked-
enclosed fist back. The brutal blow smashed in the
janitor's left ear.

Shocked by the relentless onslaught, the janitor
staggered backward. Bob was all over him, stab-
bing, punching, and slashing repeatedly. As long as
the man stood upright, Bob would pummel him
with the spike. Large gashes appeared all over his
arms, head, and upper torso. Blood gushed out of
both nostrils and several of his front teeth were broken. Even though his disfigured face was little more
than a giant bruise, the janitor tried fighting back,
but that first blow had been too much. With a savage
fury, Bob cocked back and blasted the janitor on the
side of the head, knocking him down to one knee.
Still clutching his hammer, he raised his hands to
protect his ruined face.

"I love you," Bob declared as he raised the spike,
ready to deliver the final blow through his defeated
foe's forehead.

Using the last of his strength, the custodian swung
the heavy hammer like an uppercut punch into
Bob's right kneecap, cracking it. The sound of steel
breaking bone echoed loudly in Bob's ears. Even the
roach screamed. Waves of electrified agony shot up
through him as his spike flew out of his hand and
clinked away. Dropping to the ground, Bob let loose
a banshee wail that was drowned out as a police car
came to a screeching halt.

"FREEZE!" yelled the pistol-toting officer. Sil-
houetted by the flashing red-and-white sirens, the
janitor and Bob held their positions. With a pistol

fixed on his head, the janitor, who more than anything in the world wanted to smash Bob's demented face in with the hammer, reluctantly tossed aside his weapon. His partner ran over to the prone woman with her pants and underwear around her ankles and began administering CPR. It was useless. Her life had been snuffed. The repulsed officer noticed the drumstick that was still inside of her and fought valiantly not to gag. He'd been on the force for over eight years but he had never seen a sex crime like this.

"HE TRIED RAPING HER!"

The janitor couldn't believe his ears. The lunatic was trying to pin this mess on him. He tried arguing but couldn't. His face was ravaged, his jaw shattered. He was forcefully placed in handcuffs while waiting for an ambulance to arrive.

"He—"

"Shut the fuck up," the arresting officer barked right before the janitor passed out. Invisible Bob laughed cruelly, hoping the custodian was dead. Bob saw his spike and tried to retrieve it. He tried to stand but couldn't. He put pressure on his knee and let loose a painful scream. The policeman standing over him also saw the spike.

"Take it easy," the officer consoled. Bob forced out a weak smile. The officer returned one, thinking he was assisting a hero. He walked to the wet spike, picked it up carefully, showed it to his partner, and put it away as evidence. The policeman who'd been attending to the dead woman felt something wet and sticky on his fingers. Wounds like these could not have been administered by a hammer.

They were stab wounds.

The veins in his forehead bulged with rage as he left the dead woman and walked over to Bob. He

couldn't believe that in the heat of the moment he'd
almost been duped. A cold sweat glazed his face as
his hand fell to his service revolver. Behind the silver badge that he'd worn proudly for many years,
every fiber of moral ethic turned to hatred.

Looking up, the smelly man forced his odd smile
at the policeman. He resembled a naughty dog timidly looking at its master. But this dog was way beyond scolding or reprimand. With all his strength
and hostility, the cop kicked Bob's ruined leg. Bob
never felt so much pain in his life, not even when
he'd had to jump out of the second-story apartment
he'd been robbing and landed face-first on the cement. That time nothing had been broken. Instinctively, his hands fell to support his shattered knee,
but by trying to hold it, he only hurt himself more.
Every muscle cringed, every nerve twinged in agony.

It was indescribable ecstasy.

Although the temperature had dropped into the
low thirties and he was in paralyzing pain, Bob had
never before experienced such exhilaration. The
feeling that presently consumed him was better
than drugs. A sick smirk escaped his tortured, distorted face. He tried hiding his pleasure but
couldn't. The cop pounced on top of him, bending
his arms back painfully and vise-grip handcuffs
were clamped on.

"Asshole, you're under arrest and being charged
with at least one count of murder. You have the
right to—"

Crazy Bob shut out the sounds coming from the
hostile cop's mouth. Again, he smiled his deranged
smile. Drool pittered off his chapped lips. *Where was
his dinner?* he wondered.

"*Fuckheads* . . ." Bob said smiling, wishing Ugly

Eugene were here to see his moment of glory. The policeman couldn't bear to look at the filthy psycho with the hideous smile. He would much rather put a bullet through Bob's heart. His partner had to restrain him before he hurt the suspect again. Loud whining ambulance sirens told Bob more demons were coming. He silently prayed that Invisible Bob would hand him another weapon, maybe one of the cop's guns as well as the keys to the cuffs, so he could take out a few more devils. Although any movement hurt, he forced himself to look up. Both cops were keeping a close, ready eye on him.

The ambulance stopped and two attendants jumped out. The police told them that the woman was dead. They quickly attended to the janitor, who had regained semiconsciousness. Just by looking at him they knew his mangled face needed reconstructive and plastic surgery.

Bob began to wail like a banshee as he was forced onto a stretcher. He resisted with all of his crazed strength. Freedom was much more than just another word for nothing left to lose and it didn't take a rocket scientist to figure out that he was going to prison for a very long time.

An inexperienced medic made the mistake of getting too close to Bob's snapping mouth and before she realized what had happened, her forearm was trapped in Bob's jaw. It felt like someone had wrapped her arm in razor wire and was pulling with all his might. The medic tried shaking free but that only caused Bob's teeth to sink deeper into her arm, breaking the skin. He was trying to cause as much damage as possible without the benefit of his hands. Strands of bloody flesh caked up in his rotten mouth. The first thought that came to the screaming attendant's mind was AIDS. Then her self-defense classes (and manicured fingernails) paid off as she fiercely sank her index and middle fingers into her assailant's right eye. A deafening scream escaped, unlocking Bob's mouth, and setting the wounded attendant free.

No, this can't be happening, Bob thought, unable to comprehend how dinner had turned into all this. With thick tears streaming down his grimy cheeks, he wondered if he'd ever regain vision in his right eye. He knew he saw her pull away but it felt like there still were fingers digging in his eye socket.

The warm feeling brought on by pain earlier had disappeared. He suddenly felt very small, trapped. The word *life* echoed through his pulverized mind. A life sentence was an extremely long time, even for one of God's chosen. And even with the possibility of being reunited behind bars with Ugly Eugene, prison held very little appeal.

"GOD HELP ME!"

God ignored his request.

Together, the cops and medics tried holding Bob down and strapping him to the stretcher. He fought rigidly to keep his head up. Straining, the last thing he saw out of his one good eye before being tied down was Invisible Bob, still running for freedom.

The Immortals

The scent of passion was replaced by fear when he saw the oncoming head-lights. Although common sense told him to get the fuck out of the way or at least slow down, he could not get control over the situation. Racing toward oblivion with Death as his passenger, laughing silently into his ears, the enveloping brightness had just about consumed him. This was the worst part; waiting to crash and burn, waiting to be mangled, waiting for the inevitable and the mysteries that lay beyond.

He knew he should swerve either left or right but his arms were locked and his right hand was frozen solid to the motorcycle's throttle. Looking at the speedometer right now would be useless since his field of vision was decimated by the overpowering whiteness. He thought this couldn't possibly be happening. Like some sort of mantra of the damned, he kept reassuring himself that it wasn't. But the light beams were on top of him, getting ready to swallow, and there was nothing he could do but sneer defiantly. It was what any true outlaw biker would do. And with his last bit of energy and strength, Sid thrust himself deeper into his lover.

This seemed to be a recurring theme: He would

get wrapped up with Natalie, and as the passion of two bodies melding into one intensified, the dread would take over. Dread, shit, it was outright horror. A horror that was more than loss of consciousness and rationality, it was black terror personified. It was slow-dancing with the Grim Reaper.

It was the end.

But the end it wasn't, as Sid's vision returned to normal and he was back in the safety of a warm bed. The end of his life was not yet here, but the dread and the lovemaking were over. His breathing slowed down and he felt a sense of normalcy returning. Covered in a light glaze of sweat, he rolled off the slender woman beneath him and reached for his crusty black Levi's jeans. The bell-bottomed jeans, like Sid, were tattered and hard. There was a certain amount of undeniable style beneath his terse exterior.

Natalie's stomach cringed as she watched her man get dressed. Resentment and hostility filled her. She didn't want to feel this way but couldn't help it. Besides, who the fuck was he to pump her, then split like nothing happened?

"Where ya off to?" she asked, trying to disguise her hurt as concern.

"Business."

"Honey, it's after midnight."

"I keep odd hours," Sid replied, amused with his dry wit.

"That's no excuse," she countered, running her fingers through her shoulder-length auburn hair. Sorrow had stolen some of her natural beauty but Natalie was still quite a lovely young woman.

"I don't need any excuses for what I do."

There was an invisible anxiety lurking in the darkness of their bedroom. The couple, who were never too far away from an argument or an outright fight, knew the warning signs. The tension would remain dormant for a while and then would eventually explode. Sid hoped he would be dressed and heading for the door before he had to smack the bitch.

Physically he wasn't very large, not nearly as big as some of the beasts he called his friends, but he was intense. Most people could feel his presence when he entered a room. He had an overpowering aura of self-confidence. Sid Webster was not a man to be taken lightly. He did up the buckle to the heavy chain belt that he wore around his waist. A large Buck knife was attached to the belt and this knife had been used on many occasions without hesitation or remorse. He threw Natalie a look warning her that he wasn't in the mood, but she refused to take the hint.

Her head was cocked downward, and through her reddish hair, which was parted on the side, Natalie watched her man get dressed with heavy eyes. Sid slipped his head and tattooed arms through a T-shirt. He then put on a gray-and-white flannel shirt.

"You must think I'm really naive or something. How can you just finish making love to me, then leave like nothing? It's not right and it's not fair. You wanna know what it is? It's bullshit! Fucking bullshit! I have feelings too, ya know. But you wouldn't. *You couldn't.* I ain't some 'wham bam thank you ma'am' scooter tramp whore. I'm your wife, goddamn it."

"I know who you are but you knew who I was and what my life was all about when you hooked up with me," Sid explained with no hint of remorse in his voice.

"I also thought that you'd outgrow this . . ."

"And let down my brothers?" Sid asked angrily and appalled. Without realizing it, his fist had clenched up into a ball.

"The brothers this and the brothers that . . . I can't tell you how it makes me feel when you screw me, then go off and do God knows whatever it is that you do. You break my heart night after night, but then again what would you know about feelings? What could you know?" she asked with tears streaking her olive-tone cheeks.

Sid finished getting dressed, ready to leave. Right before he put on the final piece of his attire, his motorcycle club colors, Natalie bitterly declared, "Coldhearted is an understatement. Sid, you don't even have a heart."

He thought about how he should discipline her for being disrespectful. Not a full swing or anything, just a little bitch slap to let her know her place. He took a few slow steps toward the bed. Her entire body stiffened up. She knew what was coming and braced herself.

The sterling silver skull rings he always wore added even more impact to the quick blow. Natalie held her right cheek as Sid stood over her, daring her to get out of line, but she knew better. Just like dozens of times before, the biker waited to see if she had any other stupid remarks to make before he left the silent house.

Right outside of the front door was his motorcycle. With any luck he could make it to the clubhouse before 1:00 A.M., he thought. Sid lined up his right boot heel with the kicker pedal and kick-started his bike to life. Burning rubber on the sidewalk that led to the street, he took off with a thunderous roar. The harder he rode, the easier it was to forget the grief Natalie had just given him. Within five minutes, he'd gotten it all out of his system and was a third of the way to his destination. But even after he'd slowed down to law-abiding speeds, luck would not be with Sid tonight.

Surrounded by the red-and-white flashing lights of one of Berkeley's finest, the biker reluctantly pulled over. The echoing reverberation of 1,200 cubic centimeters of Harley-Davidson horsepower came to a coughing halt. Sid, in an unusually docile mood, had decided that it was better to pull over and find out what the police officer wanted rather than try to outrun the law. He'd been doing that for the past fifteen years.

The road's shoulder was gravel-strewn and Sid almost dumped his sled. Dust and dirt flew everywhere. The lone officer pulled the patrol car up behind him and the biker wondered whether the cop had seen his near fuck-up. He could hear the officer speaking over the police radio from behind rolled-up windows.

Beneath a moonlit puzzle of connected stars, August's warmth was several hours away. Nighttime may be the right time but that doesn't stop cold from creeping in. The bearded biker silently wished he had worn his suede riding chaps. The policeman got out of his car carrying a large black flashlight. His free hand was over his holstered gun.

"Lemme see your license and registration," the handlebar-mustached officer barked. Using his high-powered flashlight, he inspected the road-beaten motorcycle. A disgusted look swept his face.

" 'Scuse me, Officer, what's the fuckin' prob—"

"License and registration . . . *and lemme see your insurance card too,*" the officer lashed out, shining the bright light in the biker's face. He kept it there for several long seconds, challenging the biker to get out of line. Sid kept his cool and searched through the mess of papers he passed off as a wallet. Finally, he found the right ones and held them out. The cop snatched them out of his hand, cautiously turned around, and returned to the warmth of his patrol car.

Sitting on a cold leather seat was not Sid's idea of fun. He was trying his damnedest to keep his composure. He'd encountered this type of cop before: a pseudo-tough guy who wasn't very tough without a badge and gun. This kind of bullshit would never happen in downtown 'Frisco or Oakland but this was a small town and he had to play by the rules. Maybe if he got close enough he would slice the pig's throat and ride away.

The familiar steamy smell of gas, oil, and grime filled his senses. All he wanted to do was get off his motorcycle and join up with his bros at the clubhouse. There was always action at the clubhouse.

Sid's brown hair fell past his shoulders and complemented his fair complexion. His chiseled face was handsome according to biker standards, revolting to most of society. Over his flannel shirt was a black leather vest with the insignia of The Immortals Motorcycle Club, to which he belonged. The top rocker, or patch, read: THE IMMORTALS in bold black lettering with a silver outline. The bottom rocker declared: CALIFORNIA, the small but strong chapter to which he belonged, and in between the two rockers was the club's center patch, an ominous black inverted cross with a silver 1% symbol in the middle of the cross. He'd worn these colors for years and could never foresee taking them off. He had served his country in the Marine Corps and done time in prison as well. The Immortals were his family and he'd die for his patch, for his brothers.

He had made a commitment to the club that didn't expire until he did. The flannel covered his tattooed arms and a dirty T-shirt that read: SO HORNY, EVEN THE CRACK OF DAWN ISN'T SAFE. Unusual appearance did not give the officer the right to pull Sid over but in certain parts of America being a biker is reason enough.

His bike suited him just fine. It was the worldly possession he was most proud of. The radical ride was his identity. The gas tank was primer-black with an emblem from the Raiders football team on each side. The heads were ported and polished and the cases wrinkle-black. The S&S Super carburetor perfectly complemented the well-balanced animal pan/shovel engine. Every winter he tried to find something new to modify. He usually succeeded.

The wishbone frame was raked forty-five degrees and stretched eight inches, which made it quite long and sleek. The drag exhaust pipes were painted black and cut short to make the bike louder than a rolling freight train. Black ape-hanger handlebars were the perfect touch to make the ride even more radical. Strapped to his wide-glide front, underneath the headlight, was a leather tool pouch. Inside the tool bag was an adjustable wrench, several sockets, a Phillips screwdriver, a flathead screwdriver, a roll of black tape, a pair of spark plugs, and a loaded two-shot .22 derringer that police ballistics could match up with several unsolved murders.

Checking out the surrounding scenery, he noticed that on the opposite side of the road was a yellow sign that read: CAUTION SLOW CHILDREN. Chuckling to himself, Sid began to picture himself racing alongside David Carradine in *Death Race 2000*, trying to mow down a group of slow-moving fat kids.

Much to the police officer's disbelief, the biker was clean.

The sound of a car door slamming snapped Sid out of his daydream before it got overtly graphic. The officer returned with a dejected look on his face since he would not have a story to tell his girlfriend and drinking buddies about how he brought in a wanted biker. Nevertheless, he kept his hand over his service revolver as he handed Sid back his papers and snapped, "Everything's in order, you're free to go."

Sid thought about making some wiseass remark regarding cops and doughnuts but common sense told him not to. The prick was letting him go without a ticket. After a few unsuccessful kicks that managed to awaken the next morning's phlegm, Sid kicked down hard and the Joe Hunt Magneto did its job. The bike roared back to life. Sid was slightly surprised that he didn't get a ticket for loud pipes. Revving up the engine and listening to the finely tuned machinery, Sid started enjoying himself ever so slightly. Every time he cracked the throttle, the bike seemed to bark like a pissed-off pit bull.

Looking him dead in the eyes, the outlaw biker considered his foe. Here's a man who's been given a badge by the people, who pulls him over for no apparent reason, and runs a license check on him. If he had any unpaid tickets, he would go to jail until one of his club brothers bailed him out. Now aren't the police supposed to serve and protect the guaranteed rights everyone shares as an American?

Hell, he doesn't have the slightest idea what it's like being free, Sid thought to himself, grin spreading, as he readied himself to roar away. He slipped the gearshift into first and slowly let out the clutch. Then like a bullet, he was gone. It was only moments before the police officer was little more than an unpleasant memory.

The cold wind felt good, alive, as he hammered down to an easy, comfortable cruising speed. Small quaint houses made up the landscape as massive trees loomed over both sides of these heavily-wooded roads. The biker knew these poorly lit roads, as well as most of northern California, quite well. During the past two years, these roads had claimed the lives of three less skilled riders.

Clem Dawson fiddled with a portable AM/FM radio while his kid brother chain-smoked Marlboro cigarettes. Trying to get any sort of reception this far from the city was next to impossible. Trying to get reception tucked down behind thick bushes on a dark tree-covered curve was ridiculous. When the biker was little more than a dot of light off in the distance, the two young men prepared themselves for action.

"Listen to that," the smoker declared, quite impressed that he could hear the engine this far away. The motorcycle was over a half-mile away.

"Yeah, Dead Eye, he is one loud fuck," his brother said, shaking his head in agreement, still trying to get the radio to work.

"Wanna go home?" the retarded boy with the wandering right eye asked as he removed a bolt-action Steyr SSG 69 from inside a carrying case. Until recently, he hated the rather cruel nickname that Clem had pegged him with, but after it was established that he was a better shot than his older brother, his nickname took on a new meaning. Hell, now he even introduced himself as Dead Eye.

"Nah, I'd rather watch you take target practice."

"Just checking," the fifteen-year-old chipped in,

244 *Del James*

mentally noting that tomorrow's headlines would once again pay homage to the fourth unfortunate motorcyclist who accidentally went off a hazardous road.

Dead Eye took aim through a Kahles ZF69 infrared scope that was graduated to a range of 875 yards, scoring ten-shot groups within a sixteen-inch circle at the maximum range. This was of the utmost importance since the object was not to hit the biker directly, but rather, to cause him to have an accident. The motorcycle's twenty-one-inch front wheel was the target.

The biker sensed something up ahead. He'd taken this hairpin turn before and knew it was quite dangerous. That's what made it fun. Although he normally threw caution to the wind, he acted upon instinct and slowed down to a steady forty miles per hour before he was back in his nightmare.

Like some biker version of the Bermuda Triangle, he was blind and being drawn against his will into the oncoming lights. The lights were calling him by name, drawing him closer and closer toward them. He was being overpowered by forces he had no control over. He felt hypnotized, trapped in a luminous void. He tried turning but couldn't avoid the inevitable. He'd had this dreadful sensation so many times before that he played his role perfectly, smirking defiantly as destruction swept over him and covered him in the blinding lights that he recognized as those of a truck.

He made it through the lights but before he could celebrate, he was twisting and being ripped apart. The sound of ruined machinery grating against the road drowned out the biker's grunts of agony. Large sparks shot out in every direction as the Harley-Davidson and its rider tumbled and skidded. Upon impact with the road, Sid's left kneecap cracked in half. He felt his flesh being ground into the cement as he and his ride slid along the asphalt for over one hundred and sixty feet. Bone and gore became visible as the left side of Sid's face was stripped off. After an eternity, the skid, which left a good portion of him spread along the road, finally came to a halt.

"Nice shot," Clem declared enthusiastically just as the AM/FM radio properly tuned. He didn't recognize the song.

"Thanks," the shooter replied bashfully as he put the rifle back inside the carrying case and hid it in the bushes. He removed a pack of cigarettes from his coat pocket and lit one. The Dawson brothers jogged out of the bushes toward the writhing biker who, try as he might, could not get up.

"Is the meat wagon on its way?"

"Better be or I'll have to put a cap in Uncle Dave," Clem said, smiling evilly. He lifted his sweater up so that Dead Eye could see the automatic pistol tucked into the front of his pants.

"When I get to the hospital . . . you fucks are . . . motherfucking dead," Sid groaned through broken teeth. This amused both teens. Clem carefully approached the sprawled-out, heavily bleeding biker. He removed the mangled man's wallet and pulled out his license.

"You fucks are dead," Sid declared, still trying to figure out what had happened to him. And why? Who were these two country fucks and why did they choose him for target practice?

Ironically, instead of worrying about his personal injuries Sid was most concerned with whether the skid had totaled his motorcycle. He felt closer to his bike than he did his wife and cared more about the scooter. Seeing his bike on its side wounded was blasphemous. He actually felt a sense of sorrow at being unable to help the motorcycle. Rage surged through him but there was nothing he could do. He tried crossing his torn fingers so that some of The Immortals would show up but deep down he didn't believe in wishes.

"Sydney Michael Webster. Blah, blah, blah. Oakland. Hair: Brown. Eyes: Brown. Height: six-one. Weight: One hundred ninety. Date of birth: six-six-sixty-two," Clem read aloud. He turned the driver's license around and read, "Pursuant to the Uniform Anatomical Gift Act, I hereby elect upon my death the following option(s): to donate any organs or parts."

"I ain't no fuckin' organ donor, you cocksucker," Sid barked in protest and spit out a mouthful of crimson. Off in the distance he heard something. He painfully turned on his side and saw an approaching truck that closely resembled an ambulance. His body went cold as he recognized the lights that were coming closer and closer toward him.

"You are now," Clem said, removing a ballpoint pen from his pants pocket. He made the necessary changes on the license and would let the attendants in the organ truck, one of whom was Dave Dawson, the mastermind behind the organ-donor scam, do the rest. A complete set of internal organs could fetch between five and ten thousand dollars. The brothers had no problem greasing their palms since they were the ones bringing in the donors.

Dead Eye and Clem saw the truck coming and, just as a precaution, ran back to the safety of the bushes. They watched closely as two attendants came out of the truck, picked up their passenger, and sped off.

"Uncle Dave sure looked happy tonight," Dead

Eye offered but Clem didn't reply. He was too busy tinkering with the radio again.

Sid's once-perfect vision was fading fast. He'd already lost sight in his left eye, as well as most of the flesh from the surrounding area, but it was what his right eye saw that concerned him. The back area of the ambulance was too clean, too sterile. Everywhere his good eye scanned he saw gleaming chrome. The tools his eye saw were not those used to preserve lives, but rather, to end them. Embalming fluid, tongs, bone saws, cleavers, scalpels, surgical knives, and other instruments used by coroners overwhelmed his sight and senses.

The racing ambulance slowed to a complete stop. The relentless agony shooting through his entire body made Sid reconsider that maybe he should not have gone out tonight, but it was too late to repent. And deep down he knew he never would. He'd lived as a stand-up kind of guy and he'd go out that way too. Then, much to his dismay, he realized what he was lying on. He tried his best to swallow but couldn't. His dry throat refused to cooperate. Then again, who could get comfortable lying on a mortician's table, complete with grooves for draining blood?

Two attendants dressed in white surgical attire hovered around Sid, and he tried fighting them off. He'd been in many encounters against larger foes, but the accident earlier had just about sucked away all of his strength. More bones than he cared to count were broken, more muscles than he knew he had were shredded. He was now fighting on instinct alone, but it was better than nothing.

"Fuckin' no-good rats," the busted-up biker groaned as the attendants tried to hold him down.

"We've got a fighter on our hands," the smaller of

the two attendants said. He was barely five feet and most people who came in contact with him regarded him as "weasely."

"They all think they're tough until they meet their maker," the second, and larger, attendant replied smiling. The two men were almost identical in their mannerisms. They both had been around dead things for too long. The few friends they had besides each other viewed them as weird and women usually called them "creeps," the ultimate compliment. And they were definitely creepy. Death was humorous to them and they often giggled when someone had a bowel movement after dying.

"Think he's gonna shit himself?" the first attendant asked, trying to restrain his obvious pleasure.

"There's only one way to find out, Dave."

"FUCK YOU!" Sid snapped, and threw a wild haymaker that missed its mark.

"That wasn't very polite," the second attendant said dryly, angered.

"You shouldn't get Ray mad," Dave, the weasley attendant, explained matter-of-factly.

Ray and Dave were all over Sid, trying to remove his vest. Sid put up a valiant effort. These were his colors, *his pride*, they were trying to strip him of. It took some effort but eventually the colors and his flannel shirt were both in Dave's sweaty hands.

"Don't fuckin . . . touch my . . . colors."

"Don't tell us what to do," Ray snapped as he grabbed Sid by the neck of his T-shirt and ripped. The shirt offered little resistance and now Sid's chest was exposed.

"Lookit that," Dave said, discarding Sid's colors and pointing at the tattoo on the biker's chest. In Old English–style lettering, the letters I.F.F.I. were tattooed directly over Sid's heart.

"Ain't that sweet," Ray snickered as he slowly removed a short but rather thick surgical knife from one of the many racks. The shining silver blade was no more than three inches long but was equally wide with a serrated edge.

"Careful now," Dave quickly said, then added, "Ain't no good if you get carried away and slice up the organs."

"Who are you, my mother? I know what I'm doing. I'm a highly skilled professional."

Both attendants snickered.

Sid scooted over as much to his left as pain would permit and then with all of his might, which wasn't much, kicked Ray with his right boot. The blow had little effect other than making Ray angry. Dave leaped into action and held Sid down by his shoulders as Ray prepared himself for some dissecting. His beady eyes were locked on Sid's chest, in particular the tattoo.

"I.F.F.I. Immortals forever, forever immortal? That tattoo should stand for *I'm fucked, fucked I am!*" Ray sneered before sinking the blade into the top of Sid's chest. Blood spurt out in all directions as the attendant forcefully ran the thick blade down the biker's sternum, toward the bottom of his rib cage. A wet ripping sound filled Sid's ears as a low long moan escaped his lips. He tried to stay upright for as long as possible, but that was only a few seconds. Soon afterward he crumpled and sagged into the comforts of the death he'd cheated so many times before.

"He lasted longer than most do," Dave said impressed, and then added in his best imitation of John Madden, the pro-football commentator, "Good hang time."

Ray did not reply as he began opening up the

corpse. The object of organ and limb preservation was to get them out of the body and into proper storage as soon as possible. The warmer and fresher the organ, the better.

Loud squishy noises were audible as Ray expertly opened up Sid's chest. Even in death Sid proved to be difficult, as his alabaster flesh offered resistance to the blade and Ray's rubber-gloved fingers. But Ray was not easily discouraged. Using the right amount of strength and leverage, he worked the skin back so as to give him a better view of the black-market organs that would help pay his car notice. Then he suddenly stopped.

"Dave—"

"Yeah, pal."

"Something ain't right."

"You need some help?" Dave asked, wondering why Ray looked so pale. Maybe he'd turned soft and the rigors of the job were finally getting to him.

"I think we both need help."

"Wha?"

"This guy . . . This guy's missing . . . This guy ain't got no heart."

"Real funny, man," Dave countered, and at that very second Sid sprang up off the table. Using his left hand, he grabbed Ray by the throat and put the squeeze on. With cat-quick grace, Sid unsnapped his Buck knife from its sheath and ran the sharp blade across Ray's throat. The attendant immediately covered the gaping wound with both hands, leaving his paling face too tempting a target. Sid viciously jabbed his deadly point in all the way up to the handle. The once-boisterous attendant crashed loudly to the floor and immediately lost control over his bowels.

"Where's my bike?"

"RAY!" Dave shrieked like a frightened school-girl.

"Ray's gone away," the smiling ghoul replied in a raspy tone as he approached Dave. Sid picked his colors up off the floor and put them back on.

"But you're dead!"

"You can't kill an Immortal," the undead biker informed the petrified attendant as he put his dripping blade back into its leather case.

Although his body was ravaged, Sid's mind was clear. Even as a child, he had known he was different than the other kids. He was special, unique. He never fell for Santa Claus or the tooth fairy. He was a hardass who couldn't grasp the concept of love or goodwill. After all, there was no such thing as an eye for an eye if you hit your opponent first and made sure he never got up. Sid had always been true to who he was and to his inauspicious nature. Treachery was a quality he admired but so few had. That was why he ran around with other kindred outlaw spirits. His soul had been very violent for a very long time and in a brief moment of clarity, he remembered the dark history that was his. He remembered the sense of who he was in his SS uniform as his neck swung from a noose in Nuremberg, quite dead and smiling. He remembered deflowering virgins, whipping and beating them for pleasure, and how sweet their tears tasted just as vividly as he remembered the stench of burning skin as the stake he was tied to held him until his eyeballs burst and he no longer screamed. He remembered the smell of black powder after being gunned down by some legendary lawman, and despising—not the man who had shot him—but rather the five-point star that was pinned to his rival's chest.

Sorry was not in his vocabulary but revenge was.

He didn't mind so much that someone had killed him for a quick buck, hell, he'd taken out more than a few contracts in his day, but where the two teenagers went wrong was they didn't finish the job properly. Sid also understood that he didn't have very long before this reanimated body deteriorated into uselessness. He also knew that he would be back someday. As long as there was virtue on this earth, there would be a need for evil.

"Who shot my fuckin' bike, asshole?" Sid demanded in his new, evil voice.

"The kids did it, man," Dave answered as tears formed in his bugging eyes. Sid picked up a large bone saw from the counter. He was quite curious whether this tool would cut as effectively as his trusty Buck had. Dave held up his shaking hands, trying to keep the biker away from him but that proved useless. He kept repeating that his nephews had shot the motorcycle, like suddenly Sid would forgive him and let him go, even as the bone saw cut through his thick skull.

"Where would bored teenagers be at this hour in this one-horse town?" Sid wondered as he started up the ambulance and pulled away.

The large plate-glass window of the 7-Eleven offered no challenge against the speeding organ truck. Twisting and crashing steel echoed throughout the open-all-night convenience shop. Where there once was peace and tranquility, havoc and mayhem now reigned. A giant glass wave rolled, then crashed heavily as the truck tore through the window and the front counter, impaling the unsuspecting clerk.

Shock swept through the two teenagers, who until seconds ago, were busy pumping quarter after quarter into a Jurassic Park pinball machine, trying to get the high score. Sid hobbled out from the ambulance's cab. He slowly dragged his ragged left leg behind him as he approached his enemy. It would have been impossible for any living person to walk with a leg as badly mangled, but Sid was beyond the rules of the living.

He stopped several feet away from his violators. Sheer hatred flowed through what was left of his torn-up body. The ghastly biker crept toward Dead Eye, and with renewed strength and vigor grabbed the mongoloid by his large head and twisted, snapping the bewildered boy's neck before he could react. Dead Eye fell to the ground, imperfect eyes bulging out.

"Where's my bike?"

"You're dead!" Clem yelled as he reached for the Glock 17, a nine-millimeter pistol with a seventeen-round magazine that was tucked into the front of his blue jeans. Automatic firepower lit up the night as the horrified teenager fired repeatedly at the ghoul. Large-impact clouds of flesh and blood rose off the staggering target. Bullet after bullet tore through Sid. Ruined muscles, organs, and intestines fell out of torn slits in his flesh. Slugs cracked and broke his bones but the sinister biker with the ruined face kept advancing forward.

"I'm dead?" he asked.

"Yeah . . ." the stunned punk replied.

"Ya sure?"

"YEAH, MOTHERFUCKER!" Clem barked before unloading the rest of his rounds into Sid. The powerful blasts bounced Sid around, knocking him back, and doubling him over in pain, but he fought gamely to stay on his feet. The bullets, the accident, and the dissecting had just about completely destroyed his features, but his will and determination were indestructible.

Sid slowly returned to a full upright position. The high school dropout tried fleeing but couldn't move. His legs were frozen with fright as the angry corpse slowly dragged himself closer and closer. The biker removed his bloody blade from its sheath and viciously sunk it into Clem's heaving chest. Screams and gurgling noises echoed inside the decimated convenience shop as Sid twisted and turned the blade until there was a large enough hole for him to stick his dead fingers into.

Natalie didn't hear the bike pull up, but that was no big surprise. She'd been in a deep uneasy sleep. It seemed like most of her rest was troubled but who could blame her? Sid and men of his ilk were the hardest to tame. *And the most rewarding to love*, she thought as she heard heavy boots clonking up the steps and across the front porch.

"Baby, is that you?" she called out, tired but never too tired to make love to her man. Then she heard him making his way toward the bedroom and a smile crept on her face. Regardless of where he was, he always came home to be with her. And if that was his way of expressing love, then she would accept it and the domestic violence that came with it. She couldn't go back in time and she couldn't change the past, especially the argument that had gone down between them earlier, but what Natalie could do was make the immediate future a little bit better, like as soon as Sid got into bed with her.

Exhausted, he made his way to the bedroom doorway. Sid felt his strength being drained with each passing step and it would not be long before his dead body was completely useless. That fact had little effect on him and he wouldn't miss anyone from this life, he'd only miss riding his motorcycle.

"Yeah, I'm home . . . And you were wrong earlier. I do have a heart," Sid said hoarsely, trying not to grin. He had a heart all right. It was in his red-stained right hand, and yes, in order to find it he had to dig quite deep.

The Melrose
Vampire

The gallery was empty. It had been every day except for the opening weekend when all the trendy Los Angeles artists, actors, and musicians made their cameos, hoping to be mentioned in the *L.A. Times* calender section or the *L.A. Weekly's* La Dee Da column. All press, including bad press, is good, even if it's at someone else's expense. Occasionally someone strolled in off the street, but all in all, things were quite dead.

Perry LaFontaine stood bored, doing his best too-tough-to-dance imitation, chain-smoking Lucky Strikes. He'd attended every day for the past thirteen days and it showed. Instead of a celebration of modern art, this felt more like a wake. Stress wrinkles tugged at the edges of the black circles beneath his eyes. Tension showed all over his twenty-eight-year-old face. He looked sickly translucent but he had to be here. It was his art.

His love for artistic expression was deep-rooted, almost sincere, but the only thing he truly loved was himself. He'd always been drawing, creating, and when "regular" school didn't work out, Perry found his calling. He enrolled in an alternative school and took every art class he could. He studied hard and was eventually accepted to Otis Parson's School of Design. True to form, that didn't last very long.

He always had different views on things. It wasn't so much his differences in opinion but the way he debated that eventually got him expelled. He was constantly being reprimanded for his "bad attitude." The Parson's School taught him more about technique than he'd ever imagined, but in his own opinion he was beyond learning. Perry believed that there are those who are naturally gifted and school is just a waste of time. Besides, the City of Angels was taking its toll on him. He was trying to change art according to L.A.'s unusual standards. His views and values were quickly changing. There was so much to experience in art that he left school and fell into the ranks of the starving artists' society.

Perry's killer good looks could get him through almost any situation. Until recently, he looked as though he could've been a model in full-page black-and-white ads for Guess? jeans or Ray-Ban sunglasses. His slicked-black hair was stylishly messy, neither too long nor too short, and strands of it often dangled in front of his face, but instead of looking messy, it looked cool. High cheekbones, perfect teeth, and a narrow nose with a small silver hoop in the right nostril perfectly complemented his pastel-brown eyes. His eyes were neither soft nor harsh, *just mysterious*, and the perpetual five-o'clock shadow gave him a sexy appeal.

Casually dressed in a black sleeveless Bill Blass T-shirt, faded 501's, and ostrich cowboy boots, Perry reminded most people of a soon-to-be-major star. It wasn't only his appearance but the way he carried himself. He was slick to the point of being enigmatic. Few could tell what he was thinking and he liked it that way. Unfortunately, he was prone to outbursts of unusual, nonconformist behavior and was never too far away from a temper tantrum. Perry could pitch a fit with the best of them. As far as he was concerned, the world was his if he wanted it, but standing alone in the gallery, he wondered when the hell his big break was coming. Many of L.A.'s movers and shakers had already discarded him as just another pretty face with an attitude. His artistic means of getting rich at a young age weren't working. He'd done the routine: starved, rejected society's mores, done theater, drank recklessly, lived out of his car, scammed welfare, kicked heroin, and slept with people he despised to get this exhibit.

In his opinion, the time was right for a new, entirely innovative art movement. Art went through many cycles and if history proved true, the world was eagerly anticipating the next major movement. It was something that, with a little luck, Perry could be a part of. The concept of being a modern-day pioneer drove him and he would do anything to surf that wave. *Anything.* Even his closest friends viewed him as thick-skinned and coldblooded when it came to getting his way; thus, Perry was appropriately nicknamed the "Vampire of Melrose." As he stood alone, surrounded by his paintings, sculptures, poetry, he wondered how he could have been so naive.

The art wasn't bad. Actually most of it was quite good and he'd already sold several pieces at reasonable prices, but money wasn't what he lusted after. *Not really.* It was recognition as a bona fide artist and the fame that went along with it. He wanted to achieve something monumental, the respect of other modern-day renaissance men. The only thing he felt he had achieved was several favorable reviews from critics who had attended during the opening weekend.

The large double doors swung open, allowing annoying sunlight to enter the dimly lit gallery. Another one of Perry's vampiric qualities was his disdain of sunlight. A six-foot-plus man walked in alone, clicking his walking stick with every step, making his entrance known. He stared at the artist hypnotically before turning away slowly. A lump of resentment swelled in Perry's throat.

What the fuck does this asshole want?

The large man removed a pair of dark sunglasses and began to stroll leisurely around the gallery. Perry's eyes followed the man in the antique-looking trench coat. Saying that the man was huge was an understatement. His broad shoulders could have belonged to a football player. His thighs were monstrous but he wasn't overweight, just large. *Very large.* Perry knew he was staring but couldn't help himself. He stubbed out a half-finished cigarette in the palm of his callused hand and continued following the stranger with his eyes.

The large man stopped at a sculpture entitled "Cuff Links." Within a glass case, cut at the elbows, two extremely detailed white marble arms were displayed. Complete with protruding veins and scars, the two arms were joined at the wrists by a pair of silver handcuffs. After that there was a television set showing nothing but multicolored static. Yellow police tape declaring: DO NOT CROSS was wrapped in an X-shaped pattern across the screen.

Next up was a mannequin wearing a leather S&M hat and a black leather motorcycle jacket. A large bullwhip hung from the right side of the jacket. The mannequin had its back turned and written in silver paint on the back of the leather coat was one of Perry's poems.

Most of the time I feel like I'm falling apart at the seams but that's all right because it's the unraveling that keeps me together. Extreme circumstance uncoils extreme meaning and there's a truth in desperation that only the desperate understand. I'm not afraid to push the limits of your reality and fears. I'll rape your self-respect and leave you wanting more. I'll kill your God and then cover him with a burning flag. I'm not afraid of the pain and its subsequent turn-ons. I laugh in the face of love since I'm not afraid of dying anymore. Actually the challenge of death is more enticing than any other because no one knows what the rules of that game will dictate. It's the mystery of the challenge that makes me curious . . . very. Do you still want to play with me?

The large man slowly walked past the jacket, past several paintings and sculptures, all of which were trying to make some sort of social and artistic statement. He'd stop and go through the motions of examining each display but he'd seen this type of art before and it did nothing for him. His narrow black eyes scanned and, within a matter of seconds, observed, ravaged, and consumed over three years of Perry's strain and misery. Neither the eyes nor their owner found anything substantial within the art.

It was the man's disinterest that made Perry unable to take his eyes off him. He wanted to know what the man thought of his work. He could stand snide comments or even laughter, but indifference was intolerable. This stranger was rude. And rude people were the lowest of the low. The fact that people often found Perry rude was irrelevant. Double standards were allowed. After all, this was his sanctum.

The large man reached an oil painting and stopped. It was a painting of a dark blue woman lying on a bed, holding a telephone. Beneath it was a tape recorder. The large man pressed PLAY: It was Perry's raspy voice.

"My dreams and inhibitions are lost in the soiled panties of another nameless lover. None of this is real except for one fleeting moment when our eyes speak and our bodies respond. Then it's understood and we temporarily bond. It's carnal. It's sacred. It's over as soon as the bed is made and phone numbers are exchanged never to be dialed . . . Good-bye."

Unamused, the large man made his way to the large display that was supposed to be the grand finale.

Making his way toward Perry.

The man appeared to drift. Perry felt himself growing uneasy, and anything was possible. *Who the fuck was this guy and what gave him the right to come into this gallery, act bored, and look down his nose at the works like he was holier than God shit?*

The large man stopped and observed. Sitting on the edge of an unmade bed was a marble statue (which had taken Perry several months to perfect). A complete male figure, elbows on thighs, large hands holding the face as though crying. Behind the bed was a redbrick wall. Inside one of the bricks, a hidden hose was attached. Every five minutes or so, a quick spray of water was released, keeping the bed, the sheets, and the sculpture doused. On the wall there was poetic graffiti. The tall man read the golden letters: *Bittersweet memories drowned in the wishing well while a small child runs from the shadows of yesterday. Redbrick buildings were the paper, chalk my pen, and everything was green. So was I. My innocence was pure, inexcusable, since I bought the fairy tales and never got a refund. I cried a lot, I dreamed a lot. I loved a lot but received little. I can remember it as if it were only twenty-four hours ago but I don't care to go back that far. Loneliness is a toy best left alone.*

The large man felt nothing. Some of this stuff was so self-indulgent it was absurd. There was no substance in this. The displays were a lot of pseudo-intellectual mumbo jumbo. In actuality, art as he saw it had lost most of its substance, most of its integrity, hundreds of years ago. Trendy, chic bullshit now consumed galleries everywhere. Art had gone soft trying to be hard.

The large man turned to leave and spun right into Perry, who was standing behind him, trying to look supercool.

"Good day," the tall man said, trying to avoid conversation with the artist.

"Wait a second," Perry said, smiling.

The tall man nodded. "Are you the one they call the Vampire?"

Perry nodded, not knowing whether to take it as a compliment. He pulled out a crumpled pack of cigarettes and lit one. Realizing he might be speaking to an art critic, he offered the tall man a smoke. The man declined.

"So what'd ya think?" Perry asked half-intimidated, half-cockily.

There was a long moment of silence, then the tall man shrugged, snubbing Perry, and started walking away. With every step taken, Perry felt his rage starting to swell. It was as if the man was stepping on his art, crushing it underfoot. No one, absolutely no one, insulted his work. The man took about ten steps before a barrage of insults started flying.

"FUCK YOU, YOU STUCK-UP DICKHEAD! ALL

I ASKED FOR WAS YOUR OPINION, ASSHOLE.
SMALL TALK PERHAPS? NOT BLOOD, JUST AN
ARTISTIC FUCKING TIP OF SOME SORT."

The tall man turned around slowly. The room
grew smaller as he walked right back to where
Perry stood. The artist felt himself being dwarfed.

"You want a tip, boy?"

Perry firmly stood his ground although he was
quite worried about what was going to go down.
The man could squash him if he wanted; it wouldn't
be the first time his mouth had gotten him knocked
around. But this was his exhibit. No one, absolutely
no one, would piss on his parade.

The tall man dug into his alligator wallet, removed a crisp one-hundred-dollar bill, and handed
it to Perry.

"Don't take yourself so seriously," the stranger
offered. The two men stared at each other, challenging one another to get out of line and respecting
each other for not backing down. When the danger
passed, the stranger started walking away again.

"Hey, mister," Perry called out. The tall man
turned around and saw the one-hundred-dollar bill
in flames.

Some things never change, he thought before returning to Perry.

They never formally introduced themselves. They
just began chatting, verbally sparring, feeling each
other out. The blows were soft and easily blocked as
neither man wanted to go for the throat. Not yet
anyway. They exchanged artistic views, debated,
and so forth. Perry found that the only friends he
found interesting were the ones who could stimu-
late him mentally. He enjoyed a good challenge and
by the time they'd left the empty gallery, they almost
felt comfortable together.

Xavier Prest had a subtle warmth beneath his solid exterior. He wasn't the type that easily warmed up to strangers. He was knowledgeable on just about every topic and had a certain old-world charm to him. His black eyes reminded Perry of onyx. He had a long crooked nose and rarely smiled. When he did he meant it and when he started laughing it was hard to stop him. A gray-streaked head of thick black hair topped his six-foot-nine frame. Perry had no idea how old the man was but was sure he was at least twenty years his senior.

A cab took them downtown to a trendy bar called Insider Trading where only chic, beautiful people, were welcome. The air reeked of young money and the patrons were the epitome of plastic. Danceable twelve-inch versions of songs by 3rd Bass, the Clash, and Salt N' Pepa pumped out of the bar's high-tech sound system. Fashion statements by Armani, Ralph Lauren, Gucci, Polo, Calvin Klein, etc., were the status quo as were top-shelf drinks, cellular phones, hard bodies (enhanced by steroids), and imported beer.

Perry and his new friend made themselves comfortable at the end of the bar, away from most of the chaos while a PM Dawn groove made the women sway around them. Their conversations ranged from artists they respected and whether art imitates life or vice versa to whether the Dodgers had a chance of winning the pennant. Politics, religion, and classic cars were debated. Several people at the bar knew Perry, but when they tried to break into the conversation they were quickly cut off. He was too captivated to share this dialogue with anyone.

Then Nova strutted over.

The large man eyed her from across the room and almost hypnotically dragged her to them. Perry actually felt Xavier's breathing get slower and heavier, like he was having a hard time getting enough oxygen. In a matter of seconds, Xavier had taken a serious fancy to her and this angered Perry.

"Hi, Perry," the sexy twenty-two-year-old said, her seductive voice deep. She was dressed to impress in a slinky black Giorgio di Sant' Angelo wool knit dress, fuck-me pumps, Armani sunglasses, and a pair of James Savitt diamond-and-gold earrings. Perry was unimpressed by the tall, lanky blonde. He barely even acknowledged her. Offended, the bombshell quickly left after spotting someone else she knew.

"Perry, that sure was one pretty woman you offended."

"It was a guy."

"*No,*" Xavier said, completely shocked.

"Yes, my worldly friend. That was Nova, Nova China," Perry replied, smiling knowingly. Perry dropped another drink and let the large man absorb what had just happened.

"What?" he asked, thoroughly puzzled.

"That was Nova China, *say it fast . . .*"

They both broke out in laughter and ordered more drinks. Whoever this old fucker was, he sure could pound booze, Perry thought, graciously accepting another shot of Finlandia and a Grolsch. Simple motor functions were becoming more and more difficult to perform as the drinks took their toll.

"You don't mind if I just call you 'X,' do ya?"

"As a matter of fact I do," Xavier declared, slowly sipping a brandy.

"Good," Perry replied cockily, and they both laughed again. The bar was thinning out before the two men had had enough for one evening. Like an enthralled couple on their first date, neither wanted to call it an evening but unfortunately it was getting late. Several hours had passed in what had felt like minutes.

"I feel like I already know you," Perry explained awkwardly.

"You do, my friend . . . . Another drink?"

Perry accepted.

In the weeks to come, the friendship between them grew rapidly. It wasn't just a casual friendship, but rather, an intense relationship. The attraction was unusually powerful and so far both men had decided to just go with it. Perry's old lovers were dropped like bad habits and the two rarely went a day without seeing one another. There was instant loyalty and intimacy.

But no sex.

Perry sat on the floor of his studio apartment, stroking his pet skunk, Pepe, and wondering why Xavier hadn't made a pass at him. Dressed in a white Comme des Garcons T-shirt, a black baseball cap with the words DINOSAUR JR. on it, and Polo boxers, the artist was visibly upset. He'd been with X almost every day for four weeks and it wasn't like they hadn't thought about sex. In one way, he was glad that Xavier hadn't tried to put the moves on him. He didn't want to go through the postintercourse guilt that was inevitable after friends became lovers. But then again, it did bother his sexual ego. In his mind, anyone, woman or man, who didn't desire him was fucked in the head.

The door rattled, startling Pepe. Perry held it close to his body as his guest walked in. Xavier's ever-present walking stick clicked loudly, announcing his arrival. As usual, he wore a trench coat and dark shades. He'd brought Perry a bottle of 1800

Cuervo Gold as well as Courvoisier for himself. Greetings were exchanged. After removing his coat and sunglasses, and experiencing some difficulty from his lame leg, Xavier joined the artist on the hardwood floor.

"How's Pepe?" Xavier asked as he reached out to pet the skunk. Perry shrugged as the skunk freed itself and trotted away.

"Is something bothering you?"

"Yeah, X, something is bothering me. For the past month you've been my best friend. I've told you everything yet I really don't know a fuckin' thing about you. What's up with that?"

Outside in the hallway, another couple was arguing loudly as they walked down the stairs. Xavier sensed the inevitable, the insecure side of Perry's personality was showing itself. *Artists are such simpleminded creatures*, X thought to himself.

"I've seen you almost every day and night yet you insist on going out one night of the week alone, why?" Perry asked, unsuccessfully trying to hide his jealous anger.

There was a long silence. Xavier definitely was not in the mood for this, not now anyway. He felt too damn good. He opened his bottle and took a long swig. Perry stood up. He felt something increasing, the pressure was coming to a boil. It wouldn't be long, just a matter of seconds before the artist exploded. He tried to control the demons inside his head but couldn't.

"I saw you last night with that fuckin' sleaze! Of all the freaks in Los Angeles, Nova China turns you on? Wha'samatter, I ain't good enough for you? You fuckin' no good backstabber!" Perry spat.

"You wouldn't understand."

"Lemme guess, *you're a junkie.*"

"No," X replied, trying to keep from smiling.

"Then try me, motherfucker!"

Xavier took another long hit off the bottle. The booze felt soothing. Now was as good a time as any to come clean.

"Take a drink first."

"FUCK YOU," Perry barked, and threw the tequila bottle against a wall, shattering it everywhere.

"Typical."

That answer hurt. Perry wanted to fight but thought twice about it. Instead, he took off his hat and flung it at Xavier.

"Remember how I told you we'd been friends before? It's true. I wasn't lying or making it up to get into your pants. Getting in your pants would've been easy," X calmly explained.

"My name changes every time I want it to. Yours would too if you were almost three hundred years old. Why do you think I know so much about art? I've watched true art created as it was meant to be. Not by some arrogant punks who thought they were pushing new standards, but by the greats. The Russian, Konstantin Dmitriyevich Bal'mont, Friedrich Nietzsche, and Ishikawa Takuboku all said more in one verse of their poetry than you've been able to accomplish in a lifetime. Why? Because they understood the passion of expression. Before you try to imitate Salvador Dali, Picasso, or Claude Monet, you should first understand their works."

Perry wished he had not smashed the tequila bottle. X had hurt him where few people dared, by challenging the integrity of his work. X offered his bottle. Perry snatched it and chugged the smooth-tasting brandy. After a few pulls from the bottle, he felt more together.

This is bullshit, he thought, wiping his wet lips.

He wanted a real explanation about why X was
fucking another man, not some Shirley MacLaine
bullshit about past lives and reincarnation.

"What's your real name then?

"My original name, my birth name?" asked Xavier, caught off guard. It had been a very long time.
Perry nodded but received no answer. The silence
was broken by the skunk darting across the floor.

"Remember when you were a little kid and
thought God was being unfair, not letting you par-
ticipate in sports because you had asthma? That's
because in a past life you had this very stupid thing
for having people stub cigarettes out on your chest,
especially when you were stoned or drunk."

Perry's hands tightly clutched his chest and were
slightly trembling. The massive man moved closer
and hugged him tightly, firmly. X hated seeing his
friends hurt. Silently, they shared the bottle until it
was almost dry. Then the artist stood up on wobbly
wheels, fetched two ice-cold Heineken bottles from
the refrigerator, and returned. Although still quite
reluctant to believe anything X said, he was starting
to regain his strut. No old-timer would bring him
down that easily.

"How do I know you're not just jerking my chain?
I mean, you've seen me take hits off my inhaler. Big
fuckin' deal."

"Because I know more secrets about you. Shall I
continue?"

Perry nodded.

"When you were little you used to cry hysterically
in cars. For no apparent reason, you hated cars. All
the other kids loved cars, especially fast ones, but
you were scared of cars. Even now, I'd wager you're
still uncomfortable riding in a car," X said.

"And if my instincts are correct, which they usually are, I'll bet your father used to call you 'the little bastard,' " Xavier added, knowingly.

Perry's jaw fell open. He couldn't believe what he'd just heard. He hadn't heard that phrase, that nickname that his mother hated so, since he was five years old. That was the capper. X was not some con artist pulling a cruel hoax to get out of being busted for cheating on him. There was something to all of this. Exactly what he wasn't sure but too much was true to be a coincidence. He listened silently like a small child to his incredible past. He felt fascinated and depressed at the same time.

"We were best friends back then. Sure we fought and you did a lot of nasty things but it was usually you that got hurt in the long run. And that hurt me. Seeing you hurt. It's taken me a long time to get over that day."

"What day?" Perry asked.

After a long pause, Xavier cleared his throat and, slightly intoxicated, explained, "I was there when you died. You were literally torn in half. I limped away. That's why I need the stick."

Xavier shifted his body trying to find a more comfortable way to sit on the floor, took a sip from his beer, and continued, "We were on our way to see the car races, you loved the races, and we had a terrible fight. As usual, you were stoned and kept rambling on and on. Even when I didn't fight back you kept pushing the issue. We were late and you were driving like a maniac. Then you went nuts! You said 'I'm gonna kill us, I'll do it.' I dared you so you drove head-on into a curve, *smiling the whole time.*"

Perry lit up a cigarette. Xavier wished he smoked. This was extremely painful. He'd carried this secret around like the permanent damage he'd done to his leg that day.

"What was my name?" Perry asked.

"What difference does it make?" X yelled, feeling anguished and frustrated. The booze was taking its toll on him and the only people who don't lie are small children and drunks. Xavier was getting ready to spill his guts.

"Because I want to know."

"I shouldn't have told you this much. Not yet," Xavier explained, hoping Perry would drop the issue.

"I have to know," the younger man replied, his glazed eyes demanding an answer. Xavier wondered whether he should tell. Most people can't handle things they don't understand. They won't accept new teachings. And even worse, he could lose Perry altogether.

"Dean," Xavier reluctantly mumbled. As the name came out, he felt regret over what he was doing. Things had gone too far.

"Wha'?"

"Jim."

"Spell it out, X," Perry drunkenly insisted.

"Jimmy Dean . . . ."

Perry was afraid that was what he'd heard yet hoped it was true. It reaffirmed his belief that he was destined for greatness. He had always identified with the counterculture cult hero, the romantic outlaw. He knew inside his heart he was an unappreciated star. X's information proved that his beliefs were true. He sighed heavily, vainly. He stood up, looked across the room, and proudly stared at himself in the mirror.

Fuck, he was James Dean reincarnated.

Then reality kicked in.

What kind of asshole did Xavier take him for? Any James Dean fan knew all of that information. He'd probably told Xavier about his fear of driving. A tremor of embarrassment shook through his body and froze a reluctant grin on his lips. Perry felt like smacking himself. What a story, and even worse, he couldn't believe that he almost swallowed it.

"Then how come you didn't die?" Perry asked coldly, arrogantly.

The tone of Perry's voice offended Xavier. This snot-faced kid had almost brought him to tears, forcing him into telling something he'd tried erasing for so long, and now he had the nerve to cop an attitude.

"Because, my long-lost friend, they may call you the Vampire of Melrose, but I truly am a vampire."

Perry quickly made his way to a window in the living room. This charade had gone on far too long. It was bad enough he'd snagged him cruising with a skank like Nova China. Now he was Bela Lugosi.

"You're tapped out, Grampa. Go back to your sweetheart's crib, you fuckin' old freak."

"Quit it, you big baby. After all, I'm not the one who wore some gallery owner's greased fist like an obscene bracelet," Xavier countered.

"The only reason I told you that story was so you'd know what I went through to get that exhibit."

The sufferings of the artiste.*"

"Don't use that condescending tone with me," Perry snapped back. He contemplated kicking Xavier in the face while the big man was still on the floor. At least this way he'd have a fighting chance.

"You're right, I should feel sorry for you. Poor baby had to sleep with someone he wasn't attracted to . . . Isn't life miserable. You've always been a hedonist. A selfish, jealous, self-centered hedonist. You think I don't know about your others? I've seen the tramps who come here after I've left, so don't give me any flack."

How did he know? Perry wondered. He thought he'd been slick, leaving no clues or evidence. He grew angered and defensive as he took a swig off his Heineken bottle.

"What the fuck, you expect me to keep waiting for you? It's been a goddamn month," Perry countered. He took a sip from his beer.

"Try forty years."

"This is bullshit, man. Fuckin' bullshit, so take your bitchin' Nosferatu self the fuck outta here and stay out of my life," Perry snarled, serious as a heart attack.

"*What?*" Xavier said, shocked, deeply hurt.

"You heard me, asshole, I said get the fuck out."

"I've traveled all over the world trying to find you and now you're throwing me out?"

"ARE YOU DEAF? AM I STUTTERING? GET OUT!"

"You don't believe me, is that it?"

"GET THE FUCK OUT, DAMMIT!"

"NO!" Xavier yelled, and, using the walking stick for leverage, pulled himself up off the floor. It took some effort but once he was up, he was fine. He took several angry steps toward the cocky artist and backhanded him so quickly that Perry didn't see it coming. X's hand felt like it was wrapped in steel and floored Perry. Blood dripped from his right nostril. One particularly thick droplet dangled but refused to fall from Perry's silver nose ring.

This just isn't fair, X thought. *First the little prick gets me all wound up emotionally, then he starts bleeding on me.* Hard-to-control urges swam through his body and it took every ounce of self-restraint not to slurp the crimson out of his friend's nose.

"GET OUT OR I'LL CALL THE FUCKIN' COPS!" Perry yelled, sounding frightened yet determined, wiping the blood from beneath his nose with the back of his hand.

"I've searched all over the world for your return. I've waited . . . I should have made you a vampire last time when I had the chance to but I didn't. *That was my mistake*. You've got to understand, I've been around for a long, long time. It's lonely losing your friends every fifty or sixty years, but then again, would anyone want the same lover for three hundred years?"

Perry quickly got to his feet, then sat down on his couch. He forced himself to listen to X's living dead rap. He wasn't falling for it, but he didn't want to get hit by the huge man again either. He wondered when Xavier would cut the Dracula bullshit. It wasn't an alibi, it was an insult to his intelligence.

"You're my best friend, always have been. I wanted you to live forever—"

"So why didn't you do something?" Perry snapped, holding a Kleenex to his bleeding nose.

"This isn't the easiest decision in the world to make. I've met thousands of people through my travels. *What if I bit Karl Marx and made him invincible? What about Hitler?* What about you? For the past month I've been trying to decide if you're ready for something like vampirism. I have to kill innocent people and that's a difficult decision to make every week. I kill to survive. This isn't like those Anne Rice novels. Everyone wishes they could live forever but to what extent are they willing to go? I kill people . . . . I choose who dies and who doesn't . . . . I hate playing God!"

"C'mon, Count Chocula, or is it God, bite *this*," Perry disdainfully snapped, holding his crotch.

"You've always been a selfish, one-way brat, imagine if you were immortal? Getting rid of you would be nearly impossible. I don't know if I could put up with you forever."

"I don't want to be immortal. Especially by someone as immoral as yourself. Eat my fuck, fuck you, *and get the fuck out!*"

Xavier was stunned. It had been a long time since he'd felt this empty or alone. His massive body felt hollow. Here he was offering his best friend immortality and due to blind, immature, petty jealousy he was being rejected. Perry's vicious tone ripped him and left him cold. Colder than he normally felt.

Dejected, X turned away. Once again he'd lost his true love. He began wondering if he'd ever find happiness in the eternal life he was condemned to. He'd seen and experienced a lot, too much for most mortals to comprehend, but regardless of how interesting someone or something was, the thrill eventually wore thin. That is, with the exception of the soul standing in front of him. And X hated himself for being so attracted and interested in someone who was poisonous. Someone who was selfish, self-centered, and downright conceited. Someone whose perpetual hoity-toity attitude drove him to drink even more alcohol than he normally did. And he drank a lot. Like it or not, there was something mystical about Perry's arrogance that completely enthralled X.

And besides, he was too damn sexy to resist.

Approaching the front door, Xavier decided to give Perry one final chance. A solemn silence filled the living room as the tall man turned around and treacherously smiled. An icy chill tickled Perry's spine. He couldn't believe what he was seeing. No matter how hard he blinked, the vision remained. Coming toward him, with his mouth stretching as wide as it would go, was Xavier. So taut was his mouth that his thin lips were turning a purplish-blue. Much like the rest of his anatomy, even his teeth, and especially his incisors, were large.

When Xavier, or any vampire, bites into someone, the euphoric effect is beyond words. It is comparable to a powerfully potent injection of crystal meth mixed with dilaudid. The more blood consumed, the higher the vampire gets. The higher it gets, the more of a feeding frenzy it goes into. It's an uncontrollable bloodlust that can only end when the victim is dead. If the victim survives the bite, he or she becomes undead, a vampire. Xavier always made sure he didn't slip up and let any undeserving victims survive. Perry was one of the few people whose life he wouldn't completely drain when he bit him. It had been over one hundred and thirty years since he'd last "made" another vampire. Once started, feeding was almost impossible to control, let alone stop, but for Perry, his best friend, he'd give it his best effort.

"Get the fuck away from me!" Perry barked weakly, and picked up a heavy marble ashtray. He could hear slight growls coming from his undead friend. Perry baseball-pitched his almost empty beer bottle as hard as he could. With his solid oak walking stick, Xavier swatted the bottle in mid-flight, shattering it. A spray of glass pebbles rained down loudly on the hardwood floor.

"I love you," declared Xavier, dropping his cane, stalking forward.

"You don't want to do this. I'm warning you,"

Perry pleaded but he didn't have a chance. "X, you don't want to do this . . . . No, please . . ."

Xavier grabbed Perry, wrapped him up in a bear hug, and sank his sharp incisors into Perry's jugular vein. He gently gnawed while his tongue lapped in a combination of biting and kissing. Although it only took Xavier a few seconds to swell into a full erection, this wasn't about sex. He had never felt closer to, or more nervous about, anyone than he did now. Would this be the love he'd searched the world over for?

There was only one way to find out.

He hoped he wasn't being too rough on his friend's neck. Rich thick crimson filled up Xavier's mouth but instead of gulping, he slowly sipped, trying to keep his reason. If he gave in to bloodlust then his lover would certainly die. Somewhere between fear and ecstasy, X fought to maintain his concentration while keeping a steady grip on his squirming victim. More coppery burgundy went down his throat. Regardless of how hard he focused, his mental circuitry was erratic. Seduction wanted him to give in to his addiction but he valiantly fought off the urges to frenzy.

Perry couldn't believe this was really happening. A never-ending tide of perplexing thoughts flooded his panicky mind. X wasn't lying about anything. Unbelievable as it might seem, everything he'd said was true. Unlike the gothic legend, there was nothing (other than certain eccentricities like his disdain of organized religions and garlic salt) that would've made him suspicious. Xavier's flesh did not burn upon contact with the sun. He didn't have to sleep in dirt. As far as he knew, Xavier couldn't fly like a bat or turn himself into mist. He was a normal person. Well, as normal as a person who periodically needs to feed on blood can be.

And most important, he'd told the truth.

All of Perry's efforts at resistance were abandoned as he gave in to immortality. Every nerve tingled as each fiber of flesh danced in an electricity all its own. He softly panted as his knees grew weak. This was an unusually sensuous sensation, somewhat like reverse orgasm. He closed his eyelids and felt himself slipping euphorically away. Perry felt a tidal wave of joy rush through his body, a body that was destined to live forever.

Then his eyes sprang open.

He tried shaking his large friend off but no blows had any effect on the vampire. Xavier sucked the blood out easily, not trying to drain, but rather to preserve. Two thin streaks of blood dribbled down Perry's neck as did two large tears on his face.

In a rare moment of humility, he actually felt something for someone other than himself. Perry, who prided himself as being obdurate, couldn't believe that friendship and love as pure as Xavier's actually existed. More tears came. These past few minutes were tragically enlightening. Perry had learned more about himself in the arms of Xavier than he ever cared to know. He wanted to see the world and share the love that X spoke of but he had his reservations. There were no perfect worlds. Dreams swirled and crashed before ever having a chance to take off as Perry realized he could never be monogamous or faithful to anyone other than himself.

The Nerve

The forest was old growth that had been there for hundreds of years. Moss barnacles covered every tree's bottom and spread slowly, methodically, draining the life from their hosts. Moisture filled the air, causing a miniature greenhouse effect; therefore, every tree, bush, and plant in the forest was larger than ordinary.

The sound of birds arguing among themselves was predominant. Occasionally a plane would zoom by, or off in the distance a truck's horn would blare. Nature loomed overhead, threatening to swallow Sandy and Daryl as they traveled a well-worn trail. The summer had been filled with more than its share of one-hundred-plus-degree days as well as all-night keggers. As long as the forest guaranteed privacy, high school boys would go there to shoot BB guns, smoke pot, and feel up girls. Local police had given up on trying to keep kids out of the woods. There were too many escape routes. NO TRESPASSING signs had been posted (and used as targets by pellet gun sharpshooters) but to date no one that either boy knew had actually been busted for trespassing.

Deep within the heavy forest, the boys had

planted their yearly supply of illegal cannabis seeds.
If nobody had accidentally stumbled across their
crop, the plants should be plentiful and ready for
picking. Last year's tallest plant was four feet tall
but with the heat wave currently going on, a new
world's record could easily be smoked.

Daryl Nieuwendyk's long strides were beginning
to tire the out-of-shape Sandy Sanderson. At sixteen, Sandy had been smoking at least two packs of
Marlboros a day for the past four years. He was
starting to show early signs of emphysema although
he didn't realize it. Sweat ran off his brow as well as
down his back. His breath was shortening and his
pulse pounding.

He needed a cigarette.

Sandy's red-and-green flannel shirt was missing
two buttons from the midsection and the red T-shirt
underneath poked through like a stoned pupil. The
boy's medium-sized frame was showing signs of too
much beer and pasta. His round belly hung down
over his waist. Faded Lee jeans hugged his thick,
stocky legs and clung tightly around the ankles of
his dark brown hiking boots. Even in the dead of an
upstate winter, these steel-toe boots kept his large
feet warm.

Sandy's facial features were unspectacular. He
looked like thousands of other faceless students. His
tiny eyes were buggy and usually red. His small
nose was wide and puglike. Zits usually decorated
his mug. His skin often broke out after taking too
much LSD or mescaline but right now it was pretty
clear. His haircut was uneven but at least it was
free. Greasy strawberry-blond hair, which was short
trying to be long, fell alongside his chubby face.
Like so many other high school students, a large

pirate's hoop dangling from his left earlobe declared his rebellion.

Sandy prided himself on being his class's waste case, but living up to his reputation was taking its toll on him. He often forgot things, even in the middle of doing them, and simple schoolwork had become impossible. He'd been kicked out of Lincoln High for selling pot. At the time he thought getting busted was kind of cool, especially since he thought it might help get him laid, but now he was having second thoughts. There was nothing cool about having all your friends return to school and go through all the normal teenage rites of passage, while you're at home alone.

"Dude, we ain't in a race," yelled Sandy, who was carrying a rolled-up Hefty garbage bag.

Daryl turned, stopped, and placed his hands on his waist. His muscular V-shape was that of Mamaroneck High's junior varsity football and lacrosse team captain. While Sandy still looked like a boy, Daryl was showing the first signs of manhood. His brown eyes were warm, intelligent, those of a leader. His nose was neither too long nor short and his unblemished cheekbones added strength and character to his features.

At times, especially during the summer when he tanned bronze, he resembled an American Indian. His shaggy, light-brown hair rested on his shoulders. The usually quiet, slightly shy boy stood five feet eleven and a solid one hundred sixty pounds. There was no body fat anywhere. He was the athlete every cheerleader lusted after. Although he tried concealing his extracurricular activities, his coaches knew he partied, but as long as he produced on the playing field, they would turn a blind eye.

Like clockwork, Daryl's attire consisted of one of his many jerseys. Today he was wearing his white mesh lacrosse jersey with a black number 7 on it. It was last year's jersey but the coach let him keep it for leading the team in scoring. He wore multicolored Bermuda shorts that drooped past his knees and high-top Reeboks.

The two boys had grown up together, Sandy being a few months older, and were rarely apart longer than Daryl's sports practices or games. Wherever one was, the other was sure to show up eventually. Daryl protected Sandy from hostile jocks who wanted to rip off his money or drugs.

Sandy walked up to Daryl and blew a large cloud of cigarette smoke in his friend's face.

"Does that mean you wanna sleep with me?" Daryl asked, fanning smoke away. Like many hypocrites, he loved marijuana but hated cigarettes. Sandy had declared war. Daryl stuck his finger up his right nostril and dug until he scooped out a large-sized booger. He showed it to Sandy, then began chasing him.

"Fuckstick, get the fuck outta here," Sandy yelled, running, trying not to laugh. Sandy huffed as he stayed less than a foot away from the green snot. The tormenting smirk never left Daryl's face. He chased Sandy until they reached the plants. Then they both stopped dead in their tracks. The smallest plant was three feet tall and the largest was well over five. Sandy couldn't believe his eyes. He'd found heaven.

"Holy oversized vegetation, Batman," Sandy said in awe, not forgetting about the green nugget on Daryl's finger. The jock wiped the slimy booger on a plant leaf, leaving it in open view.

The minutes passed by quickly. Sandy kept moving, shuffling, doing things while Daryl waited nervously. He had never seen so much pot. What if the cops knew about these plants and were staking the area out? What if they got caught carrying a garbage bag full of marijuana back to Sandy's house?

What ifs and paranoid jitters were something he could deal with for this much grass.

Still in awe of their small plantation, Daryl watched a sparrow overhead. Quietly, so not to startle the bird, he picked up a rock and took aim. His quarterback accuracy was close but not on the money. He missed the bird by less than four inches. Noisily, the bird flew to the safety of another tree, voicing its displeasure and warning other birds of the unfriendly intruders. Surprised that he missed, Daryl shrugged his shoulders and rejoined his gleefully smiling partner.

THUD.

A noise close by awoke him from his state of dormancy as the craving filled his primitive senses. His nostrils picked up faint scents that moments ago were not there. Saliva filled up his mouth. He could feel an arousal sweeping through his entire body but mostly in his stomach.

Soon his hunger would be unbearable.

His shelter was a makeshift underground cave that he'd burrowed years ago. The hidden cave was always damp and moldy but suited his needs. It enabled him to sleep away the days and, every so often, hunt.

Moisture seeped through his tattered red-and-white plaid pants although none of the colors except dirt were really visible. The bottoms were ragged and flapped around his muscular calves. The pants stretched around his large waist but were unbuttonable. It didn't matter, he didn't know how to button pants. Scrapes and old cuts festered on his scarcely covered legs. Dark brown and blackish residue remained on his dirt-soiled, leathery flesh. The bottom of his callused left foot was infected with gangrene and itched badly. He hunched into the fetal position and scratched relentlessly at his infected foot.

There was no relief.

He scratched harder but the irritating sensation would not go away. Yellow pus remained under his claws from the scabs he'd broken with his three-inch-long fingernails. Blood, pus, and dirt mixed on top of his fingers. He raised his moist fingers to his chapped lips and gently sucked.

White clouds rolled over the tree-hidden boys. It would take someone unfamiliar with these woods hours to find his or her way back into town although the road was less than a half-mile away. Getting lost (and staying that way) was quite conceivable. Due north, deeper into the woods, was Hampshire Golf Course. A ritzy whites-only course that the boys often trespassed on in search of stray golf balls or harassable golfers.

Feeling like an illegal-alien migrant worker, Sandy uprooted plants, examined the thick inch-long buds that decorated the five-foot plants, and loaded up the Hefty bag. He had saved only the best seeds from his best pot. These plants were hybrids of Thai-stick, Maui, Indica, Vietnamese, and other exotic reefers. Why grow garbage? he reasoned.

Daryl stood silent, watching for intruders. Like anyone involved in a criminal act, the longer they spent, the higher the risk of getting caught. The amount of free marijuana they'd managed to grow was absurd. Everything—the location they'd selected, the hot weather, and their timing—had worked out just right. They'd be stoned for months, he thought, grinning.

Then his thoughts drifted to Karen and the grin disappeared.

She'd been his girl, his cheerleader, his steady, until recently. Why they'd broken up was still a mystery to him. Daryl swore he'd knock the first guy's head off who tried scamming on her but so far no one had. At least no one he knew had. He'd been with other girls since they'd "officially" broken up but that wasn't his fault. If she wasn't willing to try to work it out then neither was he. According to this logic, it was her fault he was screwing other girls, mostly her girlfriends.

The couple had gone steady since the beginning of eighth grade. Almost three weeks had passed since they'd broken up. If she wasn't already seeing someone, which he'd heard she wasn't, it wouldn't be long until someone made some moves on her once school started. Karen's silky blond hair and gorgeous sky-blue eyes were enough to drive any schoolboy wild. She was beautiful, like the girls in *Playboy*'s college campus edition, but by no means an easy slut. Hell, it took her over two years to decide she was ready to lose her virginity. Using his wandering imagination, Daryl pictured her slim waist, tight stomach, and pert titties. She was smart, sexy, sweet, and available.

"Man, you'll never believe who I seen yesterday hanging out at the mall," Sandy said, still busy with the plants.

"Who?" Daryl replied, believing he knew the answer.

"Karen. She was looking hot too."

"*So?*"

Sandy read through his friend's front so he

dropped the topic, knowing Daryl would bring it back up in less than ten seconds. Seven seconds passed before a fidgety Daryl finally asked who Karen was with.

"Two seniors," Sandy replied, lying.

"Lemme get this straight, you saw *my Karen* with two motherfucking, cocksucking seniors. *Who the fuck were they?*"

"Your Karen??? I thought you said you were, like, way over that?"

"Yeah, well, I'm just looking out for her," Daryl replied, unable to hide his jealousy.

The warning light was on. Sandy's cruel joke had obviously gone too far. Hell, he hadn't been to the mall since he got caught shoplifting during Christmas. A nervous trickle of sweat ran down the side of his face. He lit a cigarette. Daryl read his friend's nervousness.

"Fatty, if you're lying . . . If you're lying about Karen, I'm gonna rip your tiny, microscopic pecker off and feed it to the squirrels."

Sandy began to giggle nervously. "Okay, okay, I was only joshing. *Oh look at me, I'm Mr. Tough guy, totally over my ex-girlfriend. Just don't talk about her.* Sheesh, what a grouch! Can't you take a motherfucking joke, eggbert?"

Daryl cocked his fist back and slowly walked over to Sandy.

"I'm gonna punch you in the neck."

"C'mon bro, A.C.A.C."

Daryl shrugged his shoulders but didn't really agree with the statement that "All chicks are cunts." To Sandy, his clenched fist looked huge. He knew Daryl wasn't going to really beat him up or anything but a dead arm or a dead leg appeared to be in the immediate future.

"I only said it 'cause I knew you were thinking about her."

Daryl stopped his forward progress and looked at Sandy. He dropped his fist after making Sandy swear to God he'd never pull that shit again. Sandy would have sworn to anything not to receive a few punches, and just as quickly as it had started, all was forgotten.

"But I did see your rubbernecked mama turning tricks at the bus stop," Sandy barked, neck bobbing up and down, and raised his fists. Daryl laughed at his chubby friend's remarkable ability to push any issue too damn far. "Too bad I didn't have a dollar or I would've got in line."

"Yeah, your mother's so old that when I told her to act her age, the bitch died," Daryl quickly countered.

"Your mama's got so much hair underneath her arms she looks like she got Buckwheat in a headlock!"

"Your mama's like a hockey team. She takes a shower after three periods!"

"What's the difference between a catfish and your mama? One has whiskers and smells bad. The other's a fish."

Both kids started cracking up.

Loose dark brown dirt fell off the plants' roots as Sandy yanked them out. The smell of thick earthy dirt became more prevalent with each plant removed. It wouldn't be very long before he was finished. Like a man possessed, he systematically uprooted each plant as quickly and carefully as possible. Daryl watched unamused. His mind was stuck on Karen.

* * *

In his own bizarre way, he looked like a mutated golfer. Nick Faldo from Hell or something. The red-and-blue patterns on his sweater were nearly invisible due to ground-in blood. Huge holes had worn through the wool sweater, exposing his callused hard chest. He wasn't very well-defined, but at seven feet three he was enormous. His ball-shaped stomach protruded nine inches farther than his fifty-two-inch chest, and scars, untreated abrasions, and festering scabs from previous battles decorated his massive torso. Fluids ran from his open wounds and had co-agulated, leaving little red patterns. His antibodies were extremely powerful and what would have killed an ordinary man was merely an irritation that he'd grown accustomed to.

He awoke groggy, wiped the dirt from his face, and stretched as far as he could in his tiny shelter, which wasn't very far. His joints ached from having slept in this damp place for so long. They always ached when he first awoke. Also, not having stretched out in nearly a month didn't help any. His muscles felt rock-stiff and sore. Tendons and cartilage in his knees cracked loudly as he slowly, carefully stood up. He removed the bushes that camouflaged the entrance to his subterranean shelter.

He stood up, feeling slightly revitalized. It had been a good sleep but enough was enough. Thick veins bulged out of powerful forearms, arms that could snap a full-grown moose's neck in half. Dirt-drenched claws extended from his wiggling fingers. The blood in his veins was starting to flow faster, more regularly. His metabolism, slowed during his sleep periods, was now picking up.

Although he had no eyes, he sensed that it was still daylight. Tiny scraggly white hairs hung off his pointed chin. He had no external ears but possessed

*an acute sense of hearing. Where he should have had
ears, there were dirty sunken crevices surrounded by
thick clusters of brown wax. His flat piggish nostrils
were rimmed in mucus. He tracked his prey using his
hearing and smell. With these two well-developed
senses, he hunted and survived. Judging by the wind
and the temperature, it would be safe to start the hunt
in approximately an hour. He ducked back down into
his cave and waited.*

Sandy reached into his back pocket and produced
a decent-sized piece of aluminum foil. While fidgeting with the wrinkled-up foil, he stopped and looked
up. The azure sky was beginning to darken and
pleasant summer temperatures were beginning to
drop. Pretty soon it would be safe to leave the woods
under the cover of darkness. He looked at Daryl,
who was off in dreamland.

"Hey, Romeo, help me, ya dumb fuck."

"What?" Daryl replied, his mind still elsewhere.

"Get some twigs and stuff."

"Go fuck yourself."

"I'm serious. Be useful or you ain't getting any."

Reluctantly, he began scrounging up twigs and
sticks. He wanted to leave. There might be a message at home from Karen or something. Beneath his
lacrosse jersey he could hear his heavy heart pounding, the chains wrapped around it loudly clanking
together. After a few minutes of gathering, it
dawned upon Daryl that the faster they tested the
grass, the sooner he could split. Besides, a little
buzz never hurt anyone.

A small fire sent black smoke spiraling into the
dimming sky above. Sandy had wrapped several
buds of homegrown in the foil and was carefully
letting them cook. He knew he should let the plants

completely dry out but why wait? When he got home, he'd dry the pot in his parents' microwave oven. This was just an experiment brought upon by impatience. His thoughts flashed to last year's crop. It had been smokable dirt weed but nothing exciting. There was light yellow and red sprinkled among the green buds, a good sign.

Ten minutes or so passed. Sandy removed the aluminum foil from the flame and inspected its contents. The buds were a lot drier than before but by no means perfect. Testing time. Sandy packed his ever-present pipe and stuffed as much in the large bowl as possible before packing it down.

The sweet-tasting smoke filled his lungs and much to his amazement tasted almost like Indica. He couldn't believe it as he blew out the smoke and took another hit. He passed the pipe to Daryl, who sucked deeply into his athletic lungs. His chest expanded and his face turned red. Tears swelled in his unsuspecting eyes. Then he coughed a loud bronchial cough.

"Holy fuck . . ."

"Good shit, huh?" Sandy said enthusiastically, eager for more. Daryl nodded and passed the pipe back. He couldn't believe that this was homegrown. *Shit, they could sell this stuff.*

"You gonna try to get back in school this year?"

"What the fuck for?" Sandy barked, wishing that Daryl hadn't asked. A part of him really wanted to be back in school but unfortunately he didn't know how to go about being reinstated without losing face.

"I just figured you might wanna."

"Why? I always got people coming by my house to score pot and then they party me out afterward. I got cable, a VCR, food," Sandy explained, trying to

make it sound like his situation was his by choice.
Daryl had known him long enough to know better.

"Yeah, but what about the future? What are you
gonna do then?"

"Fuck the future," Sandy countered, and took another hit.

They passed the pipe until all of its contents were
gone. Afterward there was a long silence. The
sounds of tree branches swaying and wildlife getting ready for another night consumed the stoned
boys. Stoned and hungry, Daryl informed Sandy
that he had to leave.

"You're fuckin' buzzed out," stated Sandy with
tiny red eyes and a cheesy smile tacked to his lips.

"*I'm too high*," replied Daryl slowly, and laughed.
His exposed legs were starting to get cold. The Bermuda shorts weren't cutting it.

"Check it out," Sandy said, pointing at a tree
branch. Daryl's eyes followed Sandy's finger upward. This pot was more potent than any grass
they'd smoked all year long. He pointed to a tall oak
tree where a squirrel chased its companion in a fast-
paced friendly game of tag. Both boys watched mesmerized as the squirrels defied gravity, leaping from
branch to branch, until they disappeared.

"The li'l fella wants some poon," Daryl declared,
and laughed.

"*Yeah, looks like you chasing Karen*," Sandy said,
and received a well-deserved punch in the arm.
Then he started loading another bowl.

"Dude, I'm stoned enough," Daryl declared.

"Dude, you can never be stoned enough," Sandy
explained, and continued packing the pipe.

*Thick, oil-like saliva frothed out of the sides of his
mouth and slowly crept down about a half-inch.*

Blistered sandpaper lips held in a tiny row of badly yellowing-brown razors. A thick bluish-red tongue sat deep in the well of his mouth.

Ancient skin, weatherbeaten from years of surviving freezing temperatures, protected his large skeletal structure. Off his face, jowls sagged and hung down loosely. His brown flesh looked like charred leather. A thick eight-inch flap of dead skin hung down from the top of his massive cranium and dangled above his flaring nostrils. When he turned his head to the side, the flap also swung to the side. The flesh flap looked like a grotesque miniature elephant's trunk.

Tiny dirt-caked rolls of flesh were piled on top of each other bringing his humongous head to a dull point, completely covering his eyes. The summer's heat loosened the soot in the crevices and rolls on his head, causing black beads of sweat to flow. Across his grotesque face, varicose veins were visible beneath his leathery skin, big blue veins that tracked all over his head, forming no legible patterns, ending nowhere.

Inborn mutated instincts compelled him to survive. And that was all he knew how to do: kill, eat, and rest. When he hungered, a hellfire desire drove him. He'd jumped into lakes and torn apart ducks. He'd cornered wild raccoons, skunks, and rabbits, and stomped them. Any adversity that nature had thrown in his path, he'd met and conquered. The deep forest of Westchester County was his terrain and the other inhabitants knew it. Birds warned one another with their squeaky songs of danger. Small mammals avoided his hole and mated on the other side of the golf course's lake. The wildlife knew of his existence and dreaded his monthly awakening, because nothing was safe.

* * *

The woods were getting quite dark and neither boy knew how long they had been gone. They sat on a fallen log smoking more pot, debating the merits of the latest Almighty compact disc and how cool it would be if the four original members of Kiss decided to put their makeup back on for one final tour. Daryl took one last hit off the pipe and was beyond toast. Handing the pipe back to Sandy took a lot of effort but the mission was successful. Sandy continued toking until every speck was gone.

Their stoned heads hummed like minute pressure chambers. The woods were intense, fascinating. There were so many details to space out on. Sandy urinated on the small campfire and a cloud of piss smoke floated away while twigs crackled and popped. After finishing, he picked up the garbage bag full of reefer and hoisted the bulky sack over his shoulder. To Daryl, he looked like a degenerate Santa Claus.

"What was that?"

"What was what?" Sandy asked, lazily looking around.

"That noise."

"Who gives a rat's ass?"

"I heard something," Daryl declared, insisting he wasn't just being stoned and paranoid. He'd smoked enough pot over the past few years to know the difference between unsubstantiated fears and real danger, and he'd distinctly heard something. His pulse raced as his nervous eyes scanned about.

SNAP.

"See, I told ya." Daryl said. Sandy heard it too and the duo ducked down behind the log. Maybe the DEA had been waiting all summer to find out who was using these woods to grow marijuana. Sandy already had a police record. Daryl began scouting

the area Rambo-style. More rustling noises came
from deep inside the woods. The boys ducked behind the log they were sitting on earlier, waiting like
a pair of bumbling Ninjas for any unusual movement. The noise had come from deep in the woods
where there were no paths, just thick bushes. Daryl
could hear his chest pounding, threatening to give
him away, and his bladder threatened to burst. At
that very instant, he spotted a decent-sized rock and
snatched it up.

The sound of twigs breaking and approaching
footsteps grew in volume. Bushes were being
pushed aside as whatever was coming made its way
toward the boys. Sandy's stoned smirk had faded to
distress. The suspense became too much to with-
stand. Both boys poked their heads over the log to
look.

"Holy shit, it's Jason Voorhees," Daryl gasped,
trying to keep his tone down to a whisper but being
quite vocal.

"That ain't Jason, *it's the Nerve!*" Sandy replied.

The infamous Nerve. . . . Neither boy could believe what they were seeing but this wasn't some
sort of drug-induced vision. Approaching them was
the living embodiment behind the wives' tale about
the deformed unwanted baby that was left in the
woods to die but who lived on as a forest monster.
No one actually knew where the Nerve came from
or how it came to be. The story of the Nerve was
generations old, changing slightly from storyteller
to storyteller. There were dozens of variations, the
most popular being about an inbred deformity who
was left in the woods by ashamed parents. Instead
of starving, the Nerve had somehow survived, legend had it. No matter how ridiculous it seemed,
someone was always willing to swear on a stack of

Holy Bibles that they'd seen or knew someone who'd seen the Nerve. Now, here in the flesh, was the real-life boogeyman.

Both boys began praying to deaf gods as the beast trudged toward them. The thing with the grossly misproportioned head had followed the scent of burning marijuana, unaware of what he was hunting. Again, the Nerve stopped for a moment and sniffed the air like a dog. He'd smelled this scent before and it often led him to good-sized easy prey. After a few seconds, it started toward the fallen log. The fleshy flap bounced back and forth. Its footsteps were heavy and obtrusive. After lying low for as long as he could, Sandy stood up and flung the garbage bag filled with marijuana at the Nerve. With one quick instinctive swat, the Nerve shredded the plastic bag and sent marijuana showering about.

"FUCK IT!" Sandy yelled at the top of his lungs before taking off down the familiar trails. Bewildered, Daryl stood up, still holding a rock that was roughly the size of a softball. Like a blanket that offers no comfort, cold air tightly wrapped itself around him. How could his best friend leave him like that? Less than eight feet separated the Nerve and Daryl.

And then the Nerve charged toward him.

With all his strength, Daryl used his quarterback accuracy and nailed the Nerve in the stomach. It doubled over, holding its midsection. A little lower and the rock would've put the giant freak out of commission. Distorted screams filled the air as Daryl took off running, following his buddy's footsteps. Within thirty seconds, he overtook his slower out-of-shape friend.

"COME ON, YOU FAT FUCKIN' TUB O'LARD!" Daryl hysterically offered. With every stride, he felt the distance between him and Sandy increasing. The chunky kid was running as fast as he could. Regardless of how much effort he put forth, it seemed like he just couldn't get out of second gear. Hopefully, the rock had put the Nerve down long enough for the boys to escape.

The monster quickly regained its bearings and angrily chased after the boys. Using its instinct to guide him, the Nerve had a steady beat on the boys and was making up ground with each stride.

"DARYL!" Sandy yelled as the Nerve maneuvered within twenty feet of him. For as large as he was, the Nerve's strides were deerlike, long and graceful. He avoided any obstacle in his path with ease. With every stride, Sandy's lead shortened. With less than ten feet separating them, the chunky teen stopped running.

"SANDY!"

Sandy saw the Nerve's flap flapping as he approached him. *How the hell could something eyeless track him down so easily?* With one more stride, the Nerve would be on top of him.

"FUCKIN' SANDY!!!!" Daryl screamed, and stopped.

Just as the malformed brute was ready to pounce, Sandy threw a haymaker right fist that connected with the Nerve's unsuspecting jaw. The blow had little effect. It hurt Sandy's hand more than it slowed the giant's pursuit.

The Nerve picked the fat boy up and viciously slammed him face-first to the ground. Rolling waves of agony shot through his soft body but there was no relief. Dirt shot into his screaming mouth. The earth tasted like an unknown delicacy and brought a faint smirk to his dry lips. It was during that precise moment that Sandy realized that he and dirt would soon be one.

He tried rolling over and getting back to his feet but it was no use. The monster had him and wasn't about to let him escape. Human flesh offered little resistance as the beast sunk its dirty claws into the boy's throat and ripped outward. A disconnected jugular vein hung about and warm arterial spurts covered the monstrosity's feeding face. Sandy's esophagus was torn open by the Nerve's chattering teeth. He tried breathing but could only wheeze. It tickled him with disgust as air escaped through his torn throat. He fought for as long as he could. When the squeals ended, so did his misery. After he finally stopped kicking, the Nerve raised its gore-drenched hands over its conical head in victory.

Daryl felt everything in his stomach fly out. He took one final look at his best friend being eaten before resuming his sprint and kept running for all he was worth.

His legs acquired a mind of their own, cutting and darting around obstacles. The paranoid boy saw all kinds of misshapen monsters lurking in the shadows. Branches grabbed at him as he ran. He stumbled over every obstacle but nothing was going to stop his forward motion. Huffing on the brink of hysteria, Daryl made it out of the woods.

Why isn't there a cop around when you need one? he wondered, and began stumbling toward his house. When he got to the road that led to his house, he started screaming.

He lived less than ten minutes from the forest. Only two cars passed him on the scarcely used Flynn Road and neither paid the stunned-looking boy any attention. On Flynn Road, he passed

Sandy's house and started to run before tears could come.

After every few steps, he looked over his shoulder. His eyes refused to blink in case they missed anything, but it was obvious that the Nerve had given up on him. He continued jogging, one eye watching his back, until he arrived home.

The cream-colored two-story house was enclosed by six-foot hedges all around. *Finally safe*, he thought but not believing. He silently made his way inside, sneakers squeaking on the freshly waxed floor. His mother offered him dinner but he ignored her and walked to the bathroom, still stoned and in shock. After finishing the piss he'd been fighting since the woods, Daryl took a long, hard, studious look in the mirror. In the past twenty-five minutes, he'd aged and grown old. Wrinkles formed at the creases of his red eyes. He pulled the mirror open and looked inside the medicine cabinet. He thought about using Visine to get the red out but what was the point?

Recklessly, he began swallowing pills, any kind, by the handful. All different kinds of chalky M&M's melted in his mouth, not in his hands. He washed down whatever he was unable to dry-swallow with tap water, then quietly snuck out of the bathroom and into his bedroom.

The room was adorned with beer ads featuring bikini-wearing beauties, trophies, and framed newspaper clippings about himself. Until today, he'd loved the life he had. It was the suburban American dream in Surround Sound. Now he just wanted the fear to end. He sank deep into the queen-size bed and pulled the covers over his head.

Annoyed by her son's lack of courtesy, Mrs. Nieuwendyk knocked on the bathroom door. Daryl wasn't in there. *The nerve of some kids. The least he could do is reply when spoken to*, she thought. He was probably with that good-for-nothing Sanderson kid, the doper from down the street.

She walked down the hall to his bedroom door and asked if he was hungry. When she received no reply, she walked in. The boy was under the covers and looked like he was trying to hide from something. He was bawling hard and that wasn't like him at all.

Growing up is so difficult, she thought, assuming her son was still broken up over splitting with Karen. She started walking toward the bed to comfort her son. Startled, Daryl removed his head from beneath the sheets. He began to shake violently. His muscles twitched and spasmed. Then he smiled crazily at his mother.

"I didn't do it . . . I tried to help but he couldn't keep up. I didn't do shit . . . The Nerve killed Sandy . . . ."

She ran out of the bedroom and grabbed her husband. By the time they both ran back into his bedroom, the boy was unconscious and dying.

Daryl awoke in the quiet serenity of a distant land. It was an uncomplicated safe place that smelled of sterility. Everything was softly lit. Harsh colors were against the law. He didn't know where he had landed but as long as he felt as good as he did, he didn't care.

A plastic tube snaked into his wrist, drip-feeding him nutrients and vitamins. It had been quite some time since he'd last eaten. Half-open sedated eyes scanned cautiously. His parents and two doctors were present. They spoke to him but their words made no sense. Someone needed to adjust the speed control inside their throats. Or turn up the volume. Or maybe adjust the tracking?

A nurse wearing a McDonald's hat minus the golden M entered the room. She was old, dry, and unappealing. A twinge of panic swept through him as he wondered if she was related to the beast that lurked in the woods. Then, as soon as the thought registered, it was forgotten. Powerful mood drugs will do this to a person.

Slightly confused but unafraid, Daryl let her touch him with her cold withered hands. She removed the pan from underneath him. Smiling falsely, she quickly left the room. Dazed, he smiled goofily back in her direction. After she was gone, he continued smiling.

Several minutes, hours, days passed. There was no change in his condition. After lapsing in and out of a coma during which irreversible brain damage occurred, Daryl was catatonic, unable to communicate with anyone except himself. His mind was shattered. And he liked it that way. It was deep inside himself that Daryl found bliss. It was here that there was nothing to fear. Nothing lurked with dripping veins and meat hanging from bloody fangs. There were no trees or bushes inside his space. No wildlife. No trails. No goddamn birds yapping. Daryl realized that as long as he kept to himself he'd remain safe. And Karen was in here too, right beside him, holding his hand.

With an imaginary knife, he went about carving DARYL LOVES KAREN, FOREVER TOGETHER inside his skull. The grating noise caused a sharp migrainelike pain behind his temples that made him wish he had used a Magic Marker instead. It took forever to finish but had been well worth the effort. Despite the pain, a faint smile crept to his lips as he rolled over and kissed his impressed girlfriend.

Hours, days, minutes later he awoke. Patients sedated on lithium, Thorazine, and other powerful drugs, passed aimlessly, peacefully by his door. He smiled at them, not knowing why. As long as everyone's head was round, the teenager would continue smiling.

A two-day manhunt in search of Floyd "Sandy" Sanderson was launched. The search was conducted by state police and local law enforcement. Canine police, volunteers, and even a helicopter offered their assistance but Sanderson's body was never recovered. Only scattered pieces of it. A torn garbage bag filled with marijuana was also found and authorities speculated that Daryl had killed his best friend over a drug deal turned sour. Local press also played it that way. No charges were ever formally pressed. With Daryl in the state he was, it was best to leave him with trained physicians in the state's care. Morose, his parents signed the papers making Daryl a ward of the state. If he ever recovered, charges could be pressed.

He leaned forward feeling the need to urinate. So he did. It felt warm and made him sleepy. He knew it was not his time to rise again. Not yet. It had been a little less than three weeks since all the commotion had occurred. He was happy when they'd all finally left, especially the bloodhounds. It shook him up at first but now his underground shelter felt safe again. Before going back to sleep, the Nerve took a large bite out of Sandy's decomposing thigh and cuddled up next to his kill.

* * *

The sound of screaming brought two nurses and an aide running. Shrieks were highly unusual. The most common commotion on F-Ward, the wing in the state mental hospital for the physically and mentally disabled, was a sedated patient dropping a food tray. Language had been abandoned by these unfortunates a long time ago. Especially the language of fear.

Screams?

By the time they reached the room, the teenager was no longer screaming, but rather grunting painfully, trying to hold back his distress. He sounded like a small animal caught in a large trap. All three members of the hospital staff had broken into light sweats but it was not from the thirty-or-so yards they'd sprinted. It was the shrill desperation in the boy's tone. Just by looking at him it was quite obvious that the kid was in extreme pain.

Daryl's face was flushed and frozen. He was covered in a thick sweat. Drool pittered out of the side of his locking jaw as his eyes bulged woefully. He was squirming, trying to flee, but making no progress. The drugs held him in place. There were no restraints around his wrists or legs but the boy could not lift his arms no matter how hard he tried. He looked like a quadriplegic trying to move. His heart and his efforts were valiant but his body could not respond.

The first nurse, a no-nonsense Asian, shuffled over to the bed. She released the iron handrails and pulled the top sheet off him. The second nurse, a light-skinned black woman, grabbed his arm. The boy tried explaining, without the ability to communicate, that someone, or something, had managed to grab hold of the nerves in his right thigh and lower back and twist them up violently. He was telling this to her through his sad eyes. It was a form of communication as old as time. The black nurse gazed into his soul's mirror but couldn't read the message. All she saw were tears.

He'd suffered minor back pain from years of athletics but never had he felt anything like this. Nerves tangled and muscles spasmed into tightly wound barbed wire as excruciating pain rolled up and down his lower right side in waves. Only after he bit deeply into his tongue did the primal grunts subside. They became pained whimpers. The aide, a husky man with a neatly cropped beard, pointed at the boy's legs. Daryl's gown had hiked up and his thigh was showing the first signs of bruising.

"Must have banged his leg in his sleep," he said, looking around the room for any signs of foul play. There were none. The aide and the Asian nurse nodded in agreement as Daryl's wide eyes desperately tried to explain that the monster that had hidden so well in the woods was back. Only now it hid inside his head.

"Or had a nightmare," piped in the black nurse, preparing a powerful injection of liquid Valium for the boy. Judging from the panicked, fear-filled look on his face, he needed one.

Without You

Although he wanted to share the dance, Mayne could not bring himself to interrupt such beauty. Her well-toned body swayed childlike, peacefully, slowly moving to the rhythm. Her innocence was enchanting, her beauty breathtaking. Mayne knew she'd be angry at him for sneaking about, watching without letting her know, but the teenage voyeur inside his adult body encouraged him and didn't care about the consequences. Besides, this was for his eyes only.

Her eyes sparkled, reminding him of the ocean, vast with beauty and mystery. A slight breeze danced through her lion's mane. A full-length see-through dress covered her shapely body and a light glaze of sweat made her glisten. She seemed too beautiful to be real. During this split second of visual euphoria, Mayne conceded that she was the only woman he'd ever truly loved.

Her eyes flickered.

She must have heard me, he thought as she turned toward him. He didn't want to ruin the beauty, only to enjoy it. Her thick lips smiled sympathetically. Then the song started growing in volume.

A sharp twinge of panic shot through him when

he realized which of his songs it was. Cold sweat
seeped out of his pores and dread consumed him.
His vision spiraled as reality distorted. Breathing
became difficult, complicated. Desperation attacked
and twisted every muscle in his thin body. Much
worse than the pain was his fear. Unsuppressable
anxiety swept through him as he started toward the
stereo. Everything lost its natural texture; the walls,
the floor, the air became surreal. The louder the music, the more difficult he found it to move. He had to
remove the compact disc but his feet felt like large
concrete blocks. He couldn't move fast enough. She
already had the pistol's barrel against her temple.

BLAMM!

Mayne awoke covered in sweat, a mute shriek still
lodged in his throat. The past six hours had been
spent in a drug-and-alcohol-induced coma that he
put over as sleep. Sleep was a rare commodity and
was impossible to achieve without some assistance.
It didn't matter whether he slept six hours or six
minutes, the nightmare always managed to creep
in. No sleeping pill or antidepressant could spare
him. He had written the song and was forever
damned by it.

With unsteady hands, he wiped sweat from his
brow and rubbed his fingers against the satin sheets.
His silver and gold bracelets clinked together. Rolling onto his side, he stared at the digital alarm clock
on top of the black night table that had a built-in
refrigerator as its base. On top of the clock was a
half-empty pack of Marlboros. He stared at the
green digital numbers but they made no sense. It
really didn't matter what time it was anyway, his
time was other people's money. Next to the clock
was something more important than cash or time.

Slowly he sat up. Tortured eyes scanned the black

marble tabletop, searching for any leftover precious brown powder. There were burned matches, bent cigarettes, and empty bindles, but no dope. It didn't matter. He could always have more delivered.

Sitting on the edge of the bed, Mayne reached down and opened the night table's refrigerator door. Inside were several Budweisers, baking soda, and a chilled bottle of Dom Pérignon. He grabbed a cold can, killing half of it in one sip. He did this every morning. Instantly, his aching head began to feel better. Although he didn't want to admit it, the time had arrived to rejoin the living. He knew he had to be at the studio soon but didn't feel up to it. Besides, the recording of his latest album, *Alone*, had been finished over a month ago. The album was now in the final mixing stages. If Mayne liked what he heard, he'd approve it and the record would be released on schedule. If not, it would have to be remixed until he did approve. *So then, what the fuck did they need him for?* He procrastinated for as long as he possibly could before finally standing up.

Much like his bedroom, the bathroom was a disaster area. Discarded clothes, creams, trash, cassettes, and towels dominated the view. Using radar to locate the bowl, he found the porcelain, fought off the urge to puke, and relieved himself.

He reentered the bedroom, not really feeling human, more like a robot dressed in rented flesh. There was a dull pain in his abdomen that he'd grown accustomed to. It, like many other flaws in his health, could be attributed to his excessive lifestyle.

Besides his jewelry, Mayne only wore Jockey briefs. He stumbled over to his dresser, removed a pair of custom-tailored black leather pants, and changed. He found a dark purple silk kimono hang-

ing in a walk-in closet and put it on. In a dresser
drawer was a gram vial of cocaine. Scooping with
the long fingernail on his right pinkie, the tattered
musician snorted eight blasts of rock 'n' roll aspirin.

The kimono felt cool against his warm flesh. He
wondered if he was feverish and concluded he probably was. He was always run-down, as if with a perpetual fever. That is, of course, until he got his chip.
He finished his beer, tossing the empty can in the
general direction of a wastebasket that was already
crammed with empties.

Staring into a full-length mirror, the run-down re-
cluse didn't recognize the reflection. Sure, the long
blond hair and tattoos gave him away, but he looked
so frail. Mayne looked like someone who was ready
for hospital pajamas. His once attractive face was
blue, taut, and expressionless. A scraggly beard covered his chin and his emerald eyes were no longer
authentic gems, but rather costume jewelry.

He needed a drink.

For the past fourteen of his twenty-eight years,
he'd spent the majority of his time inside a bottle.
Teenage beer and wine parties turned to vodka and
rum at nightclubs, which in turn evolved into
straight whiskey. Exiting the bedroom, he said a silent prayer to his patron saint, Jim Beam, asking
that there be some in the liquor cabinet.

An illuminating golden glow surrounded the thick
blackout curtains. A small war had gone down in
the living room the previous evening. Full ashtrays,
assorted liquor bottles, empty and half-empty packs
of cigarettes, and beer cans were strewn everywhere. Several CD covers were caked in cocaine
residue. Mayne tried remembering who had been
partying there and couldn't. An empty pack of Kool
cigarettes meant that one of his many dealers, Jamie

Jazz, had delivered something. It didn't take very long before he made the connection between the empty bindles in the bedroom and Jamie. Jamie (pronounced Jay-mee) was typical Hollywood trash who hand delivered coke, toke, crack, or smack to troubled celebrities, exploiting their vunerablities. Mayne searched for more clues as to who else had been over partying but came up blank.

He slid behind the bar that was adjacent to the kitchen and opened a cabinet. There were several unopened bottles of assorted white liquors. A nervous surge shot through his small stomach. What if there was no whiskey? He shuffled the bottles around until he found the proper one. A sigh of relief escaped him as he twisted the cap off and made a mental note that he needed to restock. The whiskey's aroma was his equivalent of fresh brewed coffee.

"Here's looking at you, love," Mayne said aloud, raising the bottle to his lips.

Like every day, one sip led to another. After several sips, he started feeling right. He put the bottle on the counter and made it to the refrigerator. If he was lucky, he'd be drunk before the day started. He removed another Budweiser and went back into the messy living room.

There was a dull hum inside his cranium. He couldn't differentiate whether it was cocaine-induced or the central air-conditioning. If only he could remember what day today was, then he'd know if a maid was scheduled to come by. She could bring booze. The musician sat on the couch, picked up the phone, and dialed 411.

"Operator. What city, please?"

"L.A."

"Yes?"

"What day is it?" Mayne asked sincerely, lighting a Marlboro.

"What?"

"What day is it?"

"Sir, I'm an operator."

"Ma'am, you're Information and I asked you a question," Mayne corrected her. A snide laugh escaped him. After a silent moment, she answered his question.

"It's Wednesday, sir."

"Thanks," he said, and hung up. There would be no maid service today. This was not the way he wanted to start the day. He polished off the beer, finished his cigarette, and snorted more cocaine.

After several confusing seconds, he remembered where he kept the large green garbage bags and began straightening up the mess. Moving around the large one-bedroom condominium, he picked up anything that wasn't bolted down and threw it out. Bottles and empty food containers stretched the garbage bag to a point where it threatened to rip open. After ten minutes of straightening up, the apartment began taking shape.

Besides this condominium, he also owned one in Manhattan and another in Houston. He rarely frequented his Hollywood Hills mansion, or for that matter, his house in Maui. Both brought back too many memories of her. It was in the Hollywood Hills house where he and Elizabeth Aston had spent most of their quality time. As his thoughts began betraying him, thinking more about her, Mayne instinctively went to the bar and retrieved the whiskey bottle. He could think of her as long as he had a safety net.

With all the money, fame, and success he had attained, it was the simple things like friendship and love that were the hardest to keep. He never meant to hurt anyone, especially those closest to him, but for some reason that's who he usually hurt the worst. He never set out to be malicious, but by living under a microscope with the world scrutinizing him, any wrongdoing, public or private, tended to blow up in his face and often wound up as Nightly News. Personal flaws and fuck-ups are not allowed of the elite. He often suffered silently, trapped by his own fame, until he needed out of his cage.

But the cage was as wide as his eyes could perceive.

All Mayne had ever tried to be, right or wrong, was himself. With all the doctors, specialists, therapists, fans, and everyone in his organization trying to help him, he just sank further into his cocoon, alienating himself even more. He often wondered who he really was. Was he another regenerated social security number automatically inherited at birth or a genuine reflection of society? Was he a phenomenon or just a facade? Was he a product of his own imagination or just another brick? Would he ever understand his own destiny?

Inside his mind, he analyzed why his relationship with Elizabeth had failed more times than were countable. Like the scholar he wasn't, he dissected situations, pondered things he should've said and shouldn't have been caught doing. When it came to sex, why couldn't Elizabeth understand that just because he occasionally strayed from their bedroom didn't mean he didn't love her? Sex was like role-playing. He never forced her to be monogamous but deep down he knew that if he found out she was fucking someone else it would have hurt. A lot! Even with that knowledge, he couldn't confine himself to only one woman. He wanted to have his cake and eat it too. He tried being open with her but concluded that certain things should've remained secret. Sex was an ego addiction similar to the one he felt onstage. Different audiences, like different partners, were more challenging and made him work harder for the applause. Like drugs, he was addicted to the rush. Even with an empire at his disposal, money couldn't buy him love, nor happiness, nor peace of mind.

Nor Elizabeth.

Looking around the large living room, a very disenchanted artist absorbed the modern decor. None of these possessions except a few token items had ever meant anything to Mayne. None of this shit was real. He was surrounded by trophies of a game that had no meaning.

And he was tired of playing games.

A sharp pain in his left ear sent him back to the dark corridor that led from stage to dressing room. Inside his ringing head, speakers feeding back ignited and exploded. He was experiencing another rock 'n' roll side effect, ear damage. The dull hum lasted only seconds but the memories of his final show with his former band, Suicide Shift, would never fade.

For reasons he couldn't remember, Elizabeth had been unable to attend the tour's final show. The band had been on the road for the better part of fourteen months, over 285 concerts. Every few weeks Mayne had flown her to whatever city he was performing in and she'd stay for a few nights. The final concert of any tour is an important night. It was Suicide Shift's first headlining tour and Mayne wanted to share the experience with her. It was the culmination of many miles traveled, many hours worked, and the celebration that went on afterward was well deserved. He called her several times to offer her plane tickets, trying to persuade her, but she couldn't make it.

The gig was well over two hours of electric ferocity. Of course Mayne consumed plenty of drugs and alcohol before and during the show (he did every gig), but it was the Florida crowd's enthusiasm and knowing that he'd be able to sleep for a month that gave him extra spark. Every time he took a solo, he tried to best any previous soloing effort. Every time he approached his microphone to sing backups, his voice surged with whiskey vigor. For him, this was rock 'n' roll at its best. The 4,000-plus crowd acknowledged this with deafening applause. After the final encore, it was time to celebrate.

Mayne wound up with two eager females in his hotel room. In the privacy of his bathroom he injected a little heroin. Not enough to make him nod out but enough to get him good and high. The two nubile females would only make him feel better. After struggling to get his wet brown suede pants off, he joined the nude women, and thus the revelry began.

The dope clouded his not-so-good memory but Mayne remembered a very drunk Peter Terrance walking into the room. The band's drummer had mistaken Mayne's room for his own. In the spirit of celebration, Mayne offered him a girl. Terrance declined saying he'd find his own and left. The ménage-à-trois continued. Shortly afterward there was a knock on the door. Thinking it was Terrance taking up the offer, Mayne called out, telling whoever was at the door to enter.

Standing at the door with an overnight bag was Elizabeth. On the spur of the moment she'd flown from L.A. to Miami to be with him. A very bad scene played itself out. Elizabeth left broken and hysterical. That was the beginning of the end for their relationship.

Mayne snapped out of the past. His left knee popped loudly as he straightened his legs and headed for the phone. He pushed a button. Elizabeth's number was still programmed and every now and then he pushed it just to hear her phone ring. Also in the phone's memory was his record label, his manager, the three members of his current band, the Mayne Mann Group, and several drug dealers. After receiving no answer at Elizabeth's, he pushed another button. His many bracelets clinked together and a few seconds later there was a reply.

"Yeah?" spat an unenthusiastic voice from a car phone.

"It's me," Mayne said, swallowing, cocaine dripping down his throat.

"My main man," Jamie's voice declared like a cash register ringing. "What can I do ya for?"

"Uptown and downtown." Cocaine and heroin.

"No problem. You remember what I did for ya last night, right?"

"Yeah." He didn't.

"You owe me three bills from that shit, brother man," the dealer explained just in case memory failed.

"I'm sure I got some change floatin' around. If I can't find some I'll give ya my Versateller card and you can get what I owe."

"Bet. I'll be right up," Jamie said as if he was doing Mayne a favor and hung up.

"Fuckin' prick," Mayne mumbled to himself. He lit up a cigarette and got himself another beer. The lid popped loudly and foam rose to the mouth hole. He watched, amused, then walked over to the black-

out curtains and pulled the lever, letting bright sunlight invade his living room.

"Fuck you very much," he loudly announced,
squinting, and raising his middle finger to the sky.
The view from his balcony was vast, displaying the
City of Angels below, yet more often than not Mayne
kept the curtains shut, preferring not to be a part of
the world outside. It was safe inside his apartment.

Against a far wall, tucked in the corner so that the
ivory keys faced out toward the living room, was a
vintage Steinway. He spent many pleasure-filled
hours on the instrument, and even when he wasn't
playing, the piano gave him visual stimulation. It
was an instrument of precision and grace. Next to
the piano, resting comfortably on stands were half a
dozen vintage guitars: Les Pauls, Stratocasters, and
Telecasters. The guitars he kept in the apartment
were the ones that meant the most to him.

The buzzer sounded, waking Mayne from his
drifting thoughts. He went to the intercom and
pressed the button that unlocked the front door. A
few minutes later, Jamie Jazz was inside his apartment.

Dozens of platinum and gold records adorned the
walls. Hours upon years of planning, writing, recording, and struggling had reaped these round rewards. His songwriting stemmed from inner pains
and his slower, more blues-influenced songs often
dealt with personal hardships. Those were the songs
he was most proud of and believed might stand the
test of time. The faster, more hard-rock-oriented
songs often had little significance or wore their
meanings on their sleeve. Unfortunately, the awards
were no longer awards without Elizabeth.

Mayne excused himself and went into the bedroom. Hidden behind yet another platinum disc was

a safe. He removed the disc from the wall, twisted the combination, and opened the safe. Inside were jewelry, documents, over four thousand dollars cash, a freebase pipe, and a loaded .357 Magnum. He grabbed a few C-notes and went back into the living room, leaving the safe shut but unlocked.

Jamie was seated on the black leather couch, feet up on the marble coffee table, looking casual in Suicide Shift sweatpants (that he'd gotten from Mayne) and a matching sweatshirt. He'd helped himself to a beer.

"What's the total?"

"Including last night? Six," Jamie replied, fidgeting with the beeper on his waist.

Mayne handed him six bills and put the rest in his pants pocket. Judging by the look on his face, the dealer understood he wanted to be alone and took the hint.

"Call me if you need anything else," Jamie offered, exiting the apartment. The moment the front door clicked shut, Mayne's mind rushed into overdrive but his body refused to move. He had drugs in hand, but instead of finding a syringe, he went back into the bedroom. Something in the wall safe more powerful than his addiction had caught his eye.

He walked to the safe and pulled the door open. Inside was a photo album containing precious Kodachrome memories.

Placing the drugs on top of the messy night table, he fell on the bed, and began flipping through the leather-bound book. Captured in photos were images and feelings so intense that it made him warm as well as suicidal. Elizabeth had challenged him intellectually while stimulating him sexually. She'd mothered him when he was sick, which was quite often. She'd set free inner feelings that he'd often tried avoiding. Her beauty, both inner and physical, was something he wanted, yet when she was his, he did everything conceivable to lose her.

He turned to the second page.

He had no idea how many times he'd masturbated to this photo. Every other day perhaps. It was just a snapshot he'd taken of her while on vacation in Las Vegas. In photo form, the wind blew her long hair away from her face and she was smiling. Behind her was the Caesar's Palace hotel where they'd spent the better part of two weeks in the penthouse suite. It was a typical tourist photo but it was her smile that turned him on. It was so free from pain. *Mayne would do anything to have her smile for him like she had in the photograph.* He'd do anything to have her lips, her body again.

He unbuttoned his leather pants. Before beginning his self-stimulation, he pulled himself over to the night-table refrigerator and removed an unopened bottle of Dom Pérignon champagne. The bottle opened with a loud pop and smoke billowed from the top, but no liquid spilled. Sipping deeply from the bottle, he flipped through the photo album that was all too short, carefully avoiding the final page. He rarely looked at the last page. As always, he wound up back on page two.

With the bottle two-thirds empty, he pulled his pants and briefs down to his knees and poured the remaining champagne onto his palms. This was part of the ritual. Fine champagne was something he and Elizabeth enjoyed sharing. *He could still share it with her.* As he took hold of his wet erection, his thoughts began to slip.

It was during one of their final dinner dates that she had said something that inspired him to write the most beautiful song of his career.

"I can't live with you and I can't live without you," he could hear her saying as if it were just yesterday. Words flowed from pen to paper faster than he could write. Mayne concluded that this was his private way of explaining all that had happened between them. The song "Without You," was not an apology, it was his side of the story. It was rock 'n' roll sincerity that sold over three million copies in the U.S., topping the record sales charts and putting the Mayne Mann Group on top of the rock world. He offered Elizabeth half of the royalties from the song because without her there would be no song. She politely declined.

A sold-out Mayne Mann Group tour ensued. When the tour arrived in Los Angeles, Mayne desperately wanted to see her. No matter how many women he had, no matter how over her he told everyone he was, he'd do anything for her except let her permanently slip out of his life. He'd called her a dozen times over the course of two days, leaving message after message on her answering machine. Even though she never responded, he'd left her ten All-Access passes at Will Call. She never showed.

After the show, Mayne vowed he wouldn't make the same mistake twice. He quickly showered, changed into dry clothing, and left, avoiding all the backstage hoopla. He and his driver headed for Elizabeth's apartment.

Using the phone in the limousine, he dialed her from the street below her apartment. Again he was greeted by a recorded message.

"Elizabeth, I know—I hope you're there. I'm downstairs and even if I have to break down the door to see you, I'm willing. If you're gonna call the cops, well, call 'em now . . . I don't expect anything from you. I don't deserve anything . . . Fuck,

I don't even know what I'm trying to say other than I still care about you. Words can't heal what I've done but, fuck, the past is done . . . I really need to see your face again," Mayne softly explained after the beep. The words still echoed in his mind as he wondered if he could've possibly phrased things differently.

It was too late now, he thought, already inside the building. This was one of the rare occasions after a gig that Mayne was sober. As he arrived by way of elevator at her floor, he heard familiar music. The closer he got to her door the louder the volume grew. Then his world began to spin uncontrollably as a loud gunshot echoed through the hallway.

He ran toward her apartment, lowered his shoulder, and with reckless abandon crashed through the wooden door. He'd found Elizabeth on the couch, bleeding profusely, most of her head splattered on the wall behind her. On the blood-sprayed coffee table in front of her was the answering machine, a ballpoint pen, and several crumpled balls of writing paper.

He stood destroyed before her corpse. How could this have happened? All he had ever done was love her. Devastated, he slowly walked over to the blaring stereo. A CD single of "Without You" was programmed to repeat. He wondered how many times she'd listened to the same song and shut the power off. Then he noticed that next to the answering machine was a note.

Number one with a bullet, the red-speckled note read.

Shaking and convulsing, his tears falling freely, Mayne began screaming at the top of his lungs. It sounded like someone had unleashed a wild animal. His shrieks threatened to break the windows. A migraine pierced his throbbing temples and his entire head was overloaded with pressure. Did she kill herself because they had failed or because he wouldn't leave her be? Was it the song, one of the few things he'd ever done autonomously, that had driven her to this? Was this really happening? Then another thought came to mind. He removed the pistol from her hand and put it against his temple.

He was going to join her.

CLICK.

It was empty. Elizabeth had known she would only need one bullet.

Mayne snapped out of that nightmare and was thrust into another memory. He recognized the familiar room as the honeymoon suite in Las Vegas and almost felt at ease. The bed was in disarray and Elizabeth was smiling mischievously.

"What do you want to do?"

"Wha'?" Mayne responded, confused. They'd already drunk several bottles of champagne and made love twice.

"What do you want to do?" she replied softly, daring Mayne to answer.

Mayne caught wind of her game and decided to play along. If she was giving him an option as to what they'd do next, he was definitely going to take advantage of her generosity.

"You can either come up here and tell me that you love me or go down on me."

Elizabeth's face registered joy. Words like love were the hardest to get out of Mayne's mouth. Once again she smiled as she began her descent toward his waistline. It didn't take her very long to bring him back to life. Several minutes later, when she sensed that he was as excited as he was going to get, Elizabeth looked up at her man and with the sexiest expression she could conjure, softly said, *"I love you."*

Mayne came with a slight grunt. The powerful surge had given him something to work at but there was no pleasure in the orgasm. There never was anymore. He tossed the photo album aside and lay on the bed feeling dead, staring at the ceiling. For a split second, he thought he heard musical strands of "Without You" but it was only his imagination. His tired body lay there for what felt like a year before he sat up. At least the drugs on the night table were real.

Everything he needed was on the table. Hidden beneath the clock radio was a syringe and a blackened spoon. There was a half-empty glass of water and a lighter next to it. In the spoon he mixed the proper amounts of heroin and water, and then, using the lighter, heated the bottom of the spoon until the mixture cleared up before placing a tiny piece of cotton into the spoon. With unsteady hands, he added some cocaine and his speedball was complete.

Being a high-profile celebrity, he couldn't afford to have his withered arms tracked up too badly. He usually shot into the back of his forearms or his feet. He also injected into his neck but the way he felt right now, he had no time to dillydally. Like an expert acupuncturist, he fixed into a bulging vein in his forearm.

"Cool," he mumbled, carefully examining his arm, as he felt the speedball coming on. He fell back down on the bed. Between the drugs and his emotions, he was exhausted. It was a good thing drugs numbed away most of the pressures. He was rushing out as the drug hit him in powerful waves. It

took several moments before he realized his left arm was touching something. He slowly rolled over.

The photo album was opened to the last page.

The last page contained Elizabeth's obituary and a sympathy card. Tears he'd held in since that day began to flow down his cheeks. His pale face flushed as he felt his strength evaporating. He was drowning in sorrow but didn't believe in self-pity and that made him feel even worse.

He sat up hyperventilating with a question echoing inside his head. *Why did she have to die?* He had no answer and stood up too quickly.

Why was everything so fucked?

He went back into the living room. He needed whiskey.

Why?

He loved her so much.

Why?

He'd offered her half the royalties. *Half.* That was a financial empire, but she'd refused.

Why?

He'd tried to make amends. He'd tried being good according to society's standards. He wanted to understand everything that had happened to them. He wanted her to love him but no matter how hard he tried, he fucked it up.

Why?

He wanted to be normal again but that wasn't possible.

Why?

He wanted to feel closer to Elizabeth but she was dead. That tormented his fragile soul but for a split second of insane logic, Mayne concluded that his body should not be spared either.

"Arrrrrrggghh!" he growled, attacking his living room like a pissed-off brawler. Fists and feet attacked defenseless walls and furniture. He cocked his right fist back and a large hole went through plaster. He snatched an Oriental lamp off an end table and hurled it across the room. He violently threw a marble ashtray into a plaque, ruining both. Breathing heavily and drenched in alcoholic sweat, he grabbed a platinum record and smashed it, spraying glass shards everywhere. The shattered glass on the floor twinkled like sun-reflected sand.

No matter how many hotel rooms he trashed during his career, Mayne had never harmed a guitar. That was strictly taboo until today. He walked over to the row of guitars, grabbed a '68 Stratocaster by its stringed neck and swung, smashing the mahogany body until it was little more than firewood.

With each self-destructive act, he felt slightly better. He walked over to another platinum disc, readied himself and put his right fist through the glass. Blood spurted from the hand that was heavily insured by Lloyds of London.

For the first time that day he smiled.

Mayne grabbed the Jim Beam bottle off the bar and guzzled. The liquid painkiller warmed his heaving chest and eased his bleeding hand, which looked like it needed stitches. He walked over to his Fischer stereo, and, using his good hand, turned on the receiver. The digital readout was locked on a classic rock station. It was the only safe station on the dial, since it never played any of his songs. Mayne Mann was too new, too current. The station only played material from the 60s and 70s. He instantly recognized the song playing; it was Humble Pie's "I Don't Need No Doctor." It was raw rock like this that had inspired him to become a musician. Following the Pie were the Allman Brothers. Mayne could relate to what it felt like being tied to a whipping post.

During the commercials, he went into the kitchen to grab another beer. Out of his stereo speakers a record store chain announced its prices as the lowest in Los Angeles. The background music accompanying the record store commercial was "Without You."

His eyes stung but no tears fell as he realized that no matter where he was, he couldn't hide from himself. Like a man on a mission, he walked over to the stereo, grabbed the receiver, and yanked with both hands. It took several strong tugs before the digital lights went off.

With the receiver in hand, he stumbled backward, ripping wires and knocking over one of the large Bose speakers. Distraught and panting, he made his way to the giant sliding safety-glass door that led to the balcony. He casually dropped the high-tech receiver and undid the latch that kept the heavy door locked. Fresh air attacked his senses. The cool breeze felt invigorating as he stepped out onto the balcony and looked over the edge. His jet-black Bentley sat gleaming in the parking lot directly below.

He picked the receiver up, held it over the balcony, and aimed it at the car. After several seconds of wondering if his aim was accurate, he let go. Glass spidered wildly when the receiver hit the car's windshield and broke through.

He went to fetch the beer he'd been distracted from and ripped the refrigerator door open as hard as he could. It crashed open, spilling several items onto the floor. The door dangled by a hinge. Mayne grabbed a beer, chugged half, and like a strong-armed baseball pitcher threw it at his guitar collection, barely missing his favorite: a vintage '57 Sunburst Les Paul. He grabbed another can from the crippled refrigerator as his eyes returned to the guitars.

The guitars were like adopted children and he loved each one in a different manner. Certain guitars held certain memories but each guitar had the ability to create magic. It was that potential he respected and admired most about these guitars until this afternoon. Now, no matter how much he loved a certain guitar, or how valuable it might be, all he wanted to do was feel pain. Pain brought him closer to reality.

It brought him closer to Elizabeth.

He gave the world music, very good music, and asked for little in return. *A little space to create, some kicks thrown in, and how about peace of mind?* Instead, he had more material goods than he could ever use, more money than he could count, and nothing worth fighting for. There was a time not too long ago when he'd fought like hell for all of this. Now that he owned a piece of the rock he wished he could give it back. The view from the top wasn't as picturesque as he'd imagined. What he did as his artistic expression, the record company sold for capital. He'd quickly grown disillusioned with the system but what else could he do? Without the industry he couldn't share his music. No matter how hard anyone tried explaining it to him, musical notes would never equal dollar signs. He made music because since his early childhood, he truly loved rock 'n' roll. It was the people, his people, he wrote music for after he finished writing for himself. So then, why couldn't he sleep at night?

He stared at the answer.

He was going to kill his guitars. If it wasn't for these guitars, he wouldn't have the problems he did. And he'd save the goddamn '57 Sunburst for last.

He guzzled the beer, raising it away from his greedy mouth. Budweiser rained down the side of his face. When the can was almost empty, he crushed and spiked it like a football. Enraged, he grabbed a Les Paul Black Beauty and dealt it a quick but savage death against a wall. He raised a rare Telecaster over his head and clubbed the coffee table, breaking both. Then he picked up another Les Paul and, swinging it like a baseball bat, clobbered a lamp and several other objects before the guitar's neck snapped off.

"Fuckin' cheap shit," he grumbled.

He heard something that had a bit of rhythm to it. Was there a drummer playing in his head? It took several seconds for him to realize that one of the neighbors was pounding on the wall.

"WHAT, A LITTLE TOO LOUD FOR YA?" Mayne shouted at the direction the noise was coming from.

It didn't stop.

"YER PISSING ME OFF, ASSHOLE!"

Knock-Knock-Knock-Knock-Knock.

"Motherfucker, I'm giving ya fair fucking warning," he said.

Knock-Knock-Knock-Knock-Knock.

Mayne walked into the bedroom and over to the night table. He grabbed his cocaine and poured a decent-sized mound on the back of his hand that wasn't bleeding and snorted. Afterward he licked residue off his fist, numbing his teeth and gums. There was a pack of Marlboros on the table. He grabbed one and lit it. He took a deep drag and listened to his surroundings.

The neighbor was still pounding.

The ashtray was an overflowing mountain of dead butts so Mayne placed the cigarette on the edge of the night table. He had tried to avoid a confrontation, but the shithead next door wouldn't let it lie. He went to his wall safe, grabbed the Smith & Wesson .357 Magnum, and charged out of the bedroom.

"OKAY, HOMEFUCK, WANNA PLAY GAMES?"

Knock-Knock-Knock-Knock-Knock.

KABAMMM, KABAMMM, KABAMMM.

He unloaded three shots toward the already hole-ridden wall. The pounding stopped instantly. Again he smiled. He aimed the pistol at one of his platinum discs on another wall and blasted the shiny sphere. He aimed at his TV and blew it to kingdom come.

One bullet left.

He held the silver-plated pistol in awe. He could easily join Elizabeth; all it would take was one quick squeeze of the trigger. The idea appealed to him. Maybe he'd get it right in his next life. Slowly, eyes closed, he raised the pistol. The trigger teased his scarlet index finger. The barrel felt good against his temple.

Readying himself, he reopened his eyes. In front of him, *mocking him*, were two more Les Paul guitars. There once was a point in his life when these musical embodiments were holy. The dedication and years of practicing were a labor of love. Guitars were his passion, his expression, and his ticket out of obscurity. But all of that changed with one song. Now these guitars were reminders that Mayne could never regain his innocence.

"Can't I fuckin' die with some dignity?" he wondered as rage consumed him. He couldn't even commit suicide without music somehow interfering. His shaking arm lowered and took aim at one of the guitars. There was heavy recoil as wooden fragments flew everywhere. He put a massive hole in the guitar, then walked over to examine his accuracy. It

was definitely dead, but that wasn't enough. He
picked up the remains and threw them against the
safety-glass door. He walked over to the balcony's
edge. Below, a small crowd had gathered around
his ruined luxury car.

"Anybody want an autograph?" he asked, tossing
out the fragmented guitar.

*"Wait a minute, wait a minute. I got another pres-
ent!"* he yelled, and ran into the bedroom. His heavy
footsteps jarred the cigarette he'd forgotten off the
night table. It smoldered on the thick rug. Mayne
dug inside the wall safe, grabbed a handful of hundred-dollar bills, and ran back to the balcony before
his audience could scurry away.

"Don't say I never gave you anything," he announced, letting the money fly. Several wary spectators stepped backward but as soon as it was obvious
that the confetti was currency, they rushed forward.
Mayne waved to the small crowd and went back inside.

One guitar remained.

He stared at the '57, marveling at the beautiful
colors. It was appropriately called a Sunburst.
Reds, oranges, and yellows swirled in the wooden
body. This one had gold trim as well as golden pick-
ups. The Sunburst was his preference of all guitars.
He had another two dozen in storage but this guitar
was the first thing he bought after Suicide Shift was
signed to a recording contract. It was how he'd re-
warded himself for having "made it." This was also
the guitar he'd written the music to "Without You"
on. He approached it with caution and respect and
gently picked it up. He sat down on the floor Indian
style. Deep down, he was glad he hadn't destroyed
this ax.

His picking hand hurt badly, but he wanted to

play. Blood dripped off his hand and dripped down the guitar's body. Enthralled, Mayne watched it run. No matter how intoxicated he was, his fingers never betrayed him, and this particular guitar always responded to his call. He began picking something that sounded like Hendrix.

He paused abruptly. Something about that last guitar run shook him up and he couldn't continue. In a vague way, it reminded him of a part in "Without You." After taking a deep breath, Mayne partially regained his composure. Multimillionaires like Mayne Mann aren't supposed to cry. They're beyond tears or at least that's what society wants to believe. Mayne Mann was just Stephen Maynard Mandraich, a talented kid who could run his nimble fingers along a piece of stringed wood. He began to strum one of his favorite riffs, Thin Lizzy's "Don't Believe a Word." Even though the guitar wasn't amplified, he could hear it as if it was.

He let the last note ring out as he stopped and reflected. He used to love the feel of this instrument in his hands. He used to love making the strings come to life. He used to love just holding this guitar. Then his mind viciously reminded him that he'd also loved the way Elizabeth felt. He quickly rose off the floor and tossed the guitar aside. It landed with a loud *DWWWAANNNGGGG*.

He stared blankly at the guitar and thought of her. Both had given him so much pleasure, but he'd never been able to properly express his gratitude. He never told her the truth about how she made him feel, about how much he loved her, and when he did, the song reaffirmed that he should've kept his mouth shut. *At least she'd still be alive.* But the song was pure and he wanted to play it for her. Even if her physical body wasn't present, he could still sing to her in heaven. He wanted to jam but was afraid to touch the guitar.

Then Mayne saw an alternative.

He scooped up the almost-dead whiskey bottle and finished what little was left. It slipped silently from his hand. Very drunk, very drugged out, he staggered over to the piano.

The smoldering cigarette on the bedroom rug had burned its way over to the goose-down comforter. The cover caught and flames quickly spread throughout the bedroom. Discarded clothing acted as kindling and soon the bedroom was on fire.

Until several hazy hours ago, Mayne's life, no matter how miserable, had been something most people could only dream about. It was all an illusion, and he was one of rock 'n' roll's elite, a hero. Now, he'd been reduced to his basic self and nothing really mattered. He felt the thorns wrapped around his heart and for the first time in far too long, felt human again. He'd smothered his spirituality in drug abuse. He'd stunted his health and personal growth with vice. He'd blinded himself because he was afraid to see that his purpose, his gift in life, was to be true to himself. And the only time he was able to find that inner truth was when he played his music.

He softly tapped the ivory keys, making melodies come to life through his fingers. No matter how badly his hand hurt, he persisted in making music. He was determined to play for Elizabeth and all the other angels. With every fluid run, every harmony, every musical accent, his inner pain subsided a little. With each passing musical note, he became one with the music.

Sweating profusely, Mayne felt something stirring behind him. He tried ignoring it for as long as possible. Finally, he turned and saw large flames billowing out of his bedroom. At first he thought it was a hallucination but the fire was scorchingly real and heading his way. His favorite guitar was already engulfed and dying. He wanted to save it but couldn't. He refused to let his jamming be interrupted. Elizabeth was listening.

Every time his fingers pressed the Steinway's keys, crimson stained the ivory and smeared. He ignored the small red spots, sliding his long fingers through them. Scarred-up veins bulged from his forearms as sweat ran down his face. All he'd ever wanted to do with his life was play his music and now he was. For the moment, he felt free from his demons. He built up the courage and began singing "Without You" in his natural gruff voice. The thick carpeting quickly became a wall-to-wall inferno as a giant wave of fire rose up and spread around the piano. He couldn't have cared less. As flames swallowed the apartment, Mayne never screamed and never missed a note.

DISCOVER THE TRUE MEANING OF HORROR...

Poppy Z. Brite

☐ **LOST SOULS** .... 21281-2 .... $4.99
☐ **DRAWING BLOOD** .... 21492-0 .... $4.99

Kathe Koja

☐ **THE CIPHER** .... 20782-7 .... $4.99
☐ **BAD BRAINS** .... 21114-X $4.99
☐ **SKIN** .... 21115-8 .... $4.99

Tanith Lee

☐ **DARK DANCE** .... 21274-X $4.99
☐ **HEART-BEAST** .... 21455-6 .... $4.99
☐ **PERSONAL DARKNESS** .... 21470-X $4.99

Melanie Tem

☐ **PRODIGAL** .... 20815-7 .... $4.50
☐ **WILDING** .... 21285-5 .... $4.99
☐ **MAKING LOVE** .... 21469-6 .... $4.99
    (co-author with Nancy Holder)
☐ **REVENANT** .... 21503-X $4.99

☐ **GRAVE MARKINGS/Michael Arnzen** ..... 21339-8 .... $4.99
☐ **X,Y/Michael Blumlein** .... 21374-6 .... $4.99
☐ **DEADWEIGHT/Robert Devereaux** .... 21482-3 .... $4.99
☐ **SHADOWMAN/Dennis Etchison** .... 21202-2 .... $4.99
☐ **HARROWGATE/Daniel Gower** .... 21456-4 .... $4.99
☐ **DEAD IN THE WATER/Nancy Holder** ..... 21481-5 .... $4.99
☐ **65MM/Dale Hoover** .... 21338-X $4.99